THE water had no level. It surged up to the roof of the pipe and yawned open below the swaying, freezing cable. It had no surface. Between air and water there was a whipping tangle of spray. The smell of subsoil flooded into Corander's chest. The nerves of his eyes seemed to have snapped from his brain.

He could not find Wells. He could not hear his own screams. The water rose. He flung himself to the right with his back to the cable—and felt her fingers locked on icy metal. One hand. He could not find the other. Was it her dying grip?

A PLANET in ARMS

by DONALD BARR

FAWCETT CREST • NEW YORK

To C.J.B., W.P.B., H.B.T.B., S.M.B.

A PLANET IN ARMS

Published by Fawcett Crest Books, a unit of CBS Publications, the Consumer Publishing Division of CBS Inc.

Copyright © 1981 by Donald Barr

ISBN: 0-449-24407-5

Printed in the United States of America

First Fawcett Crest printing: May 1981

10 9 8 7 6 5 4 3 2 1

CHAPTER 1

AT 0800 Colonel General Pradjani bent over a small folding table on the weedy margin of the space-field and signed the articles of surrender. He straightened. His glance, flickering over the knot of Colonials drawn up in important attitudes on the other side of the table, fixated for a bare instant on three elderly civilians in dark, old-fashioned coats who stood together in the middle of the throng. The defeated Imperial commander gave them a quick, tight nod that was somehow a salute. Then he executed an about-face and marched out onto the field, ignoring a grinning Colonial trooper who offered him a lift in a groundcar. For twenty minutes the lone, diminishing figure moved in a straight line, and with an unvarying cadence, across the scorched flats toward the gray spire of the Imperial flagship, the *Yi Sung Sin.*

At 0973, the *Yi Sung Sin,* with the last of the disarmed legions in its webbing, rose on its chemicals. At 1002, its fusions cut in. At 1007, for the watchers on the planet below, it had become one of several bright, uncertain motes in the clear sky. Then, as the DaSilvas of the Imperial fleet set up their geometries, the planetary watchers saw the ships' plasmas wink out one by one.

The second planet of Epsilon Struthionis—Rohan's Planet—was independent.

At 1100 the streets of New Nome were filled with processions singing "Rohan, arise!", at 1700 with drunken men and women and children, at 2200 with chaotic violence.

Looting began, but after three years of warfare there was little enough to loot. In the once fashionable shops of the Second Quadrant, a few scraps went; the looters stripped the automannequins and sent them swaying down Boulevard Planck, where more idealistic patriots seized them, painted them with huge wild pudenda and political symbols, and bore them aloft, still undulating languidly, impaled on sticks.

Rohan, arise! The ambulance-copters hovered over the First and Third Quadrants like flatulent, carrion-eating birds.

A naked, elderly woman climbed up the wall of the Central Crematorium and harangued the mob in Maxwell Square for thirty minutes before she fell, split her skull, and died. A blind man tried to climb up in her place. The crowd cheered his unavailing efforts. Rohan, arise!

Earth-President Cetshwayo IX DeWet was burned in effigy on a hundred street corners. Some of the effigies were fireproof; the flames of the fuel-cell compound and stinking raw bog-pitch licked at them with orange tongues throughout the furious night.

Out of sheer joy, one mob of a dozen or so citizens had been looting and burning the homes of suspected Loyalists in some of the quiet streets in the Fourth Quadrant. They swooped around the corner from Hamilton Street into Dedekind. A wall-eyed youth in the lead happily screamed, "Peterson the Earthie lives right down here! Peterson next! Here we come, Peterson!"

A tall, knobby young man in militia uniform studied them in the light of a street lamp as they passed. Their faces were blissful with hatred. "'Chapter Two,'" the militiaman murmured, "'The Cannibal Children Go to a Birthday Party.'" He turned and joined them, running with long, efficient strides. He pulled abreast of the leader and roared with apparent enthusiasm. "Here we come, *ready or not,* Peterson!"

On the front walk of the unlit Peterson house, the knobby militiaman sprinted ahead, flung himself against the locked front door, and slipped aside as the rest came up and beat at it with their bodies. He vaulted a neat but corroded fence, found a large window overlooking a garden, backed off, and, covering his face with his arms, hurled himself at it. The sheet of lucimorph was designed to resist the destructive radiation of a hundred planets, but not a projectile.

Some of the mob started toward the burst window. A light went on inside it. The militiaman stuck his close-cropped red head out of the burst pane and called to them, "I'll let you in at the front." The rioters surged round to the door again.

Inside, a chalky-faced woman, with two small girls clinging to her, was watching the militiaman from the shadowy kitchen door. "Got a basement?" he asked.

The woman nodded.

The militiaman said, "Get down there and keep quiet." Through the shattered window he saw one of the rioters come staggering along the street between two heavy canisters of fuel-cell compound. "I'll join you in a moment," the young man added in a gentler tone. "I'll knock like this: ta-*dah* ta-*dah*."

She and the little girls disappeared.

The militiaman ran through the dark house to the front door and began to fumble noisily with the hardware. Already a jagged line of light from the street lamps shone through a gash in the door panel. "Hold it! Hold it up!" the militiaman bellowed. The pounding stopped. He rattled the lock. The assault recommenced. The young man waited till the jamb began to crack, then bellowed again, "Hey! Hold it up! How can I get this thing open?" The assault subsided once more, the knobby militiaman opened the lock, and the rioters swarmed in. "Somebody's upstairs!" yelled the militiaman, leading the way at a run.

They followed him, turning on lights, smashing the same lights, smashing ornaments, and pocketing objects that glittered. The militiaman went up the stairs three at a time, gaining a lead of several meters, hurtled around a corner, pulled the key from inside an open bedroom door, closed the door, locked it from outside, pocketed the key, and when the rest of the rioters stumbled into view was hammering at the door with his fists and yelling, "Come out! I know you're in there!" They joined the attack on the door. "Hear that? Listen!" roared the militiaman. They fell silent. "I heard a woman crying in there," said the militiaman. They resumed the attack joyously. The militiaman slipped away, found the stairway clear, and sped down.

He knocked softly on the basement door, rat-*tat* rat-*tat;* the lock rattled; the white-faced woman moved aside as he stepped through. He locked the door and, controlling her between his big hands, pushed her down into the dimly lit basement.

There was something like a repressed sob and then a voice, scarcely more than a sigh: "Oh, please, please, not in front of the children..."

He cut in as if he had not heard: "Is there an outside hatch?"

"Yes. Also a tunnel to the power-unit out back."

"Better still," said the knobby young man. "The three of you go that way. Don't break into a run. Get over to Hilbert Street."

"But the house," protested the woman, "who'll take care of it?"

"They will," said the young man. "They'll burn it. They raped a woman a few minutes ago. Their leader was joking about it just now in the street." His harsh candor restored her self-control. She pushed the children toward the tunnel. "Hilbert Street," said the militiaman. "Two-three-oh. Say, 'Mrs. Corander, your son sent us and he told us not to answer any questions.' Two-three-oh Hilbert. Corander. Goodbye, children." He kissed each of the children on the tip of the nose. "Now Mommy." He held her shoulders and kissed her on the nose.

"When can we come back?" she asked.

"To what?" said the young man.

When they had scurried out, he crept up into the house. The smell of fuel-cell compound was dizzying. The raiders were filing out the front door. The wall-eyed leader was helping strew the compound through the halls and rooms. The red-haired militiaman hung back out of sight.

When the last of the fuel had been smeared on the old books in the parlor, the wall-eyed youth sent his accomplices outside and scuttled up the stairs, feeling in his loot-stuffed pockets. He brought out an igniter and bent to light a trail of compound. "Ssst!" said the militiaman behind him. The youth whirled. "Before you light it," whispered the militiaman quickly, "look what I found." He put his forefinger mysteriously to his lips and started to lead the leader toward one of the bedrooms.

The wall-eyed youth ducked down, fecklessly lit the compound, and followed.

"Hurry then," whispered the knobby young man, maintaining his calm. Behind them the compound crackled into flame. Smoke pursued them. The knobby young man pointed into a bedroom overlooking the front. "In there!" The leader peered in; the young man rabbit-punched him, knocking him unconscious, dragged him into the room, locked him in, and ran toward the stairs. The hallway was filling with smoke from the books and decorations, and the flame of the compound sent gusts of scorching gases against his face. Fire had crawled across the stairhead. The militiaman made a short, fierce run and broad-jumped over the flames; he landed awkwardly several steps from the top; his left boot slipped and he barely kept himself from falling down the rest of the flight. At the foot, he looked back up to where the melting, sputtering compound was dripping from step to step. The house was doomed. He pulled an igniter from his own pocket and clattered to the front door, lighting trains of compound as he ran; as he hurtled out into the gathered mob, he whooped, "Look at her *go!*"

The rioters gasped with delight as flames unfurled from several of the windows. "Hey!" yelled the knobby young man. "Where's the kid that brought us here?"

There was a fugue of "Where's Mick?" "Hey, Mick!" "I saw him a second ago." "I didn't see him." "Mick, where are you?" "Where's Mick?"

"*There* he is!" cried the militiaman. "He's caught in there. Look! Up there!" At the window of the locked bedroom, the figure of the youth came waveringly into view, struggling with the window latch. "Mick!" the knobby young man called anxiously, "what are you doing up there? Hey!" he said earnestly to the men around him, "he better get his ass out of there fast."

Mick got the window open, threw one leg over the sill, recoiled from the drop, looked inside, shrank from the glow, threw himself out, and lay moaning, his legs smashed under him. The rioters looked for the young militiaman to take charge again. But he was nowhere to be seen.

Meanwhile, on Hooke Place, in what during the First Settlement had been the Opera House and more recently a theater showing dubious threedees, the Chamber of Deputies was in session. Outside, the momentary masters of the planet chanted and vomited and burned out the families of the old elite. Inside, under the flaring houselights and the ratty old vainglories of the decor, the creators of the new state worked in a kind of fleshless passion: seconder gravely followed mover, speech followed speech, measure followed measure, in a long solemn ritual of organized consent.

"Those in favor will signify in the usual manner."

"Aye!"

"Opposed?"

A vigilant silence.

The Premier stumbled as he rose to introduce the Comprehensive Health Services Bill; the old man had not eaten for eleven hours. The Finance Minister seemed really to be in the grip of some private emotion as she listened to the young Minister of Propaganda; her lips trembled and her still comely bosom rose and fell quickly, as if she were listening to a serenade instead of a speech in support of a highly technical currency measure she had brought up; there was nothing to that, of course; she was the wife of an army doctor and the mother of three grown children.

It was during this speech that the first of two unseemly incidents took place. The Minister was deriding the "pathetic outcries of the rich, the secretly powerful, the skillful profiteers who have so long lived so well off the toil of others. The Revolution," he said, "is not sorry for them." There was a loud *crack* of metal giving way. It seemed that a deputy sitting with the conservative minority, a very large, seamy-faced old man, had twisted sharply in his seat and broken it. In the ensuing pause, he was heard to say to his neighbor in a growling aside, "So! Now! The Revolution has become a living thing. It will consume us all."

"The Revolution will not be intimidated in a whisper," said the Minister superbly and continued his speech.

Shortly afterward, the same large discordant old man could be seen arguing less audibly with the Minister of Justice in the shadows under the loges; and then he left, as did some other deputies. The majority went on with their enactments.

CHAPTER 2

NINETY-SEVEN days later, John Corander was in a waiting room on the tightly guarded fourth floor of the Ministry of Justice. He had an appointment with the redoubtable female who headed the Internal Defense Department, which was technically a division of that Ministry.

Corander was himself an IDD agent, but having been recruited and used "in place" in a hard-pressed and half-mutinous militia unit on the northern front, he had only twice before set foot in headquarters. He had never, so far as he knew, seen his chief.

The Ministry and its hated Department were still housed in a converted garment factory in a scarred, depopulated industrial suburb. The anteroom was so bare that seven of the eight people in it had nothing to fasten their eyes on but one another; so small that they could almost feel one another's stares like breaths. The one occupied person was a burly young man in a gray infantry uniform without insignia, seated behind a gray metal desk guarding the chief's door. He wrote steadily without glancing up.

The others, except Corander, played a bored, furtive game of eye tag: the aging young man with fingernails bitten to the quick would look covertly at the elderly woman with fine-boned, lacerated hands and the putrid breath of the starving; she would look up and catch him, and he would hastily shift his glance and meet the gaze of the listless workman who had eaten synthetic hard sausage for lunch; the workman's pale sad eyes would turn guiltily away and rest on the girl who might be a squeed addict, until her peevish glance darted toward him; and so on around the stifling room in endless permutations. Corander was a spectator.

The game dispersed abruptly as the massive alloy door of the chief's office slid open and emitted the citizen who had been inside for the past ten minutes, a top-heavy man with a melodramatic black mustache mounted on his prognathism. He stopped dead, as if struck by a recollection, hunched his shoulders convulsively, and blundered out of the anteroom. Corander could see the streaks of tears on the brutal face.

From the doorway of the inner office, a clear, reedy female voice called, "Send in Citizen Corander, please."

A silent nod from the guard. Corander, passing the desk, glanced down and saw that the burly young soldier was legless.

Her elbows on her desk, her chin on concentric fists, the Chief of the Internal Defense Department watched Corander with an intent half-smile as by habit he reached over to slide the door shut. It resisted him; he gave it a surreptitious wrench; it would not move. He faced his chief's smile and was disgusted to feel himself flush.

She said pleasantly, "It's *my* door."

Corander: "The People's door. The People's soundproof door."

Without taking her eyes off Corander's face, she shifted one elbow to depress a button on the desktop. The door rumbled shut behind him.

Citizen Wells was known (in undertones) throughout the Department's lower echelons as "the Little Bitch." Nothing factual was known of her except that before the Revolution she had been in the underground and during the early fighting had operated behind Imperial lines with a murderous daring that earned her, still a very young woman, a place in the generally colorless Rohanese leadership. Everyone had heard stories of how, by substituting doctored maps in the headquarters of two enemy battalions in the Ostwald, she had got one to storm a position held by the other; how, dressed as a boy, she had sauntered into the staff men's toilet at the Imperial Commission of Inquiry, walked up behind the atrocious First Secretary Kraitz as he stood at a urinal, cut his throat with a pocketknife, and sauntered out again; and how, leading an improvised commando of eight patients from a nearby mental hospital, she had rescued Judge Issachar from the Terrans' interrogation center at Quine. Then she was put in charge of the Revolutionists' counterintelligence and suddenly receded into the shadows; where she still, for all her reputed power, remained.

She was handsome, with dark hair and eyes, and skin like a pale Arcturan rose. She might be two or three years older than Corander, but there was a tracery of weary humor around those unrelenting eyes that made her seem older than that; suddenly he felt an intense, resentful desire for this dangerous young woman.

She said, "As you say, Corander, a soundproof door. If just anyone could walk in and close it, how long do you think I'd live?" She pointed to a plain steel chair. "I apologize for the chair."

It was indeed an uncomfortable chair; it was in keeping with the office. The entire Ministry, as Corander knew from the other visits, was drab and cluttered, and IDD's floors drabber than the rest. The green factory walls were unchanged except where heavy alloy plate had been riveted, or bready-looking soundproofing sprayed on, as in this office, which was the drabbest room of all. The chief's desk might have been an assistant bookkeeper's, the chief's own chair a straight steel affair no assistant bookkeeper would have submitted to. She sat straight-backed on it; she sat, Corander thought, like a young soldier driving a surface-cruiser in combat.

He said, "No apology needed. No creature comforts. Here we're still at war, citizen. Revolutionary self-discipline. I appreciate the thought you've put into the didactic setting here, citizen. The legless man outside, and so forth."

The dark ambiguous eyes widened. "Dirck? The job supports him while he writes his novel."

Corander nodded. "He can write his novel while he gives each of your visitors a little touch of castration anxiety. As preparation."

"Corander, please!" Pure amusement bubbled out of the

Chief of the Internal Defense Department. "I really have no intention of castrating you. You're quite safe from me." Then: "Agent Corander, there are certain reasons why I wanted to give you your new assignment myself instead of having the Briefing Room—"

His look stopped her.

Corander had come not for a new assignment but to resign from the Department. Citizen Wells, it appeared, had meanwhile sent for him for her own purposes. There was a brief contest of urgencies.

Citizen Wells, persisting: "Corander, there's a very important—"

Corander, offensively: *"Wells, it's useless."*

She gave him an astonishing little moue and then stared past him into space at her very important problem, whatever it was. She was treating him as if he were an old friend with whom she was accustomed to discuss her work. When her eyes were shadowed by care, they were the most beautiful eyes he had ever seen.

The eyes in question returned to him. "You want out of this Department. I can't think why. Deceit, killing, distrusting everyone—the work is light. I suppose you want to get back to—psychology, wasn't it? You were going to be a clinician. Maybe some day you'll take me on as a patient." The eyes fell. "But just now, you see, there's a matter—which isn't an ordinary Departmental matter—for me it's a personal matter—it's a—it *isn't* personal—it's—it's a matter of planetary consequence."

To his consternation, Corander heard himself say, "Do you want to tell me about it?"

Citizen Wells: "Not if you're about to leave the Department."

Corander: "Consider me your psychologist."

Again that ebullition of pure amusement. "Well, doctor, I have this friend, see..." Somberly: "No. In your *present* profession, Corander, we have a principle: never trust anybody you can't kill."

Corander: "And you trust me?"

Citizen Wells: "Oh, implicitly. But they've made it illegal for me to kill anyone outside this Department."

Corander: "All right, I'll take one more assignment."

Citizen Wells: "Are you familiar with the expression 'word of honor'?"

Corander: "You have my word of honor."

She began slowly. "There's a man who has to be brought in here, *to me*. He'll have to be arrested. He's a fugitive." She seemed about to take the word back, then: "Leave it at that, a fugitive. But he is *not* to be turned over to the—to the regular authorities. Under any circumstances. You are to arrest him and you are to bring him here; only you, and only here. And that will be a great deal more difficult than it sounds."

"Who's the man?"

"Simon de Ferraris."

Corander stared at her with erupting disgust.

It surprised the dominant species of Sol 3, as they drilled deeper and deeper into space, to discover no other intelligent life in the galaxy. Men fully expected to meet up with witty crustaceans, saurians with a full complement of ethics, culture-bearing vegetables, and the like. In system after system, however, they found very little living matter, and all of it rather mindless.

Planets in many systems could support advanced life, even human life, but to evolve it, it seemed, called for an odd environment which could support life but not support it in luxury. To produce complex organisms, very complex changes in environment were needed. On some planets, the changes had evidently come too fast; the rocks of Caramoor held a record of creatures with specialized organs, even nervous systems; but nothing was left alive under the dull green skies but some bacteria, a sort of vetch, four fungi. On others, the changes had come too slowly, and organisms had accommodated hardily, like the worms of Gaeus. Here and there, organisms would change their environment by crawling or flying from one place to another, and there were even a few that changed their environment by building or burrowing elaborately. The social insects of Procyon 4 could make fire— as primitive humans made it, by friction—but they did it out of instinct; in the cold warrens of that wretched planet, there was no time, no spare food, and no safety for helpless infancy. And so men found no six-legged Socrates or leafy Faraday in the Milky Way. In fact, they found no placental mammals. They found no altricial species whatever.

Having no natives to deal with, the leaders of Earth thought they would have a peaceful time colonizing the galaxy. At first they did.

The trouble was, by the time Chandra Gopal and DaSilva

(15)

had burst through Einstein's lid and mankind had reached deep space, no one could quite remember how to run a far-flung empire. For a hundred years the epicenter of Terran politics had been in the East, where the vast empires of the past, the Mongols' and the Russians', had been connected empires; sprawling, not scattered. The scattered empires had been the Western ones, the Spanish and the British preeminently; and now five generations of Terrans had been allowed to learn nothing about these except that they were bad.

It had been the fate, as often as not, of the old European imperial governments to clash with the grandsons of the colonists they had planted rather than with the autochthons they had supplanted: the English with the Americans, the Spanish with the Creoles. When this happened in space, the high-minded Terran administrators were dumbfounded. They had been taught virtue, not history. Soon they were sedulously repeating the mistakes of ancient Englishmen and Spaniards of whom they had never heard. Before long, the edges of the Empire were ragged with disorder.

The first full-scale colonial revolution broke out on Epsilon Struthionis 2, the most Earthlike of all the colonies. The Terran commander, Colonel General Pradjani, was able; his troops were steadfast; but his superiors on Earth lost opportunities faster than he could win battles. The rebel militiamen on Rohan's Planet deserted by platoons and ran away by regiments and sometimes found their generals home before them; and this only baffled the Imperial strategists the more.

Nearly four Earth-years of war all but wrecked the planet's precarious agriculture. A new class arose, numerous and bewildered: debtors. A situation like theirs had never existed before, so far as anyone knew. The Earth government had always (i.e. for eighty-three years) been the universal creditor, and interest rates had never (i.e. not for sixty-six years) been more than a means of motherly regulation. The Revolutionary regime, slow to think like a regime, had faltered, and credit had slipped, unnoticed, into private hands. An unheard-of economic animal, a mutant, the moneylender, appeared. The Revolutionary authorities themselves resorted to bonds and Freedom Loans and became a debtor. As risks grew, interest rates soared.

Worst of all, General Pradjani ordered his forces to pay in full for all supplies they commandeered on Rohan: they pumped money into the market and drained off goods, creating an inflation in every ward and village they held. In the third year of the war, farmers in some districts paid for a stere of seed-grain with a stere of banknotes.

In the last year of the fighting, the Imperial troops were in steady retreat, and wherever the guerrillas and the tattered patriot army drove out their well-heeled enemy, prices collapsed. The farmer who had borrowed 120 units when a drum of monopotassium phosphate cost 12 units had to repay 120 units when 1 unit would buy one drum—and when half the market for his produce had gone lumbering off into the great gray transports of the Empire. The debtors raised a piteous outcry.

The Kalino Cabinet proclaimed a great currency reform. The old unit-notes were called in and new notes issued—and issued, and issued, spilling from the presses in a green-and-russet flood, and fed back into the presses and overprinted with lengthening black rows of zeros. During the second inflation, a man could wipe out a lifetime of debt with a banknote that would not buy three cigarettes.

Creditors tried refusing to take the new money in payment. They lowered the interest rate to the vanishing point. They tried offering negative interest. They organized a Reconstructionist Party in opposition to the dominant Freedom Party.

A talented minority of members of the newly formed Chamber of Deputies threw in their lot with this new party. Their leader was one Simon de Ferraris, who represented a once prosperous New Nome constituency and was himself reputed to be still wealthy. Eccentric, sulphurous-tempered, a lumbering, wheezing, insulting giant of a man, he was unimpeachably patriotic. He had given money to the Revolutionary cause in its first days, when it seemed certain to fail ludicrously, and had lent money to the Revolutionary Government at nominal interest when its resources for carrying on the struggle had seemed exhausted. The sanguinary but indecisive campaign in the Plain of Runes had fed on him. He commanded enormous respect among the rich and had used it then and always to keep his class, who leaned toward the Loyalist side, from working actively against independence. But there were many who supported him now who had certainly not listened to him then: Loyalists who could not bring themselves to retreat with Pradjani's armies and had let the battle lines roll over them. To these grim, shamed remnants of a proud community, the Reconstructionist Party appealed irresistibly. They emerged as spokesmen for the New Poor.

In the ceremonious precincts of the Chamber, their support was powerful. Outside, in the debased give-and-take of mass politics, it cost the Reconstructionists dear. The Freedom Party had, in Carl ap Rhys, its Propaganda Minister, a youthful master of slashing sanctimony; it had no trouble in tacking the pro-Empire label on the whole Reconstructionist movement. As for the self-styled "patriot" de Ferraris—why, naturally he supported the moneylenders, explained the Freedom Party: hadn't the old usurer lent money to the fighters of the Freedom Party?

"Your tactic will work, Herman. No one," said Simon de Ferraris the last time he ever spoke to his old friend Premier Kalino, "ever lost an election by underestimating the intelligence of the People."

Kalino and de Ferraris stood together on the tarmac at the spaceport when Pradjani signed the Articles. Their friend the Minister of Justice stood between them. He was on speaking terms with both. But the three old men in dark coats were silent.

That night, debate in the theater on Hooke Place was strangely one-sided. De Ferraris and half his faction were in their accustomed places when the session began, but sat in unprecedented silence, abstaining on every vote. And in the small hours of the morning, as the Legal Tender Bill moved toward passage, the great bulk of Simon de Ferraris abruptly rose and started toward the exit. The Minister of Justice intercepted him in the shadows and could be seen extending his hands in supplication. De Ferraris caught one of the hands in his big left paw and wagged it; then he was gone. There was not one Reconstructionist left in the Chamber when the bill was passed into law.

The law seemed simple at first. Henceforward it was a felony to refuse to accept the new units in payment of a legal debt. There was the usual Schedule of Sentences to guide the judges: according to the size of the sum one refused, one might go to prison for a few months or be banished to the terrible subcontinent of Laing's Land for a term up to twenty years—which in Laing's Land meant for life.

The next morning began the strange spectacle of creditors hiding from their debtors, and debtors hunting them down and paying them without mercy. Four days later, the citizenry hit upon the clause numbered I.36(a).12. It defined the word "debt" in highly technical language that somehow included too much. Thus began the destruction of the magnates. Over the next weeks, as a divided Cabinet failed to amend the law, fortunes were annihilated in minutes. Great houses went under the hammer for food and clothing. Ladies with pale faces and soft, small hands could be seen among the New Poor waiting outside the Labor Exchanges. Men doing casual labor could be seen stopping to ask each other for instruction in the simplest operations. And gradually the seats of the Reconstructionist deputies began to fill again in the Chamber. The old occupants returned, but they were not the same. They came wearing patched, stained clothing; their smiles were tight and faint; they spoke only to one another, and in short, inaudible phrases; they voted but never debated. They seemed to be waiting. At last virtually all their seats were occupied, except one.

Simon de Ferraris did not return. He had not been seen in his seat, in his flat or his office in New Nome, or on his lands in the Kuban Valley, in the ninety-seven days since the first night of independence, when he had stepped through the exit of the old theater on Hooke Place.

It was clear that the fool was about to die; perhaps he had a weak heart; at any rate, the pain had been too much for him. He had stopped his feeble pulling at the cords and lay on the bed, spread-eagled, his breath seeming to scrape in and out of his lungs irregularly. His right hand, which Kullervo had tied slackly, lay soft, unclenched, perhaps already numb.

Kullervo picked up the pencil angrily and jammed it into the unresponsive hand. The man could not or would not hold it; Kullervo, restraining his fury, checked the gag in the man's mouth, reached over to the man's groin, and tightened the clamp there once more. This time the man did not even moan, but when Kullervo returned the pencil to the loose fingers, they closed gently on it.

Kullervo said, "If you tell me the truth, the pain will stop."

The man did not try to answer.

Kullervo picked up the cheap writing tablet on which the man had previously scrawled in a deteriorating script: "Laing's Land Laings L Its the truth Lai. L. Please LL LL LL Pls L"

Kullervo tore off the used sheet and stuffed it in his pocket;

he held the tablet near the man's hand and said, "Where did the old man go? Write the truth this time."

The pencil wavered: "La." Then it fell from the inert fingers and rolled onto the floor.

Kullervo felt for the man's heartbeat. There was none. His own heartbeat, however, thrummed in his ears. He was still feeling the excitement. And he had made fairly sure that the man had been telling the truth from the beginning.

He tore off the sheet of paper with "La" on it and put that in his pocket; undid the clamp, cleaned it on the bedsheet, and put it in the same pocket; scrambled on the floor, retrieved the pencil, put it in the pocket, and in doing so became aware that something had happened to his right eye.

He hurried into the dingy little bathroom to check his appearance in the mirror; and the disguising contact lens had in fact dropped out, revealing the telltale red iris; he now had one hazel eye and one albino eye. He returned to the bedroom and searched around the corpse; he could not find the lens; he knelt and peered around the floor, but his color blindness made it impossible to find the small object on the cheap, spotty design of the floor covering. His excitement was ebbing. A prickle of fear supervened. He ran his fingers through his hair; in withdrawing his hand, he saw that the sweaty palm was streaked with black. The hair dye was temporary, of course, meant only to disguise the white albino hair for an hour or two, but it did not have to come off that easily. Had he smeared his forehead?

It was at this moment that a man stepped into the room. Kullervo had carefully locked the door but the intruder had somehow opened it noiselessly—and now stood taking in the corpse, the crouching form of Kullervo, Kullervo's hair, and Kullervo's eyes.

"Morgan. Internal Defense Department," announced the newcomer calmly, and flourished a small plexic shield. "You're Deputy Kullervo. Or at least part of you—"

Kullervo killed him with a single burst from the little ray pistol he had drawn, rose, thought for a moment, transferred the pencil and the scrawled sheets of paper to Morgan's pocket, put the clamp in Morgan's hand to pick up his fingerprints, and tossed it on the bed.

He used the corner of his jacket to keep his own prints off the hardware on the door and went out, down the dark, filthy staircase, and out into the squalid streets, keeping his right eye closed.

The beam that seared through Agent Morgan's right temple, his throat, and the left portion of his rib cage missed by a few millimeters a microtransmitter taped to his chest under the left nipple.

Known in the Internal Defense Department as a T-Transmitter, it was standard equipment in the Imperial police services across the galaxy and had been issued, out of the spoils of the Revolution, to IDD personnel on especially dangerous assignments. It recorded sounds on a tiny loop of wire, so that the latest two minutes of the wearer's experience were always on the wire. The device was kept in the "RECORD" mode by the wearer's heart. The instant it was pulled from his chest— or his heart stopped—the circuit switched to the "TRANSMIT" mode and sent its last two minutes of data, compressed into one second, to Room 32 in the Department.

The Chief of the IDD faced Corander's glare of shock and revulsion and said nothing.

Corander began, *"In the Ministry of Justice—"*

He was interrupted by a little snarl from a buzzer in the chief's desk. Citizen Wells pressed a button, and without turning from Corander asked, "Very important?"

An insect-voice from the desk: "You said to tell you if—"

"Bring it." She pressed the door control. A man in civilian dress came in at a run and the door ground shut. He thrust a data-disc at Citizen Wells and she mounted it on the spindle of a reader unit. "T-Transmitter unload," said the man. He looked at Corander and back to his chief.

Citizen Wells, bleakly: "Yes, he should hear. Training. Agent Morgan, Agent Corander." She switched on the unit.

Confused sounds, the loudest the heartbeat of a straining man, and, once, a creak like a loose stair. The heartbeat alone. A vague stirring. Then words, close: "Morgan. Internal Defense Department. You're Deputy Kullervo. Or at least part of you—" A crackle—a radiation weapon, Corander thought—and, so close that it exploded like a bellow, just a fraction of a gasp. The heartbeat stopped.

The audio switched itself off. The chief and the man she had introduced as Agent Morgan looked at each other. "Oh God, Morgan, I'm sorry." She held out the data-disc.

He took it with a shaking hand, which she briefly held in both of hers. "Did we locate?"

Agent Morgan responded dully, "We're on our way."

Citizen Wells: "I think you want to go, Tim."

Agent Morgan: "I think I do."

"Go. Musca will relieve you. And Tim, tell Musca...the Little Bitch said to leak this to Billioray."

Agent Morgan nodded, then burst out, "My brother was with you in the Ostwald, remember? He would have died for you," and left.

Citizen Wells whispered to no one at all, "He did." She turned to Corander with misery in her eyes. "You were saying, 'In the Ministry of Justice...'" A pause.

Corander: "I forget what I was going to say."

Citizen Wells: "You were going to say you were shocked that I would order you to run a filthy political errand." A pause.

Corander, defiantly: "Yes."

"It has to look like that," the young woman said. "Because I *can't* explain." Then with the unconscious melodrama of a child: "Corander, I swear to you, I swear to you *on my honor*—" She broke off and started to blush. Corander felt an enormous dim-witted desire treacherously rise up inside him. "Damn you," she said. "I *swear* this assignment is not...what it looks like. Am I blushing?"

Corander nodded.

"I apologize for rubbing your nose in my little sincerity. I wish this would go away." She felt her cheeks with her palms, grimaced with exasperation, and then, crimsoning still more, came around the desk and stood over Corander, whose desire obeyed a kind of inverse-square law as she approached.

Citizen Wells: "I want to tell you why I thought you were the man I could trust with this assignment. To do it right, that is. Your record is quite—distinctive. Haldane Ridge. The Hammersville salient. The retreat from the canal. It was obvious you knew how to kill a man, but we all know how to do that; you also seemed to know how *not* to kill a man."

Corander made a perfunctory joke about practice making perfect. She stopped him and described an invisible war where the only safe thing was to kill one's enemies. "Except," she said, "you never really know who is your enemy and who is your friend. You served on Sarkis' firing squad—"

Corander said in a creaking voice, "And as you know, he was my oldest friend." He began to shudder with rage but went on seeing the intimations of thigh muscle and pelvic bone under the coarse white linen trousers fifty centimeters from his eyes.

Citizen Wells: "I knew it when I had you assigned to the firing squad."

Corander finally raised his eyes to her face. It was a very pale face. "Oh. You're going to tell me everything, item by item, that might make me hate you. You're a formidable woman, Citizen Wells."

"Sarkis was guilty. You said—was it to Mrs. Penstock?—'I suppose the simplest way for them to make me think Sarkis' sentence was just was to force me to execute it.' (I was impressed with that.) But Sarkis *was* guilty...On my honor."

Corander stared up at the pale, lovely, complicated face. "Mrs. Penstock. Go on."

Citizen Wells did not go on.

Corander: "And I thought I was irresistible."

Citizen Wells: "They all said you were."

Corander: "All?"

Citizen Wells: "All the ones that reported to me. Elaine. Molly. Lucille. Mrs. Penstock."

Corander: "That's all of them. They reported to you?"

Citizen Wells: "In detail. Well, they had to. I assigned them to you." That unruly laughter of hers seemed to tremble around her lips. "You have to admit, Corander, I may not be a great policeman, but I'm a—a formidable madam."

Corander, meanly: "Are you ever sorry you went into administration?"

Citizen Wells: "As regards killing, yes."

Corander remembered First Secretary Kraitz.

Citizen Wells: "As regards *not* killing, I *am* an administrator and I want you to arrest Simon de Ferraris and bring him to this room *safe*—as safe as Lucille's paralytic husband when you crawled into the fire at the Locks and pulled him out, Corander—as safe as Mrs. Penstock's little boy when you took him to the doctor at Pradjani's headquarters, Corander."

"I can *formally* arrest him?"

Under the tunic, a long, silent exhalation; no other acknowledgment of his surrender. "You'll have to find him first."

Corander: "I'll find him."

Citizen Wells: "Then you can arrest him formally."

Corander: "On what charge?"

Citizen Wells: "Violation of the Legal Tender Act."

Corander: "How can he have violated the Legal Tender

Act? If I recall, Simon de Ferraris disappeared before the act was passed."

Citizen Wells: "He disappeared completely."

Corander: "Then he has *not* refused to accept payment in legal tender."

Citizen Wells: "He has not."

Corander: "You're saying he *will* refuse?"

Citizen Wells: "You will offer to pay him. I think he will refuse you."

Corander: "Is he insane?"

Citizen Wells said with a curious sadness, "His motives are excellent."

Corander: "Where is he?"

Citizen Wells: "Where would *you* have gone if you were Simon de Ferraris?"

Corander declined to play Three Guesses, and at length the Little Bitch explained. "As soon as Simon de Ferraris heard in the Chamber that the punishment for refusing this trash we issue would be banishment to Laing's Land, he stood up and went where he could refuse payment and not be banished. He went to Laing's Land."

Corander: "You sound as if you admire him for running away from his debtors and leaving his friends in the lurch."

But it appeared that in fact de Ferraris had saved his friends. Knowing that the Legal Tender Act would come in some form, he had prepared. He was immensely rich—"in solid things like land and machinery," said Citizen Wells, "not in what they call liquid assets. In the Valley of Kuban...never mind the details." Simon de Ferraris did not belong to the creditor class at all.

Corander: "He lent money to the Revolution, didn't he?"

"He lent us money as long as no one believed we could ever pay it back. He could have just given it to us; but that, you see, wouldn't have shown confidence."

When the Act came, the old man had dropped from sight and got in touch with his friends, who between them were holding instruments of debt with face values in the millions— practically worthless paper. He had bought up those instruments, paying for them with hard property. What he paid his friends was not what they had loaned out, but in real value it was ten thousand times what they would have got from the debtors. Simon de Ferraris' friends could come out of hiding and sit in the Chamber; and he held the instruments and went into hiding. "He had to," said Citizen Wells. "The

Act forbids 'speculation' in debt instruments, and if you can convict the 'speculator,' you can seize whatever he paid for your debt instruments."

Corander: "Where exactly in Laing's Land?"

"That I don't know."

Corander: "But you do know he's in Laing's Land?"

The Chief of the IDD said, "I know Simon de Ferraris."

Corander: "A lot of men might consider the thought of being paid by angry debtors less unattractive than the thought of being murdered by an angry vegetable. Anyway, how safe from the *big* debtors is he? He's not the only man who'll go through a lot for money."

"They wouldn't go through Laing's Land."

The cry was far away but distinct, the cry of a human in mortal pain.

The old man rolled his huge frame out of the hammock and stood up with a speed that belied his shock of white hair and his heavy paunch. "Cath!" he roared. "Cath!"

A young woman in the last stages of pregnancy came hurriedly out onto the porch of the cabin, fear mingled with the inquiry on her face.

The man was already pointing. "Out there. Listen."

She shook her head, hearing nothing.

Under the frowning black brows that had never whitened with his mane, the old man's eyes were fixed on his wristwatch. His long, seamed, bulbous old face was rapt. The scream came again, hardly more than a thrill of the motionless atmosphere.

"Over a minute," said the man. "It's just started." He picked up one of the metallic boots beside the hammock and began to work an enormous stockinged foot into it.

"Simon!" burst out the young wife.

"It's another of them, all right," the old man rumbled. "We'll never run short of fools."

"Simon!" The girl clutched tensely at his arm. "Simon, you mustn't go."

"But, my dear..." The old man looked up with a sardonic smile. "My dear, he may be a fool, but he's our guest! He's come a long way just to see me. I can't leave him out there."

"You mustn't go, you mustn't go. The last time you were nearly caught yourself, and the man died anyway."

Simon finished with his boots and straightened. "Cath dear, my little girl, I cannot leave that poor devil on the vine.

Whatever he is, he's human"—the scream again, higher-pitched—"and...so I must help him."

"It's worse this time. If you don't come back, it isn't just me now. What will become of us? Don't go."

He glared down at her tenderly and touched her stomach with a feathery motion of his huge paw. "Don't be frightened, little love. If I don't come back, break radio silence and call McIntyre. But I'll be careful." He whirled her up in an embrace, seized a heavy metal rod leaning against the cabin, and ran down the kopje with his great rolling stride.

The girl watched him in pride and anguish, both hands to her hair, which spilled like dark honey through her fingers. At the foot of the slope he turned, flourished his glistening, staff over his head, bellowed, "Back in a minute!" and disappeared at a run among the yellow plant gases of the swamp.

Citizen Wells: "They wouldn't go through Laing's Land. But you still miss the point. What if they did find him there? He'd refuse to accept payment."

Corander: "And you'd have him."

Citizen Wells: "The Legal Tender Act wasn't drafted in this Ministry. Deputy Kullervo, who did most of it, is a great friend of the People but not a competent legal draftsman; he forgot to abrogate the old Imperial law that a man must be tried in the district where he committed his crime. Simon de Ferraris refuses payment in Laing's Land, he's tried in Laing's Land—well, at the station on Spion Island off the coast—and then, according to the Schedule of Sentences, he goes back to Laing's Land."

Corander: "And this debt I'm to non-pay? Same result."

Citizen Wells: "This is a small debt, thirty units—two months in jail under the Schedule. There's no jail in Laing's Land. We couldn't keep people out of it if there were. Consequently, he comes back. Under guard. You're the guard; that's essential."

Corander began to laugh and could not stop. "By the Lord, our plot is a good plot as ever was laid," he gasped between whoops, wiping his eyes; "our friends true and constant: a good plot, good friends, and full of expectation; thirty units," he crowed; "an *excellent* plot, *very* good friends. Thirty units. Excuse me, citizen; it's the feeling of degradation. And what do we do when Simon de Ferraris accepts them?"

"I don't think he will," said the young woman in a curious

voice. "I don't think he'll accept them. But if he does, you will say he didn't."

A silence fell.

"Whose debt am I paying?" asked Corander.

Citizen Wells: "Mine." She issued him a true copy of her debt instrument, the money to pay it, her quitclaim to Corander for it, an undated warrant for Simon de Ferraris' arrest ("This was hard to get!"), Departmental orders, miscellaneous passes and papers, and a sealed note to a "poor Frizzell" at the Caserne on Spion Island. He signed for them all. "Here are the discs on Simon de Ferraris. You will now go to Room Forty and study them under mnemergine, a moderate dose. The techs are ready for you. Then to Room Twenty-one downstairs for your travel money, your transportation data, and the rest. Then to the Geographical Office in the Annex; they'll brief you there on Laing's Land; but to them you're Abraham Kemp, a chemist who has permission to visit his brother in exile. That's your cover until you make the arrest. Next, come back to this floor and in Room Thirty-one get your special equipment. That includes the N-Transmitter. You've never had one."

Corander: "No."

Citizen Wells: "*You* won't have any trouble with it. It operates two-way scrambled audio on a fixed wavelength, a protected wavelength which is your own. One of the receiver-senders in Room Thirty-two is tuned to it, to you and no one else, with a man detailed to it at all times. Your whorl-plate will switch the set. When you get the N-T, you're on your way. You'll get running instructions once you find de Ferraris. Clear?"

Corander: "Clear."

Citizen Wells: "Corander, listen to me. This is essential. It is not, repeat *not*, the policy of this Department to share information or responsibility with any other bureau or agency in the Government. Do you know what this means?"

Corander looked steadily at his chief. "I know what it means."

CHAPTER 3

WHEN Simon de Ferraris was out of sight of the little berylloy cabin, he took a less jaunty and more practical grip of the raystick and studied the path with darting eyes, as he half-ran, hunched forward. The path was dry, but the greenish sand had a soapy consistency and smeared underfoot. On either side festered the pools and pocks of the maremma; the plant gases hung over them. Here and there, black specks skittered in low arcs: the bog-flitters, little beaked hexapods with membranous foreclaws like wings, flying in silence because it was daylight. The whole scene was silent, except for the screams.

These were coming faster and seemed nearer, but their direction was less certain. The old man had chosen his path from the summit of the kopje and was committed to it but, as always in the swamp, had begun to doubt it. He lifted the raystick, his thumb rolling the knurled wheel in the shaft to open out the collimator. A dense mustard-yellow cloud of vapor was hanging across the path, and he destroyed it methodically. His teeth were bared.

Two kinds of vegetation had given Laing's Land much of its evil repute. Plant gases were the lesser of the two. They were not really gases, but cloudlike networks of brown filaments electrostatically holding a thick, oily yellow vapor; they were rooted almost like Terran plants and grew from a kind of fluid seed; they were not lethally poisonous but produced a tenacious and sickening itch.

The other and far worse growth, E.Str.2.183.03 in the old Imperial Classification, locally known as "the vine," was a reticulated creeper that sometimes covered an entire hectare with wrist-thick tendrils sheathed in a glossy gray substance; from these grew flexible offshoots, some spearing into the ground and becoming roots, others twining across the stems. Needing, apparently, the by-products of certain kinds of putrefaction to which proteins were liable on this world, it lived in a terrible symbiosis with the Laing's Land fauna. The bog-flitters dropped their egg-slime around the roots and on the heavier stems of the vine; their spawn or larvae were parasites on the vine until they formed hard membranes around themselves like birds' eggs; and when they hatched from these they became the prey of the plant. Let a bog-flitter flick against—or even near, some said—a tentacle, and the tentacle whipped up and around it; the gray sheath, ionized or chemically altered, became both adhesive and corrosive, and soon the bog-flitter was dead; and the vine imbibed the nutrient from its rotting carcass. Almost any sort of animal protein—Terran as well as Rohanese—attracted the tentacles. A man once caught could never break loose by his own strength; the fibers etched through his clothing and into his flesh; and it was the special horror of the vine that they did not do so continuously. The grip was steady, but the electrochemical attack was rhythmic. The agonies came a minute apart at first, then faster and faster, mounting in intensity, until each spasm drowned the release of the last—like the pains of a woman in labor. Some biologists maintained that the bog-flitters were not in pain, but in ecstasy, that a principle of inversion or algolagnia ran through Rohanese life; but it was no Liebestod for humans—such as the poor wretch whose screams were now coming at half-minute intervals. Simon de Ferraris had recovered bodies from the maremma...

He focused the raystick to a tight beam and set off at a run. The path twisted and doubled and doubled again maddeningly. A false step, or a misjudged try at a shortcut, and he would end in one of the glutinous pocks where the vine flourished. Once he took a wrong turn and found himself at the end of a long, winding spur a little more than a meter from the true path. The shrieks were only a few seconds apart now and changing their note. The grim old face trembled.

"God," the old man muttered, "but this one can stand a lot!" He gathered his forces and jumped. One foot dragged across a tendril, and it cracked upward; but the metal of his boot had delayed the reaction and his leg was clear. He landed on the other foot, twisted his ankle, staggered, caught his balance in time to keep from plunging into the next pock, and pounded down the path, throwing off the pain.

The screams were coming as fast as his own pulse and had lost all human quality. He scanned the swamp, skipping back and forth on the path to see around obstacles. He glimpsed something dark, almost hidden by a plant gas. It writhed.

It was at least thirty meters away, too far to burn a clear path to it in time with a light raystick. The rescuer must pick his way through the great gray net of the vine, trusting to his metal boots to damp the stimulus of his flesh, and every step for sixty paces landing within a centimeter of death. Or—leave the man on the vine.

"I'm coming!" he shouted. "I'm finding the heart!" The vine had no heart; the term was used for a polysynaptic node over each of the main root clusters. Burning out a heart stopped the electrochemical activity in a large area of the vine and allowed a victim to be pulled free, but the heart might be meters away from the victim.

The wretch gave no sign of having heard. His cry was almost continuous. De Ferraris poked the outermost tendrils of the vine aside with the raystick and gingerly set his foot down. He took a second step; a third. On the fourth, a new sprout which he misgauged lashed across his toes; he burned the strand off.

Here and there the vine was speckled with the decomposing bodies of bog-flitters and other creatures, most of them no longer recognizable. The old man had a horrifying vision of two large new lumps of compost rotting in the gray-and-mustard desolation. After eight paces, he could see what he thought must be the fibrous knob of a heart. He managed to get four steps nearer to it and trained his raystick on it. The target sputtered and gushed a luminous vapor for a few moments. It was a heart, but governed neither the place he was standing nor the victim's trap. Bog-flitters dropped off where the vine went dead, indicating a safe area which reached the path at one point. This would be his way back, if he went back.

Working forward with a prancing, hobbling gait, he saw another heart. In his haste he landed carelessly on his twisted ankle, which buckled and touched a fiber. With a whistle and report, a tentacle whipped at his leg, catching him above the boottop. A flash of agony went through him, and a worse flash of terror, for the impact sent him off balance and for seconds, flailing with his arms, he hovered between standing and falling.

A chance stab with the raystick against a clump of hard soil righted him. His leg was numb, which made it more dangerous to burn off the tendril close to the flesh. A better chance lay in destroying the heart before the minute elapsed and his own agony began. He seared at it tremblingly.

The victim fell loose. The contorted form rolled over. The shriek went on for a moment and then made a kind of sobbing glissando to a low animal croon. An instant later, the rescuer felt the torment blaze in his own side; he himself was still on the vine.

Frantically, he turned the ray on the tangle of stems around him. One after another, fibers sputtered and parted. The rubbery grip on his thigh did not relax. He brought the whining tip of the raystick closer and closer to himself, shaking uncontrollably. He felt the surge of the vine begin again, then stop abruptly. The tendril slid off. His eyes filled with tears.

He blinked them away and examined his thigh. Blood oozed where his breeches had been turned to pulp. The fiery numbness subsided, and he could already feel the raw wound as a wound.

Between him and the recumbent victim lay only a few meters of live vine. The injured leg made it impossible to pick his way across; the man was safe enough for the moment, having enough life to keep up his keening, now broken by efforts to mouth words. De Ferraris began to cut a pathway.

Some minutes later, he looked down at the limp, crying form. "You're all right," he said dully. "You're all right."

A long, gasping sob answered him. Simon de Ferraris lowered himself painfully to his good knee, his other poking out awkwardly in front of him. He unclasped the man's tunic and shirt and bared the flesh. He would have retched but for the bracing pain of his own wound.

"S——" began the man, trying to bring his eyes into focus on his rescuer.

"Yes?"

"Simon d——d——" It was to be a question.

"I am Simon de Ferraris."

"I owe you my l——" The eyeballs locked upward and the man fainted.

Simon de Ferraris muttered, "That's not all you owe me." Under the open shirt he found the usual belly-belt and slipped open the pouch. Inside were a bank-banded wad of high-denomination notes, a standard copy-of-instrument form, a quittance prepared for his own signature, and odds and ends of papers. "Sad little fool!" the old man growled. He replaced the papers, the debt-instrument, and the quittance; he flapped the money thoughtfully and hurled it into the scum under an undamaged part of the vine.

Most of the spaceport departure facilities were shut down, disused, but a new row of gates bore stenciled signs, erratically lit, reading: NEW NOME AUXILIARY AIRPORT.

While Rohan's interstellar communications had all but ceased, its domestic traffic had swollen with the postwar dislocation. Outside one corner of the terminal complex, on the terrace over which the goose-shaped loaders once had trundled passengers and goods toward giant spaceliners three kilometers away, stood two rows of neat, aging copters. In the night chill, amid the flare of lights, porters in chipped red helmets shuffled to and fro with lists and luggage; passengers waited in groups, fumbling with their documents.

Corander, his youthful, bony frame costumed in the respectable seedy tunic and breeches of a professional or scientific worker, stood near one of the groups. He excited no curiosity; his kind were a unit a hundred, men and women who had watched their hard-won youthful savings, all the hopeful beginnings of their prosperity, wiped out and were now struggling to live on salaries less and less responsive to the inflation.

An official came up, printout in hand, the bored peremptoriness of government showing through the time-honored bogus optimism of ports. At his back came a little man, unmistakably a busy, trying to maintain a look of great significance on naturally insignificant-looking features.

The official peered at his printout and intoned, "Belaker Ulysses." The little man behind him stood with eyes rolled piously up to the green-black sky, apparently miming the silent patience of the state.

A portly man in the field uniform of the Geophysical Corporation stepped forward and honked, "Right here," extending his sheaf of documents.

The official flapped them perfunctorily into the small man's line of vision, intoned, "In order," and handed them back. "Coomaraswami Sam...in order. Gibbons Harold...in order. Kullervo Kosti...good *evening*, Deputy!" The official fawned on a heavy-set man with the colorless hair and red eyes of the total albino, and the little busy puffed out his chest and coughed importantly. The official: "In order, of course. Gregorowicz Clara...in order. Kemp Abraham..."

Corander walked over with his papers. The small man cleared his throat. The official handed the papers over to him without looking at them. The small man said in a thin portentous twang, "Will you step this way, Citizen Kemp?"

Chapter 4

AT the head of the table in his own villa, Premier Kalino faced his ministers warily. Something was wrong: the rhetoric which had interfaced a thousand political understandings seemed to have failed eight or nine times already this evening.

"Olivia," said the Premier earnestly, almost pleadingly, "this is in your Department. Surely you can suggest something which will meet—"

"I'm sorry, Herman. Carl said it all," replied the Finance Minister in her rich voice. She glanced softly toward the Propaganda Minister for a fraction of a second. The Premier saw the look, and his heart tightened.

The Premier: "Carl, Carl, have you really said it all? Policy is not exactly doctrine. Surely there is more to be said than these—"

The Propaganda Minister: "I'm sorry, Herman." There was a flush on his cheekbones above the lean blue-black jaw.

The Premier: "'I'm sorry, Herman.' It seems to be a formula tonight. And you, Mustafa, are you sorry-Herman too?"

The Minister of Justice looked not at his old friend but at his two opponents across the table. The Propaganda Minister returned his stare. The Finance Minister looked down; and the aged judge gloomily surveyed her soft shoulders and ripe bosom. "With me it is not a formula," he said dryly.

The Premier: "We had better recess. I'm beginning to feel sorry for myself."

The Cabinet members drifted in pairs and trios out into the dark garden, and their host, the Premier, sat alone at the head of the long table, restlessly sketching on a pad with his fading-pencil. This device wrote a clear black line which lasted four minutes and then rapidly faded away without a trace; it was sold as a child's toy, but the Premier found it invaluable at meetings. He could sketch endlessly without leaving a pictorial record of his thoughts and pass notes that ceased to exist once they had been read.

He had drawn Rohan's Planet, a neat circle, and the western outlines of its main land mass, Van Vainor's Land, and its great peninsula, Laing's Land. A heavy jagged line represented the River Bohr, the water-filled fissure which marked off the subcontinent of Laing's Land. He shaded in the continent and subcontinent with a deftness he owed to his early years as a geology master in a girls' boarding school. Now, as fast as he penciled in the details, the outlines faded and vanished. He touched up one stroke; another was gone. The old fighter for Rohanese freedom smiled despondently. It seemed a symbol of Herman Kalino's lifework.

The Cabinet was split and the Freedom Party would soon break apart. The moderate faction was led by an elderly retired judge, the Minister of Justice, Mustafa Issachar. The radical majority was led by the youthful Minister of Propaganda. This Carl ap Rhys, with his high color and dark intensity, his adolescent virility, his oratory too full of effects and touches, mystified the Premier, whose heart was with Mustafa Issachar. Kalino had an old man's desire for warmth; he longed for the unity of the first days of independence, when the same vision was strong upon them all...no, his real nostalgia, if he was to be honest, was for the period of struggle and war, when there had been no Reconstructionist Party and when Simon de Ferraris still roared in the Revolutionary councils. And where was Simon at this moment?...However, the party rank and file were on ap Rhys' side, and a certain logic too. The Propaganda Minister proposed to continue the inflation, ruthlessly using the state's power of issuing money to wipe out once and for all the "creditor" class, who existed only because the state's early blunders had forced them into being. (But Carl ap Rhys did not dwell on these blunders, for which his devoted ally in the Finance Ministry was responsible; he merely mentioned them—it increased her devotion, Kalino supposed.) The moneylenders had appropriated the planet. The People would expropriate the moneylenders.

The moderates urged a policy of deflation. They distinguished between creditor and capitalist. They would impose heavy taxes and retire the currency thus taken in, cutting expenditures almost to nothing. This meant giving up the great public works program the Propaganda Minister delighted in; the clearing of Laing's Land would have to wait. Even the health-insurance benefits would have to be revised. Otherwise, Judge Issachar said, the inflation would destroy private capital, destroy all capability of self-renewal, and force the planet back into economic dependence on the Empire.

For three hours the Premier had argued, wheedled, and manipulated for a modest retrenchment that would save the most urgent public works, and spare the industrialists further punishment.

Something was wrong. It was as if someone at the table had secretly decided to force a crisis. Herman Kalino rose to walk in the garden before reconvening the Cabinet. He would make one more effort.

The small man led Corander through the ringing, tall, half-darkened vacuities of the terminal, down a motionless escalator, into a service area.

"My office," said the busy. It was a cubicle with sound insulation sprayed thickly over makeshift partitions, neat in a way that Corander associated with functionaries who had no real functions. In offices like this, they always began by telling you smartly that you had to hustle to make way for the next appointment, then they kept you forever. Corander could not afford a long delay. There was only one flight left to New Tavistock, the only town beyond the River Bohr with scheduled air service. The copter was due to take off in twenty minutes. Missing it meant a nine-hour wait—perhaps longer if tomorrow morning's passenger manifest was full of junketing bureaucrats. New Tavistock was not very far inside Laing's Land, but far enough to have a "frontier" atmosphere, and since Independence it had become a popular resort of petty officialdom out for a thrill.

The little busy: "I can give you a few minutes. I have an appointment at"—he looked at his watch and did some arithmetic, moving his lips—"twenty-four sixty-three."

Corander: "I don't want to take up your time at all."

Ignoring this, the busy spread Abraham Kemp's documents out on his desk and sat down to contemplate them.

"You Abraham Kemp?" he said at length.

Corander: "Yes. How did you know?"

The busy: "A plant chemist?"

Corander: "Yes." He sat down unasked.

The little man opened a drawer and fingered through a bunch of bluish pamphlets. They were the old Imperial Army Q-and-A books. Every personnel worker used them to check the claims of professed specialists. Not six hours before, Corander had studied one under mnemergine. The busy pulled out the one labeled "Chemistry, Plant," opened it, and, elaborately concealing the text from Corander, asked, "What is...colchicine used for?"

Corander, contradicting the manual at random: "Nothing much. It used to be used pretty extensively for doubling chromosomes in hybrids so as to make them fertile. That brochure you have there must be pretty old."

The busy: "Hm. What is the difference between... flavanones and...flavanols?"

Corander tried to answer the "Q" without using the exact words of the "A." "The flavanols have an extra double bond and a hydroxyl group which the flavanones don't have."

"Hm." The little man put away the booklet and asked, "Brother of Carroll Kemp?"

Corander: "Yes."

The busy: "Ah—um—I've heard of your brother's case."

This was more than Corander could say. He said nothing.

The little man looked at him with what he obviously hoped would be a penetrating glance but, failing to effect penetration, dropped his eyes and said, "I've sometimes thought your brother was harshly treated."

Corander said nothing. He could hear a recording device creaking defectively in a desk drawer.

The busy: "Going to New Tavistock?"

Corander: "Yes." He added mildly, "The copter leaves in fifteen minutes."

The busy: "And from there?"

Corander: "I'm going to contact my brother there."

The busy: "Private reasons?"

Corander: "Yes."

The busy: "What are they?"

Corander: "I like my brother."

The busy: "He was a Loyalist."

Corander: "He's my brother."

The conversation wound its way slowly to the point at which the busy said, "Know many of your brother's friends?"

Corander: "We weren't that close."

A few tortuous minutes more, and the busy asked, "Would you like to do something for your brother?"

Corander: "Yes."

The busy said thoughtfully, "I think your brother was harshly treated."

Corander: "So you said."

The busy: "I might be able to get his sentence shortened, if I thought it was too long."

Corander: "You already said you thought it was too long. _I_ didn't."

The busy: "Your brother sees a lot of Loyalists."

Corander: "There are a lot of Loyalists in Laing's Land—for some reason."

The busy: "We'd like to know a little about his friends, the Loyalists."

Corander: "Who is 'we,' citizen?"

"The Internal Defense Department," said the little man, and with a conjurer's flourish produced a glossy styoprene badge.

Corander stared. He had heard that the Department employed quasi-overt agents at airfields and other centers, and he had realized from the outset that this must be a particularly debased specimen of these, but he was appalled that the man should so openly name his connection with the Department. "So?" he said.

The busy: "Do you love Rohan?"

Corander: "Sure. Fine."

The busy: "You could write a little report on these Loyalists who see your brother."

Corander: "I'm a plant chemist, not a spy."

There was some discussion of this tactless sentence. Then the busy tried cajolery: "It would be helping your brother."

Corander: "I won't spy."

The busy tried sternness: "You want to be on that copter tonight?"

Corander: "My papers are in order."

The busy: "You're what is called a Category C passenger, family of a banished convict."

Corander: "I know I am. I can read."

The busy: "Category C passengers have to have what is called pilot's clearance."

"So then? You're not the pilot."

The busy: "I am the Acting Security Officer of this airport."

Corander: "You're not the pilot. My papers are in order. My ticket is paid for. I am not unruly. The pilot can't refuse me clearance."

The busy: "On my recommendation he can."

Corander looked at his watch and brought matters to a head. "Recommendation! Recommendation!" he shouted. Then more quietly: "So you *admit* it's a recommendation only. Tell you what I think, citizen. I think you've badly exceeded your authority."

The Acting Security Officer stood up. "You think that, do you? We'll see," he said with weak bluster. "Wait here," he added nervously, as Corander began to rise. "I'm going to get the pilot." He strode out.

It was three minutes before flight time.

"Where's Kid Freedom?" said a voice from the door.

"Who?" asked Corander, turning.

"Keyhole Johnny. Acting Security Officer Thekman, the flower of our liberties," explained the newcomer rapidly. He advanced with a cordial smile on his chubby, weatherbeaten features.

Corander: "He went off to look for the pilot of the New Tavistock flight."

"Went off to look for me? Went—ah! I see it all. Off the old gridlines at last. I knew it would happen. That's what comes of him guarding our freedom night and day, citizen. Sad. Sad. You see," the pilot went on, noticing Corander's face, "I always meet him here five minutes before flight time. Always. Gone off to look for me! Well, well."

Corander: "He isn't crazy."

The pilot: "'Isn't crazy'! Who are you, coming here with these indiscreet, not to say Reconstructionist-type, observations about our beloved Acting Security Officer?" He was sidling over to the desk to get a glimpse of the papers on it.

"Hah! My missing passenger, Abraham Kemp, the pride of Category C. Come along, Abraham. Unless you've committed syphilis-G," he rattled anxiously. "No? Murder, arson? No? Rape, refusal of payment, felonious assault with a deadly weapon, common sense, sodomy, high treason? No? Come along, then." His speed of utterance was astonishing, and his face beamed all the while in the most placid repose.

Corander: "I need pilot's clearance."

The pilot: "With unerring instinct, you've come to the right man. Flight Officer Desmond Henry Feigenbrod clears you while he flies you. Pleased to meet you. Come along."

Corander: "But he said he would recommend that you refuse me clearance. That's why he went to fetch you." He stared fixedly at the desk drawer that hid the defective recorder.

The pilot: "Fetch me? Recommend? Ah, Abraham, I see you are but a child in these matters...Yes, Abraham, I hear it chirping its little song of love."

Corander opened the desk drawer and said loudly, "Why, somebody's left a little machine running! What do you suppose it is?" He turned it off. "Thekman, I take it, went to intercept you so you wouldn't come here and find me."

The pilot, his ink-pencil poised over a form, peered at Corander and said without flippancy, "Intelligent plant chemist. Here's your clearance."

Corander: "Wait. Won't this get you into trouble?"

The pilot: "Trouble? Me?" He scrawled a firm *D.H.F.* "No trouble at all."

Corander: "But I'm Carroll Kemp's brother."

The pilot: "The name is new to me."

Corander: "He's a Loyalist."

The pilot: "I think your brother was—oh ah uh hem hem—harshly treated. Eh?" Feigenbrod laughed shortly. "Was that it? Love Rohan? Just a little report. Mere fratricide. Horace Thekman wanted you for his very own spy, eh?"

Corander: "That's it."

The pilot: "Well, friend Kemp, I really never heard of your brother, eminent seditionist though he may be, but I'll do a great deal for a man who won't sell out to IDD." He picked up Kemp's papers. "Let's gather up these blessings of freedom here and leave before Captain Sneak of the Nose Patrol comes and delays the flight another half hour." He lowered his voice as they went out: "Ever hear of Simon de Ferraris? Well, my father was old Simon's farm manager out at Kuban Valley, and if it weren't for old Simon I'd be a stinking little state-trained hydroponics hand right now, shoveling magnesium sulfate till I was ready for my pension. I'm telling you this so you'll know. My father got killed by a rogue plow-robot, you understand, and I always wanted to go to space, but Surabaya wanted the locals to shovel magnesium sulfate. And Simon de Ferraris paid out of his own pocket to send me to Earthside flight school. Out of his own pocket. Couldn't get me a job on spacegoing stuff. All Earthies in those days. But you wait. One of these days they'll throw out that wind sock Kalino and put in old Simon and we'll have a real government and a real space fleet and *I'll* be on the Antares run."

They came to some side doors opening on the field.

Corander: "Wait a minute."

The pilot: "Wait? Certainly I'll wait! Haven't I waited patiently while you regaled me with the most shameful and loose-mouthed treason—"

Corander: "Do me a favor?"

The pilot: "Right."

Corander needed a place where he could use his N-T, which was strapped to the inside of his left thigh, and report himself to Room 32. "Is there an empty room somewhere? I won't be a minute."

The pilot: "Crew's head. I'll let you in with my key, and there's a bolt on the inside. Then come straight to Position Six. And, Citizen Kemp...pull the flush before you leave. Verisimilitude, you know. Place is crawling with patriots."

Everyone at the table knew the crisis had come. The Premier could see swallowing movements in Olivia Keye's mature neck. Carl ap Rhys was more vivid than ever. The Minister of Armies and Marine, Francis Bentinck, had his eyes closed and was damply pale. The Minister of Health, Ch'ien Wu-hsien, was scribbling with his head down. Mustafa Issachar alone looked calm, a withered sea-eagle, motionless and fierce. And that, thought Kalino, might be the worst sign of all.

The Premier: "Well then, we *have* made progress, haven't we? Wu has agreed to get us a Departmental memo on possible reductions in health-insurance costs."

The Minister of Health: "Under protest." He looked up. "Reluctantly."

The Premier: "I mean savings, not crippling cuts."

The Minister of Health: "Under protest." He resumed his scribbling.

The Premier's tactic was to divert everyone's attention to the small practicalities of Departmental budgeting and ease both sides into compromise. Both sides knew that. For a moment, nevertheless, it seemed as if the maneuver might work.

Just as Kalino was forming the name "Francis" on his lips—he was beginning with the less political ministers—the voice of Carl ap Rhys glided into the pause. "May I ask what help Mustafa is ready to give this big program of little economies? Will he—"

"Carl," began Kalino desperately, "I think I should put the—"

"Will he perhaps cut out that very expensive item," the Propaganda Minister asked in a ringing voice, "the Internal Defense Department?"

Everyone looked at the Minister of Justice. The Premier wondered: Will Mustafa cut off his right arm for me?

The Minister of Justice: "I shall ask the chief of that Department how much of its activities we can now do without." He was not forcing the break.

The Propaganda Minister was. "I for one can do without your gun-girl entirely."

The Premier whispered: "Carl—"

The Minister of Justice said calmly to ap Rhys: "My 'gun-girl', as you call her, discovered General Ibrahim's treason. My 'gun-girl' stopped the North Front desertions. My 'gun-girl' broke up Shigahara's gang. My 'gun-girl' caught Fenstermacher. And when"—the aged voice dropped still further and became still more precise—"I ask my 'gun-girl' whether you with your damned publicity for fairyland and your damned policy of chaos can be kept in power without a secret-police establishment or not, she will tell me the truth."

The Propaganda Minister: "You seem rather exercised. I have sometimes wondered—"

The Premier: "Carl!"

"What have you wondered?" asked Issachar in a voice like the drip of water.

The Propaganda Minister: "I have wondered at the abnormal influence over you of a girl young enough to be your granddaughter."

The Minister of Justice: "Is that what you wondered? Yes, my gun-girl is your age, Citizen Minister. She is young enough to be my granddaughter." His glittering old eyes moved from Carl ap Rhys to Olivia Keyes and back again. "At least she is not old enough to be my mother."

The Propaganda Minister sprang up, registering wrath and scorn. "And what, citizen, do you mean by that?" From beside him came the sound of the Finance Minister repressing a sob. The young man's expression splintered. The histrionics were swept away by sincere fury. The red lips lost their discipline. "You'll suffer for that."

Mustafa Issachar slid a blank sheet of paprite toward himself, picked up an ink-pencil, and began to write.

Carl ap Rhys flung out of the room into the darkness of the garden.

"I'll suffer," said Mustafa Issachar. He did not look up from his writing. "Oh, young men in love!"

The figure of Carl ap Rhys was trembling in the doorway again. Everyone looked around, except the Minister of Justice; even the mewling of Olivia Keyes stopped.

"I'm resigning," said the young man. "And others are resigning too. Goodbye." He vanished again into the garden.

Olivia Keyes emitted a rich concluding sob and said to the Premier, "My resignation will be on your desk in the morning, of course."

The Minister of Justice: "No, no. We've had quite enough bad farce tonight. There's no way from that garden to the street, as you know and Carl knows." He raised himself from his chair, picked up his piece of paprite and his dispatch case and walked down to the Premier. "Here is a *real* note of resignation, Herman, effective tomorrow at twelve fifty, noon. By that time you may have an even more formal document if you like. Goodbye, old friend." He wrung Herman Kalino's hand and went out—into the hallway that led to the street door of the house.

All faces turned toward the garden door, and through it ap Rhys strode to his seat.

Francis Bentinck rose heavily to his feet. The Minister of Armies and Marine: "I will make my resignation effective twelve fifty tomorrow." His dispatch case under his arm, he went out the hall door.

The Premier: "If there are no others...I will see each of you about the reconstruction of the Cabinet, if I may use that term, before the Chamber sits at fifteen hundred tomorrow. We will adjourn now."

On the bed in the berylloy cabin, the man stirred and

whimpered. Cathy de Ferraris went over to look at him in the orange light of the Barstow lamp. "Simon, he's coming to."

De Ferraris joined her, limping. "Bah, what a mess he is! What a disgusting mess you are!" he roared down at the man, who now lay looking up at them with blank, wide eyes. "You can't see me, though, can you? Blinded with pain. Cath, hand me that Kendall's compound F. This is going to hurt. Cath, look away."

A moan and then, "S——"

The old man: "Simon de Ferraris."

The hurt man: "Simon de Ferraris…Simon de Ferraris."

The old man: "That's right. And you? I say, and you?"

The hurt man: "Walter Vanderwol. Simon de Ferraris."

The old man: "Still here."

Vanderwol: "You are my creditor…" The hurt man stopped, exhausted.

De Ferraris: "I am your creditor?"

Vanderwol: "You are the holder of an instrument of mine for two hundred and seventy-five thousand units."

De Ferraris: "Who lent you the money?"

Vanderwol breathed heavily for a few moments, every dilation of his thorax making him grin with pain. Then: "Herbert Magellis."

De Ferraris: "I hold a good deal of Herbert Magellis' paper. Wait." The old man limped over to a shelf and, with a key on a cord around his neck, unlocked a filing box from the heavy hasp which moored it down. He carried the box nearer the lamp, opened it, and leafed through its contents. "Magellis. . . . Vanderwol. I have it. Two hundred and seventy-five thousand units." He dangled the instrument before Vanderwol's face.

Vanderwol: "I hereby…" The man's hands fluttered around the loosened belly-belt. "I hereby tender you two hundred and seventy-five thousand units plus four thousand five hundred units in arrears of interest in legal discharge of that…debt." He gasped and worked a hand into the belt.

De Ferraris: "Are you sure you can afford it just now? I don't want to press you." He laughed, a single hoot, turned, and limped out onto the porch. There he swung in the hammock for a long while, listening to the crying of the man inside.

CHAPTER 5

OLD Hosig was frightened. His rotten brown teeth were too few to chatter, and his dark yellow eyes always rolled in the wagging skull the way they did now, as if he feared someone behind him; but the wried figure crouched under the basement steps of the building, completely still except for the inextinguishable tremor. For once he had stopped running. He had to think...

Had to think because, loping and hopping through the maze of roofs, alleys, subcellars, and communicating passages which was his universe, he had come upon a noise. Had come upon a noise, and had followed it to the bulkhead on the roof of a tenement building where he often came for scraps; and had peered through a crack where the frame of a skylight was sprung; could see nothing; but the noise, a hard purring noise, had been loud.

Then voices had sung out nearby: "Phase Six." "Phase Six." The purring noise had shaken. "Phase Five." "Phase Five." On the next roof, two of them bent over something from which the noise was coming, a tangle of metal and wires and misshapen lanterns that gave a light the color of drying blood. One of them had sung into the tangle, "Phase Four." "Phase Four," the other had answered. The noise had shaken.

Pressed to the crack, old Hosig's eye had rolled so badly that he could scarcely see.

Also, there had been others on the roof, listening to the singing and the shaking. "Phase One."

"Lock phase!" and the noise had purred out strong and steady. The others had had—

Had rayguns in their hands. Old Hosig had scuttled back into the darkness...

Now he had to think, because, just afterward, he had blundered into others, in one of old Hosig's own favorite burrows, in the disused Crile Road Water Station where, ever since he could remember, ever since the terrible days, he had little by little gathered together one of his most comfortable beds.

He had almost been in the room with them before he realized they were there, for they had had no lights with them and had been sitting silently. But as he was scrambling through the rubbish-choked corridor toward the room, a low voice had called out, "That you, Ark?" Instantly old Hosig had shrunk into stillness, in the stale darkness, behind a huge, dusty sack full of something soft.

After a long while, the voice had muttered, "Guess not."

"Well, it's someone," a second one had whispered.

"Vermin," the first had said. "Spider-rats."

"Better look," the second had said.

"Look yourself," the first had said.

The second had not answered that.

"I wish Ark would come," the first had whispered.

"Why do we have to wait?" the second had said. "There she is. It's thirty meters. I could get her with this right now."

"Rays would have to work on the window first," the first had said.

"Only take a couple of seconds at this distance."

"Make enough noise with that lucimorph. Absorbs everything but the Terran spectrum. Fizzes. Might give her a couple of seconds' warning," the first had whispered.

"She's a nice piece, though," the second had whispered. "Look... What's this gun Ark's bringing?"

"Old chemical job. Gas expansion. Pushes a solid plug of metal. Never tried one myself. Ark says the plug will go right through the window and her. Hey, look at her now!"

"Ho!" There had been a silence. "Won't Ark be sore he missed this!"

"Sh...what's that? That you, Ark?"

"Spider-rats," the second had said.

It had not been spider-rats but old Hosig creeping out...

Old Hosig thought about it. Old Hosig was always frightened of men and women, though he could not remember why. He thought men and women had done something to him before the terrible days but did not know what it was; could not remember anything before the terrible days; except sometimes a few things, but when that happened, he stopped remembering. Old Hosig sometimes thought he was really a man himself, but was not sure. If he had been a man, he would not be frightened of them. He would feel the same as they. That was so. Mostly he was sure he was not a man.

He lived among men and women, and often went very close to them; outwitted them, especially his particular enemies, the men who came and took away the scraps of food; would set little traps in the disposal shafts to catch the food on the way down; ran through the hallways at night and stopped to hear sounds of pleasure or pain. He could understand all the language men and women used; could speak aloud to himself; thought that if he had not been frightened he could even speak to one of them, even to the Woman; but was always frightened.

But then there was the Woman, across the street. Old Hosig would sit on the floor by his window and watch for her, and when the light went on in a certain window opposite, she would be there. This every night, and old Hosig would wait for it. Often she took off her clothes and put other clothes on, but when she had no clothes on it was very beautiful and strange for old Hosig. Then he would think he was a man; would almost be sure. She could not make him feel so strange if he were not one of them. At such times he would sit on the floor by his window and cry.

But when he was creeping away from his room where the men had been waiting for Ark, old Hosig had been frightened with a new fear; and something else; had been angry. He had wanted to go to Ark, who was coming to hurt the Woman, speak to him in the language he knew, and tell him not to do it; thought he could speak to him.

It was when he was creeping angrily away that he had seen the—

Darting sideways out of the alley door of the water station, he had seen—

Had seen a figure standing in the street; a thin, straight, black figure with its edges blurred by the light, like a long black spider-rat swimming in whitish water. Old Hosig had thought it was Ark. The man had stood uncertainly, looking up and around at the buildings, and had not seen old Hosig, who had made noises at him soundlessly with fear and anger.

Old Hosig had known he could not speak to the man Ark; was too frightened; and Ark had come to take away the only beautiful thing old Hosig knew about, and there would be nothing left for old Hosig except running in his dark places.

Old Hosig loped out of the alley, but the one he thought was Ark had not turned around; had reached the stationary figure; had spoken. "Ark—"

The man had turned.

It was the Judge. Ark was the Judge. Old Hosig had seen this even before he remembered who the Judge was, and when he remembered, a sob of horror and bafflement had burst from him. Before the terrible days, men and women had done something to old Hosig; he would never remember what; but would remember the Judge. The Judge took him away from the other men and women and set him free. Old Hosig remembered the Judge as a stern, frightening presence in a big room, high up near the ceiling; but the Judge was good to him. Yet the Judge was also Ark.

So then old Hosig had run away to think, head pumping on the end of the twisted neck, eye rolling; and he had seen as he ran that the Judge crossed the roadway. Away from the water station.

As old Hosig ran, he knew that *the Judge was not Ark;* Ark was a man, the Judge was a good man. But he did not go back; found his safe cellar steps; thought.

The preternaturally dark street outside, and the palsied, reeking old derelict who had run away from him, had shaken Mustafa Issachar.

"Come in, Judge."

At that moment, the old Minister of Justice wished ap Rhys' innuendo could have been true. The Chief of the Internal Defense Department, straight, swift, keen, female, with that odd glow of world-weary asceticism in her face, greeted him with a handclasp like a man's. In her left hand she held a ray-pistol as lightly as she might have held one of the small fashionable pipes that girls smoked, and she put it down with as little embarrassment. Her tab-collared black tunic and white linen trousers were a sly, elongated, swelling parody of her soldierlike office garb.

"I'm honored, Judge, of course. But something is wrong."

"I've resigned."

Characteristically, she neither disguised her stare of dismay nor wasted time in exclamations. "Effective as of?"

"Tomorrow noon."

Her dark, searching eyes closed. "And your successor?"

"No name yet. Herman's giving in to Carl."

After a few instants the eyes reopened. "We have the whole night to maneuver in, then. I'll alert Room Thirty-two." She plucked an N-T set from the pillows of the couch where she had been reading and held it to her ear. "Phil? Phil?"—but she was already frowning. She flung down the little set, marched to an old console 'visor in the corner, snapped it on, looked at the twinkling blank of the screen, snapped it off, reached for the radiophone on the wall, listened, replaced it, and said, "I was wrong. They've thrown a standing deadwave over this place. Can't be anything else. They're ahead."

Mustafa Issachar smiled desolately. "So that's why the street outside was too dark . . . I thought there'd be an attempt. If Carl hadn't overdone things this evening, his whole plan might have worked. They would have killed or caught you tonight and me in the morning. All unsuspecting. But he showed his hand . . . Oh, young men in love!"

"What's our move, Judge?"

"We go to Room Thirty-two. We ought at least to warn your agents."

"Even if we got there alive, they'd only clamp a field on Room Thir—"

Something buffeted the window explosively, there was a loud report, and a tall old glass mirror fell in shards from the wall. The girl bent, seized Mustafa Issachar around the waist, and brought him down. "Crawl!" she ordered. The two crawled toward the window and lay below its sill. The shot was not repeated.

The judge broke the silence. "Are you all right, my dear?"

"Better than that, Judge. And you?"

"You tackle hard, my dear."

"Did I hurt you?"

"I am suffering from nostalgia."

"Thank you, Judge . . . Room Thirty-two is out. Probably

Carl already has every kind of dead-wave generator there is, sitting right on top of our pants factories."

"As a matter of fact, there were workmen 'fixing the heat pumps' all day...All day." A pause. "Sue," Mustafa Issachar said in a low voice, "if you think what I am going to suggest is treason, I will drop it and never think about it again."

"Earth?" asked the girl, even more quietly.

"No," said the Minister of Justice. "Not Earth. I'm going to stay and fight! I will *not* give this world to Carl ap Rhys!" Then, tentatively: "Simon de Ferraris."

Sue Wells sprang up. The old judge caught her wrist as she was about to stand erect and pulled her down on top of himself. There was another *crack!* and another splintered puncture in the lucimorph window. "Careful, my dear," he said mildly.

"Thank you, Judge. I'll be more careful." She looked into his eyes for a moment, then leaned forward and kissed his forehead. "I'd rather go to Earth," she said. "Oh, Mustafa, I'd rather go to Earth."

"Sue, Sue, what *is* the matter? I thought you'd want to fight. More than anybody."

"Oh, I do!" The girl seemed to be examining her mind. "I do want to fight. More than anybody. But I do *not* want to go crawling to Simon de Ferraris."

"He's not a traitor. You know there's nothing to the 'Loyalist' charge."

"I know that," said the girl in a tense voice. "Better than anyone. Let me think." After a while she said, "We'll find Simon de Ferraris. I have—I had a new man working on it. He started today." She began to crawl on hands and knees toward a cabinet. "We'll have to catch him tonight. He's flying into Laing's Land with instructions to arrest Simon de Ferraris on a thirty-unit charge under the Schedule of Sentences."

"Sue! Why would Simon—"

"Don't ask me about it, Judge. You know you can trust me." She laughed shortly. "You're now the only person who can. If we break out of here alive, we might catch my man at the Auxiliary Airport. They fly some New Tavistock copters at night." She had opened a drawer and was plucking out various undergarments. "How's your heart? Stunner waves can cause fibrillation."

"I have a good heart."

"All the same," and she flung him a heavy-banded brassiere covered with what seemed to be metal foil. She laughed, this time a pure giggle. "I'm sorry, Judge. I used to have blouses made of the stuff, but they were too hot. Don't worry: I've another here for myself." She began to take off her tunic, but stopped. "Forgive me, Mustafa. That would have been an insult, wouldn't it?" She crawled out of the room, crawled in again a few seconds later, and resumed rooting in the drawer. "Here. This is for your head. Not completely effective, this item, but it takes the worst of it. You can usually get through."

"I have a good head."

"Pretty good, Judge, pretty good. This is like one of those stocking caps with a rolled brim. When things hot up, roll the brim down and it's a hood. The eye slits are narrow, so wait till you need it. Ever used a raygun? It's not hard...I lost my gun-virginity at twelve. Here. The safety is *off*. Ready? No, no, leave the lights on."

They crawled out the door.

"It's over us like a bell jar," came the girl's whisper in the darkness. "We can't get help. They're coming in to finish us off."

The pair crouched behind the sills of adjoining windows looking out from the third-floor hallway over a narrow alley. The wall opposite was blind. The girl rolled her mask down, stood up, mounted the window ledge, took a grip of the mullion with her left hand, and leaned as far out as her arm would let her swing.

She swung back. "Can't see." She rolled the hood up from her eyes with her free hand and swung out again, looking down the alley to its mouth on the street. "Two of them," she reported. "In this alley. Do you have a pencil?"

"Yes," said Mustafa Issachar, puzzled.

"Rub your prints off it with your tunic and drop it down there."

There was a faint clatter as the ink-pencil struck the pavement, then hurried footsteps approaching below. The girl swung out over the alley and the ray-pistol sputtered for an instant in her right hand. There was the first throat-click of a yell that got no further, another rush of footsteps, another swing and sputter, and a childlike squeak.

"Now," whispered Sue Wells, "follow me down this," taking a coil of thin wire from her pocket and hooking it to the base of the mullion. "I took this wire from Shigahara himself.

Wind it once around your pistol barrel—better put the safety on—and use the whole wave-guide for a grip. You twist to control it. Watch me," and she slithered abruptly downward.

The old judge was tremulous when he joined her on the ground. She had already turned over both corpses. "These were easy," she remarked. "From now on, though, they'll be expecting a fight. Here are their stun-guns. Take this. You aim at the thalamus. Notice, they had their blasters out and their stunners in their pockets. Recognize this one? Not much left of the head, but it's Olivia Keyes' younger son, Richard. My, he'd grown! And what a nasty little beast Carl is! Judge, this will make trouble for us with—with Simon de Ferraris." She flicked the wire loose from the mullion above and coiled it. "Around to the back, now."

The girl: "Careful down these steps. What did you say?"

Mustafa Issachar: "*I* didn't say anything."

Thus they came upon old Hosig. In the same instant there was a shout behind them: "There they are!"

A more distant cry: "Stay back, they might have rays!"

From the half-human figure which had scuttled across the door in front of them came a thin, careful tenor, the matted mouth laboring over the words, "The Judge."

From above, exultantly: "They're down there. They can't get in."

The girl forced old Hosig aside with a single thrust of her shoulder and put her full strength to the latch. "Locked!"

"You are the Judge," repeated the gentle voice.

"We'll have to burn through," said the girl. "Out of the way, you!" and, her lips invisible with effort, she tried to drag the little derelict away from the basement door. The convulsive eyes seemed to glow yellow at her; the matted face wagged speechlessly. The girl's hand went for the stunner in her tunic pocket. "No!" said Mustafa Issachar in a sharp tone.

"They're coming, Judge," said Sue fiercely. "Let me just put him to sleep."

A voice above: "Follow the wall, idiot!"

"Cannot sleep now. It is not light yet," said old Hosig wonderingly in the thin, cultivated voice.

They could hear the enemy moving, like skirmishers, above their heads. "Keep back!"—the low command was close by, and there was silence.

"I can open the door," said old Hosig suddenly.

"Open it, then," ordered the girl. Old Hosig stood, swaying. "Please open it," said the girl. Old Hosig stood. "Open it, or—"

"Wait," said the Minister of Justice; and calmly to old Hosig: "I am the Judge."

Old Hosig: "The Judge. You must tell me..."

The girl whispered, "Judge, are you insane? Let me burn the lock."

Mustafa Issachar said softly to old Hosig, "I know you. I remember your case well. Will you open the door for us? There are men up there who wish to kill us."

Old Hosig, slowly: "The Judge. You must tell me three things."

A few centimeters over Mustafa Issachar's head, the ancient steel of the baluster suddenly smoked, hissed into flame, and parted. The old judge said steadily, "I will answer three questions, and then you will save us."

The girl said savagely, "This is a fairy tale," but she fired an answering burst at random over the parapet of the stairwell. A scream told that it had taken effect.

Old Hosig: "Am I a man?" The wavering eyes suddenly locked with the old judge's gaze and were still. There was a fleeting pause.

Mustafa Issachar: "You are a man... What is your second question?"

Old Hosig: "Will you take the Woman away?"

Mustafa Issachar: "Yes. I am taking her away. And your last question?"

Old Hosig shuddered, and his eyes unfixed. He bent over as if he were in physical pain. "No, no, no." His sobs were like the grunting of a small animal.

"I *must* take her away," said the old Minister gently. "There are men here who would kill her. I will save her. Please, your third question?"

"Citizen Wells," a woman's voice called from above. "Citizen Wells."

The girl: "So you're here. What do you want, Olivia?"

The woman: "Will you surrender? We won't hurt you if you surrender."

Sue Wells answered with a laugh, and said in a low voice to the judge, "They still haven't found the bodies. What an idiot Olivia is!"

"No, no," old Hosig was crying, as if no one else had spoken, "not the third question. Do not answer it. I thought I could. Please take her away, and do not answer it." He turned and clawed at the upper hinge of the old heavy door; the pin slid out easily; flame and fumes spurted from the metal where his hand had been an instant before, but old Hosig seemed not to notice. He looked at Mustafa Issachar and said timidly, "I thought I could, you know." He tipped the door on its moorings and disengaged the lock.

The girl: "Olivia!"

The woman: "Yes?"

The girl: "Ricky is dead."

She followed old Hosig and Mustafa Issachar into the open blackness.

Simon de Ferraris: "Citizen Vanderwol, can you hear me?"

Vanderwol: "Yes."

De Ferraris: "Is the pain easier?"

Vanderwol: "Yes."

De Ferraris: "You seem to have made your trip for nothing." A long pause.

Vanderwol: "Yes."

De Ferraris: "I am glad you have stopped crying about it, Citizen Vanderwol. You are my guest, my wife is pregnant, and if you keep sniveling and complaining you will make life harder around here. Do you understand?"

Vanderwol: "Yes."

De Ferraris: "Very well. Now, suppose you tell me how you discovered where I was."

Vanderwol: "No."

De Ferraris: "No?"

Vanderwol: "No."

De Ferraris: "Then suppose I tell you."

Silence.

De Ferraris: "Citizen Vanderwol, have you thought yet why your pilot set you down on the other side of that stretch of swamp?"

Vanderwol: "Because I asked him to."

De Ferraris: "Oh, I'm sure you asked him to. But why? Who first said that the noise of bringing the copter down right on my hillock might give me enough warning to hide or run away?"

Silence.

De Ferraris: "He made you ask him, didn't he? Who put you onto that pilot?"

(54)

Vanderwol: "A patriot, who doesn't like to see poor men cheated." It was the familiar surly whine.

De Ferraris: "The same man who sold you my whereabouts, wasn't it?"

Silence.

De Ferraris gentled his voice. "Didn't it occur to you that anyone in New Tavistock who discovered where I was could make a good living selling the information to debtors—*so long as none of their customers reached me alive?* For if they began to come here, I would surely move, and that would spoil their business."

Vanderwol: "I don't see that." But his tone was less surly. "If that's what they're up to, why should they bother to tell the truth about where you are? *Any* place would do."

De Ferraris: "I've wondered about that myself, Citizen Vanderwol. That's why I thought you might help me. Maybe it's just coincidence. I take refuge in the most dangerous part of Laing's Land, thinking in my simpleminded way that I'll be safest there; and they deliver their victims to the most dangerous part of Laing's Land to make sure of never seeing them again. Or maybe..."

Pause.

De Ferraris: "...maybe they think I'll make sure for them."

Silence.

De Ferraris: "In any place but the right place, their victims might just stumble on help and get back. Eh?"

Vanderwol said tremulously: "You wouldn't."

De Ferraris: "No, I wouldn't. I didn't, in fact. But that fact might not occur to a patriot. A true patriot." Silence. "Who doesn't like to see poor men cheated." Silence. "Which of them was it? Kellowy? No, more likely Gnostou. Gnostou it was, not Kellowy, eh?"

Vanderwol: "Neither. It was Harding." The man was glad to correct his interlocutor for once.

De Ferraris: "Oh? Harding. Thank you very much. There isn't really any Kellowy or Gnostou, you know. Harding. You don't happen to remember his first name? No? Well... Never trust anyone in New Tavistock, Citizen Vanderwol. That is the moral of this whole affair. You must rest now. I've kept you talking too long. Try to sleep. You are my guest, and I must try to make you comfortable. Goodnight."

*   *   *

There was no light at all, once the fugitives had turned the corner inside the opening. The blaster-rays had melted the hinge of the door. It was a matter of moments before the attackers would venture in. Mustafa Issachar did not ask the girl if she had a torch, and she produced none.

The air was close, but clean enough. The paving was even and dry.

The blackness beat against Mustafa Issachar's eyes. "Jakob," he whispered.

Old Hosig stopped so sharply that Shulamith ran against him and he staggered, but he did not utter a sound.

Mustafa Issachar: "Jakob, let me hold onto you. Sue, where's your hand?"

It was done without another word. They went on at a good pace, old Hosig a little ahead, the judge holding the musky, twisting shoulder with his left hand and the girl's cold left hand with his right. After a hundred steps or so, they turned and turned again, and an instant later Mustafa felt old Hosig's shoulder drop in his grasp, and dragged the girl back just in time to save her from falling down a steep flight of steps.

They stumbled down, and after a few more meters, old Hosig stopped. A single swoop of the little body and he was free of Mustafa's grip. The Minister barely checked a cry of alarm. But old Hosig still seemed to be moving near them. Mustafa did not release the girl's hand, and she seemed content.

Mustafa Issachar: "Sue, do you have a torch?"

The girl: "No."

Mustafa Issachar: "Then—" He did not finish the thought. The tightening of her fingers told him she too had realized how completely they were at the mercy of their strange guide. What if old Hosig darted away? The old judge tried to recollect the turnings they had taken. He could remember only blackness.

Mustafa Issachar: "What is this building?"

The girl: "I don't know. We went into Benzion's, the old warehouse. But we must be beyond it now. The Armory backs on Benzion's. Maybe this is the Armory."

Mustafa Issachar: "Jakob, where are we?"

There was no reply.

The Armory was the oldest building in New Nome, dating from the Second Settlement—a vast, complicated, imbecile structure, built during one of the great Inhabitant scares to stand years of siege that never occurred. Corners of it had been used for making threedees before the Revolution; the judge had been in one of the studios once... After a silence, there was a click and a soft scraping like that of a metal door. Mustafa Issachar groped toward the sound and was rewarded with old Hosig's ragged sleeve and a faint squeak. The squeak reassured him. At least, he thought, the old lunatic was as frightened as they.

They set off again, in their strange human molecule. The paving had ended, and the sickly sweet smell of Epsilon Struthionis 2 soil filled their heads. Another sense blocked, thought Mustafa Issachar. They had walked only a dozen meters or so when the Minister squeaked with fright himself. A hand like a large insect fluttered over his face and pressed his mouth; it was, of course, old Hosig, and Mustafa understood that this was a command of silence. He felt upward for Sue's face to do the same for her, and encountered old Hosig's other claw clamped on the softness of her cheek. She had borne the touch without a sign.

The next moment, the reason for the command was clear. Seemingly from nearby, almost among them, came the low-spoken words, "Put out that light!" There was no light anywhere.

"And go it in the dark?" replied another voice, which Mustafa recognized as the one that had exulted over them outside. "Not me!"

"Sure, and they'll just wait and blast us when we come prancing along with your nice light."

"I'd rather take a chance on the rays, thank you. Tell you what: you go ahead in your nice safe dark and I'll wait outside with my dangerous light."

"Oh, come on, then. Kelly and Fracht are trying to get in through the Armory. *They* might jump us in the dark."

So, thought the Minister, they were still in the warehouse. Evidently they had doubled back. He blessed the chink or acoustic fault that had given him his bearings.

From that point on, the tunnel took on a downward slope and began to turn; the roof of it was lower, and Mustafa Issachar had to stoop to avoid the slender metal laths that shored up the spongy dirt ceiling. The perfume of the subsoil made him nauseous. The darkness was like a thick fluid that smelled and tasted of it; his mind struggled not to drown. The only two senses now left to him were touch and hearing, and he kept them clear with an effort of will.

(57)

The girl: "It's like hiding in an old whore's wardrobe, isn't it? But I suppose you've never had to do that. What a planet!"

Clinging to old Hosig with one hand and to the girl with the other, and plodding sightlessly into the penetralia of the old city, Mustafa had the curious feeling that there was another bond between them besides his own arms, almost as if they had begun to share one another's consciousness a little. Under his fingers, even old Hosig, without a sound, seemed somehow to have drawn closer to them; and presently the others could hear a thin murmur from him like singing. It was some time before they could make out the words, a first echo from his human past, of the immemorial song: "...three blind mice, see how they run, see how they run."

CHAPTER 6

AS soon as an orderly society had been arranged over the main land mass of Epsilon Struthionis 2, restless elements began looking for a new wilderness. Failures sought to leave their weaknesses behind, criminals to escape from justice; violent men looked for life they would be admired for destroying, poor men for wealth, women for men. These hardy pioneers pushed across the River Bohr, the water-filled fissure in the planetary rock, and where the natural horrors of Laing's Land were just beginning, they set up the Roaring Towns. The Towns were their utopias, where there was no justice.

At the same time the Towns were themselves places of a ghastly expiation, cooperative hells.

If the frontier had moved on, the Towns might have become cities. But the botany of the subcontinent stopped the frontier. There was no economic benefit to be had in Laing's Land. One Town disappeared after another. The pioneers went back. Or died. Or converged in the larger Towns, this time not to join the traffic but to prey on it.

New Tavistock stayed alive only because the Colonial

Government, seeing that self-exiled men and women could not tame Laing's Land, began to use the subcontinent as a penal colony and fed and clothed and peopled it through this last of the Roaring Towns, where, mingled with the older traditions, there developed a new sort of savage prosperity. The forces of official law were outnumbered, sometimes almost besieged. The Government itself retreated to the Caserne on Spion Island, off the coast.

After the Revolution came, the Planetary Government began to send political prisoners into Laing's Land, and New Tavistock acquired new pastimes. Outside the town, politicals and felons let each other alone. In the town, they mixed uneasily with each other and with the half-secret agents of the law, while the Old Parties, remnants and offspring of the original pioneers, served and exploited everyone alike, with an amalgam of timidity, contempt, envy, and comradeship all their own.

Such an Old Party was Cass Harding, who ran an around-the-clock eating stand in the terminal and whom, almost by chance, John Corander fell in with a few minutes after the copter set him down next to Number Three Ramp. Harding was a short, sharp-faced, ill-complexioned man with a wide but extraordinarily flat body and an expression so rankly dishonest that Corander knew just what was coming when Harding removed a flat white finger from his nasal fossae and waved it along the old-time fluorescent counter on which he was leaning: "You'll never believe this, but this pitch right here makes me more money than any of my other businesses, any, and I got several little things going, you'd be surprised, you'll find this is quite a town; and you know? Of all of them this is the one personally I care about least. You know that? I could see it go . . . like *that*. Really. But that's human nature, isn't it? People are like that."

Corander: "I believe it."

Harding: "Now take a young fellow like yourself." (Here we go, thought Corander.) "This restaurant business is all right, I've got no complaints, food's good, people from all over town come to the terminal to eat, it's good business. *But.* I like to help people. That's my weakness, we all got our weaknesses and I'm no more honest than anybody else, I'll tell you that frankly, I've got several little things going right now. *Because.*" He slapped the counter. "I like to help people. A young fellow like yourself for instance, just take you as an

(60)

example, now I don't know what you come here for..."—a hopeful pause, during which Corander regarded him thoughtfully—"that's your business, and everybody has their own different reasons for coming here, it's quite a town, but a young fellow like yourself, just as an example, he comes here and he doesn't know his way around, maybe he's looking up some political friends, maybe he's got folks here, maybe he's just looking around, though if it's women he wants," the entrepreneur added severely, "I can't help him, I do know a man who can take care of things like that...but I won't touch it myself, I'm not boasting, we all have our shortcomings, our weaknesses, none of us are perfect, you know that, but my weakness is I like to help people. I said that before, I don't want to repeat myself. A young fellow like yourself, I'd rather not know your private business, I'm not asking, I'm not inquiring. I don't want you to tell me what you personally, individually, are here for. *But.*" He slapped the counter dramatically.

"All right," said Corander, "I won't then."

Harding: *"But."* He slapped the counter dramatically again and dropped his voice. "As an example, suppose you were looking up certain political friends of yours, suppose, this is just an example, they were a certain outfit that wasn't having too good a time right now, Loyalists, I'm not afraid of the word," he whispered, "it's a political matter, that's all it is, there's a lot of dirt in politics, we all know that, we're not children, the point is, *you're* honest, that's enough for me." He picked his nose in silence for a while. Corander waited. Harding resumed: "There are a lot of favors I could do a person like that. *For* a price, *for* a price, I'm not pretending to be better than I am, I'm not in it for love but there might, now take for example, there might be somebody he wanted to see, that's not easy in a town like this, this is quite a town, and this young fellow might come in as a Category C passenger. Say that happened. There's a lot of people watching those manifests, you'd be surprised, there's all kinds in this town. *And.* It could be very hard to..."

Corander let him talk five minutes more by the clock and then, with an abruptness that seemed to upset Citizen Harding, explained that he had come to Laing's Land to find Simon de Ferraris himself, and that he would pay well—within reason—for any help.

He made an appointment for 1150 the next morning, same place. "And listen, I owe him money. I'm not a dirty Loyalist," he remarked and walked away confident that Harding, who had obviously studied the passenger manifest, would take him for a liar.

In the blackness of the tunnel, the girl said, "Have you noticed that this journey is all down and no up?"

It was true. The tunnel itself had leveled off, but there had been several more flights of steps, all leading down. Mustafa Issachar thought they were descending a gigantic helix. Although the floor now had paving blocks set in the dirt, and the walls when he brushed against them were more regularly supported, the stench was unabated. It was like walking in a hothouse ablaze with heavy, pungent flowers; but in the staring blackness the effect was more terrible. For what seemed hours, the old judge's retinas had recorded nothing except the flames of his fatigue and strain. His whole awareness was concentrated on listening to footsteps, the girl's few remarks, and the coming and going of old Hosig's "Three Blind Mice"; and now he was conscious of another sound, a steady, subdued roar like distant surf.

Old Hosig led them down another staircase. This was a tight spiral with the ring of steel to it. At the foot, the little creature opened a door, and the roar burst on their ears like a gong.

The shock of sound made the judge recoil, and he lost old Hosig's shoulder; he stumbled over the high, sharp metal threshold, and the girl staggered against him.

"Jakob!" he cried. "Jakob, where are you?" His own voice sounded faint above the beat of the noise, and he could hear no reply. For a moment he nearly gave way to panic as he felt himself robbed of hearing. The darkness, the mouth-filling reek, and the noise seemed about to annihilate him. He began to scream, "Jakob! Sue!" more to hear a human voice than to be heard. Reassurance came through the last of the senses left to him: Sue's fingers pressed his with a warning tenderness, and a moment later old Hosig's claw took his arm.

They resumed their march. The air was cold and wet, but the corrupt sweetness was strong as ever. There was no light, but Mustafa now minded neither the blindness nor the overwhelming of his smell and taste; he fought desperately to hear something above the boom and sough of the waters. He stamped as he walked; the soles of his feet rang with pain at every step, yet for all he could hear he might have been strolling on a lawn; and every step took him nearer to the sound. There would be a long, coughing, drawing noise, with the groan of heavy iron plates in it; and then a few pulses like a drum heard through fever; and then a slowly rising yell of air and water and metal, and then the sucking noise again. He felt like an insect in the brazen cone of a bell.

Suddenly he realized that his grip on both old Hosig and the girl had tightened to the limit of his strength: he must be hurting both of them, yet old Hosig drew them all ahead without a sign—was he still singing "Three Blind Mice"?—and the girl let him crush her fingers. Had he drawn a cry from her that he could not hear? He softened his pressure, and Sue at once increased hers companionably. It was enough. He passed below the surface of the sound without fighting any longer.

Mustafa's whole mind was in his skin and muscles; but he thought he was conscious of the surge of blood in his own arteries, and in the girl's and in old Hosig's; it was as if the same systole and diastole swept through the three of them. He half imagined wordless understandings imparted by his fingertips. He was conscious also of a difference in the feel of the torn air on his face. It was damper; it had a fitfulness, as if the pressure were changing constantly; it began to be very cold.

At length old Hosig halted and fell to his knees. Mustafa Issachar could feel the little figure strain, and then something gave way. Old Hosig stood and moved the others back gently with his hands. The din was beyond all sensation, but it seemed suddenly to redouble, and in the same instant freezing air and spray exploded in their faces, followed by a long, intense suction.

Old Hosig's hands guided their feet to the brink of an opening. Then he seemed to lower himself into it and from the level of the floor directed Mustafa Issachar's movements until the judge was standing above him on a metal ladder on the side of a large round shaft. Mustafa in turn held the top rung with his left hand and groped for Sue's ankles with his right, turned and placed her and pulled her to a crouch above him, guiding her until she stood on the second rung.

The spray screeched and exploded again beneath him, and again he felt panic surge through him. But he clung to the wet, biting cold of the metal and buried his face in the back of the girl's legs until the withdrawal began, felt old Hosig's

(63)

tug at his calf, and began the descent, passing the signal to the girl.

The ladder was shorter than he had expected. In a moment, they were standing on the slats of a ledge. Old Hosig pressed them against the wall of the shaft, and moved past them to the ladder—to close the lid, Mustafa Issachar guessed—and for a few seconds, they clung to each other, alone, blind, deaf, and gagging with the sweet, dirty taste of the water. They were in the Great Conduit.

The Great Conduit had been built by the Second Settlement to force a strong underground stream through the outpost's power plant; that was before the first Brangwyn Pile had been brought from Earth. It was generally thought that the crude cast-iron channel had been rusted away and the workings around it flooded and destroyed. Yet they were standing in it now.

Or rather, they were in a flue of the Great Conduit. Old Hosig rejoined them, and they began another descent.

With the hatch closed, the spray abated somewhat but the rise and fall of the pressure sent agony stabbing through their heads. For Mustafa Issachar, it was a descent into final horror. Unable to hold onto each other, but touching whenever they could, they lowered themselves to the churning surface of the water, and old Hosig transferred their grasp to a cable which was apparently stretched along the huge pipe, out of the water.

Gripping it tightly—his left arm was weak from holding old Hosig's shoulder for so long—the judge swung off the ledge into the stream. The swift current dealt him a buffet that burned the skin of his hands and made the tendons crack in his arms. For an eternity of seconds, Mustafa was alone in the howling throat of the world.

The water had no level. It surged up to the roof of the pipe and yawned open below the swaying, freezing cable. It had no surface. Between air and water there was a whipping tangle of spray. The smell of subsoil flooded into his chest. The nerves of his eyes seemed to have snapped from his brain.

Sue! Could she have kept her hold in this fury? Or was she at this instant being carried down the black current into the planetary bedrock? Mustafa twisted his right arm about the cable and with his left felt along it, hanging almost clear of the slobbering hollow of the water. There was old Hosig, water streaming off him. He could not find Sue.

He could not find Sue. He could not find Sue. He could not hear his own screams. The water rose. He flung himself to the right with his back to the cable—and felt her fingers locked on the icy metal. One hand. He could not find the other. Was it her dying grip? Then he felt the girl's other hand on his own face, in a swift caress, and old Hosig's claw signaled to him to follow. These were the last things he felt clearly.

As they began to inch along the cable in the direction of the current, Mustafa Issachar's sense of feeling began to fail. The numbness was not in his arms or in his legs, but everywhere. It filled him. His viscera were dead to him. The thought that if the frail, palsied body of their guide were swept away Sue and he would surely be doomed became a kind of distant, intellectual knowledge. The horror in his mind was of losing the last sense left to him, and under the pull of the current, as dark and swift as time itself, he felt it going.

Without sight, smell, taste, hearing, or touch, the Minister of Justice nevertheless traversed the metal strand, handhold after handhold, iron bracket after iron bracket, breath after breath, every handhold and breath an act of naked will, of separate intelligence; and all the time aware with violent clarity, not knowing how he could be aware, of the two human beings moving with him along the cable in the Great Conduit.

They came to one bracket that seemed larger than the last; and then Mustafa Issachar followed old Hosig up a ladder into a flue, a tube so small that he could hardly bend his knees to climb. He forced his exhausted frame past the hatch plate, pulled Sue to the dry surface, and fell asleep.

Rorschach Street in New Tavistock began—or ended, but began for more men and women than ever it ended for—at the air passenger terminal, a low, sprawling, glistening structure like a heap of children's toys, surmounted by a white pylon on which the reflections of the green, cerise, and orange displays below quarreled all night. The broad tuff-block pavement, with its old-fashioned raised sidewalks (for there were neither electro-curbs nor parking grids in New Tavistock), climbed a long hill, at the crest of which it divided and redivided into a delta of thin streets.

Corander left Cass Harding and walked up the slope, looking for a hotel. Both sides of Rorschach Street were furious with light and sound. Most of the accommodations were for the traveler to stay awake in, and the few which promised sleep looked as though the traveler might never wake up again. Their dingy entrances were all but lost amid the displays which rioted out onto the sidewalk from bars, gambling hells, and dance halls.

One large establishment, which obviously combined all these functions and some others, had a low, long marquee with strontium-plasmoid lights hugely reading GLO IA'S NI HTLAND. The entire front was formed of visor tanks. As Corander moved under the marquee the life-sized, three-dimensional image in color of a naked woman sprang to life in them with an electronic screech: this was Glo ia of Ni htland, a fortune in advanced electronics and gases brought, as Corander reflected, 9,240 parsecs from Earth. Glo ia had tawny hair and skin of an unstable white, faintly freckled; she walked alongside Corander, full-haunched, smiling, and murmuring low, crackling solicitations through the nearest in a row of little speakers.

Corander's tired soul was delighted. He stopped at the end of the mechanism to study its effect on the next pedestrian, an elderly drunk. The drunk paid no attention to the electronic nymph's invitations to come inside, but honked at her: "Honey! oh, you *are* a sight for an old man in a dirty world. Listen to me. Shut up. Sam Prior says he don't like your big round ass. But I say, it's becoming to a woman to have a big round ass. Sam Prior says you have dirty feet. But honey, pick them up *and* lay them down. If you pick them *up*, you got to *lay* them down, and they get a little dirty. Shut up. Sam Prior says you a'n't nothing only volts. He says he *saw* them put you in the dirt on the hill, honey. Sam Prior says you're gone now in the dirty dirt. But I say *I* saw your keester walking in front of the Nightland, and I know a bare keester from volts. Oh, the tops of your legs is fat, honey. Shut up. Never lose the fat tops to your legs, *never* lose that good strong suet, no matter what Sam Prior says. *Listen* to me. Don't lay down in the dirt. It's cold on the hill, honey. Don't lay down in the dirt. Oh, shut up, will you!"

He wove toward Corander, accompanied by the eidolon. Corander said offhandedly, "Evening, Sam."

The drunk glared at him. "Mr. Prior to you, buster." He wavered on loftily. Glo ia disappeared.

Out of a bar dashed two little pinched-faced boys. They swerved under the marquee of Ni htland and began a wild game of tag with the two identical naked women who appeared to gallop back and forth in the tanks. The boys, scrawny and uproarious in their untended latency, careened back and forth, each trying to tag the other's woman, while the audio circuits got hopelessly snarled and several men gathered to shout encouragement: "Go get her, Timmy! Show your big brother how!" "Aw, she got away! You're getting old, son."

A bald, stout black man appeared in the entranceway to Ni htland. The bystanders fell silent expectantly. Evidently this was the Real Gloria and he had had trouble with these urchins before. He glowered at the chaos they were making in his precious threedee tanks, gathered himself, and bellowed, "You better get your humps out of here, you two. Why ain't you 'n bed? I'm goin' a tell your *mother!*"

"She don't care no more," crowed one boy triumphantly. "She works for Mr. Alfred now!" The spectators guffawed.

Corander walked away, found a quiet-looking building on the other side, and stepped inside hopefully. But it was a cabaret of some kind, dark, reeking of hemp. A woman was singing in an exquisitely pure, wistful voice without any vibrato, slowly, accompanied by a single twanging instrument:

> *"If I was good and I never known*
> *What I know so well, I could go home—*
> *I'm so weary, cryin' all the time."*

She sat in a circle of orange light, black shadows where her eyes should be and under her lower lip, and plucked softly at her out-of-tune guitar, as if reverent of her own sadness. Corander found an empty table in a dark corner and sat.

> *"But there's a girl breathes in my breast*
> *Gives me no power, gives me no rest—*
> *I'm so weary, cryin' all the time."*

The customers sat like cataleptics, some alone, some paired off; nothing moved except the singer's hands, the plumes of smoke here and there, and now and then the glint of a glass lifted toward some dim, waxy, inturned face. Two more customers, males, came in, peered furtively around, and sat near Corander, averting their faces from him.

> *"If I had wings like the yellow bee,*
> *I'd fly 'cross the river to a soft country—*
> *I'm so weary, cryin' all the time..."*

An aging waitress in youthful coveralls appeared before Corander with a mournful look of inquiry.

Corander: "How much is the local absinthe?"

"Eighty thousand," whispered the waitress.

Corander laughed aloud. The sound sent a shock through the place; heads moved convulsively; the singer's plucking faltered, began again, and stopped.

In the silence, Corander explained cheerfully: "That's charging a little too much for self-pity, Mom. You got some effing crust, you know that? charging for the atmosphere— the customers bring their own atmosphere. 'Yellow bee'! That's what you used to use on the Earthie tourists." He shoved his chair noisily, and carefully blundered toward the door. The two latest arrivals continued to sit with averted faces, as if nothing were happening.

Corander selected a hefty boy who sat with a pale young girl in gingham coveralls. "Come on now, sonny!" said Corander kindly. "Trying to impress her? Trying to show her how *damned* you are? Save your money, sonny. She's been impressed before."

The youngster jumped up, knocking over his table, and drew back for a roundhouse punch. The two men who had not been noticing Corander lunged from their table and seized the infuriated boy, expertly holding him helpless. One of them rasped angrily at Corander, "Get going."

Corander said benignly, "Thanks. Sure." He went out into Rorschach Street. Orange, loud, purple, shrill—the sensory overload hit him like a blow.

He continued slowly up the hill, and soon became aware of his two rescuers, or whatever they were, moving discreetly behind him.

Mustafa Issachar was awakened by old Hosig—within a few minutes, apparently, for his clothes were still wet. The crash and sigh of the Great Conduit still drowned everything out, but the subsoil scent appeared to come mainly from his clothing.

Sue's head lay pillowed on his thigh, but she was awake; she stood up and helped him to his feet. Old Hosig pulled them over to a staircase, and they began the ascent.

The first trapdoor shut out part of the roar. They were still in darkness at the end of a few minutes of turning and climbing when Sue spoke and Mustafa found he could hear again.

"I could stand a little fire." And the astonishing girl slid her arms up and around the old judge's neck.

Except for the smell of the drying mud on their bodies and clothes, the air was close but pleasantly tart. Exhaustion began to tell again on Mustafa Issachar, and they rested after each flight of steps. The noise dwindled to a kind of snore and then a whisper behind them, and the cheerful clap of their footsteps on the paving revived his spirits.

Their dark voyage came to an end in a little chamber, where old Hosig brought them to a halt. Mustafa could see a thin line of light in the ceiling. Their guide was clambering somewhere near, and suddenly the pale crack burst into a glaring white square. After the first agony of returning vision, they could see the blurred figure of old Hosig perched at the head of a steel staircase, waiting for them.

Once they were out of the trapdoor, the light faded rapidly as their irises contracted to normal, and they found themselves in a dingy hallway, lit by a single Chevalier lamp set in an ornate wall bracket. Of the trapdoor there was no trace except a rectangular slit in the worn rose-glass carpet.

The girl: "Judge! Do you recognize this carpeting?"

Mustafa Issachar: "I—I might if I were less sleepy, Sue."

The girl: "This is Hooke Place, sleepyhead! We're in the basement of the Chamber."

A movement on the edge of his vision made Mustafa Issachar spin around. "Jakob!"

Old Hosig stopped where he had been loping into the shadows and turned slowly. The dirt caked over the wagging face seemed to crack. "Now I must run away," he said in his strange cultivated voice.

Sue said, "Come with us."

"No," said old Hosig excitedly, and then softly: "You are the Woman who takes her clothes off, but I will not come with you."

The girl opened her mouth and shut it again.

"Come with us, Jakob," pleaded the old judge. "You are a man. You belong with men. Didn't you feel that, down there? I've judged you in my court, and I know what you've been. In the dark and the danger, when you had my life in your hands, you knew you were a man. Down in the waters, when you couldn't see me or hear me or touch me, you knew there was a man with you and that you were a man. Come back with us now...I have answered two of your questions, and you have saved us. I owe you a third. Shall I tell you your story, Jakob Hosig...Jakob von—"

"No!" screamed old Hosig, turned, and ran.

"Jakob!" shouted Mustafa Issachar in a breaking voice. "If I come back, will you talk to me?...What did he say? Did he say no?"

The girl: "I think he said, 'I don't know.'" She put her hand gently on his arm. "Lavatories. Then the spaceport."

CHAPTER 7

THEY were making for a tube-station on Van't Hoff Street.

Hurrying between the storefronts blinded with dull gray metal slats, the vacuous black rectangles of recessed doorways in the dim walls of old office buildings, and the great slab faces of warehouses, they saw the frayed elbow of a tunic protrude into the yellow lamplight for an instant from a shadowed doorway ahead of them. They whirled into the shadows two doors away.

The girl's lips moved at the old Minister's ear. "Another. He's got his back to us, watching the station. They must be watching all the stations. Wait here ten minutes. If I don't get back, try to get to the Auxiliary Airport and find Abraham Kemp, a plant chemist. He's John Corander, my man."

Mustafa Issachar: "Yours, or the Department's?"

The girl: "Oh...I think mine. But he wouldn't know there's a difference." She slipped away, and the old judge felt utterly helpless. Then he heard her feet ringing unsteadily on the pavement. She was muttering to herself. Mustafa Issachar shrank back into the doorway. She reeled past him with the traditional stride of the soliciting prostitute, collapsing every few paces into a stagger. She turned neither head nor eyes toward him.

She reached the unseen sentry. Mustafa could not make out the man's mumble but heard Sue's familiar reedy voice, outrageously coarsened: "Ever been on a *vine*, honey?..." Involuntarily the old man's hand closed on the stunner she had given him.

The girl: "But honey, you don't have to stay outside *all* the time!...O-o-oh, honey...Not just a little minute? Your friends won't come for a little minute...Just inside the door—you could get that old door open, you're strong..."

So it was that Mustafa Issachar's gun was ready in his clenched hand when the whir of a groundcar swelled in the stillness and the roach shape swung into Van't Hoff.

He had no time to roll down his hood. He heard the rasp of radiation weapons from the car but felt nothing. They had missed. No, they were not shooting at him at all. The patrol in the car had mistaken him, the single figure, for their own man and instead had rayed the pair in the other doorway. His weapon was aimed and sputtering, spraying the open windows of the car, before he had decided what to do. The enemy's guns ceased. He heard one fall to the pavement. Had they been stun-guns or rayguns?

He pulled his hood down—it was still wet—got the eye-holes adjusted, and ran as fast as he could to the car, looking over his shoulder toward the other doorway. Sue and the sentinel were sprawled together, motionless.

He wrenched open the groundcar door. There were three unconscious men inside and three stunners on the seat, floor, and street. Stunners. The old judge dragged the inert forms out, tugging and kicking at them until he had lined them up on the pavement. Then he dosed each, firing point-blank into the head, as a prophylactic measure.

He walked—he could run no farther—to the pair in the doorway. He rolled Sue clear of the sentinel, a heavy-set, pustular man in a dirty green tunic, and pumped the waves into the base of his skull. His hand began to tremble. He forced himself to stop.

He made no attempt to revive the girl, not knowing whether a premature awakening might damage the brain. It was a struggle to get her to the car without dragging her.

She was not heavy, but he was old. "Oh...old men in love!" He held her inefficiently, politely.

The Chief of the Internal Defense Department shivered in her sleep. She was stretched out across three chairs in the Acting Security Officer's room at the Auxiliary Airport. The Acting Security Officer dithered tenderly. He did not recognize his own chief.

But Horace Thekman did recognize the Minister of Justice. Swelling with importance, he plucked at the pages of a first-aid manual. "Ah, um, yes. Here it is. 'Protokoloff's radiation, sometimes called 'stunner waves,' was first recognized by Fyodor Protokoloff on the fourth planet of Alpha Centauri in 2078, and first propagated artificially by means of the meson-vortex filter—'"

Mustafa Issachar: "Never mind that. What's the antidote or treatment of choice or whatever?"

Thekman: "Well...hm...oh! 'Treatment. It is inadvisable to apply any of the normal means of stimulation, chemical or physical, to the unconscious victim, as injury to the neurilemma may result. The indicated treatment is rest, preferably in a horizontal position, and the avoidance of extremes of heat and cold. The duration of unconsciousness generally varies directly as the three-halves power of the dosage and according to the age and health—'"

Mustafa Issachar: "Very helpful, Citizen Thekman. Now, while we're waiting, you can give me some information. I want to find a man named Abraham Kemp, who was scheduled to go to New Tavistock tonight."

The little man's eyes lit, but he was too good a bureaucrat to squander his news. He stroked his jawbone thoughtfully. "Kemp. Hm. Yes. The plant chemist."

Mustafa Issachar: "What do you know about him?"

Thekman: "Young man, apparently well qualified in his field, but...the brother of *Carroll Kemp.*"

Mustafa Issachar: "Who's Carroll Kemp?"

The Acting Security Officer swallowed. "Oh. Carroll Kemp. Hem. The Loyalist—you know the case, sir—but" (hurriedly) "I thought it was the brother you were interested in. Abraham."

Mustafa Issachar: "That is right. What *about* Abraham?"

Thekman: "Well, sir, Carroll Kemp is in New Tavistock at present. That is, he's thought to be in New Tavistock.

Unofficially. He's unquestionably in Laing's Land. I don't think his whereabouts are precisely known—"

Mustafa Issachar: "Is this Carroll or Abraham?"

Thekman: "This is Carroll, sir."

Mustafa Issachar: "I thought we were talking about Abraham."

Thekman: "Right, sir. Abraham was to visit Carroll."

Mustafa Issachar: "*Was* to visit Carroll. Why, what happened?"

"I wasn't altogether satisfied with his papers, sir." The Acting Security Officer began to grow more important. "There were several things about them. He was Category C—"

Mustafa Issachar: "Citizen Thekman, you seem to be spreading a very small amount of information over a very large area of words. Skip all that, do you hear? Where is Abraham Kemp now?"

Citizen Thekman realized suddenly that he did not know where Abraham Kemp was now; knew less than if he had let him go to Laing's Land. Kemp's papers—where were they? The Loyalist must have taken them away with him after missing the flight. Glancing desperately around the office, the Acting Security Officer was further unnerved to find that the pretty girl's eyes were open and regarding him steadily. "Abraham Kemp," he said, "is at present in New Nome—ah! I see your daughter has regained consciousness, sir."

S. Wells began to swing her feet down from the chairs.

"Miss," said Horace Thekman solicitously, "if you'll permit me, I think it would be advisable for you to rest in a horizontal position. I am told that you have been subjected to—"

Mustafa Issachar: "Sue, this is Citizen Thekman, *Acting* Security Officer of the New Nome *Auxiliary* Airport. He takes his responsibility very seriously and has read a big book about emergencies which *seems* to say that you ought to lie down for a while."

The girl: "All right, Judge. I'll lie down. Now: why didn't Abraham Kemp go to Laing's Land?"

Thekman: "He was refused pilot's clearance."

The girl: "Who was the pilot?"

Thekman: "Well, Flight Officer Feigenbrod was the pilot."

The girl: "Desmond Feigenbrod? Or Dennis? No, it would be Desmond. What did Desmond Feigenbrod have against Kemp?"

Thekman: "Nothing, miss—citizen. I—I recommended

withholding clearance. There were certain irregularities in his credentials."

The girl: "There were *what?* Judge, I'll have to do this sitting up, neurilemma or no neurilemma. Now, Citizen Thekman, do you know who I am?"

Thekman: "No. Yes. No."

The girl: "Yes you do but you hope I'm not, is that it? I'm the Chief of the Internal Defense Department. Do you know where those credentials were prepared?"

Thekman: "In the Department?"

The girl: "Right, Thekman. Now. What were these irregularities?"

Thekman: "I—I don't remember—they were technical— his own answers didn't—"

The girl: "His answers didn't what? Do you know where those answers were prepared?"

Thekman: "In the Department?"

The girl: "Right, Thekman. Abraham Kemp ranks you in the IDD by more grades than you'll ever have."

No reply.

The girl: "Where are the credentials now?"

There was no reply.

The girl: "Is Feigenbrod back yet?"

"I'll go and see," said Thekman, and escaped.

Mustafa Issachar: "Sue, I haven't got the point of this. Why blurt everything out?"

The girl: "Because I'm going to fire Thekman in a moment. Then he'll go home, and there won't be anybody here if Carl alerts the security posts against us. We may be able to get some transportation out of here tonight on our own. I know this Feigenbrod."

"Flight Officer Desmond Feigenbrod is here," announced Thekman from the doorway.

"Good evening, citizen. Good evening, citizeness," said the newcomer. "The local representative of justice and progress tells me that I have mysterious visitors. At least, he makes them *sound* mysterious; you don't *look* mysterious. But that's the way with the brave lads of the IDD. Always mysterious. Excuse me"—he paused in this patter to stare down at Sue— "but don't I know you? Isn't that comely face of yours linked with my past—some less sordid episode in it, of course," he hastened to reassure her. "Have you ever been in love with me?"

"No," said Sue, amused. "I don't know you."

Thekman said through dry lips, but openly enjoying the imminent prospect of the pilot's destruction, "That's the Chief of the Internal Defense Department you're talking to like that."

Feigenbrod: "Ah, good evening again, citizeness. I owe you an apology for all the bitter, bitter things I have thought about your Department. But how can you blame me? I was judging by Citizen Thekman."

Sue said amiably, "That was your mistake."

Thekman cleared his throat. "And this is the Minister of Justice."

Feigenbrod: "To do justice to Citizen Thekman, you *are* mysterious visitors. What do you mighty folk want with me, a humble plow-robot of the skies? Hah! Does that strike a chord?" he asked, swiftly catching a reaction of Sue's.

The girl: "No. I want to know why you refused clearance tonight to a Category C passenger named Abraham Kemp."

Feigenbrod: "I? Refused clearance? The mysteries deepen, citizeness."

The girl: "We understand, however, that it was on Citizen Thekman's recommendation you did so. Is this so?"

Feigenbrod ignored the sudden frightened appeal of Thekman's eyes. "Citizen Thekman? Recommendation? The mysteries are now unfathomable. Bluff, honest Thekman says he told me to bounce (if I may so express myself) the notorious syphilitic Abraham Kemp—you *did* say syphilis, Citizen Thekman? or was it misprision of treason? Whenever Citizen Thekman says to me, 'Bounce this man,' I bounce that man, yet I have the most vivid recollection of seeing the man Kemp walking up Number Three Ramp over at New Tavistock. And I could have sworn," he went on with additional distinctness, "that I never so much as saw Citizen Thekman before flight time. I did blunder in here, and found a distraught passenger waiting for the Acting Security, who I naturally supposed was in the gents' room. I gave the fellow the clearance he needed and flew him to Laing's Land."

Thekman, furious, cried out, "You cleared a Category C passenger without even consulting the Security Officer?"

"It seemed to me I did," said Feigenbrod sadly; then, brightening: "But your testimony has acquitted me of the charge...Wait! perhaps there were *two* syphilitics named Kemp."

Sue, with a trace of sharpness: "Category C means that

the passenger has Loyalist connections. You ought to have consulted the Security Officer."

Feigenbród gave her a brilliant smile. "I *tried* to. I said I came in here, didn't I? I don't come in here to wash my hands, you know. There's no sink. You can see for yourself. No sink. And also, *my* hands weren't dirty. And I might add"—he opened his eyes wide as he met her gaze—"that it's no fault of mine if dangerous Loyalists are rushing about the planet in this disgraceful fashion. The Government ought to set up some sort of agency to watch these traitors. Likewise, it would seem like a clever notion, citizeness, if your acting leg-sniffer here had orders to be on hand before flight time so that fervent-type patriots like myself could check up on these conspirators."

The girl looked at Thekman. "Perhaps he has such orders."

"As it happened, I was looking for *you,*" Thekman sputtered to the pilot.

Feigenbrod: "Leaving this traitor alone in your office? What if he had peeked into your bulging files?" He gestured to the bare walls.

"Well," said Thekman, "well, as it happened, he wasn't a traitor. He was one of our men."

Mustafa Issachar repressed a gasp. Citizen Wells' face congealed. Desmond Feigenbrod said finally, "Then there's no harm done. What's the bickering for?" His eyes were grim.

The girl: "Citizen Feigenbrod, will you wait for us outside? I want to talk with you later."

Feigenbrod: "Certainly." He gave them a comprehensive wave and turned to go. "By the way. You won't want me immediately, will you, citizeness? I'd like to go wash my hands. They're dirty."

There was a faint tremor in her voice. "Go ahead."

When the pilot had gone, she turned to Thekman. "That was the most insubordinate and moronic performance I have ever witnessed. Hand me your badge." The little man complied. "You are relieved of all duties, effective now. Take anything that belongs to you and leave the premises at once. Report to headquarters in three days."

Horace Thekman pulled open the drawers of the desk one by one, picking out paprite, ink-pencils, eradicator-sticks. "My own camera," he said defensively, raising a countenance of misery to Mustafa's as he pocketed the little instrument. "I guess I don't need this," replacing a folding rule. "This is mine," staring for a moment at the big first-aid manual from which he had prescribed for the girl.

A man came in noisily with a slip of paper and said, "Oh, I didn't know you were busy. This came for you at Communications." He handed it to Thekman and swung out without looking at the others.

"I suppose it should go to you now," said the little man, with a trembling mouth. As he extended it to Citizen Wells, his eye fell on the text, and he snatched the sheet back.

The girl said quietly, "Watch this, Judge."

"So!" crowed the little man. His joy was appalling to see. "So that's what you've been up to! Well, you're in for it now! Do you know what this is? Would you like me to read it to you?"

Mustafa Issachar: "If you please."

Thekman: "'To all Security Officers and Traffic Control Personnel. Effective immediately, Citizens M. Issachar and S. Wells are relieved of their duties as Minister of Justice and Chief of the Internal Defense Department respectively. They are not to leave New Nome. If they attempt to do so, they are to be detained and the fact reported without delay to the Ministry of Reconstruction. Signed, C. ap Rhys, Deputy Prime—'"

"Catch Citizen Thekman," said Sue. The rattle of her stunner filled the room for an instant, and the two fugitives stretched the Acting Security Officer across the three chairs.

Mustafa Issachar: "The indicated treatment is rest, preferably in a horizontal position...Poor Herman! He's still holding out against the worst, anyway."

"Not for long," said Sue.

They walked quickly out into the corridor and hurried toward the main terminal area.

"We could talk more privately outside," said a voice behind them. It was Feigenbrod. They went out with him onto the field and began to walk toward the darkness. The fact that he was with them reduced all official challenges to greetings—"Hey there, sport!" "Hey there, Red!"

The girl innocently asked the pilot, "Did you make your call to New Tavistock?"

Feigenbrod: "Yes. My hands are clean now."

The girl: "He's a good lad. I hope your friends won't be too hard on him."

Feigenbrod: "He'll find it interesting professionally."

They were beyond the lighted area of the field now; the

pocks and scars of the war were around them, huge brooding pools of shadow. They climbed down and sat on the slope of a crater, out of sight from the ground above.

At last the girl said, "I'm glad you're in a serious mood, Desmond. You weren't often."

Feigenbrod: "You were right to say you didn't know me, Shulamith. You still don't."

The girl: "I don't know myself any more, Desmond. I've been finding out things tonight."

Feigenbrod: "What things?"

The girl: "Oh, lots of things. Haven't you, Judge? Don't you feel as if you'd had a whole new education?"

Mustafa Issachar: "Not a new one. Things I'd forgotten."

The girl: "I'd forgotten a lot. I'd forgotten about your father and the plow-robot, Desmond. I've got a bad memory."

Feigenbrod: "Is it true you're outlawed now? They're saying inside that there's been some kind of putsch in your windy little government."

The girl: "We're not legally outlaws—not yet. But they've been trying to kill us all night."

Feigenbrod: "How'd you ever get into it, Sue? The whole thing, I mean. How'd you ever get to be Chief of the IDD? I never suspected it was you heading up that horror. Whose name are you going under? You're not married?"

The girl: "My mother's name. Wells. I've been calling myself Wells for years and years; it was my name in the movement, even before I left my father."

Feigenbrod: "But there wasn't a fight, was there, Shulamith? He was very proud of you."

The girl: "A wretched fight. But that was later. When I left the first time, he was proud of me. He approved of my independence, not exploiting my family connections, all that. But then...anyway, it's over. He married that girl. There's bad blood in *that* clan, Desmond."

Feigenbrod: "I heard she's nice. I know she's expecting a baby boy any day now."

The girl: "Her mother's a fat, stupid strumpet."

Feigenbrod: "Old girl's on the other side from you now, eh?"

The girl: "She's probably in bed with Carl ap Rhys at this minute."

Mustafa Issachar: "What's all this? What *are* you talking about, Sue? Who's your father? *Who's* in bed with Carl ap Rhys? I thought Olivia—"

The girl: "Judge, Simon de Ferraris is my father. Olivia Keyes is in bed with Carl ap Rhys. No...I killed her son Ricky tonight, Desmond; so maybe she isn't. Have you recovered yet, Judge?"

Mustafa Issachar: "I don't know...So *you're* the daughter Simon used to talk about!...No wonder he was so proud."

The girl's voice shook: "It's a bit of a tangle. I'm Simon de Ferraris' only child—so far, that is—so my stepmother is the daughter of Olivia Keyes, whose son I killed because he was trying to assassinate me for his mother's lover, Carl ap Rhys, on account of whom I'm going back to my father. Have you got it all straight, Judge?"

Feigenbrod: "Are you going back? Are you really going back, Shulamith?"

The girl: "If I can find him."

After a moment, the pilot asked, "What will you say to him?"

The girl answered slowly. "I shall say, 'Hello, Poppa.'"

Feigenbrod: "Will you say, 'Hello, Poppa'?"

The girl: "Yes."

Feigenbrod: "Then I'll take you to him."

The girl: "When?"

Feigenbrod: "Now." The pilot stood up precariously on the slope. "Shulamith, before tonight, you've only known me as a stubborn, loudmouthed kid. Now you'll find you're dealing with a man of indomitable resolve and unquenchable high spirits. Also, this is a good night to steal a copter. The selection is good. Do you have any preferences as to color? No? Well, wait here. When something beats its great wings over you, don't get the conceited idea you're a latter-day Leda. Just climb aboard."

CHAPTER 8

THERE were two girls, friends, who grew up together in the Valley of Kuban. One was a lean, dark child, quick and passionate, always flashing into the kitchens of the farm folk with a taunt or a keen, affectionate greeting or a bit of bluster, or crouching in silence for hours to watch the huge gray plow-robots clank back and forth across the sunny alluvial plain, for she was the only child of a great landowner of the valley; this was the older of the two. Her companion, younger by a year, was one of three children of a doctor; she was a golden, placid girl who said little and loved much and was frightened by the older child's antics, so that she would be seen smiling her slow smile in mingled apology and pride while some householder was being insulted or outrageously cajoled.

The doctor was busy; his wife was much involved in committees and causes. The landowner approved of temperament; and his wife was ailing. So the children, when school was not in session, were free.

This was a spacious existence. The war of independence

was some years in the future, and the overlordship of Earth was in the main benignant, certainly benignant for those who were too young or too old to have character on the production side of the economy. The culture of the valley was agrarian and stable, yet new enough and remote enough so that manners were easy. The arts the girls practiced were their own.

The passage of the long Rohan years brought changes in the two friends, and changes for them. The younger reached menarche first; the threat of responsibility and desire did not frighten her; her breasts formed high and large, her waist lengthened, her hips filled but remained flexible, and she passed without awkwardness into a bright, deep nubility. To the dark girl, puberty came bitter; her laugh was heard less often, her taunts grew briefer and then retreated altogether behind a flouting lip; and her mood generally was unidentifiable, a brooding question. But there was no relaxation of loyalty between them.

The dark girl's mother developed Levkranz's Syndrome, and the fair girl's father worked devotedly to shock the renegade brain cells into submission. Within a few months there were traces of pancreatic failure, and a brilliant cytosurgeon was called in from Earth to do the restoration. Inflammations fulminated around the implanted electrodes in the brain, and there was nothing more to be done. The dark girl came back from New Nome, where she had gone to work for a season and to take a leading place in the Revolutionary conspiracy.

The mother's painful, tremulous deliberation turned into helplessness. The landowner and his daughter did most of the more intimate nursing themselves, because the woman still retained her curious colorless pride. The doctor's daughter, who had sometimes assisted her father, helped her friend and became one of the watchers. The patient's husband, daughter, and daughter's friend spelled each other at the bedside.

Late one night, the dark girl went to her bed exhausted. Her father, his big body dragging with grief, was still up, getting through some work. She kissed him goodnight with less, somehow, than her accustomed reserve; perhaps what goaded her was the sight of the fair girl moving through the sickbed routine, cleaning a syringe, with that calm sweetness of hers; the dark girl suddenly kissed her too, with a pang of envy.

After an hour or two of sleep, the dark girl awoke: someone

was sobbing. Her head still sour with dreams, she arose silently and went out into the passage to listen: then she flashed down the hall to her father's room and flung open the door.

The syllables of comfort which her instincts had prepared as she ran died in her teeth.

The old man, clothed above the waist, naked below, lay across the great bed, hugging under him the naked body of the golden girl. He had, it was clear, already released his passion and his tensions into her and lay, decanted and crying, with his huge, seamed old face buried between her breasts, while the girl, even as she turned a countenance of fear toward the door, stroked him with her arms.

The fair girl twisted loose and sprang up with a soft, incoherent cry. But the door slammed.

There was no confrontation. The guilty pair dressed and went quietly down to the sickroom. It was locked. The daughter kept the vigil alone, locked in with the dying woman.

As the day was dawning grayly, the patient's pulse failed. Her attendant bent over her with a dark stare, holding the emergency hypodermic, found the vein, and pressed home the plunger. There was no reaction. Face set, the girl turned, opened the door, and walked, without a word or a glance at her father or her friend, away from her mother's corpse.

There was a burial, for the landowner was a man of eccentric beliefs. Daughter and father stood facing each other across the open grave. Tears stood in the furrows of the man's face. The younger girl was not there. There was a thin, cold, silent wind. The helpers waited.

"Veyatzitsu me'ir," began the widower in a strange voice and language, stooped and plucked up a handful of the bittergrass, and flung it into the grave as if it had burned his hand—*"Ke'eseb ha'aretz."* Something like irony, an ancient irony, lit his eyes. He stooped and scrabbled up some dust and threw it into the grave—*"Zachur ki 'afar 'anachnu."* Then he broke off and, looking at his daughter, said distinctly, "I was crying and it happened that you were asleep..." Then he shut his mouth. The girl met his gaze and did not answer. The only things alive in her face were her eyes, full of wild and hate-driven reproof.

CHAPTER **9**

CORANDER found the Hotel Montessori cringing between two hells, a squeed hell and a gambling hell, great pale blocky opacities, near the top of the slope.

"Full lup," said the dozing clerk without opening his eyes.

"I want a room with a bath," repeated Corander stubbornly; then added, "and with a brown-haired girl, real young."

The clerk opened his eyes. One sized up Corander coldly; the other drifted sideways and seemed to search for inspiration in the dark corners of the lobby. "Why dinn you say so? I thought you meant for the night. Room Twenty-five. Eight thousand units. 'Nadvants." He pushed Corander his change and flicked his cold leer on and off. "You're getting a good one. If you ask her nice, she'll get 'n the tub with ya *wash* ya. That's one hour and half *maximum*, including the bath." The armpit of his jacket was soiled and frayed where the butt of a small weapon poked up underneath.

* * *

Corander asked the young naked girl in Room 25, "What's your name, sweetheart?"

"Brandy."

Corander: "Before it was 'Brandy'?"

"Madeline."

Corander: "How many customers do you think you'll have tonight after me, Madeline?"

"Brandy."

Corander: "Brandy has the customers, hm?"

A duck of the head. A quick look, but whether of fear or impatience, Corander could not say.

Corander: "Well, how many will *she* have?"

"Four. I don't know. Five?"

Corander: "Do me a favor, Madeline. Put on some clothes and take this forty thousand units down to the desk. Tell the desk I can't resist Brandy, and he's not to bother me. Then you run quietly along somewhere—not next door, Madeline—and amuse yourself till ten in the morning. I need some sleep."

The girl, doubtfully: "Mr. Alfred won't like that, if the desk tells him."

Corander: "Who is Mr. Alfred to interfere with a man's pleasures?"

The girl: "Owner."

Corander: "He doesn't own *me*. I'm a consenting adult and you..." He stared at her. "Please, Madeline dearest?"

The naked girl, sharply: "I *woon't*." After a moment: "Anyway, where will I go? I usually get some sleep in between."

Corander's voice was gentle: "All right, little honey. I apologize. Give them the money and come back here."

"Corander calling Room Thirty-two. Come in. Over."

"Room Thirty-two. Report, Corander. Over."

"That's not David or, what's his name, Nolly."

"No," said Room 32.

"Who is it, then?"

"Nolly's off duty, and David's out sick."

Corander: "He wasn't sick when I called in earlier."

Room 32: "He got sick an hour ago."

Corander: "Why won't you give your name?"

Room 32: "Hendrix. Report, Corander. Over."

Corander: "I'm in the Hotel Montessori. I've got two characters tailing me, Hendrix. They're being helpful. Ours?"

Room 32: "They might be...I don't know."

Corander: "If they're ours, ask the chief how she expects the Reconstructionists to let me get near them with a goddamn yoke of oxen following me around. Ask her that. I want them taken off."

Room 32: "The chief's... off duty."

Corander noted that tergiversating break in the rhythm. "When she comes on."

The slightest of pauses. "All right."

Corander: "Thanks, Hendrix." Casually, "Anything I should know?"

Again the little break. "...No. That is, there are some personnel shifts here. They don't affect you, though. But you might hear some exaggerated stories. Don't pay any attention. They don't affect you."

Corander, very casually: "Just political stuff, you mean."

Room 32: "That's right, just pol—"

Corander: "Someone's coming. Over and out." He put the N-Transmitter back on the strap which held it against the inside of his thigh. "That you, Madeline? I'm in the bathroom."

The girl's voice: "It's me. Brandy. You want me to come in and wash you in the tub?"

Corander hastily stepped out of the bathroom, and found the girl pulling off the last of her clothes.

On seeing him fully dressed, she lost her decerebrate smile. Her shoulders drooped. "All right, what is it?" she said. "Whips? Corsets? Don't tell me I got to pee on you. You got to get in the tub if I'm going to pee on you. Mr. Alfred don't—"

Corander: "No, no, it's worse than that. I want to talk to you." It was the last thing he wanted to do. He desperately needed time to think about what Hendrix had let slip. He sat on the bed, took off his boots, and lay back.

The naked girl: "This?"

Corander: "*No,* thank you." He lifted her away, feeling the adolescent body wriggle angrily. "Madeline—all right: Brandy—let me talk to you. I have a different problem. It's a little—different."

The pretty little face gazed down at him with a suspicious pout.

Corander said in a low voice, "The girl has to be young and—and innocent. I can't do anything if she's not innocent—"

The naked girl interrupted darkly, "Well, citizen, you should of been my guidance counselor in sixth grade."

Corander: "No, no, I mean you have to *look* innocent. You have to be lying there, sleeping innocently—"

The naked girl: "It's a hell of a place to come for cherry, you know? What's your name, oddbaby?"

Corander: "Abraham."

The naked girl: "Cheese! Abraham."

Corander brokenly: "You've got to help me, Madeline. You've got to be lying there, looking very soft and innocent, like—like—"

The girl's eyes narrowed. "Like *who?*"

Corander: "I c-can't tell you." He trembled.

The wary little face softened. "Like what, then? Like this?" She curled up beside him and pretended to sleep.

"Yes," said Corander.

"I don't do rape stunts, you know," said the girl, twisting from her fetal position to glare at him.

Corander: "No, no, nothing like that."

She relaxed.

One thing was certain: Citizen Wells was no longer in control at the Department. Hendrix's reactions told him that. But whether—

"That enough?" The naked girl sat up perkily. "How you coming along, Abraham?"

Corander, sadly: "Oh, Madeline, you spoiled it! You've got to *really* sleep."

"Cheese!" muttered the naked girl. She curled up again.

At the kopje, the night was quiet, except that Citizen Vanderwol, in a sleeping bag on the cabin floor, mumbled now and then in pain; but Cathy de Ferraris was restless. She felt swollen and strange; whenever she closed her eyes she had the illusion of having grown monstrously big so that she nearly filled the cabin; twice, she imagined premonitory flutters in her uterus; and several times the sturdy kicking of her unborn son struck her as irresistibly comical.

The squalling of the com-set tore into her drowsy confusion. Her husband flung himself heavily out of bed. She heard him curse as his forgotten wound announced itself, then a yap of agony in another voice and a profane apology in Simon's as he stumbled over Vanderwol and plunged to the corner where the yellow light was flashing on the set.

The yellow light meant the squawking-IFF had detected

and queried an incoming air vehicle and had received a properly coded identification signal. This was not an attack, then. Unless there had been treachery.

Simon roared into the microphone: "Speak up, damn you!"

A chuckle from the audio, then: "Calling Tshombe. Calling Tshombe. This is Bumptious. May we come in? Over."

Simon: "Tshombe to Bumptious. Come on in. Over and out." He switched the set back to passive-detection mode and listened to the faint thrill of the approaching vehicle. "Citizen Vanderwol, I am about to receive more company. I offer you a choice: either I drug you or I lock you in the storage shed, where you cannot see or hear my other guests. The drug will incidentally ease your sufferings. The shed is unheated but tolerable if you stay in the sleeping bag. Drug or shed?"

Vanderwol: "Can't I just give you my word—?"

Simon: "Drug or shed?"

Vanderwol: "Drug." He was unconscious by the time the copter was overhead.

Then the flagellant sound outside ceased. Cathy sat up in bed. Simon stood with his raystick swinging in his right hand. The door opened, and Desmond Feigenbrod thrust his head in.

"Good evening, Boss. And good evening, Mrs. Boss. We just happened to be passing by and thought we might drop—" He saw Vanderwol. "My goodness! A deceased person! And in an advanced state of decomposition. Are you holding a wake?"

Simon: "Another uninvited guest. But he's still alive. Step inside. All of you. *Whoever else you are.*"

Desmond Feigenbrod stepped quickly inside, followed by Mustafa Issachar. They stood, mutely questioning the grim old giant. The door remained open.

The old men looked into each other's eyes.

Simon: "Are you my old friend, or the Minister of Justice?"

Mustafa: "I am your old friend. I am not the Minister of Justice."

"And who is still out there?"

A slim girl stepped in, studied Simon de Ferraris with keen eyes, and said, "Hello, Poppa." She looked toward the bed. "Hello, Momma."

Feigenbrod: "An affecting scene, as all will agree. I wish I could stay for more of it, but I'm sure you dear people have many things to talk about. My advice is not to talk about them. You do very well at pregnant silence. Stick to that. I must run along and think of something interesting to do with a stolen copter. Boss, I'll send McIntyre and Billioray in the late afternoon. They can relieve you of the horizontal citizen there. I'll tell our medical friends to be ready. I take it he had a set-to with a vine? We must edit his recollections. We don't want him selling your address. What memories he will have! How he will think back to those fierce, sweet days as the pampered darling of a sadomasochist cult! Ah, but you all have your own memories... Goodnight, Boss and Mrs. Boss. Goodnight, fugitives!"

It was nearly three hours since Desmond Feigenbrod had called from New Nome to warn that "Abraham Kemp" was really an IDD man sent to hunt down Simon de Ferraris. For most of that interval, eleven weary Reconstructionists—Billioray and Hadder among them—had been scouring New Tavistock for the spy. It would have been one thing to search for an impostor among men and women who led genuine lives; it was another to search for an impostor where everyone lived in a private tangle of secrets and deceits. One promising lead turned up—in a small nightclub where a man who fit Kemp's description had created a disturbance—but that trail was lost only a few meters away in a throng on Rorschach Street.

"Nobody ever saw *anybody* on Rorschach Street," said Hadder to Billioray.

Billioray's white, crooked mouth twisted in a yawn. "They're not afraid to talk. They don't see people, that's all. They're afraid to see. You don't see me, for that matter."

Hadder: "I do see you. You're an ugly fish-mouthed pervert with low blood pressure."

Billioray: "There! You see? You're seeing your own frightened interpretation. You'll be nipping round the corner soon, Hadder, I'll tell you that. You have the habitus of a schizophrenic."

Hadder: "Last month it was epistemology. Now it's psychology. Next it'll be religion."

Billioray: "I've tried religion. It kept me going a year. I'm still holding some in reserve. The *mythos* of Rorschach Street, Hadder, is the *mythos* of Narcissus. How do you like that? Not bad, for no sleep and a full bladder. Narcissus in the latrine, staring at his reflection in his own wee-wee."

Hadder: "Tell you what. I've got to go too. Let's investigate this ginzo hotel here, and maybe they have a bathroom."

Billioray: "Hundreds of Narcissi with their windowless *mythoi* is a thought that is pithy."

Hadder: "Next month it'll be poetry. Come on, Billioray, you're too shy to urinate in the street. I saw your face down there outside that strip club, the one where the naked woman comes blooping out on a swing with her legs apart. You damn near fainted."

Billioray winced. "I thought she was going to urinate on me. She had that look. What's that got to do with sex?"

Hadder: "Urinating in public is sexy. That's why *you* can't do it. So let's check this place out and use their facilities while we're at it."

They went into the Hotel Montessori.

The room clerk awoke to find two unpleasant men contemplating him across the counter. They were politicals; they had that I'm-Here-For-A-Better-Reason-Than-You-Are look he hated; all the politicals had it.

"Full lup," he said quickly.

"I beg your pardon," said the spokesman for the two, a burly, white-haired man with a pale scar on his nose and a pale, narrow mouth; "we're looking for a friend of ours, a young fellow named Kemp, who came in on the New Nome copter last night."

The clerk: "I can't help you."

The spokesman: "He's one-point-eight-six or -nine, big-jointed, with reddish hair. We missed him at the airport."

The clerk put on his I'm-Waiting-Not-Listening expression and then repeated, "Can't help you."

The spokesman, courteously: "You mean he isn't here?"

"I mean I can't help you," snapped the clerk. "Want me to sing it for you?"

The other man, a small man with a large head wavering on a long, flexible neck, giggled at this. "Why, yes," he said, "try it in E-flat major—"

The clerk whirled on him.

"...*because* you'll sing a different tune when I get through with you, you pus-filled degenerate." And before the clerk had time to be astonished at this, the larger man had vaulted over the desk and seized him. The clerk had no chance to get his hand on the stunner in his armpit. He found himself bent backward over the desk, with the thumbs of his adversary stabbing into the nerves of his neck and right arm. He choked with pain, and his attacker, with a cruel slanting smile, said,

"Don't talk, or I'll hurt you. All right"—the big man nodded to the smaller one—"give him enough to make him optimistic." The small man produced a device like a misshapen atomizer. It had a bifurcated nozzle, which he inserted into the clerk's nostrils. The big man lurched against the clerk's gut, then pulled away to relieve the pressure; the little man simultaneously clapped a hand over the victim's mouth so that on getting his breath back the clerk had to inhale through his nose; at that instant the sprayer sent a flood of lemony-tasting vapor into his head.

"Fine!" said the large man jovially and released him. The whole attack had taken a few seconds.

The clerk stood free, throbbing with fury for a moment; then, to his own surprise, he felt the hostility drain out of him; he realized there was no point in dwelling on the past. "Let bygones be bygones," he said thickly.

"That's right!" said the burly man enthusiastically. "We all make mistakes."

"But we learn from them!" cried the small man.

The room clerk liked this point of view. He looked at the two men with whom he had had a misunderstanding and felt that they had all grown as a result of the experience. "You got to give people a chance," he said profoundly. It was not so much a feeling of well-being that had taken possession of him, because the molars on the right still kept biting the inside of his cheek, always in the same goddamn place; no, it was a sense of progress. That was what counted: people were making an effort. He looked around the dim, cold, unswept lobby and for the first time saw it as the humble, necessary support of everything that went on above. It was the basis. Upstairs, right above his head, were the rows of warm rooms where girls were all squirming and twisting their warm bodies at the same time in toasty warm beds, like a great hive making honey, faithfully—

"That's right!" agreed the burly man, showing many of the small white teeth in his little mouth. "Most people are decent, if you only give them a chance."

"More than decent," the small man corrected him. "Constructive!"

The clerk was glad he had found someone to whom he could explain this new understanding he had. Madeline, for instance. A dedicated person. "You take Room Twenty-five," he said. The two men were spellbound. They hung on his words, and he realized that his new ideas meant a great deal to all of them. "She's constructive."

The large smiling man: "That's where Kemp went? Room Twenty-five?"

The clerk: "What does it matter what his name was? It's his attitude. He's helping Madeline to make honey."

The large man seemed a shade upset by this last. The clerk saw at once that further explanation was needed. "Have to think of the muscles," he said. "The different parts. Tendons. The hair is different color from regular hair, for instance." He tried to describe his vision. "Beautiful. Like your mouth," he said. "All for the honey." The large man only leaned against the counter and swallowed. All at once the clerk perceived the reason for the man's difficulty. "Not only some of them you wouldn't think they were muscles"—he touched his own behind lightly and tactfully—"but you can't see your own, so it doesn't make sense. But *then* you see— hard and soft and hard and soft—before your very eyes. All helping," said the clerk triumphantly, overthrowing the communication barrier. "Part of a plan. That's what I mean by honey."

The smaller man, at least, understood. "A tall young fellow like our friend would be a great help."

The room clerk was exhilarated. "One-point-eight-six, that's what you said? That would be about right. With big joints. Because Madeline—"

The small man: "And Madeline is Room Twenty-five?"

The clerk: "Right, right—"

The small man: "Well then, why don't we run upstairs and look at the good news for ourselves?" He leaned forward confidentially and gave a little nod indicating his friend. *"Then* he'll understand, don't worry. You wait here and take care of things. We won't be a minute."

But no sooner had his two disciples disappeared into the stairwell than two other men entered the lobby, and the room clerk caught himself about to say "Full lup" by force of habit. He suppressed the words, proud that he had progressed so far in a short time, and called out brightly, "Good morning, citizens! All the muscles are making honey, but if you'll—"

Apparently not hearing this remark, they strode to the stairwell, and disappeared after the others.

The attack on the door was so noisy that Corander knew before he saw them the intruders were not from his Department. IDD men might be clumsy about tailing, but they were issued good picklocks. The characters outside Room 25—he could now even hear them breathing curses at each other—were using something like a jemmy.

He lay on his back, making no physical move to get ready. As soon as the naked girl had consented to act the part of a sleeping child, she had actually fallen asleep; and then she had curled closer and closer to him until his left arm was lightly around her thin shoulder blades and her face was trying to burrow into his armpit. It was an amusing little face, more Brandy than Madeline. She seemed able to sleep through the preposterous racket at the door—doubtless the Hotel Montessori was full of preposterous noises—and Corander wished he could manage the impending scene in such a way that she could sleep safely through that as well.

The archaic lock broke and two men rushed in, full of menace and vigilance. One brandished a blaster, the other a curious device like a cross between an atomizer and an Earth serpent. They were not the compact, rather military types who had guarded him in the nightclub. One of these was a large, bleached-looking man with a scar, the other a spindly creature with a big skull.

Corander put his finger to his lips and said, "Shh!" just as the spindly man said with a sort of meaningless fury, "Get up and come with us!"

Madeline stirred.

Corander whispered, "Lower your voice. You'll wake the baby." Very gently he began to disengage himself from the naked girl. She opened her eyes.

The bleached man was trying to point the blaster without looking at the defenseless, unripe body directly in front of him, and the weapon shook. The spindly man seemed to flex his atomizer arm.

The half-shut door behind the two intruders quietly began to slide open. Standing outside were the two myrmidons from the nightclub.

Corander said to the girl, "Don't look round, darling. Just keep looking at me." It was the wrong thing to say. She tried at once to turn her head. To restrain her, Corander put his knobby hand around the little jaw and as an afterthought planted a kiss on the tip of the girl's nose.

One of the men outside raised a stun-pistol.

The naked girl said to Corander, "That's a boring perversion you got, you know that?" She still did not know what was happening and tried again to turn and look.

The man in the doorway fired. The bleached man pitched forward, struck the edge of the bed, and slipped to the floor. His blaster fell between the girl's thighs. She squeaked in fright. The stunner rattled again. The spindly man sank. Corander glimpsed the realignment of the weapon for a third burst and roared "No!" but was too late. The girl subsided on the bed, unconscious. Corander pulled back his hand, numb, from the slack face.

"What was the point of *that?*" he said disgustedly. He picked the blaster from Madeline's groin, holding the small, heavy weapon by the barrel, and bent earnestly over her pubic area as if to examine it for injury, running his numb hand over the jaunty little tuft. He shook his head slowly. The man with the stunner came over, slyness glinting through his battle expression, and peered.

Corander called over the peering man's shoulder to the other, who was still in the doorway looking up and down the corridor, "Come in and shut that damn door!"

The man moved inside and, in closing the door, momentarily turned his back to the room. Corander brought the butt of the blaster down heavily on the base of the peering man's skull, dropped the weapon, lunged, seized the stunner from his toppling victim, and snapped a burst at the man by the door. He gave the man he had just knocked out a short precautionary dose of the stunwaves and pocketed both the hand weapons.

He redisposed Madeline on the bed and searched the four unconscious men. In the clothing of the first pair of intruders, the bleached man and the spindly man, he found nothing at all to identify them. They were probably operating outside the law, then. But strapped to the stomach of the man lying by the door was an N-Transmitter; therefore, the second pair were IDD...And if this was so, the first pair must be Reconstructionists. That meant his cover story, the "Abraham Kemp" identity, had been blown. That was strange, so soon.

After checking to make sure all his companions were in fact unconscious, he took out his own N-Transmitter.

"Corander calling Room Thirty-two. Come in. Over."

"Room Thirty-two. Over." It was Hendrix's voice.

Corander: "That you, Hendrix? Listen, somebody's blown my cover to the Recons. Two of them came here to the hotel after me, and those two buffaloes I was telling you about before—ours—tried to protect me, and there was a little stunning and our two got it. And I took out the Recons. Now I've got four sleeping beauties here."

Hendrix made no comment on Corander's identifying his two protectors as IDD. "Want help?" he asked.

Corander: "That's just what I *don't* want, Hendrix. Repeat: *don't*. First place, our two should be coming around soon; and second place, I can keep the Recons under as long as I need to. When ours come around, we might stage a little something to reestablish my cover. But if anyone else gets in on this, my Department connection is going to be obvious to whoever is still watching outside."

Room 32: "If you don't want it, you don't have to have it. You're the man on the spot."

Corander: "Thanks. How's David?"

"Fine," said Hendrix, caught off guard, and Corander nodded grimly.

He changed the subject: "Hendrix, who blew my cover?"

Room 32: "Don't know."

Corander: "The chief? Or," he added casually, "maybe now I can say the 'Little Bitch'?"

Room 32: "Could be."

Corander signed off. He went around the grungy hotel room collecting what he needed to bind and gag the four men, and with great difficulty because of his numb hand got them trussed and silenced. He dragged the four of them into the bathroom and stacked them in the tub.

Then he lay down beside Madeline, put his left arm around her and her head on his shoulder, and dozed off, his doubts alive and his options still open.

Mustafa Issachar's presence in the hut made it impossible for Cathy, Shulamith, and old Simon to say to each other what was on their minds. They were grateful for the inhibition, and in the predawn chill, with the windows shuttered tight and the heatless golden flare of a single Barstow lamp casting shadows like glares and sneers on their faces, they launched into political talk. They were too shy to stop. Even Cathy interjected bloodthirsty opinions in a timid voice. There were never any silences.

Finally, Simon yawned, snapped off the lamp, opened the shutters to let in the gray dawn, lumbered out to the storage shed, and brought back two sleeping bags, and the exhausted judge dozed off in one of them; but by that time Citizen Vanderwol showed signs of returning consciousness.

The little man pretended to be still asleep. Sue watched the telltale movements of the eyeballs behind his closed lids.

Simon was growling: "Silly talk. A set of dreaming refugees."

Cathy: "Why silly? We could win."

Simon: "We forget we're reactionariés. We talk like mad counterrevolutionaries."

Sue shook her head warningly. "Your patriotic friend is with us again, I suspect," she said. Politics ceased.

Cathy de Ferraris had curled up in the bed, like a fetus containing a fetus, and was regarding her husband and stepdaughter with a sleepy eyê. Simon eased his heavy body down next to hers and arranged her fair head on his shoulder, crooking his arm about her.

Shulamith leaned over them, adjusted the bedclothes, impulsively kissed her father on the side of his bulbous nose, drew back, stared at her stepmother for several seconds, kissed her on the cheek, and said, "Go to sleep, fatties."

Chapter 10

"I'M looking at you," said a small voice in Corander's ear, "lying there all young and innocent, and you know what? It gives me a pain in the ass."

Corander opened his eyes. It was morning. Madeline was still nestling in the crook of his left arm, and he found that his left hand was wrapped around a hard little buttock. He did not move it. The girl's face was glaring into his from his shoulder. He kissed the tip of the nose again. "Good morning."

The naked girl: "You mean you're not too exhausted? You can do that *twice?* Oh boy! *Kiss* my *nose?* Oh boy!" Her face softened into something like compassion. In a lower voice: "I know. I'll—I'll wash out my mouth and gargle and all if that'll make you feel better...I'm *me*. You—you can't think about anything else in a place like this."

Desire swept through Corander. But the N-Transmitter was strapped to his thigh, a neat little obstacle to the drive of the moment. She could not be allowed to find it; she would not know what it was, but she might mention—

She saved him from his dilemma by remembering. "Say!"

The face became pugnacious again. "Who were those people?"

Corander: "Oh, those! Some men who came in here and had a fight. Four of them."

The naked girl: "Fight about what? What happened to them?"

Corander: "Politics. They're in the bathtub." He relinquished the buttock as the naked girl whirled up. She scampered to the bathroom, then drew back before opening the door. He joined her. "It's all right," he said. "No mess."

All his victims were alive; and two, one IDD man at the bottom of the heap and the spindly man on the top, were conscious and struggling in their bonds; but the spindly man and the bleached man had emptied their bladders; the heap was sopping. Madeline, undismayed, crowed with laughter and said, "Well, you do have some kind of balls." Then she noticed the cords and gags. "Hey! That's my bedspread." Her face crumpled. "That's *mine*. I bought it myself, it's not Mr. Alfred's. I like things pretty. You tore up my bedspread..."

Corander: "I'll get you a new one, I promise."

She cheered up at once and examined the four captives with the look of a sly child about to ask for toys.

"You can't have them just yet, little sweetheart. You have to have me first. No, no," he said hastily, "I have an appointment down the hill right now. But when I come back—"

The naked girl: "I know, you'll *kiss my forehead*." She pretended to sneer. "You can kiss—"

Corander seized her by one bare shoulder blade and one bare buttock and kissed her mouth. The numbness was gone from his right hand. He said, "You're not to touch anything while I'm away."

She giggled.

Corander: "Promise me."

The naked girl: "I promise."

Corander: "Whatever you have to do with the desk, do it, and tell them you have four bondage queers up here and they're waiting for their big friend. That's me. And you don't want to be disturbed."

"I'll wait. I promise."

"What you were talking about last night," whispered Cass Harding, pushing his peaky face close to Corander's, "now I won't make any promises, you understand, it won't be easy, these things never are, don't I know that better than anyone? I've handled, listen, I've handled—"

Corander: "Where shall we talk?"

Harding waved a pale flat hand at the eating stand. "Right here is best, out in the open, you go into a room, you don't know what's in there, anybody could of set it up, this is quite a town, I could tell you things, bathrooms for instance..."

Corander whispered, "Those two men?" There were two customers in the place, not together. One of them was the albino Deputy Kullervo, who had been on the copter the evening before, who was mixed up in Agent Morgan's murder and who had drafted the legislation under which Corander was operating. The deputy had finished his meal but did not leave; Corander inferred that he was now waiting to speak to Harding. The other man was still eating.

Harding: "Just keep your voice down, face turned they can't read your mouth, watch *me:* see? They can't catch a thing. Right out in the open nobody can sneak up on you— toilets are the worst place. *Anyway.* I've found out two things, don't be surprised, I'm a fast worker, when I move I really move, what you might call an expert, it's worth the price." He paused for this to take. "You could spend the rest of your life dragging your gumple all over Laing's Land looking for the gentleman you mentioned, we'll keep names out of it, you could spend years and then." He shook his head slowly from side to side for several seconds. "End up in some swamp, and that reminds me. *Uppp. Wait a minute. First things first.* This gentleman you're interested in? Well, I've found out where he is, don't ask me how, I won't tell you, I'm not at liberty to tell you, a man like me can't reveal our sources, you've heard of honor among thieves?—not that I'd put anything over on you, I'm not going to stand here and say I'm honest, a thing like this what I'm doing for you, it, it isn't strictly what you'd call honest, there's a lot of risk involved, I'm taking a chance, I know it, you know it, we're going into this thing with our eyes wide open, that's why I'm asking a price. *But.* I'm not going to cheat you, you can look all over this town and you won't find anybody who's been cheated by Cass Harding. *Now.* First place, I know *exactly* where he is, I have a map. You'd have never guessed where, you'd have never found him in a lifetime, but you knew that when you came to me. *And.*" He slapped the counter. The two other men looked interested. Harding resumed his whispering: "I've found you a pilot." He looked triumphantly into Corander's face. *"With* a copter."

Corander: "He wouldn't be as much use without one."

Harding: "All joking aside—ha ha, that's pretty good, you're quick, I can see that, ha ha—but all joking aside, he can fly you there, he's an experienced pilot, used to be with the lines, and that reminds me." He looked worried for a while. "There's this difficulty." He looked worried some more. "This gentleman you're talking about, it seems he's suspicious, naturally, he's got enemies, we all have, you don't want to listen to everything you hear about anybody; I always tell people show me a man who has no enemies I'll show you a failure, I don't care *who* it is, but being suspicious—he has to be, of course—but he has ways of dealing with—of clearing out quick when he hears someone coming that he doesn't know who it is, a copter or anything of that nature, they make quite a bit of noise."

Corander: "Your pilot friend could put me down nearby and give me the route on foot. That's not a problem. Get to the point. What are your terms?"

Harding looked at him admiringly. "That's a smart idea, I see you got a head for this. Very good idea." He began to haggle.

"It's all right with Mr. Alfred," said the naked girl when Corander returned.

Corander: "I know. The man at the desk offered me a job here as I came in."

The naked girl: "That's Mr. Alfred. Mornings."

Corander: "Did you keep your promise, Madeline?"

The naked girl: "I didn't *act*ually touch a one of them." She smothered a laugh, watching him. "But—but I peed on them. The funny one with the scar had just woke up when I went in there to pee, and he made faces at me, so I peed on him, and he passed right out again." Corander laughed to her satisfaction, and she went on: "Then I washed myself real nice."

Pause.

The naked girl: "Are you going to keep *your* promise?"

Corander, lightly: "I've kept it." He gave her the parcel he had brought in under his arm. "Open it. It's yours."

It was a bedspread, proclaiming itself to be of "Genuine Earth Cotton," pink, delicately ornate, and feminine. It had cost him a great deal of money and an amorous misunderstanding at the airport shop.

The naked girl stroked it and hugged it to her breasts. "It's pretty. You're nice. What's in that other one?"—Corander had a smaller parcel in one hand—"Is that for me too?"

Corander: "It's for our little boys in there. Sticky-tape. We have to change their diapers."

The naked girl snickered. "Their gags, too. I didn't realize my pee would soak into their gags." Softly: "You promised me something else."

He took her by the shoulders and held her at arm's length. She looked pathetically young between his big hands. Her eyes seemed to grow huge as he stared into them. "Madeline—"

"Brandy."

Corander: "There's this girl, you see. She did something to me, something unspeakable; and I have to have her. I can't help it. I have to."

The naked girl: "Today?"

That being much simpler than the farrago he himself had devised, he hastily accepted. "In about three hours."

"Why didn't you say so?" She studied him. "I think you're crazy, and maybe I think you're lying," she said at last; then, shyly: "But I can see you'd really like to get me. Every time you look at me, you think what it would feel like. So it's all right." She wriggled out of his grasp, darted to him, put her arms around his neck, and brought down his last defense with the tip of her tongue. As soon as the erotic urchin felt that he was helpless, she released him and asked, "What are we going to do with *them?*"

He explained that he needed certain information and outlined his plan for getting it. She giggled lubriciously.

With much wrestling and threatening and rolling of pallid hairy bodies, the two got their four prisoners stripped, rinsed, regagged, and rebound, naked this time except for the tape. The bleached man was again awake. Corander dragged him across the room and heaved him onto the bed.

The naked girl hunkered on the bed next to her victim's face. "Open your eyes," she said. The victim squeezed his eyes tighter. She pinched his nose between her thumb and forefinger, shutting off his breathing. He struggled in the tapes. His chest worked vainly. "I could kill you with two fingers," she said. "Open your eyes." He opened his eyes, and

(101)

she let him breathe. "He doesn't look in the right places," she complained, and pinched off his breathing again.

"Maybe he'll behave now," said Corander, watching the man's color with some concern. "Strange fellow. *I* think it's beautiful. It has a wonderful personality."

She let her victim breathe. "He isn't really looking. He has a funny scar on his nose. D'you suppose he got bitten by one once? *Wwoof!*" she honked, lurching.

Corander took a piece of paper from his pocket and unfolded it. "Maybe he'd rather look at this." He held it in front of the man. "I just bought this map this morning." The man's eyes showed relief and then consternation. "Recognize it?"

The man shook his head sullenly.

Corander: "Brandy..."

A few minutes later, they had broken the man's spirit enough to take out the gag. The girl bounced with excitement and said, "I think politics is interesting."

At the end of an hour, they had elicited two major emendations to the sketch map, miscellaneous facts about the Reconstructionists in New Tavistock, the function of the spindly man's atomizer, and the names Billioray and Hadder. Billioray was the man they had been working on.

Corander: "Brandy, let's open a fresh one."

They replaced Billioray's gag, returned him to the bathroom, and extracted the spindly man, Hadder.

As they arrayed Hadder for questioning, the naked girl said, "This one's the opposite. Look at his eyes."

Corander: "You'll have to work him the opposite way."

The girl was already doing preliminary work with the nail of her right index finger. "I'm going to break him with one finger, you'll see," she said; "no—with one toe." She wiggled the big toe of her left foot.

Hadder, who had been shut in the bathroom while Billioray was on the bed, and who, Corander judged, could have heard no more than a general tone of horror, soon was groaning out most of the same facts. He knew less about Simon de Ferraris' situation in the swamp and more of the Reconstructionists' reluctant underground in New Tavistock and New Nome, and there were small inconsistencies. Corander thought these showed there had been no preparation. Brandy had made good her boast: Hadder had broken open.

The two IDD men were grayer and less intellectual victims than Billioray and Hadder, and Brandy resorted to outrage. Neither agent could tell Corander anything definite about the changes in the Department. Brandy became more inventive.

Corander: "I guess I'm satisfied, Brandy."

The naked girl: "I'm not."

Corander: "Little sweetheart, you have them all to play with now. I have to go."

She clambered off the weeping agent and helped Corander bring the other three prisoners out of the bathroom. "Two on the bed *and* two on the floor," she crooned to herself, rolling Billioray across the room with her foot.

Corander retrieved the agent's N-Transmitter and the spindly man's atomizer from the underside of the bedframe, where he had secreted them overnight. He pocketed the transmitter, hesitated, then offered the atomizer to the girl. "You heard how this works," he said. She accepted it with a glistening look at Billioray that made Corander regret giving it to her. "Don't overdose them," he cautioned her. "A little makes them enthusiastic. Too much, and they might bite...Give me a big, big hug."

His last glimpse was of her sweet behind as she knelt on Billioray's stomach and tried to spear the poor fellow's moving nose with the atomizer. "Come on, now, let Mumsy give you the good medicine, make you all foozyastic. (Oops, nearly got you that time, you dumb proke!) You know Mumsy wouldn't give you any squirt-squirt that wasn't good for her baby-boy. Then Mumsy will show her good baby-boy where he came from..."

Mr. Alfred himself was still at the front desk. The buyer of souls was a slow, heavy, dark man who radiated a kind of reductive contempt Corander could feel across the lobby; it was as if the hotel hotelkeeper knew exactly what had gone on in Room 25 and exactly what to charge for it. Corander explained to him that the four bondage queers in Room 25 turned out to have no money and had gotten a free lunch.

Mr. Alfred replied in a melodious voice, "Thank you so much for telling me. I hope you are not too much out of pocket. As for the hotel"—he smiled with surprising charm as he prepared to leave the desk—"perhaps they will wash the dishes for me."

CHAPTER 11

UNDER the enormous sky of the airfield, Corander picked his way across the cluttered tarmac toward some sheds that served as hangars. He was looking among the small air vehicles for E7116G, the copter Cass Harding had "found" for him. Finally he made it out, a puffy little craft that looked like a Terran frog carrying an umbrella.

E7116G had belonged to the Imperial military. The Green Insigne had been daubed over with a single coat of plain olive-green paint, which was wearing away. Corander wondered how and when the machine could have passed directly from the Empire to a nonpolitical like Cass Harding. As soon as he saw the pilot, he understood.

The man was a Terran deserter, unmistakably. He had the bronze skin of the High Asian States and the precise, haughty bearing of a male of the traditional officer caste of the Empire, traditionally trained; but also the look of a furtive voluptuary. Inaudible amid the skirl of rotors, and with almost invisible movements of his lips, he was talking with a man with cream-colored hair. It was Deputy Kullervo.

The pilot: "Citizen Kemp?"

Corander: "Abraham Kemp."

The pilot indicated Deputy Kullervo: "Citizen Bradford." It was obvious that the renegade Terran himself knew better.

Corander: "Pleasure."

Bradford/Kullervo was silent.

Corander's original plan had been to stun or intimidate the pilot, take the copter in as close to de Ferraris' cabin as his quarry would let him, and then get the rest of the way in by his revised map. The miscellaneous facts little Brandy had winkled out of the two tormented Reconstructionists should have sufficed him for a story.

As to what he intended to do after reaching Simon de Ferraris...he had kept his options open. Which was to say, he had lied to his Department and betrayed his fellow agents. He himself was not sure why. He found himself thinking of the disturbing young woman who had sent him on this mission. Where was she now? Creeping, like himself, between two uncomprehended loyalties?

Now, in any case, with the deputy along on the copter, Corander's original plan was worthless. He clambered after the others into the machine.

Outside the hut in the maremma the sky was overcast. Inside the light grew slowly; throughout the morning, it remained gray and crepuscular and did not rouse the four sleepers.

The fifth, Citizen Vanderwol, had been awake for some hours but pretending to sleep. He could not tell whether the young woman with the beautiful reedy voice was still watching him or not. It became maddeningly hard to keep his eyes shut. Then he drifted off into a confused terror-dream, from which he awoke to find the light stronger.

Actually, Shulamith had tried to watch Vanderwol but had fallen asleep. Her dreams were rhetorical—not so much events as attempts to expostulate with some diffuse accuser, whom she associated with the light on her lids.

The two old men slept happily.

Cathy's dreams were also happy at first but toward midday began to involve some recurring pain—or a gentle, deadly apprehension of pain—which then took the identity of a vine. She was on a vine. She struggled against the rhythmic pangs and woke herself up. As she came awake, the pain subsided into unease, and she could not be sure whether she was in labor.

A stealthy movement drew her attention.

Citizen Vanderwol slid millimeter by millimeter out of his sleeping bag, agony trying to force its way out of his white mouth. He rose to his feet and tottered toward the com-set. The bliss of destruction lit his mean features. Cathy thought, He's going to smash the set. She nudged her husband, who opened his eyes with a contented smile—to see the little man hover over the set, suddenly stoop to the dials, peer, and twist.

Simon de Ferraris leaped out of bed with a bellow, and, heedless of the cold wound in his leg, lunged toward Vanderwol. Mustafa Issachar and Shulamith thrashed about in their sleeping bags and managed to sit upright. Vanderwol struggled in the bearlike grasp of the old man, squeaking toward the set, "Help! Help! Simon de Ferraris is here. He's trying to—"

Mustafa Issachar: "Stand back, Simon!" He had brought his stunner into play.

Simon shoved Vanderwol clear of himself. Mustafa took formal aim and dosed Vanderwol into unconsciousness. Simon flung himself at the set and pulled the main switch.

Shulamith inspected the dials of the com-set, and turned a worried face to her father. "At that setting, they must have picked *something* up. Long enough to get a fix, do you think?"

Simon bent to look. "Perhaps. But not a very acc—"

A muffled sound came from the bed. Cathy de Ferraris was suppressing a moan of pain.

Corander and Kullervo stood side by side and watched E7116G pull aloft and dwindle against the pale overcast. Corander was touched by the way the albino averted his gaze slightly from whatever he looked at, as if everything were too bright for those rose-colored eyes. But there was another kind of blindness in the blinking face.

The deputy was, however, polite enough. "Shall we proceed, Citizen—Kemp?" He produced a sketch map and a small inertial compass from his pocket and peered at them slantwise. He looked like a small boy on his first hike.

Corander had a virtually identical map in his own pocket, but he had corrected it in two places at the instructions of the retching, sobbing Billioray. He did not take it out. "I see you have the same map as I," he said and patted his pocket.

"Lead on." The first correction—the first of Cass Harding's traps—was still some distance ahead.

Kullervo did not ask to compare maps. Corander wondered why the deputy did not see that if Cass Harding was selling the same maps over and over, and if the maps were accurate, Simon de Farraris would have decamped long ago. Harding must have told some story or other to inoculate the politician against the obvious.

There was also the tiny pause between "Citizen" and "Kemp" when Kullervo had used the name a moment ago. That was not Harding's doing...

All around stretched the waste, its knolls protruding like bubbles on a boiling stew, and between the knolls the ambiguous surface of the swamp veined with greenish sandy ridges and tufted with the yellow plant gases. The rank-sweet scent of Rohanese subsoil hung in the still atmosphere. A diffuse heat radiated from the cloud cover. Except for the whirr of a bog-flitter's wings now and then, there was silence. Kullervo set out cautiously along the ridge. Corander followed.

Deputy Kullervo: "What is your business with Simon de Ferraris?"

Corander: "I'm sorry, but I do not know you, Citizen—Bradford."

Kullervo stopped short and whirled. For a moment he studied Corander, seeming to look past him. "Your real name is not Kemp," he said softly.

"No," said Corander, "my name is Kullervo."

The man's transparent skin flushed an appalling red. "Kindly explain that remark."

Corander: "Why should my name *not* be Kullervo, Citizen *Bradford?*"

Kullervo: "Because it is Corander."

Corander: "Quite so. Thank you, Deputy Kullervo. I wondered if you knew."

Kullervo: "Would you care to walk in the lead?"

Corander: "No, Deputy. You have the compass."

Kullervo: "I would feel more comfortable."

Corander: "Perhaps you would. I don't know your relations with my Department."

Kullervo, shortly: "They're excellent. The point is, I don't know *your* relations with your Department." He said this without humor; but at least his pathological anger was cooling.

Corander: "Why don't you ask them? Here." He reached into his tunic pocket, calmed the deputy's slight shying movement with a smile, and pulled out the N-Transmitter he had taken from the agent in Brandy's room. "We all have these. N-Transmitters. For direct scrambled audio to headquarters." Kullervo nodded. "Matched to my thumb." Kullervo nodded again. "My set," offering it. "My thumb," offering that.

When the set would not operate, suspicion returned to the deputy's face, but Corander staged a display of panicky frustration and for a climax hurled the device into a vine-infested dimple of the swamp. While the transmitter was still tumbling in its long trajectory, Corander said dully, "I'll walk anywhere you want."

"Left," said Deputy Kullervo.

"No," said Corander. He stopped, turned, and faced Kullervo across the map in Kullervo's hand.

Kullervo: "You can see here: left. That's this one here. Let me orient the map for you."

Corander: "No."

Kullervo: "Then let's see *your* map, Agent Corander." Evidently his suspicions had returned. He backed away.

Corander: *"Be careful!"*

Kullervo had backed nearly into a treacherous dip in the path. He nodded once in acknowledgment of Corander's warning, as if it had been a duelist's courtesy.

Corander: "My map was the same as yours, Deputy Kullervo. But if it hadn't been, what would you infer from the fact that Harding sold us different maps of the same terrain?"

"What do you mean, 'was'? Have you destroyed it?"

Corander: "No, I've altered it."

Kullervo: "How have you altered it? Where did you get your facts? Let me see."

With just a shade of excess in precision and detail, Corander said, "I talked to some IDD agents at noontime today, after I obtained the map from Harding. I was told the map was substantially accurate except at two points. I corrected those points. The information could have been faulty, of course." He took the map from his pocket, advanced, and held it up to Kullervo's.

The deputy turned his wincing gaze from one map to the other. Barely two meters away, in a pock of the maremma, a large bog-flitter flitted too close to a vine tendril; there was a sound like the yelp of a whip, the hexapod was caught, and the chitterings of its ecstasy began. Corander shuddered. Kullervo seemed not to be affected.

He said softly, "Your Department had these details?"

Corander: "I don't know. I didn't get them from headquarters."

Kullervo: "Quite so. Strange your fellow agents had so many facts this morning that your headquarters *still* hasn't heard of. But you didn't actually *say* the agents told you. You 'were told.' You had other visitors this morning, didn't you? Reconstructionists. You reported to headquarters that there had been shooting. The Reconstructionists stunned the agents and you stunned the Reconstructionists. You were going to wait for the agents to wake up and then work some kind of game on the Reconstructionists. But maybe things turned out differently. When I talked to your headquarters, the two agents hadn't reported in... The transmitter that didn't work. Maybe it wasn't yours."

Corander: "You think the Reconstructionists corrected my map for me?"

Kullervo: "They might have."

Corander: "Then my corrections might be correct."

Kullervo: "Now, why would the Reconstructionists help you find de Ferraris? They wouldn't if they knew you were IDD, and you told headquarters someone had blown your cover. *You* know who blew your cover to the Loyalists. Citizen Wells did, when she went over to them last night. On the other hand, suppose *you*'ve followed her over to them..."

Corander played a waiting game: "Or suppose they thought I did. I *told* Room Thirty-two I was going to make them think that."

Kullervo: "Yes. You told them that and that's what you'd have told them if you were planning to defect."

Corander, courteously: "Point One. Thank you for telling me what happened to the Chief. Room Thirty-two wasn't that frank. I didn't know we'd had a chistka in the IDD."

Kullervo interrupted: "I didn't say anything about a purge."

Corander: "You've been telling me in fourteen different ways, Deputy. Yesterday, I gathered from what the Chief said, they wouldn't have let *you* use the men's room at the IDD. Today, the Chief is gone and is being denounced as a Loyalist, and headquarters is blurting out compromising details on operations to the likes of you. I haven't defected, but

(109)

now I just might. *Here* and now. Point Two. You've been proving my corrections are correct."

Kullervo: "Not so, and you know it. Your Loyalist friends' corrections may be correct, but these marks on the map may be something else. You seem peculiarly anxious for me to accept them."

Corander: "Or they may not be 'something else.' I enjoy being an equivocal figure." There was a long pause. Corander went on: "Kullervo, I suspect you of being a very violent man. You have the emotional eruptiveness, the defective empathy, the attention to detail, the paranoid ideation. And yet you do not attack me, although you hate me. Why? First reason: because I might have the information that would save your life, and as you say, it might not be on this map. Second reason: because I am armed *and trained*."

Kullervo: "I am armed."

Corander: "But not trained. In any case, Deputy, you have two maps and an equivocal man in front of you. The equivocal man is going to lie down here and sleep for one hour. You may take your choice of the two maps."

Kullervo, without humor: "I'll take yours. It's both maps at once."

Corander: "Tut-tut, watch yourself, Deputy. You had a nasty little impulse there—to grab my map and throw your own into the vine. Now: give me yours and take mine at the same moment. One, two, three. Fine. Just a second while I jot my corrections on your map... Done."

Kullervo: "*Why* are you waiting here for an hour? If I get to Simon de Ferraris first, how do you know you'll ever get to transact your business with him—whatever it really is?"

Corander smiled. "Either I do know something that's not on the map and I'm waiting till you're out of sight, or else I'm waiting to find out what happens to you, so I'll know which map is right. I imagine screams carry a long way out here. Of course," he added, "both maps may be wrong."

The com-set in the corner of the cabin squealed and the alarm lights flashed. The squawking IFF had queried an air vehicle and found it not a friend.

Simon de Ferraris went to check the scopes. Cathy, whose pains were now fifteen minutes apart and of a wrenching, drawing intensity, watched with scared eyes. Shulamith took her father's place at the bedside, and Mustafa stood over the still-unconscious Vanderwol.

Simon: "Thirty kilometers northeast, coming in fast. I didn't think they had military flitters or copters out here any more."

Shulamith: "My Department—the Department keeps a smallish copter at New Tavistock. It's not a gunship; it has Public Health insignia."

Simon: "This is coming from New Tavistock and it's small-ish for a copter. The decoys and vaguers on the other knolls might confuse them for a few minutes, but the damn thing's on a true course. They have good field-stress optics...Ladies and gentlemen, it's time to go downstairs." He pulled the main switch and the com-set went dead.

He limped to the bed, heaved at its frame and sent it skidding halfway across the cabin, stooped, and slid back a section of the metal flooring; there was an almost vertical shaft underneath.

Shulamith: "I'm beginning to think Rohan is hollow."

Simon: "This kopje is."

Shulamith and Mustafa helped Cathy down the narrow companionway into a wide chamber, cold, patchily lit, and largely occupied by the crouching hulk of a machine. Simon moved the bed back almost to its position over the trapdoor, stood at the top of the companion ladder, then with an effort of his great shoulders pulled the bed the rest of the way into place, and slid the trap cover to. The lights in the chamber went out. The others heard Simon moving down the ladder. "Cathy?" came his growl. "Will you chance it?"

Cathy's reply was steady: "I'll chance it, Simon." Then, timidly: "I—I'd rather not have the baby in the dark, but we can leave the light off for a while yet."

Shulamith's voice: "Poppa, is this a flitter?"

Simon: "It's a two-seat flitter."

Shulamith: "And there's a launch-hatch on the side of the kopje?"

Simon: "There's a hatch."

Shulamith: "Poppa, take Momma out of here. You have time to get her to a safe place."

Simon: "It's a two-seat flitter."

Mustafa: "We can fend for ourselves, Simon. Sue said the IDD copter wasn't a gunship."

Cathy: "Anyway, there isn't a safe place...I'm the safest of any of us. Because of my mother. She always said she wanted a lot of gr—"

There was silence.

Corander to Room 32: "Hendrix, I'm out in the swamp near de Ferraris' hideout. I have a map of the paths, but I think it's defective. A deputy named Kullervo came with me, but he's gone off on his own. He had a copy of the same map, and I warned him not to trust it, but he's more suspicious of me than of Cass Harding."

Room 32: "Cass what?"

Corander: "Cass Harding, who sold us the map. He's a crook who operates out of the New Tav air terminal."

Room 32: "What kind of crook?"

Corander: "In general practice. Never mind all that. You seem more interested in my sources than in me. Hendrix, are you planning to jettison me? Keep listening. A Public Health copter passed over here a couple of minutes ago. They let me alone, and I got to thinking they might be our people. Right?"

Room 32 did not reply.

Corander: "Over."

Room 32: "I don't know."

Corander: "Well, Hendrix, you dumb surly bastard, you'd better find out. Ask around your room there. It's one thing to lose a fellow agent. It's another to lose a whole deputy. Somebody might miss him. Keep listening, Hendrix. It happens the Recons picked up our two sloppy boys in New Tav, and I'm the boy who got away and knows how to trace them. Bear that in mind, Hendrix. Keep listening. *Assuming* the copter is ours, call it and order them to pick me up, and I'll help them with Kullervo *and* with de Ferraris. Give them the following coordinates..."

Citizen Vanderwol opened his eyes and crawled painfully across the cabin floor to look under the bed. He could not see the trapdoor, though he knew more or less where it was. The man Harding in New Tavistock had said de Ferraris had a secret means for escaping if anyone approached the cabin. From this he had got his own idea of being set down out in the maremma, creeping up on de Ferraris, and using de Ferraris' own transportation, whatever it was, to leave. He had lain hour after hour hating Cass Harding for that trap; now it turned out Harding was right.

He listened for the sound of a flitter or copter, but there was no sign that Simon de Ferraris was making a getaway. Probably the criminal planned to make a fight of it from some hidden fortifications. He heard a distant copter. The government people—he was not sure what the girl had meant by her strange phrase "my Department, *the* Department"— were coming. He must warn them before de Ferraris' treacherous fire wiped them out.

The sound of the approaching vehicle grew enormously. Citizen Vanderwol stumbled on numb legs to the door. He opened it. A white copter with red insignia was sweeping in low and fast, its nose-hatch wide open. A man in civilian dress crouched in the opening, holding a ray-carbine.

Citizen Vanderwol hobbled out and halfway down the slope toward the oncoming copter, shouting his guess: "Look out! It's a trap! They're waiting—"

A burst of radiation from the copter scythed through him.

The two men on the Public Health copter were IDD agents.

The man at the controls: "Actually, I didn't catch what he said." He pulled the machine up and away from the kopje.

His partner thought for a moment. "Something about, I don't know, 'a trap' and 'they're waiting.' The first part was, I think it was, 'Look out.'"

The pilot: "Why did you burn him? He was trying to warn us."

The man with the blast-carbine was apologetic: "I did it before I, you know, really took it in, you know?" He shrugged.

The pilot accepted the apology: "Well, maybe he was just trying to bluff us off. Doesn't matter. Do we land? Or do we hang here and shoot them up a bit?"

The other man: "Shoot *what* up?"

The pilot: "How should *I* know? We can't land if it's a *trap*."

The craft's audio coughed and rasped: "Room Thirty-two calling Cadooshus. Room Thirty-two calling Cadooshus. Come in. Over."

The pilot: "Cadooshus. Boyle speaking. What now?"

Room 32: "Have you attacked de Ferraris' place yet?"

Boyle: "We just started. We blew away one of them, some ferky-jerky who ran out into the line of fire, but it isn't old de Ferraris."

"Pull off and stand by." Room 32 sounded upset. "What did this man look like? Did he have cream-colored hair and a pink face, an albino?"

Boyle: "I'm standing off. No, he was ordinary—on the runty side, Dombroff here says. Over."

Room 32: "All right, stay away from the place a minute.

Did you spot a man out on the swamp at coordinates approximately Lazy-four-three-two, Charley-oh-one-eight, with the beacon setting New Tav two-one?"

Boyle: "We saw a skitso sitting on his gloot, yes. We left him alone. It could of been around there. We figured the vines would get him soon enough."

Room 32: "Here are your orders. Go back and pick him up. He's one of ours, John Corander. And there's another man out in the swamp, nearer where you are. Did you see him too?"

Boyle: "Well, Dombroff thinks there was another way off on one of those tits they have growing out of the swamp, but I'm not so sure. Dombroff says this one was reading something. I'm not so sure."

Room 32: "First, go pick up the one you're sure of; it's probably Corander. The second one is supposed to be Deputy Kullervo. Big in the Party. Before you pick this Kullervo up, go back with Corander to the de Ferraris place and let Corander get out and go inside for you. He can do a Public Health act—tell him how. Corander has orders from—from *yesterday* (all right?) to bring in de Ferraris. Alive. *To us.* We're letting those orders stand. For him. We think Kullervo has some different ideas, so pick up the good deputy *after* you've got de Ferraris secure, and then don't let Kullervo get at him. But if Corander doesn't make it, you're allowed to—ah—do what you have to to de Ferraris. Got all that? Over."

Boyle: "Corander. De Ferraris. Kullervo. Over."

Room 32: "Incidentally, Boyle. Watch Corander. We're not too sure about him. Over and out."

Boyle: "Out." He grumbled to his partner, "'Incidentally. Boyle'! Balls. They're nervous." He punched in Lazy-four-three-two, Charley-oh-one-eight.

Dombroff: "*I'm* nervous. I think headquarters has gone into politics."

Fairly near the data point, they found the man who was supposed to be Corander. They eased in and hovered a meter above the greenish ridge, about four meters from where he sat rubbing his ankle.

Corander looked up at them with a wan smile. "Twisted it," he said. "I thought I was done for. I could never have made it through with this."

Dombroff helped him aboard; Corander thanked him, reached into his own pocket, took out a stunner, gave Boyle and Dombroff each a heavy dose, took the controls of the copter, put away the stunner, took out Kullervo's map, and set his course for Simon de Ferraris'.

Two little sheds on a bare knoll. The place looked utterly defenseless, except that a man's body, neatly cut in half, lay on the ground. Corander circled the kopje again and it looked just as candid as before. Except for the body.

Even if there was weaponry in these huts, one light missile could knock them out; and there was no room in them for any vehicle. Simon de Ferraris would have to be a fool to isolate himself like this with no means of defense or escape; and Simon de Ferraris was no fool.

On the third circuit Corander suddenly formed a different gestalt: he saw the whole kopje as structure and the cabins as superstructure. The kopje itself had been hollowed out. The means of defense and escape were inside it. Any second, therefore, he might be incinerated by one burst from a concealed aperture.

With some difficulty he set the copter down on the slope. The smaller shed was padlocked on the outside and presumably empty of people. The larger cabin was open and empty. In one corner, a com-set with extra scopes and flashers, dead; in another, a large, rumpled bed; both still warm. Three sleeping bags on the floor, still with the living human smell.

One entrance to the hollow knoll must be in this cabin, otherwise old de Ferraris would have to gallop across an attacker's sights to get to his own stronghold. Corander took out the blaster he had plucked a few hours before from little Brandy's crotch. In each corner of the floor—two in the main room, one in the bathroom, one in the galley—was a heavy bolt that anchored the cabin to footings or pilings; he obliterated the bolts. He dismantled the heavier contents of the cabin—the com-set, the bed, an excellent fuel-cell unit—and carried them outside. He started the copter, positioned it over the cabin roof, set the controls on Hover, activated the winch to lower the grapnels and cable-ladder, swarmed down, attached the grapnels to the window frames on either side of the cabin, clambered back, worked the winch until the grappling cables were taut, locked them, and threw the controls to Ascent. The cables tightened and sang; the craft strained, bucked, sideslipped, and righted; the engine bellowed; and the cabin rose with a great wrenching loose of wiring and plumbing, and began to sway and rotate under the copter.

Corander's hands danced on the controls, fighting the torque and the swing.

He succeeded in shifting the copter sideways, and saw what he expected, a rectangular opening in the ground. He set the cabin down on the slope and released the grapnels. It canted crazily and slid almost to the foot of the knoll. He landed and walked to the shaft. "Excuse me," he called into the booming chamber below, "can anyone direct me to the nearest Reconstructionist conspiracy?"

Footsteps rang on concrete; a pair of white trouser legs and a pair of pale hands glimmered in the blackness and began to climb the ladder; a black-haired head and a dark tunic took shape; the head tilted, and Corander looked into the pale face of his chief.

He proffered the grip of the still-warm blast-pistol.

"Thank you. I have one," she said.

He shifted his hand to the butt of the weapon. "I have very little to offer," he said somberly, and undid his breeches. "Except myself."

He fumbled in between his legs. "Where is it?" he muttered. "Ah!" He drew forth the N-Transmitter which had been strapped to his thigh, threw it on the ground, and vaporized it with the blaster. The snarl of the weapon elicited a girl's wail from the dark cavern below.

Citizen Wells looked speechlessly at the glassy crater where the transmitter had been.

Corander refastened his breeches. "These little symbols help one get through the day ... You entertain friends down there? Or is this de Ferraris a countertenor?"

In this blend of moods began days and nights of feverish activity.

First, the IDD had to be dealt with, quickly, before Room 32 dispatched gunships from New Nome to find out what had become of their copter, their three agents, and the redoubtable deputy. Old Simon took the flitter out and selected a knoll eight kilometers to the northeast. Corander ferried the cabin, the storage shed, the two sleeping agents, and the two halves of Citizen Vanderwol to it, and arranged them in as convincing a replica of de Ferraris' place as he could. He left the white-and-red copter with Boyle and Dombroff in it, and went back with Simon in the flitter through the failing afternoon.

Corander: "Not entirely convincing, sir, I'm afraid. They'll see through it as soon as they examine the cabin."

Simon: "It will be dark when they wake up, and I just need a few hours."

Corander: "Mrs. de Ferraris?"

"She's a brave little thing, isn't she? We're taking New Tav tonight, you see, and then in the morning, if she's still in labor, we can take her there. Otherwise . . . she's very brave. Yes," said the old man in reply to Corander's startled look. "It will spread, or else it will vanish again. We shall see whether Simon de Ferraris or Carl ap Rhys is the better political economist. I've got two men copting out about now from New Tavistock. My daughter will go back with them. We have a good cadre in New Tavistock, I think. And my daughter was the best organizer we had during the Revolution." He withdrew into memory. The dimming maremma slipped under them. Then: "Also, she knows the enemy."

"Sir, may I go with her?"

Simon: "For her to say. Does she trust you?"

Corander: "She trusted me with your life."

Simon: "That's more than she trusts me. What are you good at?"

Corander smiled sadly. "She'll tell you my record."

Just before nightfall, a man named McIntyre copted in alone from New Tavistock and apologized for being late: he had been told to bring Billioray but could not find him.

Corander: "Billioray? Pale, scarred man?" All faces turned toward him. "Billioray won't be fit for service, I'm afraid. Not for a while."

Simon: "Explain."

Corander explained, using sound editorial judgment.

As they walked down toward McIntyre's copter, a faint cry came across the swamp.

Corander: "Deputy Kullervo."

Simon, Shulamith, Mustafa, Corander, and McIntyre looked at one another in the last light of the sky. From inside the kopje, where Cathy de Ferraris was lying on a sleeping bag, came a low moan.

Simon: "One must make choices."

McIntyre followed Shulamith and Corander into the copter, and they flew to New Tavistock.

CHAPTER 12

THE copter taxied to the base of the control tower like a dog sniffing a lamppost, and Citizen Wells, followed by the two men, jumped out and started the civil war. She rushed the tower and stunned the solitary controller there. She left McIntyre in charge and ran with Corander through the oblivious crowds to Cass Harding's stand. Harding himself was not in the place; his counterman took alarm, tried to shoot it out with Corander, and was killed. The plantains burned on the stove. A miscellaneous, *sotto voce* panic spread through the terminal. Most people thought the matter an IDD atrocity, and this helped to throw the local officials off guard.

From a public vidiphone booth, Citizen Wells put the word out to the Reconstructionist cells on her father's list and, before the authorities realized what was afoot, was perched on Harding's counter amid the condiments, scribbling on a tourist map bought and duly paid for at the nearby souvenir stand, and sending out the first of her assault squads.

Corander led one of them, cleared the terminal, and posted

a headquarters guard of the slower-footed Reconstructionist actives.

All night a sanguinary émeute flickered and eddied through the streets of New Tavistock. The first Reconstructionist thrusts were at communications and essential services. A small detachment, murderously efficient, stormed the dishes on Titchener Hill, cutting off all ordinary transmission between the city and the rest of Rohan. After that, the principal links between Government elements in New Tavistock and the Government in New Nome were the N-Transmitters of IDD men.

IDD New Tavistock, fractured by the purging of its chief the night before, was now shattered by her appearance as a leader of guerrillas. Some agents took this as treason confirmed, put themselves at the head of counterinsurgent bands, and battled the Reconstructionists' shock troops in the streets and buildings. Others took it as "more politics" and replied with thin excuses to the furious commands of Room 32. And a few—the Little Bitch had her following—joined the rebellion.

The other Government personnel in New Tavistock were a scattered, corrupt, and extensively disaffected lot, because the Freedom Party Left clique in New Nome had been using Laing's Land posts to get unenthusiastic bureaucrats out of its way. Still, the Government, because it was the government, had considerable support among its technicians and in the regulatory agencies, and the Freedom Party did have a fraction of fervent supporters in the populace, so that after a few hours, the Government's effectives equaled the Rebels' in numbers. But they were essentially leaderless—New Tavistock had a mayor, an engaging, torpid old confidence man, only he happened to be in New Nome, and his understrappers waited to see which way the battle went—whereas the rebels had S. Wells.

The mayor returned, peremptorily and foolishly sent back on conventional transportation, and brought with him a Colonel Engstrand, said to be *the* expert on guerrilla warfare at the Ministry of Armies and Marine. But McIntyre, in his tower, was directing all incoming flights to the maintenance tarmac, where the passengers and crews—all except attested Recons—found themselves herded into empty hangars and locked up for the night; and Mayor Hurlbut and Colonel Engstrand were unceremoniously locked up with the rest.

"Over there's a copter going out," said the mayor to the

colonel as they were being bundled along. "Why can't they just let us go back?"

"Empty, you'll notice," snapped the colonel. "Ferrying their people in. L' Bitch knows what she's doing."

The outbound copter was one that Desmond Feigenbrod had stolen, a large and very fast one; he was shuttling in reinforcements—tough, weapon-wise men from old Loyalist families in the rangelands just east of the River Bohr.

Many of the buildings in New Tavistock had their own fuel-cell units. The city went dark patch by patch, with lit houses here and there defying the battle. Rorschach Street was extinguished. The entertainers, stripped of amplification, quavered tentatively in the blackness for a few minutes and stumbled away. The revelers drifted, too sick and frightened to take sides in the swirling hostilities.

Untended children slipped through the streets and found one another; swarms of them skittered like bog-flitters through the fire-fields, appalling the combatants.

Corander, meanwhile, asked permission to lead an assault squad in the field. Citizen Wells looked at him narrowly, assigned him Power Station Six, an MHD installation in the west-central district, and gave him five men, a groundcar, and one hour. He took Power Station Six by scurrying alone up to the front door, ringing the bell, and glancing apprehensively over his shoulder, while his squad waited out of sight, and then he waggled a blaster at the technicians inside while his squad filed in. Leaving the five men to hold the station, he swung through the deserted streets in the groundcar.

Almost everywhere resistance was stiffening. Power Station One, east-central district, manned by technicians under an IDD agent's command, was holding out against a considerable Reconstructionist force. Nearby, a crouching Rebel with a sniper's scope clamped on his laser told Corander, "This is important, see? It feeds the school. They've got a bunch in the school science lab setting up some kind of a communication dish or something. We can't seem to get into the school either. Our men don't want to shoot up their kids' things." Among the besiegers, Corander found a technician from another district. Together they pried open a manhole lid between Power Station One and the school, climbed down, and sliced the power main with their blasters. Corander continued his unofficial tour of inspection. Several times he had to swerve to avoid the incomplete corpses of men who, convinced of this or convinced of that, had been cut down in the dark streets—the tallies used in this terrible game of thrust-and-parry.

He reported to Citizen Wells. She looked drawn. The keenness had given way to sharpness. In New Nome, she told him, the Government was rallying from the surprise, assembling gunship crews—although with difficulty, because squadron administration and discipline were bad—but several craft would be air-ready in an hour or two. And the nearest regular military force, a mixed-weapons brigade at the River Bohr, had been ordered to advance on New Tavistock. "I've got word to Desmond Feigenbrod to drop the ferrying operation and go on to New Nome," she said. "He'll do what he can to fritz the gunships, but we can't count on much. There's some hope over at the river—with any luck, an incipient mutiny. So...I'm off to see old Pegrim."

Corander looked his astonishment.

Citizen Wells: "Brigadier William Hammett Pegrim. He's in command at the river. Also, he was once my history teacher. Corander, you're in charge here. Move some of the innocent bystanders from the hangars out there and lock them in rooms throughout the terminal. Especially the not-so-innocent ones. And be a little sloppy about it. Let one or two of them escape and tell the Government. That way, when the gunships come, they won't be so likely to rocket the terminal...Back in a while. If not—" She stood on tiptoe, pecked him on the nose as he had kissed Madeline the night before, and went out to the copter at the tower base.

Corander lacked the girl's bright inspiriting ferocity but had a certain dash of his own. As the hours of his command passed and his squad captains reported in, he felt his forces gaining slowly on the resistance, but there was no doubt that the Government's supporters were steady, sustained by their knowledge of the gunships and the brigade from the river.

Then McIntyre came hurtling down the tower stairs and shouted the warning across the tarmac: a large craft approaching, IFF-blinded, probably a gunship. Corander ordered the best shots in his HQ guard up to sheltered positions on the roof. To the detachment leaders he said over and over, "Hold your fire till *they* open fire. We don't really know who they are."

Several minutes later, Desmond Feigenbrod's voice crackled in the tower's audio receivers: "Is that St. McIntyre Stylites? Mac, old fellow, the Government mistook me somehow for one of its pilots, a Captain Pascal Corvi, and I have this gunship on my hands. Also, as villainous a crew of mutineers and running dogs of finance capital as you ever saw. Fetch up the Commanding Patootie, will you, so we can scheme?"

McIntyre: "The Beauteeous Gluteus has gone to stir up mischief somewhere. Man named Corander's acting. Better just come in regular."

Feigenbrod: "All right, but don't let the awkward-squad get excited and pop off at us."

Corander thought it best not to let Feigenbrod take his ship around the skirmish points demonstrating support for the Recons: the arrival of nonmutinous Government gunships later could cause disastrous confusion.

Feigenbrod: "The arrival of those gunships is subject to delay due to unforeseen circumstances, like sabotage. But perhaps you're right."

The appearance of regularly armed and uniformed troops wearing the pale blue Reconstructionist armbands sent a shock through the pro-Government forces, but they rallied and held out. There was still the brigade at the river to be heard from.

Morning approached, and the brigade and Citizen Wells were still to be heard from. Fear began to overtake Corander, as much for the young woman as for the insurrection; he kept remembering their few minutes of comradeship.

But toward dawn, McIntyre picked up a lone, small vehicle on his scopes, and then the girl's voice came in: "Wells to McIntyre. Are you still there?"

She brought with her a young officer named Pearson, Brigadier Pegrim's S-2, and announced that the brigade's tactical aircraft and four heavy ground-to-air countermeasure units would arrive within minutes to join the rebellion. The entire brigade would be in New Tavistock before daylight. "Reasonable people," she said exuberantly, tapping Pearson's sleeve with her fist. Corander felt a twinge.

A few demonstrations by Pegrim's tactical aircraft broke the Government resistance in the city. A flotilla of Government gunships, transmitting menaces, approached. Brigadier Pegrim himself went up into the tower to reply to their ultimata, and they veered off and disappeared from the scopes. Daylight found New Tavistock securely in Rebel hands.

Later in the morning, McIntyre flew out to the kopje and brought back Mustafa Issachar, Cathy de Ferraris, and a tiny baby boy; Simon de Ferraris led them in the flitter.

Over the next two days, eight other military units of various types and sizes—the largest a regiment—declared for the Rebels and made for Laing's Land or for the rangelands east of the River Bohr. Eleven copters under the command of Desmond Feigenbrod dropped hastily organized Reconstructionist partisan bands on the flanks and in the rear of two large bodies of pro-Government troops that moved uncertainly toward the river to confront the revolt. The partisans nibbled at the moving columns from the Cordillera almost to the River Bohr. Neither column reached the river. Brigadier Pegrim hurled his full strength against the more northerly column in a night attack and sent it reeling to the northeast. Then, giving his men no rest, he swung southeast, wheeled against the rear of the other column, and began to roll it up. During its scrambling retreat, two battalions defected to the rebellion.

While the war in the rangelands was turning into an affair of pursuits and surprises, Simon de Ferraris threw his prodigious skill and concentration into the task of organizing insurgent armies. His great, rolling figure was everywhere; his growl awakened junior officers in the middle of the night with promotions to independent command; his pockets fattened with papers detailing supplies—stolen, diverted, bought, cajoled—and the logistics of the insurrection grew under his sure direction.

Shulamith and Mustafa quietly vanished from New Tavistock. Only old Simon and Cathy and John Corander knew that they had gone to New Nome to reorganize the underground there. For a time, Corander served as Simon's aide; then he nagged the old man into brevetting him to Brigadier Pegrim's command as a major, and joined the caprioling in the open lands.

Chapter 13

CORPORAL McBride, the battery clerk of B Battery, 18th TRW Battalion, had a piss-cutter of a headache and his fingers kept shaking. Last night's yam-rum had been laced; he had suspected as much at the time, and this morning, late getting out the morning report, he knew it for sure. Moreover, the magnetyper was choosing to act up, and the computransmitter-console kept flashing its green, asking for the report. Any minute Sergeant Hansen, a son of a bitch at the best of times, would get off his own ass and climb on his, McBride's, about that.

McBride damn near got through one magnetic card before making a mistake, lost his place correcting it, tore it out of the machine, put in another card, and started over. The madder he got, the steadier his hands got; which showed him he was still a healthy organism. He got the crew leaders' tallies lined up a little more neatly, keyed the numbers into the machine in spite of their tendency to throb, and got through the whole humping report without error just as Hansen rolled in.

The first sergeant saw the green light flashing on the transmitter and roared, "Late again, McBride! McBride, I'm gunna bust your ass down to buck-ass private, is what I'm gunna do. Where's that piss-ass morning report?" He grabbed it from the battery clerk. "How do I know this is right?"

Corporal McBride: "How do you ever know it's right? It's right, that's all."

First Sergeant Hansen: "McBride, you're the dumbest crock I ever had for a clerk, and someday I'm going to bust your ass right down to buck-ass private. Where it belongs. Where's the CO's magnestamp?"

Corporal McBride: "Here. Where's the CO?"

First Sergeant Hansen: "Who knows? Who cares? He can go piss up a rope...Here: shove this up your transmitter. There, that'll hold'm." The green light stopped flashing. Regiment was satisfied.

Corporal McBride: "What was in that yam-piss last night?"

First Sergeant Hansen: "As a trained pharcamologist, I'd say it was dibenzylmonoaminotricruddyoxidase with an extra hydroxyl group up its ass. Who knows? The real problem around here is the morale stinks."

"Captain," said the clerk at regimental headquarters, "better take a look at this." Captain Shanzer, the S-3, came over. Sergeant Mackey, the clerk: "Look at the Eighteenth, sir. Look at B Battery. Look at C."

The S-3 pulled the whole printout loose and read it. "Sent this up the hose yet, Sergeant?" he asked casually.

Sergeant Mackey: "Yes, sir."

Captain Shanzer grunted.

Sergeant Mackey: "Well, I couldn't fudge it here, could I?"

Captain Shanzer looked appropriately shocked.

The clerk went on, "Anyways, B of the Eighteenth was late again and Division was greening all over me, so I didn't have time. And B's the worst."

Captain Shanzer: "They're all pretty bad. Get me B of the Eighteenth on the peekaboo."

The clerk punched in the code, and First Sergeant Hansen appeared snowily on the intervisor screen. "B Battery, Eighteenth TRW, Hansen. Sir."

"This is Captain Shanzer at Regiment. Where's your CO?"

Sergeant Hansen: "He just stepped out, sir." The first sergeant turned aside and called to somebody off-screen, "McBride, did you hear the lieutenant say where he was going?" A reply was partly audible through the crackling speaker and seemed to produce some kind of upheaval in the first sergeant's swollen features, but what Hansen said was only, "No. We don't know, sir. Probably inspecting the emplacements."

Captain Shanzer said somberly: "That's funny, Sergeant. I could swear I heard someone say he was pissing up a rope. Never mind. You'll do instead." He waved the printout at the intervisor scope. "Today's morning report shows your battery with twenty-three percent of its strength sick and another seventeen percent—*seventeen,* Sergeant—AWOL. Why?"

Sergeant Hansen considered. "We just report the *changes* in tally, sir. The computer keeps track of the totals. Maybe somebody buggered up the computer, sir."

Captain Shanzer: "The computer is the only thing that works in this whole regiment, Sergeant."

Sergeant Hansen: "B Battery isn't any worse than any other outfit, Captain, that much you got to admit."

Captain Shanzer: "Matter of fact, Sergeant, it *is* worse. It's *the* worst."

Sergeant Hansen: "Only this morning, Captain. That's because somebody slipped some difartylmonohydroxycrapazine into the yam-rum last night, sir, but ordinarily our morale problem doesn't stink any worse than anyone else's."

Captain Shanzer: "I shouldn't think guys that were sick on laced yam-piss *could* go over the hill."

Sergeant Hansen: "You don't understand, Captain. You think it's different guys AWOL every morning?"

Captain Shanzer: "You mean they're repeaters?"

Sergeant Hansen's inflamed eyes steadied and hardened. "I mean it's a couple of new ones each morning and they never come back...So now you know, Captain."

Captain Shanzer: "Does that go for your CO too?"

Sergeant Hansen shrugged. "You can't prove it by me, Captain."

From the colonel's office behind Captain Shanzer, Sergeant Mackey called softly, "Captain! Division calling the old...man. You'd better take it."

"The pattern is quite distinct. Quite-quite-quite distinct," said the gnome proudly. He was an elongated gnome, as tall as an ordinary man but not even as thick as your ordinary gnome, and with a gnome's large head, very very bony in back. General McGifford did not like him, did not trust him, but could not refute him.

General Holcott R. McGifford had been coopted from the staff to act as Minister of Armies and Marine. He did not like his colleagues in the Cabinet, did not trust them, and intended to have very little more to do with them, but meanwhile he had been instructed to report on the heavy rate of desertions from the armed forces and he was getting up the facts. He had sent for a mathematician to analyze the data, and he had gotten this gnome. It was all very trying.

The gnome, whose name was Professor Smeal, had put together a presentation, which comprised an inordinate number of tables and equations. To make matters worse, the general had spent some time in confusion, until he realized that when Professor Smeal referred to "the model" he meant the real world, which he appeared to regard as one of a number of surprising examples of what he called "the relation axioms."

"Let me see if I understand you correctly," said the general. "The farther any military unit gets from New Nome, the more men desert from it?"

Professor Smeal: "In the model you are concerned with, yes, that would obtain."

General McGifford: "Obtain? Oh, yes, I see. Obtain. Now, you're sure things get worse and worse as units get farther and farther from the capital, *not* as units get closer and closer to the enemy."

Professor Smeal: "Enemy? Ah, yes-yes-yes. What we have called the gimel space. It is not a Kraushofer space, you know. Quite different. Quite-quite-quite."

General McGifford: "Totally. I took that for granted." It was all too depressing.

Professor Smeal: "Let me see. As we have set up our model, the nearer one gets to the centrum of the gimel space (call it what you will, 'enemies,' 'friends,' 'sweethearts'), the farther one is from the centrum of the cheth space (that is not easy to say)."

General McGifford: "That's our side, the cheth space."

Professor Smeal: "As you wish."

General McGifford: "The closer a unit gets to the enemy concentrations, the farther it gets from New Nome: is that what you're saying?"

Professor Smeal: "You may use any names you wish, of course. So that whatever obtains as one gets farther from cheth-sub-zero-zero will necessarily obtain as one gets closer to gimel-sub-zero-zero."

General McGifford: "Not necessarily, Professor. Suppose the bastards sneak up on *us*."

Professor Smeal: "Would you rephrase the question?"

General McGifford: "Suppose the gimels move closer to a unit, but the unit doesn't get any farther from cheth territory."

Professor Smeal: "You wish to refine the model? Easy." He pondered. "A simple Yamasaka-Katz transform will do it. Almost a pseudo-Euclidean mapping." He pondered some more. "Beautiful." Silence ensued.

General McGifford: "This is all very exhilarating. What I want to know is this, Professor Smeal: let gimel stand for the bad guys and cheth stand for me—"

Professor Smeal smiled. "No. No-no-no. Let 'the bad guys' stand for gimel and 'me' stand for cheth."

General McGifford: "Yes, that's much clearer. Tell me: does it matter how near my soldiers are to the bad guys or does it only matter how far they are from me?"

Professor Smeal: "Oh, these relations are not reflexive. This is the beauty of an interpenetrating-mixed-space system—"

General McGifford: "I take it that I just can't send my troops too far from New Nome. It doesn't matter where the gimels are."

Professor Smeal: "As you have set up your model, yes, it doesn't."

General McGifford: "That obtains, does it? Thank you. Somewhere in this masterly presentation of yours"—he gestured toward the fat binder waiting on the professor's skinny knees—"does it tell me how to calculate just how many kilometers away from New Nome I can send my boys and still keep down desertions (and I think you said the Sirian clap obeyed the same equations) to a given level?"

Professor Smeal smiled again. "It is only a matter of plugging in numbers, General. And of course, the same relation axioms can be illustrated by a clap model too."

General McGifford: "One more thing. Can gnomes breed with humans?"

Professor Smeal: "Would you rephrase the question?"

General McGifford: "As you were. Never mind. Professor Smeal, I can hardly thank you adequately. You have been of the greatest assistance to the Government. You may in fact have saved it from the gimels." He reflected for a moment and added in a low voice, "Unfortunately."

"...cannot, therefore, keep any substantial number of troops for any extended period of time beyond this line, unless there is enough set-piece fighting to keep their minds off *you*."

General McGifford bowed slightly but comprehensively to the Cabinet.

"As this map shows, Professor Smeal's theoretical line corresponds roughly to the line of the Peurifoy Mountains and the near edge of the Plain of Runes.

"Gentlemen—and ma'am—I do not consider even one desertion 'acceptable'; but if we keep our forces well inside this line, the desertions, defections, and suicides, and the cases of venereal disease, psychotic fugue, and delirium tremens will not seriously impair the potential fighting effectiveness of the units.

"This means we cannot play a cat-and-mouse game at the edge of Laing's Land. That is a pity. It would have deprived the enemy of the psychological initiative that insurrectionary warfare needs, and might even have starved him out.

"As it is, either we must fall back on New Nome and stand siege, which would be a losing game for us because the siege could not be lifted from outside, or else we must operate just where we shall be most open to classical guerrilla attack. I take it you know what that means: the enemy concentrates and disperses at will, and we, if we are to have a chance of fighting any battle on equal terms, have to keep several times as many men in the field—and, with the present state of the art, that coefficient is usually taken to be six-point-three.

"We can safely assume that the enemy's leaders are more intelligent than ours, and that they have already grasped the situation. They will not, you may be sure, be lured into large set-piece battles. They will not fight steadily enough to give our militia that sense of comradeship, that commonality of dependence, which, in the absence of a good cause, is the only cohesive force we could have. The enemy is going to hit and run, hit and run, while we go clanking after him, endlessly, in well-armed and costly pursuit.

"Lastly, I advise you, Mr. Premier, to keep a certain number of your troops in New Nome at all times, under careful but rather indulgent supervision. You should compute that certain number as follows: add the number of troops you have outside the Capital District and the number the enemy has, and take two thirds of that sum. Anything less will invite praetorian treason on the part of your officers in the field. Such has been your leadership that the allegiance of your effectives depends entirely on your power to overawe them from behind. End of report."

General McGifford glared at the Cabinet members seriatim, shook his head slowly, and sat down. "It is all very tedious," he said aloud to himself.

"Thank you, General," said Premier Kalino, and fell silent.

The Deputy Prime Minister had a question: "General McGifford, you have told us that our crucial problem, the one that robs us of our freedom in picking strategies, is entirely a problem of morale. Is that correct?"

General McGifford: "I hope you got more than that out of it, Mr. Rhys."

Carl ap Rhys: "Nevertheless, that was fundamental to your case—"

General McGifford: "Thank you. Are there any other questions?"

Carl ap Rhys: "I haven't finished my question, General. It would seem logical, therefore, to attack the problem from which all the other problems arise, the problem of disaffection. And I propose that we appoint to each military unit a political officer, whose especial responsibility it would be to look after the welfare and morale of the men."

General McGifford: "When are you going to ask your question, Mr. Rhys?"

Carl ap Rhys: "The question is, what do you think of this proposal?"

General McGifford: "I think it's a thoroughly bad proposal."

The Finance Minister asked why.

General McGifford: "The commanding officer of a unit is responsible for the welfare and morale of his men. That is the command transaction."

Carl ap Rhys was smooth. "I'm sure he'd be grateful for expert assistance. That would free him to deal with—ah—logistic and military concerns. To continue—"

General McGifford: "Would this commissar report to the military commander?"

Carl ap Rhys: "Report? Yes."

General McGifford: "'Report' is a technical term. I'll put

it in more primitive language for you. Could the 'political officer' be replaced *at will* by the military commander?"

Carl ap Rhys smiled deprecatingly. "That's a detail we'd have to work out, General, but I was about to say that the political officer would in some degree provide a safeguard against the 'praetorian treason' you've warned—"

General McGifford: "In other words, you want to set up a system of dual command—each military commander spied on and second-guessed by a political agent who would have the real—"

Carl ap Rhys: "Come, come, General. You're putting words in my mouth—"

General McGifford had reached flash point. "Mr. Rhys! I have been at some pains to prepare my report, and I don't believe you would have selected a known incompetent to fill this chair; otherwise any one of you might have added my portfolio to his trove. Professor Smeal, however repulsive and unplugged he may be, is eminent in his field. It seems very odd to me that anyone at this table should miss his main point (and mine), *which is* that the morale problem has little to do with the activity or propinquity of the enemy. It has something to do with this government. The pattern is distinct. This is the pattern: as a man gets farther and farther out into the operational field, he hates what he is doing more and more. Your proposed solution is to send out spouters and snoopers to *remind* him of what he is doing. That, Mr. Rhys, is a bizarre idea."

The Finance Minister moved the question, the Deputy Prime Minister's proposal was carried, and the Minister of Armies and Marine tendered his resignation *viva voce*.

CHAPTER **14**

EIGHTEEN days later, Pegrim's brigade, feeling its way slowly across the moldy floor of the valley west of the Peurifoy Mountains, brushed against the pickets of a strongly entrenched force and set off a storm of very accurate fire. The brigade promptly executed the maneuver called "soaking into the ground"; and Pearson and Corander crawled out through the rain and dank foliage to reconnoiter the enemy's outworks.

"Whew! Either these buggers have heavy machinery or they've been here a long time," whispered Pearson. "Look at those textbook emplacements."

"We'll never get through that stuff. That's a lot of stuff. Incidentally, Peep, you're lying on a spanking new sheep turd."

Ordinary Terran sheep would trip even the best-calibrated personnel-emission-detection gear if they got close enough, and Brigadier Pegrim had issued each of his infantry units a flock with which to jam the enemy's sensors before attacking. Pearson and Corander had commandeered two elderly ewes from Kyne's battalion and had coaxed them on ahead, themselves keeping well rightward of them to be out of the line of fire when the defenses reacted.

Corander: "They're staying in the lee of that hummock. If they'd just move a little farther to the left...Olivia's a fine figure of a sheep, don't you think? Look at that dignified posterior...Ah, she's going to move."

The two men slid into the cold muddy water of a sinkhole.

Pearson: "It'll wash off the turd, anyway."

Corander: "The mud smells worse. Ah, there she goes."

With a shrieking rattle, radiation erupted from hidden weapon nodules around a good fifty yards of defense perimeter. The two men gulped air and pulled their heads below the surface of the foul water.

The noise cut off. Both men raised their heads cautiously. Olivia was gone altogether. The front half of Mrs. Murgatroyd, who had just emerged from the protection of the hummock, was charred away. The enemy's side of the hummock itself was a glowing, smoking expanse of dirty glass.

Corander: "Here comes the janitor to investigate."

A man in militia protectalls rose from one of the entrenchments to the rear of the casemates and loped toward the target area, hand-blaster ready. Corander aimed his laserpistol at the man's leg and brought him down.

"Now," he said, "let's beat it. They won't turn on the juice again while he's out there alive."

"Here's the particle road," said little Brigadier Pegrim, glowering at the map as he had once glowered at his students' history themes. "Here's the particle pass. Here we are. And here *they* are, sitting on the particle road between us and the particle pass—dug in, casemated, equipped with every particle thing old Pradjani left behind, and with an open supply line to their base *and* a whole chain of mountains protecting their particle rear. Is that the picture you're giving me?"

"That's the picture," said Corander. Pearson nodded.

Brigadier Pegrim: "Hell's fire, I can't force that position. I couldn't if I had ten times what I've got. Can I turn either flank?"

Pearson: "Doubt it, sir. Why wouldn't they be tight to the mountains?"

Corander: "We could send up a couple of boomerangs and make sure."

There were three boomerangs available—little rockets that carried cameras over a flat trajectory and were supposed to return to where they started—and two of them did return.

Pearson reported to Brigadier Pegrim. "Tight as my auntie's anus, General. You won't pry those flanks loose."

Brigadier Pegrim: "There's the Morlang Pass, seventy kilometers south. There's Yasmy Notch to the north. They'll have them plugged the same way. They're going to hold the line of the Peurifoy Mountains from end to participle end. So they think...Are you thinking what I'm thinking, Peep?"

Pearson: "Afraid so, sir."

Corander: "Let *me* do it, General."

Brigadier Pegrim: "If you can tell me my plan."

Corander: "I take a party of men up *over* the mountains, come along the road *from* the other side, and goose them up their own supply line, while you distract 'em in front."

Brigadier Pegrim: "Full credit on the first question. Question Two. Where do you go over the mountains, north of the pass or south? Compare and contrast."

Corander studied the map. "North, sir."

Brigadier Pegrim: "Why north?"

Corander: "Because from the north I can get down onto the road closer to the pass. Also, it looks good and rough, but passable, right to the road's edge on the northern side; along the southern side there looks to be some flat open space."

Brigadier Pegrim: "Question Three. How many men?"

Corander: "I'll need, oh, two companies, sir."

Brigadier Pegrim: "*I* could do it with two, of course, but I'll give you three." He stared reflectively at the map. "Thermopylae," he said. "We'll give them a royal Persian gerund."

The rain had stopped again. A cold, opaque fog had settled over the valley. At 0975 Bravo and Fox companies moved out into it with a vast, muffled rustling and squashing.

Each man could vaguely see the shapes of two or three others near him and the ground for three meters ahead. The longer-range radiation weapons and the countermeasure gear had been dismantled and the parts distributed as extra load to the men, who loomed through the murk in spiky, hunched, fantastic shapes as Corander passed among them.

The plan was to move the units in wide connecting arcs, so that if the fog lifted, the enemy could not look down and see tracks leading to the point of attack.

The men began to lose cohesion as he worked them round. Corander trotted around them like a shepherd's dog. At 0990, he called a halt and heard his bark repeated all around him in the milky atmosphere as if he had waked up a kennel. He moved alone out beyond the head of the column and stood waiting.

Presently he heard a diffuse watery rustling again, and Pearson brought up Dog. "Here's your third company of Immortals. At least, I think they're around here somewhere. Good luck." He took six steps, and disappeared.

Corander: "Company commanders, front and center!"

They got the three companies dressed into a single long skirmish line, with the officers and noncoms regularly interspersed, and Corander sent the company commanders to whisper "Azimuth forty-five" to each lieutenant and sergeant carrying an inertial compass, and to pass "Use password two" down the line: "Use password two. Pass it on... Use password two. Pass it on..." They waited.

At 1025, a tumult arose a few kilometers to the southeast: the shriek and rattle of ionization, the crump of radar-jamming canisters, and the faint baaing of sheep. Corander bellowed, "All right, get your immortal asses in gear and—*let's go!*" and the whole line wavered forward orthogonally through the pearly haze.

Plodding damply through the whiteness, Lieutenant Holtz, second platoon, Fox company, caught one glimpse of a scuttling figure through a rift in the fog.

When challenged, the figure said it was "Macdougal, Bravo company," and gave the password, "Xerxes."

Lieutenant Holtz: "The *second* password, Macdougal. How come you didn't get the order to use password *two?*"

The figure hesitated. "Persia."

Lieutenant Holtz: "Where's my electrician? Corporal Binswanger!"

"Sir?" called the tech from somewhere to the left.

Lieutenant Holtz: "Got the bolometer?"

"Right here," said the tech, materializing.

Lieutenant Holtz: "See this humper? Use the meter on him, Corporal. Keep marching, Macdougal. Hut, hup, trip, faw."

The captive was emitting a long-wave beep every twenty seconds.

Lieutenant Holtz: "Fox Two wants the major. Pass it on."

"Fox Two wants the major. Pass it on. Fox Two wants the major..."

Major Corander veered out of the fog. Lieutenant Holtz explained.

The major: "Find the beeper, but don't disturb it."

Lieutenant Holtz: "March, Macdougal. Hands steady. Hut...hut..."

After a while, Binswanger laughed. "Found it. It's kind of dug into the skin on his chest."

The major: "Can you tell if it's self-pulsed, or pulsed by his heartbeat or something?"

There was a gasp from the prisoner.

Binswanger: "I *think* it works off his heartbeat, Major."

The major: "Right. If we kill him or try to shift the beeper to somebody else, they'll know...So, Macdougal, you're not a traitor, you're a spy, a radioactive tag."

The captive burst out: "That's right, Corander, *you're* the traitor."

The major: "Ah, I *thought* you were IDD. Binswanger, take all his clothes off but leave the beeper."

Lieutenant Holtz: "Keep marching, Macdougal. Hut . . . hut . . . We'll tell you when to stop."

They stripped the prisoner naked, found no other communication gear, tied his wrists to the back of his neck with some of Binswanger's spare wire, knocked him down, wired his ankles, and fastened him to a bush so that he could not give the enemy a direction by crawling.

When Binswanger and Corander caught up with the line, Corander said quietly, "Lieutenant, you said he knew two of the passwords? I made all four of them up *at* the briefing this morning. But *this* fellow didn't join till *after* the order to use the second password. So: we've *also* got a traitor with us somewhere."

Major Corander's little force rested for the ascent in a ravine at the base of the mountain chain. The mass of vapor drifted slowly upward, and tufts of reality began to take shape around them and grew and coalesced until Corander could see most of the valley floor stretching away to the west. It was like looking under a bed.

Corander called in his three company commanders and told them about Macdougal and the unknown traitor. "Have every platoon leader dress his men in rows, and have each man keep an eye on the man to his right."

The skirt of the fog was retreating up the barren rubble of the slope. At any moment it might recede past an enemy scout or picket in some ledge or coulee above them, the alarm would go in, and the three companies would be slaughtered.

Captain Trescia of Bravo: "We'll have to follow the fog up the mountain, now, and flush them as we go."

First Lieutenant Kessler of Fox: "We'd end up shooting each other."

First Lieutenant Fordyce of Dog: "I've got a few boys that can climb and shoot. They're from the Cordillera."

"We'll do it that way," said Corander. "And I want techs to keep directional bolometers trained on all the climbers. The first sign of any signal, jam it hard."

Five men from Dog started up the mountain face following the fog. Corander waited with Binswanger in the second platoon of Fox.

A few minutes later, the corporal said, "Here it is," reached over to the jammer set and pressed the stud, and pulled off his earphones. "Hot as a whore's ass, sir. One of those two over on the right. Scrambled voice. Strong."

That sounded like an N-Transmitter; the spy would have known at once he was being jammed and now would demurely bide his time. Corander began to climb.

Panting and painfully abraded, he overtook one of the suspects scrambling up a diagonal gully, but Lance Corporal Pilliman submitted to questioning and body search and turned out clean.

Corander nodded in the direction of the other suspect. "Who's that?" he asked softly.

"Hancock."

"How well d'you know Hancock?"

Pilliman: "He's sort of new. Six weeks? Seven?" Yellowish eyes studied Corander from a weathered, freckled, ageless face.

Corander: "Pilliman, if he kills me, kill him fast." He mustered his strength, slithered over the lip of the gully, and made his way toward where Hancock had disappeared into a narrow couloir.

When he could hear his quarry scrambling nearby, he called softly, "Halt, Hancock!" The noise of climbing ceased. "This is Major Corander. I need your blaster. Would you hand it out, butt first, please?"

There was a pause. Corander crept as noislessly as he

could to a position two meters from where he had spoken. A tense voice: "How do I know you're the major?"

Corander: "The four passwords are Xerxes, Persia, Thermidor, and Sanity. Please hand out the blaster." He shifted again.

"Here, Major." The wave-guide appeared and turned toward the point where Corander had last spoken: then the soldier launched himself out of the cleft, bringing the weapon to bear. Corander, not quite where Hancock expected him to be, had a fraction of a second to kick upward, knocking the muzzle aside just as Hancock squeezed the trigger. A burst of radiation vaporized the stones next to Corander's face; gases seared his cheek. Corander kicked again, catching Hancock on the elbow. A reflex opened the man's fingers. The weapon fell, slid on the gravel, and went clattering down the mountainside.

With a sound between a grunt and a sob, Hancock rolled onto Corander, got a clumsy purchase on Corander's helmet and jaw, and tried to push Corander's face into the half-molten rock. The man was maniacally strong. Corander felt the helmet fastenings give way; he twisted his head free suddenly and, bareheaded, butted his enemy under the jaw, at the same time stamping with his left foot at Hancock's ankles.

Hancock lost his hold, slid a meter downward, flailed and clutched, and, with a thin mewing, began an accelerating, bouncing fall. Corander's helmet bounced down alongside him. Corander started a cautious descent.

There was blank silence to the south. Pegrim's feint had been pulled back. The enemy, therefore, was now able to pick up the jamming and might well guess from it what they had failed to learn from their spy.

Trescia and a medic greeted him below. "Dead, sir," said the medic.

Corander: "Stop the jammers...Let's see what he had." It was an N-Transmitter taped into his left armpit and, by a wild chance, undamaged. "Left armpit. Medic, amputate Citizen Hancock's right thumb."

The four remaining mountaineers pursued the last wisps of fog up the lower slopes and found no signs of the enemy. They hand-signaled the "all clear," and two of them went on ahead to scout while Pilliman and another Cordilleran showed the Immortals the way up.

Bravo company, under Captain Trescia, was to stay in the

ravine until Dog and Fox were in control of the terrain above and then, covered from above, was to follow in reserve. Corander assigned the fourth mountaineer as their guide and, with Pilliman, led Dog and Fox up the brownish, rankly sweet acclivity. A light wind had sprung up, and the haze was being driven from the sky.

Corander: "Pilliman, could you imitate Hancock's voice?"

"Not too well, Major. I'm hoarser than he is—was."

Corander: "Can you do his style?"

The Cordilleran considered. "He was nothing special."

Pilliman: "That's Hancock's transmitter?"

Corander: "An IDD transmitter."

Pilliman: "And what's *that?*"

Corander: "A piece of Hancock's right thumb. This set won't work without it."

Pilliman:-"Gahh!"

Corander: "It's *his* set. It talks only to *his* case officer at IDD Room Thirty-two. Ready? Do you have the story? Oh, one more thing! Hancock may not have been his real name. Slur as much as you can and keep off the name till you're sure."

Below them, lying and sitting on ledges three hundred meters above the oily green of the valley floor, men from Dog and Fox companies watched.

Lipless with distaste, Pilliman put his thumb over the piece of Hancock's thumb taped to the set, pressed, and whispered faintly and breathily: "Amrigramasooms memmering Room Mermynoo. Ullibramanans nergering Room Herbydoo. Hobblig. Oble."

Room 32: "Hendrix. I can't make you out, Burmiss. Can't you speak louder? Or is your scrambler on the fritz? Over." Pilliman and Corander exchanged triumphant glances.

Pilliman, a little more loudly: "Hermiss remorning, Room Nerdydoo. Ham you hear me nomm? Oble."

Room 32: "Not very well. If this is important what you've got, Burmiss, better take a chance--and speak up a little. Over."

Pilliman responded in a harsh, petulant whisper that was almost a voice: "*All* right, Hendrix. Why don't you try washing your ears? But *I'll* take the chance. Good old Burmiss, *he'll*...Never mind. I'm sitting in a stinking crack in the mountains about forty kilometers south of Yasmy Notch.

We're moving north, eight, ten kilometers an hour. I suppose they'll try to flank the Yasmy. Two battalions, with—"

Corander, two meters away: "Hancock! What's that you're doing?"

Pilliman gasped frantically, "Out!"

"It was chancy," admitted Corander to Trescia when Bravo company came up. "One of their copters might pass here on its way to where we said we were. They could burn us off the hillside."

Captain Trescia: "They never seem to send gunships out here."

Corander: "They don't trust the crews. But get all your antiaircraft stuff screwed together, find yourself a nice gulch, and defilade your men and gear. I'll take Dog and Fox on up. Try to cover us if anyone comes along. It'll take us the rest of the day to make the top—*if* we make it. We'll sleep on our arms and attack at oh-seven-fifty. You stay down here till oh-five-hundred and then start up to support us. You'll have the shadows of the mountain to move in, but the sky will be light...Of course, we don't know how the bastard has organized his ground up there. Do you realize, Trescia, he might have a couple of regiments sitting behind that hogback up there waiting for us?"

He cocked an eye at the summit, jagged and golden in the glancing light.

CHAPTER 15

THE officers and men of Dog and Fox companies—their skin and clothing torn, their bodies and packs heaving as they strained for more of the thin air, their eyes staring whitely out of dust-caked faces, and blasters in their lacerated fists—crawled in a long, ragged line toward the edge of shadow that marked the naked crest.

At Corander's hand signal, the slithering ceased. Corander searched the shadowed declivity ahead with infrared field glasses. Nothing moved. The reverse slope seemed quite empty.

Pilliman said softly, "Somebody's out there."

"Hold your fire!" shouted Corander.

Misdirected or ineffective fire would be suicidal. Whoever was "out there"—and wherever—in two or three seconds the enemy hardware could target them all. Corander conferred in whispers with Pilliman, who knew only that someone had lately been over the ground ("See there where the lichen is scored?"), and with Binswanger, whose equipment told him nothing ("I personally don't like that rocky area, sir, but this gear can't see through rocks").

Corander glanced right and left at his troops. All were watching him. He signaled them to stay back, then shouted at large across the stony ridge, "I want twelve volunteers to rush that cleft and spray it. Sergeant Pike, pick your men!"

There was a long moment in which only the clouds moved, and then, as if it were rearing from the ground, a white rag tied to a blaster muzzle began to wave rhythmically among the rocks. There *was* a cleft. Across a hundred meters, a voice called thinly, "How's your fire discipline up there?"

Corander called, "First-rate. How's your morale?"

The voice: "Questionable. But we do have grounds for hope. We have the sweetest little audio here."

Binswanger: "They're not using it, sir."

"We can't decide whether to report you or not," the voice went on. "I suppose if we do, you'll kill us."

Corander: "Immediately."

The voice: "And if we don't, Mr. Pollack here will be simply furious. Mr. Pollack advises us on politics. Meanwhile, if you try to rush us, we'll have time to call base. Then you'll all die too."

Corander: "What if we jam you?"

The voice: "That would save us the trouble of reporting you, wouldn't it? I call this little drama 'Impasse on the Roof of the World.'"

Corander: "You could kill Mr. Pollack."

The voice: "That motion was made and seconded, but failed of passage. I voted with the minority, but the majority happen to have the audio. Just a minute...They say if *we* rush them to take the audio, they'll report you, you'll have to kill us all, and their friends will kill you. Do you think they have a point?"

Corander: "Yes. Can I come over and talk to you?"

The voice: "Just a minute...The motion was made and seconded, but failed of passage. Just a minute...However, I'm authorized to meet you halfway."

Corander whispered to Lieutenant Kessler, "You're in command unless and until." He stood up, slid out of his pack harness, placed his hands on top of his helmet, and walked slowly forward.

A tall, thin figure simultaneously straightened up among the rocks, stretched luxuriously, carefully dusted its knees, and began to climb toward him, its face seeming to catch fire in the glow of the sinking sun.

This face was singularly ugly—too wide in the jaw, and with a crumpled nose—and singularly intelligent. It seemed on the point of exploding into wry laughter. Corander smiled.

The two men, each with his hands mortised on his head, stood silent on the crest of the Peurifoy. The cold, attenuated air slid past them into the dark east. The Peurifoy chain was the last great natural barrier between the Rebel brigade and the capital; the pass was the key to the Peurifoy; and that little cleft and its occupants—with their transmitter—might very well be all that stood between Corander's force and the rear of the pass.

Like hounds sniffing, the snouts of four hundred and fifty radiation weapons rose along the hogback, some trembling down toward the tall skinny soldier who faced Corander, some restlessly sweeping the rocky patch, from which Corander could now hear the growls and sibilants of a surreptitious dispute.

"My name is John Corander."

The skinny man's shaven head sank in the suggestion of a bow. "Mine is T. Walter Hines, at the moment." He continued in a low voice: "I want to get out of the army. What do *you* want?"

Corander replied in the same low tone, looking blandly up at the sky: "I want to destroy that transmitter of yours. I don't want any signal to go out of here."

Hines: "A modest wish. And, of course, it's not my transmitter... You understand, I'm not changing sides. Your army is just as unsuitable as the one I'm in."

Corander: "I take it you don't object to the killing as much as to the being killed."

Hines: "Not nearly as much. Oh hell, am I going to be offered *that* choice again?"

Corander: "Last time. Positively. Help me kill Pollack?"

Hines: "How?"

Corander: "Describe your nest over there. But kindly don't glance toward it." He took his hands off his head.

"What do you take me for?" said Hines, grinning and lowering his hands. "My dear Mr. Corander, I was for years the cynosure of every policeman in New Nome. My associates will now see me order you to leave our mountain at once." And he began to gesture indignantly up at the Immortals, who frowned at him over their gunsights. "It's a gully," he murmured; "shape of a boat, a little more than, oh, a meter deep..."

At the far end, Pollack and "a big tub of lard named Harfinger" were sitting with the transmitter on the ground between them. ("Pollack will be the one that looks like an Aldebaran sea-stoat. I'd rather you did the killing.") At the near end was Private Hinckley ("a man of very sound views"). In the middle was Sergeant Henry B. Punter. ("Henry B. is dumb but strict. He won't let Hinckley and me desert or kill Pollack or anything the least bit illegal. But he *has* stopped Pollack and his fat friend from killing *us*. So I'd prefer you let him live, if your current plans permit.") Hines rattled through this account, gesticulating at random.

Corander made contentious gestures. "Thank you. Who has what weapons?"

Pollack had his blaster, of course. Sergeant Punter had *his* blaster—it had a white rag tied to it. The rest of the blasters were lying on the ground—"under the great neutral buttocks of Henry B."

Corander: "Walk over and tell them I offered to pull my troops back to the valley *if* they'd give me the transmitter first, but you refused. While you're talking, I'll come over to argue with you some more. We'll see what happens." Without waiting for a reply, he raised his voice furiously: "That's my offer, and that's the only way you'll get out of here alive!"

Hines roared back, "We'll see who gets out of here alive!" He turned, and strode down to the rocky patch.

Hines hunkered down at the lip of the gully and reported for a moment or two to his comrades. Corander shouted, "How do I know you're telling it right?" and started briskly toward them.

From the gully: "Get back!"

Corander ran toward the gully, bellowing, "How do I know you're telling it right? You didn't get the point. You clod, you're going to get everyone killed!" He pounded on down, ignoring a crescendo of shouts and warnings from the gully. "Let *me* explain it, damn you!"

He came up behind Hines, snapped "Save Henry," heaved Hines into the gully on top of the gaping sergeant, and leaped on the larger of the two men at the far end. His right boot took the fat man in the face and hurled him to the ground. Corander jumped with both heels on the fat man's larynx and jaw, jumped forward onto the mud-colored case of the transmitter, feeling it crunch satisfactorily, and dived at the man he took to be Pollack, who had brought a large blast-pistol to bear on him. He got a grip with both hands on Pollack's wrist and forced the weapon upward.

Pollack suddenly let his arm go up, so that Corander stretched forward, and Pollack kneed him in the groin. Nauseating pain overwhelmed Corander for an instant, and Pollack almost succeeded in bringing his weapon into play. Corander strained upward again, and the wave-guide slowly turned toward the dim sky.

Behind Corander, Hines was crooning, "Come on now, Henry old dear, be a good soldier and stay out of politics. Hinck, my lad, slide one of these popguns out and make sure of Harfus-Barfus."

Corander caught a glint of cunning in his opponent's eyes; Pollack brought his free left hand up, took the weapon from his trapped right, and brought it down; simultaneously, Corander lunged sideways and with his body pinned Pollack's left elbow to the scarp of the gully, so that the blast-pistol was again pushed out of play; and then, twisting around, Corander seized the weapon and sank his teeth into Pollack's left wrist. The blaster came free; Corander backed away, turned it on Pollack, and killed him with a burst.

Hines' voice said, "A vote of thanks to Mr. Corander was moved and seconded. It was passed, two to nothing."

Corander, turning dizzily, saw a small, timid-looking private, presumably Hinckley, next to him, bending over the fat, inert body of the man Corander had first attacked; the head lay at an impossible angle. A meter away, a dazed sergeant was sitting with his legs spread out straight and some weaponry scattered between them, like a plump little boy with his toys. Leaning with one elbow on the lip of the gully and contriving to look elegant despite a torn uniform and a bleeding face, stood Hines. "With three abstentions," he added.

In a vast, ragged arc, Corander's men came bouncing like toads through the gathering darkness.

The light before sunrise showed little except the road itself, a broad pale streak across a kind of colorless harsh uncertainty. Corander, Pilliman, and Hines crouched behind a tilted slab of basalt and took turns scanning the terrain through the infrared glasses. Behind them, distributed in the lee of the rocks, lay Dog and Fox companies.

Corander hand-signaled, and a moment later, Binswanger whispered at his elbow, "Major?"

Corander: "Got their quacker working?"

Binswanger: "No, but I've mickeyed one of ours to simulate it."

Corander: "Pilliman, do you think you can do a dumb sergeant?"

Pilliman: "That's the only kind I *can* do, sir."

Corander: "Hines, this is a pass through our lines. You can have it in return for one last favor."

In regimental HQ just east of the pass, the peekaboo was rasping away. Corporal Barnett windmilled off the row of chairs where he had been sleeping through his duty. He stumbled across the half-lit bunker, kicking aside a particularly obstructive chair, and looked at the clock: 0741 already. He grabbed up an ink-pencil and clipboard to look busy with. But the caller was only the goldbricking commander of B Battery, 18th TRW.

Lieutenant Meehan was unusually testy. "Where the hell is that stinking little Pollack? He's got four of my men with him, including the only nonalcoholic sergeant in my whole battery."

"They haven't called in, sir. The whole perimeter up here's on manual, sir. It's been on manual all night, sir." Corporal Barnett had a wonderfully offensive way of saying "sir" of which he was very proud. "And there's nothing on the screen, sir." He glanced nervously over at the perimeter display to see whether he had told the truth; but he had. The steady yellow light was still on for Detection Only mode. The rotating green sweep in the scope elicited so many echoes from the broken terrain that Barnett could make nothing out; and the superimposed red affine grid of the personnel-emission detectors glowed softly at ground state.

At that moment, the perimeter display broke out with a shrill beeping. Some intersections on the red grid had brightened to orange, but behind it the green phosphor of the radar showed only the same crazy quilt of reflections as before. Whatever—or whoever—had set off the presence indicator had a low silhouette.

Out of the colonel's darkened office careened Captain Shanzer, the OD, knuckling his eyes. He swerved to the display and peered at it.

The display was out of range of the peekaboo's camera.

Lieutenant Meehan said, "Somebody want to tell me what's going on?"

Captain Shanzer: "Back from your card game, Meehan? . . . *Could* be them. Right area. I don't know, though. *Look* at the damn thing! Too goddamn much emission over too goddamn much space—we've only got one five-man patrol out."

From the com-desk monitors, two voices began at once.

One said, "Attention, all units. This is Fire Control. This is Fire Control. Presence showing in the K to M, Twenty-three to Eighteen area. K to M, Twenty-three to Eighteen. We are targeting the area. Report any personnel you might have out there. Report at once any personnel you might have in K to M, Twenty-three to Eighteen. We are targeting now. We will hold fire for ninety seconds."

The other voice crackled, "Calling Optimist. Private T. Walter Hines calling Optimist. Citizen Pollack, are you sure this set works? Calling Optimist. Come in, Optimist. Over."

Corporal Barnett: "It's them, sir. That grid is buggered up, sir, that's all. Maybe it's tuned to Pollack's halitosis." He asked the peekaboo, "You got a T. Walter Hines on that patrol, sir?"

Lieutenant Meehan ruminated in the screen. "Hines, yes. But what happened to Sergeant Punter? Or Pollack himself? I don't somehow trust Hines."

Fire Control: "Seventy seconds."

Captain Shanzer left the display and elbowed Barnett aside. "If you stall a little longer, Meehan, you'll get rid of Pollack. That the idea?"

The lieutenant said apprehensively, "No, it's not. Well, it's a good idea, but I got four *men* out there."

Private Hines' voice: "Calling Optimist. Yoo-hoo, Optimist! *Would* you take your finger out, please, there's a good Optimist?"

Fire Control: "Sixty seconds."

Captain Shanzer: "Barnett, ask Fire Control for two more minutes."

A small, half-clad man ran in. "You can't leave Pollack out there!" he cried.

Corporal Barnett: "I *told* you those snoops listen in on everything . . . sir."

Chapter 16

CORANDER, squatting among the second platoon of Fox, said, "Lieutenant Holtz, I'm casting a show. Pick me four smart, nervy men. One tall and skinny; that's for Hines. One small; that's Hinckley. One bulbous; that's their sergeant. One medium-to-scrawny; that's Pollack."

Lieutenant Holtz: "Wilbrick, Flinders, Kettelbart, and—ah—I'll be Pollack. With permission, sir."

Corander: "Permission granted. In three minutes, bring the Fox Light Opera troupe over where Binswanger is. Meanwhile, get yourselves up as regulars who have been through a bit. Regulation blasters only."

He crawled back to where Binswanger, Hines, and Pilliman were crouched over Pollack's transmitter. Hines was saying plaintively, "But *sir!* We killed all eight of them. But they got Harfinger. There's no one out here but us. Pollack—excuse me: *Citizen* Pollack—took a bolt right in the ass and he can't think—I mean he's sort of unconscious. And Sergeant Punter's jaw is burned, as well as his left foot, the one on the left ... If you *insist,* Captain. Sarge, can you talk through that bandage? Ooo, don't, it looks terrible. Ugh, put it back. All right, Sarge, mumble something typical for the nice man."

Pilliman's eyes showed orange as he rolled them toward the first sunrise and said hollowly, "Hydifuggle hamwee hiddafuggle woe? Naddanuh? Hedgerassing-gear."

Hines: "You're so right, Sarge! *We're coming in!*"

The Fox Light Opera troupe staggered out of the shadow cover onto the road and started toward the pass at 0746, tall, skinny Wilbrick and diminutive Flinders carrying Lieutenant Holtz, bulbous Kettelbart hobbling after them.

The sunrise sent enormously long shadows dancing ahead of them and, despite the caution of the attackers, picked out here and there a helmet or the dish of a countermeasure piece as Corander led Dog and Fox companies stealthily through the jagged terrain alongside the four actors. Suddenly the advance stopped. The turbine whine of a groundcar had become distinct.

A black command car nosed up over a distant maximum of the highway and sped toward the four. Not until it was near did it slow, then it stopped shriekingly, and just as the squeal of its treads died, Corander stood up, stepped out from behind a rock, and fired a long burst from a heavy stunner into the open ports of the vehicle. He announced, "Binswanger and Corander in for Flinders and Wilbrick! Binswanger, bring your gear. Kettelbart, hop in but take your time. Attract attention. They may have vis-optics on us."

Kettelbart made great play with the difficulty of climbing in with a wounded foot, hopping about and yelling "Hoo!" and "Hah!" while Flinders and Wilbrick duck-waddled away into the shadows.

Corander ran forward with Binswanger: they picked up Lieutenant Holtz and tenderly put him into the car. "Holtz," said Corander, "drive. Kettelbart, how many sleeping beauties?"

Kettelbart: "Three." He pulled the helmets off the unconscious men and whacked each on the head with his blasterstock. "Ouch!" he said. "That last one could have been too hard. I heard something crunch."

Corander: "Lieutenants Fordyce and Kessler? Can you hear me? We're going in to shoot up their controls. You'll have four minutes to get your heavy stuff assembled. Soon as you see my signal rocket, attack. If there's no signal rocket in seven minutes, *you* send one up and attack anyway...Holtz, drive."

The vehicle sped back toward the pass.

The flock of sheep kept drifting forward through the succulent ground cover, baaing stupidly. Brigadier Pegrim scowled into his field glasses and muttered to his intelligence officer, "Those sheep are ahead of schedule. No way to make 'em stop, I suppose? Peep, what do shepherds do?"

Pearson: "Shepherds don't *have* schedules...Don't worry, General. Corander's rocket'll go up any second now."

Brigadier Pegrim: "Actually, it's Corander who's *behind* schedule...Can you *call* sheep like cows and hogs?"

Pearson: "I imagine the enemy's sensors are better than the sheep's."

Brigadier Pegrim slid into the sinkhole, rolled over, and glared at his watch as if it were insubordinate. "Oh-seven-forty-participle-eight. Where *is* Corander?"

Captain Trescia gave Bravo company a short respite and, sitting on a ledge with his arms around his knees, conferred with his Cordilleran guide. "It's oh-seven-forty-nine, and we're nowhere near the top." He looked along the great shadowy face of the range. "What if we turned forty-five to the right and went up *that* way?" He gestured southeast.

The guide: "Might save time, sir. Some...Unless we ran into a crevasse. Or a radar picket."

Captain Trescia: "We'll chance it."

As Lieutenant Holtz took the command car westward at 120 km./hr., Kettelbart checked his weapons, Binswanger huddled over his detection gear, and Corander examined the untidy heap of men on the vehicle floor. One, with a staff captain's insignia and a strip over the right breast reading "Shanzer," was shallowly unconscious. Another, evidently the driver, was a private labeled Murescu; he seemed likely to be out for a long time. The last wore a uniform but no insignia at all and was probably a commissar; there was a hideous cavity in his temple where Kettelbart had hit too hard. Corander gently turned the dead face up—and did not have to look for the name strip. "Well, well, Citizen Thekman. Poor little shit!"

He took the heavy weapon from the groundcar's rack—an SOS gun, which sent a collimated beam of molecule-disrupting radiation and then a little homing rocket that went through the blast hole and exploded chemically behind it.

Binswanger: "Their radar's over to the left."

A second later, the road began to descend. They were in the pass.

Holtz: "Left, you said? Hold on."

The vehicle swerved with barely slackened speed onto a ramp freshly chopped out of the rock escarpments to the left, fishtailing wildly on loose fragments.

Corporal McBride carefully smoked the two centimeters he had marked off on his genuine smuggled Terran cigar and looked around the mess bubble. The problem was that his skull started and stopped rotating an instant before his brain did; this made him wince. B Battery was still dragging its collective fat ass in to breakfast. It was 0750. They were late. So was he. Most of the men wore grubby, tattered fatigues: they had traded out their fresh issue for yam-rum and tobacco. Many of them were red-eyed and sallow. So, he knew, was he. It was getting so his hangovers started with the first swallow he took; and the piss you could get now was the worst yet; if things kept up this way, he would get his hangovers *before* he started drinking; at least that would save him the trouble of cheating the supply sergeant at cards.

He exhaled slowly, ending with a luxurious long belch, carefully extinguished his cigar on the tabletop, and stowed it in its macromol container. He might as well wake up that— who was it today?—Ferrucci in the orderly room and take over before Old Mineral-Ass Hansen got there. He rose. His brain sagged momentarily in his skull as he did so; which made him wince.

He got as far as the out-lock.

Then the whole freaking thing caved in. Some clown had blasted away the bubble top, and all that crud-colored membrane came floating down over everybody. Everybody in the bubble exploded into shouting and laughter, which made him wince, but he flung himself out through the doors to see who the clown was.

A hundred meters or so away, a command car had stopped, and one clown was firing a blaster through its roof-port at all the bubbles; two other clowns were snapping bolts through the side-ports into Fire Control and the radomes; and a fourth, a tall, knobby clown, jumped out, set something that looked like a little rocket on the ground, reached in and got an SOS gun, and began to punch Fire Control with it as he raced toward the hatch of a regimental bunker. The little rocket went up with a prodigious fart.

Brigadier Pegrim kept just below the lip of the sinkhole. "...the first time I was ever commanded in battle by a participle flock of—"

The enemy's defense perimeter erupted. The air seemed to come apart. It was as if geometry itself were screaming with pain.

Pearson shouted, "Keep down, sir!"

Brigadier Pegrim: "I *am* down."

Pearson: "*All* the way down, sir!"

Brigadier Pegrim: "When I see the rocket—ah, *there she is!*" He kicked his way down to the bottom of the sinkhole and watched the black locust shapes of his assault-force arc overhead, shielded in their heavy skirmish suits and propelled by the fat bursts of vapor from their jet-packs.

Pearson rested the head of a small visible-light periscope on the lip. "They're getting in amongst 'em. The enemy's fire is awful sloppy."

The brigadier took his turn at the periscope. The skirmishers were fighting their way into the enemy's service trenches behind the casemates.

"I think," said the brigadier, lifting on the helmet of his own skirmish suit, "Corander's got to their fire-control setup.... Now they'll have to slug it out on manual too. My boy, tell the second wave to go in with some heavy stuff. I wonder, could you and I get into those pods and turn 'em around?"

Captain Trescia saw the puff of the rocket, half orange half gray in the sunrise, and almost at the same moment became aware of a howl of radiation to the south-southwest.

"All right, Bravo," he shouted, "straight for that rocket smoke. Take your bearings and move!"

Lieutenant Fordyce grinned up at the rocket puff and to Lieutenant Kessler: "Sammy, my boy, we're in business."

Lieutenant Kessler: "See you later, Porkbutt."

Lieutenant Fordyce: "All *right*, Doggies, let's *move!*"

Lieutenant Kessler's voice rose and cracked boyishly: "*All* right, Fox, shake your jocks!"

*   *   *

As Corander raced toward the hatch of the bunker, his eye identified the peculiar dull sheen of high-dislocation steel and he nearly broke stride. He could use up an SOS gun's charge on this tough armor and have nothing to finish off the Fire Control center with. He could open a rathole for three men—and himself—and leave Dog and Fox to face a withering fire.

But there was no time to change plan. Here in the open he had only a few seconds more of life. He steadied the gun for a burst—and the hatch slid smoothly open, revealing a moon face framed by two hands raised deprecatingly.

Corander dove down into the opening, whistled shrilly between his teeth, put aside the SOS, and drew his own blaster, preparing to give Holtz, Kettelbart, and Binswanger covering fire. He watched the whalebacks of the other bunkers, but their fire-slots were black and still.

Binswanger scurried toward the hatch. A bolt of radiation, fired from behind the shards of a radome, struck the parapet of the steps just behind his heels. Corander flinched from the vapor but picked off the enemy marksman. Kettelbart lumbered across safely, attracting inaccurate fire from two distant bunkers. Corander sprayed these slots to cover Holtz; the fierce needle-beam of a laser stabbed out of one of the perforations in Fire Control and took the lieutenant below the left knee, and he pitched forward into the dust.

Corander: "Cover me." He thrust his blaster at Kettelbart and plunged up the steps. He picked up Holtz by the armpits and dragged him to the steps, while Kettelbart, teeth bared, emptied the blaster into Fire Control.

A figure scrambled out of the command car, started toward the hatchway, and then, apparently seeing it in Rebel hands, spun round and began a frantic, weaving run toward another bunker. It was the officer, Shanzer.

"Hold your fire!" snapped Corander. He snatched up the SOS. There were six or seven missiles left in its magazine. He surged up the steps and loped toward Fire Control. The officer running ahead of him cast a wild look back, and there was one shocking instant of eye contact. Corander gasped, "A bargain?"

The only response he heard was a cough.

He dogged the officer for a few more seconds, keeping Shanzer between the nearest whalebacks and himself. Then he veered toward an undamaged portion of the Fire Control turret and emptied the SOS into it. He dropped the dead weapon, flung himself on the ground, and crawled toward the reeking skin of the turret, fumbling for the small laser-pistol carried in his thief's-pocket. He lay flat on his back, inserted the muzzle into a still-glowing hole, and held the trigger back, slowly twisting the little gun to cauterize the insides of the dome.

The whaleback into which the officer had disappeared was forty meters away to the right, and its fire-slots commanded the ground where Corander lay. Corander's chest was heaving, the thin air insufficient. Over and over, his glance flickered toward the fire-slots. They remained empty. Once what looked like the wave-guide of a weapon poked out but was abruptly withdrawn. Shanzer had kept the bargain.

The handgun grew blisteringly hot and sputtered out. Corander heaved himself up and began his run back, trying to steer a drunkard's-walk course without losing his footing. He desperately fought down the impulse to make a straight run for the captured bunker. His lungs were starving for oxygen. Kettelbart and Binswanger sent bolt after bolt at the other bunkers but could not altogether blanket the enemy's fire. Corander felt the scorching passage of a burst that missed him by millimeters. A laser beam exploded the gravel beside his boots.

The steps were ten paces ahead. He swerved and swerved again; then he tumbled down them, and someone helped him through the hatch. He vaguely heard it clang shut.

In Division bunker, Captain Shanzer faced the wrath of two colonels and the lifted eyebrows of a major general, while to one side a sergeant jumped up and down and yelled, "I could have killed him easy!"

Colonel Gorburn said, "Sergeant Miles could have killed him easily!"

Colonel Zielen said, "Why did you stop him? Why?"

Captain Shanzer: "It was a bargain."

Colonel Zielen: "What bargain? A bargain with the enemy?"

Colonel Gorburn: "He didn't kill *you* out there, so you came in here and saved *his* life. Where was the bargain? *You were already safe.*"

Sergeant Miles: "I had him right in my sights."

Colonel Zielen: "Aid and comfort to the enemy."

Captain Shanzer rubbed his head where somebody must have tapped him; the resulting twinge made him blink.

Colonel Zielen: "Don't start malingering. It won't save you."

The general went "sshh" like a mother calming a baby. "Captain, you were right to *keep* the bargain. (Sergeant, get over to the turret and shoot at something.) Colonel Gorburn, are you accusing the captain of cowardice for *making* the bargain?"

Colonel Gorburn: "Yes, I am. It was his duty to protect Fire Control *at any cost.*"

General Fordyce: "Captain Shanzer, was your life worth more than Fire Control?"

Captain Shanzer: "Yes, sir, because—"

Colonel Zielen: "To you it was, because you're a coward!"

Captain Shanzer: "Also to you, you quivering sot. Because I'm the only man who knows *what's out there.*" And he pointed eastward.

Two hours later, advance elements of Pegrim's main force had silenced the outworks and begun the ascent of the road. They were taking severe casualties, but the enemy's technology was out of control.

On the east side of the pass, Kessler had brought Fox company snaking through a jumble of broken rock to a point where his snipers could pick off targets in the enemy's camp.

Across the road, Dog company had had harder going against an arc of the defense perimeter that seemed to work well on manual, and Lieutenant Fordyce was probing to his right, end-over-ending his platoons. He had all but lost contact with Kessler.

In a regimental bunker in the northwest quadrant of the enemy's camp, Corander, Holtz, Kettelbart, and Binswanger, with the wounded Holtz recharging their weapons, and their prisoner—or host—Corporal Barnett neutrally serving them coffee, had beaten off four attacks; it was only a matter of time before the enemy made a serious effort to finish them off.

Bravo company was still working its way up the slope.

From the Government side, the situation looked more complicated. The presence in a command bunker of a few of the enemy was a nuisance but did not justify accepting more losses; the damage was done. Rebel fire from the broken terrain to the east could now sweep part of the open area between General Fordyce's bunker and the Rebel-held one.

Demolishing the bunker with heavier weapons at longer range would endanger the hospital bunker nearby.

At 1250 pressure on the Government position intensified. Dog company had sidled around the northern face of the defenses and held the crest one and a half kilometers north of the road, with an excellent field of fire southwestward down much of the slope, enfilading General Fordyce's right as he faced the ascending Pegrim. The Rebels occupied the lower concavity, the Government the upper convexity; and the Rebel Dog was threatening to push the Government main force off into the gunsights of the well-covered Rebel main force. Colonel Gorburn pointed out to his commanding general that a division could hold out against a mere brigade, and Colonel Zielen contributed something about interior lines of communication. The general replied, "Get Captain Shanzer."

Captain Shanzer assembled a striking force, something over battalion strength, from headquarters details and the disjecta membra of beaten units. It thrust suddenly northward, hurling Lieutenant Fordyce's little Rebel force back along the mountain crest about four kilometers. Fox company came in behind the new grouping and seized possession of their camp, freeing Corander's group, but could only harass the Government rear; it could not induce General Fordyce to turn and give battle from the wrong side of his own defenses.

At 1320, the situation of Dog company seemed desperate. The headquarters striking force would soon destroy or scatter it, then turn and destroy Fox, and the pass would be held. Pegrim's main body was all in the concavity of the lower slopes but, in the face of deadly fire, had made little progress past the inflection point, either north or south of the road.

At 1322, Captain Trescia, climbing with difficulty at the head of Bravo company, hand-signaled his men to rest and crept forward on his stomach. He heard movement ahead of him and moved closer stealthily. What he saw was the oblivious flank of a Government striking force, moving north. Turning his field glasses rightward, he saw the main elements of the Government division about two kilometers downslope *with their backs to him*. If it was not a trap, it was a glorious hiatus. At 1324, Trescia's men flung themselves into the gap and against the flank of the striking force, howling their battle cry of "Brah-voh" like an opera audience. Their voices reached Dog company, who counterattacked recklessly; and an audio signal from Trescia reached Binswanger, still at Corander's side. Corander and Kessler led Fox yelping into the rear of the striking force. The Government troops on the mountainside were pinned down by a raging burst of activity from Pegrim's main force, who had been signaled by Binswanger; and at 1430 the battle was over. The pass was open. The capital was in hazard.

The commander of the Government division, Major General Walter B. Fordyce, Sr., surrendered to the commanding officer of Dog company, First Lieutenant Walter B. Fordyce, Jr. The general said, "You took too many chances, boy."

CHAPTER 17

THE word in the captured camp was: the Rebels were
going to "process" them all in the mess bubbles. Everybody
was rushing around like an idiot asking, "What does that
mean? What does that mean?" Corporal McBride kept having
this great image of a bunch of cannibals sautéing the whole
division...He wondered if the bastard who ate *him* would
get his headache...They could freeze them up and sell them
as pork; they could *buy out* the freaking Government with
what they'd get for just one division of pork. At this point,
some moron lieutenant asked him, "What are they going to
do? What do they mean, 'process,' do you know?"

Corporal McBride: "First they sauté you in corn oil—oh,
excuse me, sir, officers in butter—and then they freeze-pack-
age you."

The imbecile lieutenant kept saying, "Yes, yes," as if he
was listening.

Corporal McBride: "They charge by the rank, sir, except
sergeants cost more than captains—they're not scarce, but

they're so hard to clean. And colonels' balls are a great rarity. Though they want a good Burgundy to bring out—"

And the poor imbecile lieutenant said, "Yes, yes," in his scared voice and drifted away.

Then it turned out that most of the division had got away eastward, and Corporal McBride supposed a good many others had been killed...so, as things stood, it was not crowded in the bubble he found himself in.

Then there was the usual Attention and As You Were and Attention again and At Ease and crap, and a little brigadier-type general like a schoolteacher stood on a bench and made a speech to the effect that he was Mr. Pegrim, a civilian at heart, and maybe they had heard that the Rebs didn't take prisoners; yes, he could see that some of them had.

"Well," said Pegrim, "it's true." He was the first brigadier general with a good sense of humor Corporal McBride had ever seen.

It was his policy, Pegrim explained after eighty-seven poor cowardly bastards broke wind, to let soldiers go. The soldiers in *his* brigade were there because they wanted to be. Any one of them could pack up and go home anytime. Well, *almost* anytime. (For some reason, many poor cowardly bastards present found this hysterically funny, but it was not up to Corporal McBride's standards.)

"Similarly," said Pegrim, "*you* are now free to pack up and go home, or anywhere else you like, even back to *your* army."

Someone: "Just leave?"

The brigadier: "Leave. Haul ass. Go home. Go to the nearest recruiting office. The only things you may not take with you are weapons or vehicles of any sort. You will be checked for those. But before you go—"

"Awwwwww."

"—I have one request to make. To each of you. If you should ever find yourself in battle against us again, and you're aiming at some poor slob, just remember, *he let you go*...Dismiss."

Corporal McBride was walking eastward.

The way he had it reasoned out, the parts of the division that thought they had got away were about three hours ahead of him, busting their hump to go homeward down the mountains, with the Rebs shooting at their asses and the good old Government without a doubt lining up some "politically reliable" units in front of them to make the poor bastards turn around and fight some more; whereas the ones that *didn't* get away, such as for instance himself, were...

That, on careful analysis, was what gave him a stabbing pain in the giggy. How much better off *was* he?

He broached the subject to the man he happened to be walking with, a knobby-looking, reddish-haired character in officer's protectalls but with no insignia of rank. "Where are we going?"

The knobby character: "Where do you *want* to go?"

Corporal McBride: "Haven't made up my mind."

The character: "Then you'll never get there."

Corporal McBride: "Where are *you* going?"

The character: "'Over the hill to the poorhouse.'"

Corporal McBride: "You'll get there." He became more direct. "What happens when our friggers bump into the happy political friggers and then the Reb friggers jump on them both? Where do we go *then?*"

The character looked back at him with a half-smile. "That's when you'd better know where you *want* to go."

McBride had been assuming that the character was either an officer cutting out or an enlisted man who had stolen an officer's outfit, but now another explanation of the rankless uniform suddenly offered itself: what if this was a political officer?

The character must have seen McBride's eyes searching frantically for signs that the officer's insignia had been removed, because he said, "I lifted these. They're too small for me. I'm told they belonged to a busy named Pollack...Oh? You knew the late Pollack?"

Corporal McBride: "Didn't you?"

The character: "I didn't get along with him."

Corporal McBride: "How do you know he's dead?"

The character: "I saw his corpse."

Corporal McBride was repelled. "You took those off his body?"

The character: "Death isn't catching. But no, I took them out of a locker."

Corporal McBride: "The Rebs *let* you?"

The character: "Look, friend, I'm going to tell you my secret. Two secrets. Secret One. People need time to think, so if you want to do something, do it very fast, and they won't work themselves up to stopping you. Secret Two. People feel guilty already; start with that. Now you know my secrets."

They trudged on in silence for a while.

Suddenly, out of nowhere, a line of Rebel troops appeared ahead of them—two lines appeared—three lines—and coming their way. It was a disgusting sight.

Corporal McBride: "You got a secret way through *that?*"

The character smiled. "You worry too much." He walked forward as if he owned the mountains, and McBride could think of nothing better to do, although at the moment he felt his own title to the mountains was clouded.

As soon as the Rebels were within hailing distance, the character interwove his hands on top of his head and called out genially. "Aren't you fellows going in the wrong direction?"

McBride put his hands up without this goddamn banter.

Some Rebel yelled, "No, you are, Major!" and somebody else laughed. Then another Reb said sharply, "Shut up!"

McBride muttered to his companion, "What was *that* about?"

The character muttered back, "It's humor. You have no sense of humor?" He called out to the Reb who had first answered him, "All right, *General,* what's behind you? *Why* is it so funny we're headed that way?"

The man replied with surprising seriousness: "The Government boys have a dragnet out for their own men. They're rounding 'em up back there and putting them into all different outfits."

In the same serious tone, the character asked, "Isn't anyone getting through?"

The Reb: "Hard to say."

Another Reb: "If they get through, there's worse behind."

Corporal McBride asked, "What could be worse?"

The Rebs looked at him. "There's a way to find out," said one. "Aah, tell him," said another. A third, the serious one, said, "We hear there's a government cordon out in the lowlands. When the provost marshal catches you down there, boy, he don't put you in one of their regular outfits. He puts you in a punishment battalion." The second Reb said, "Safer to come in with us."

The character said, "It's a latrine rumor. I'll take my chances."

"I'll think about it," said Corporal McBride.

They pushed on unmolested through unit after unit of the Rebels, all coming back up the hill. McBride could not understand why the Rebs were not down there jumping on the Government boys.

The light reddened; they followed their elongated shadows through the desolate scree. McBride noticed the sky for the first time in years. It was very large. He felt as if his lungs were too small, or perhaps congested.

The character said abruptly, "I'm tired and I'm hungry."

McBride would never have known it.

They sat down on rocks and silently ate cold rations from their thieves'-pockets. The shadow of the mountain lapped at their ankles. "You could go wading," said McBride shyly. "Only, your feet would get purple."

The character looked at him with the most peculiar expression, like compassion, but said only, "I'm going behind that big rock."

Corporal McBride, politely: "Hope everything comes out all right." He stood, stretched, laid his ass down on the ground where his feet had been, and propped his feet on the rock where his ass had been...

"On your feet!" said a voice in very harsh tones.

Corporal McBride was startled by the change in his companion. "What's the matter, you constipated?"

The voice: "Better get up, buster."

Corporal McBride opened one eye; it looked straight up the wave-guide of a blast-weapon. He opened the other and saw as mean a specimen of the wild army sergeant in *must* as he had ever encountered; it was holding the carbine on him, and a horrid little private-like creature, with another weapon, ran up blinking and squeaking and stood beside it. "Hump yourself," said McBride, but scrambled to his feet with alacrity.

The sergeant: "Where's the buddy you thought you was talking to?"

Corporal McBride: "What buddy? I thought I was talking to a sergeant who's full of shit, and I find I was right."

The private type squeaked, "I saw somebody behind that big rock, Sergeant."

McBride's erstwhile companion strode briskly out from behind the rock and said, "Nope, nobody behind *there*." He was now wearing a major's insignia. "You're seeing things. Don't stand here all night, Sergeant," he snapped. "It'll be dark before you know it and you'll be shooting at your own men. If you haven't already," he added contemptuously at the private. "Corporal"—he turned to McBride—"my advice

(162)

is, get them to put you in the MP's." He gestured toward the Military Police patch on the sergeant's uniform. "They must be hard up for men in the MP's." He strode briskly away into the darkening landscape, eastward.

CHAPTER 18

THEY were, Corander saw from his hiding place in the musk sedge, using air vehicles this morning, flitters and copters, to round up the remaining fugitives from their own army. He smiled grimly. If they had risked using a few of these craft in the mountain battles, they could have destroyed his three companies and would at this moment be rounding up Pegrim's brigade out beyond the Peurifoy range.

The copters beat the early morning air with that fractured snorting noise they made. Their primary mission was to direct the cordon as it made its sweep across the farmlands, but once in a while the searing beam of a laser would wink from one of them, and then from a hedge or spinney would come a shriek and two or three survivors would waver out with their hands over their heads.

After leaving the corporal, Corander had veered northeast, hoping to slip past the Government dragnet. In this he had failed and had been chivvied through part of the night. He had found the little river rushing across the scree and had followed its winding course as it widened in the alluvial plain. For two hours after the arrival of the air vehicles, he had walked in a crouch along the deepest part of the stream with only his head above the surface. His neck ached.

The copters were now raying every copse and thicket as the cordon came on, about two kilometers away. They would soon ray the sedge.

The old house was his chance. It stood fifty meters up a gentle slope, across what had once been open lawn; now the untended grass, Terran grass, was high enough so that it might give him some cover. He wriggled forward.

Someone in a flitter or copter must have seen the grass move. There was a hiss and a blinding laser flash, striking where he had been a second before. Another to his left. Resisting the impulse to run, he slithered along as smoothly as his failing body could manage. Five more meters—one more meter to the corner of the house, past which he would be cut off from the view of the watchers aloft—he was past the corner. He stood up and ran for the door. It opened to his hand easily, with no more than a creak. He stepped inside into dimness and the gentle smell of dust.

From somewhere, an ancient, cracked voice—too old for Corander to tell the gender—called out, "Now, who the' hell is that?"

"Where are you?" shouted Corander.

"Good Christ! It sounds like a young man! I'm upstairs in bed, darling. Come and join me." Then a laugh like a demented chicken's.

Corander raced up the stairs and found a spindly form under faded covers in a vast archaic bed, the ornate, massive posts of which supported a great wooden canopy hung with the tatters of what had once been white or peach-colored silk. The creature was probably a woman, it was certainly in the second century of life, and the face that turned to Corander amid the heap of pillows was like a white pudding raisined with liver spots; but the eyes were black, bright, and focused.

They swept up and down his wet protectalls. "I'm undressing you mentally," said the crone. "Do you sense it?"

"No," said Corander. "No."

"But I also notice you've been in the river. How did you manage that?"

Corander: "I was hiding in the river, ma'am."

The crone: "When I was a Girl, we took off all our Clothes before jumping in the river. Sometimes we took off all our

Clothes and never reached the river at all. The object of the Game—"

Corander: "This was serious hiding, ma'am."

The crone: "You are a Fugitive. How romantic! And from Justice?"

Corander: "From the military authorities."

The crone: "The Military Authorities! They used to be a form of Justice. I don't know how they would be classified at present."

Corander: "They will be here shortly, ma'am."

The crone: "Are you a Chocolate Soldier? Never mind. You wish to hide?"

Corander: "That was my plan."

The crone: "In my bed?"

Corander: "Well, ma'am, I don't think they would mistake me for a part of you."

The crone: "At least you didn't shudder... You would be surprised at the capacity of my bed. When I was a Girl... However, if you will promise not to scratch the bedpost with those Boots of yours, you may climb up and hide on top of the Baldacchino." A cackle of laughter.

She seemed to be referring to the canopy. "I'm afraid it won't hold me, ma'am."

"Darling," said the crone. "it has supported many a better man than you. I used to swing on the crossbars of it with four stalwart young Lechers pulling at me from below with all—"

Corander mustered his forces, jumped, caught the carven wood, and hoisted himself up. The old creature was right: the structure was steady. He lay uncomfortably across the heavy crosspieces; between them, some sort of wickerwork supported the desiccated remains of the silk, which were adequately opaque, he thought; he was probably invisible from anywhere below.

The crone: "Splendid! One would never know you were up there. When will the Myrmidons arrive?"

Corander: "In a few minutes, I should imagine."

The crone: "Are they oppressive?"

Corander: "Quite, ma'am."

The crone: "Perhaps they have oppressed my maid. She is not actually my maid; she is the great-great-granddaughter of an Indentured Convict who used to be my Lover. She has not appeared this morning to prepare my breakfast and give me the bedpan. Perhaps they have raped her."

Corander, reassuringly: "I doubt it, ma'am. They're too busy rounding us up."

"'Us'? Who are these 'us'?"

"There's an insurrection going on, ma'am." He twisted to relieve the numbing pressure of the slats. "I'm one of the insurgents, but the military authorities think I'm a deserter from their own forces."

The crone: "Time to turn the steak. It was more painful naked, believe me. So, you're a Rebel in Arms! This is very gratifying."

Corander: "How long have you been left alone?"

The crone: "Since bedtime last evening. Bedtime!" She cackled. "Mine is the longest bedtime in History, I daresay. Just is the Wheel, swerving not a hair! Sally comes over four times a day to tend to me, poor thing."

Corander: "And betweentimes?"

The crone: "My days among the dead are passed, darling; around me I behold, where'er these casual eyes are cast, the mighty minds of old; my never-failing friends are they, with whom I converse day by day. Unless you meant Sally. She, it is true, pursues the Lies of Life instead of the Truths of Art betweentimes, but I should imagine you'd be too caught up in the excitements of being a Fugitive to do justice to little Sally."

Corander: "I meant you. I didn't see any books or tapes near your bed."

The crone: "I already know what's in them, you see. I shall improve your mind up there with a Great Novel while we wait: '*He sat, in defiance of municipal orders, astride the gun Zam-Zammeh—*'" The psittacine voice broke off, and instead there was a terse whisper: "Be still now, darling, or you'll compromise me," then silence in the room.

A diffuse pounding arose downstairs, shouted orders to look in the cellar, sounds of breakage. Two sets of footsteps thumped up the stairs with a sort of hesitant truculence.

"Well," complained a rough voice, "what are you waiting for? There ain't none of 'em *yet* been armed."

A second voice profanely invited the first speaker to proceed if he was so sure. There was some stamping about, and then the two men found their way into the room. Not till then, and then only in a half-audible quaver, did the old creature ask what they wanted.

"Who the frig are you?" demanded one of the roughnecks.

"That is the Question I should be asking *you*, child."

Second roughneck: "We're looking for a deserter. He came in here."

Crone: "In here? In my bedroom?"

Second roughneck: "In this house."

Crone: "I'm alone in the House. They flee from me, that sometime did me seek, with naked foot stalking in my chamber. I have seen them, gentle, tame, and meek, that now are wild... Now that you're looking under the bed, dear, would you give me the bedpan?" Then: "Would you put it under me, please? I can do nothing for myself. Thank you, child. My Spine has rotted away with some Disease. They offered to make me into a nice cyborg, squeaking around needing Oil, but I refused to give up my Body. I trust you have found no one in your Search under my bed? I'm finished now, child."

First roughneck: "Forget it, Alf. Let's get moving... If you're so sorry for her, knock her on the head and put her out of her misery."

The crone's voice was faint but calm: "It would make very little Difference to me, my dear, after One Hundred and Fourteen Years. But it might make a great Difference to you. It would distress my great-granddaughter Olivia, who likes to come visit me; and she works for the Government."

There was a note of caution in the roughneck's voice: "What's her last name?"

The crone: "She married a Physician. I believe his name is Keyes. Would you be so good as to remove the bedpan? Thank you. Just place it under the bed."

There was a clatter of footsteps from the direction of the door, and then a roar of obscene menaces. Some superior—a sergeant, by the vocabulary—was recalling the two roughnecks to their duty.

The crone: "Lovely, dear boy! How refreshing to hear the Language used well! It was just the way my Mother spoke." (A smothered sound from the direction of the two roughnecks.) "These two delightful children have been looking for a friend of theirs. They did not find him here. I have so few visitors these days. They are all gone into the world of light! Only my little Olivia..."

Corander could hear a self-serving mutter from one of the roughnecks as to who "little Olivia" was. The sergeant was obdurate: "*Some*body came in here. Our copters rayed him as he crawled through the grass."

A wail came from below Corander so sudden and piercing

that he nearly betrayed himself. "Leona-a-ardo! You brutes! My Leonardo! You have killed my puppy!" She began to keen.

The three men retreated in audible consternation, the sergeant protesting that no body of any dog had been found.

"Brutes! Brutes!...Darling, you had better stay up there a little longer, in case they return. —*'the gun Zam-Zammeh, opposite the old Ajaib-Gher...'* I am so proud of remembering poor Leonardo's name after One Hundred and Three Years. *'—the Wonder House, as the natives called the Lahore Museum.'*"

CHAPTER 19

BEFORE the passes fell, Rebel forces ranged at will west of the Peurifoy-Runes line, making no attempt to govern—in fact, inhibiting any political entities larger than townships. In the scattered, head-scratching little hegemonies that grew up, farmers and mechanics used Government thousand-unit bills for scrawling notes of hand, which mayors then countersigned so that they could be traded as commercial paper. Within weeks these notes were all measuring debts in "Old Units." That fact (as Premier Kalino pointed out to the Cabinet in one of the comments he now rarely made) showed an ominous change in the political temper of the debtor classes.

East of the mountain chain, New Nome was at that time in control. "Political officers" were attached to local units of government as well as to military units. There was a ceaseless coming and going of "teams": agronomy teams trying to restore food production, teams of economic policemen detecting "profiteers" and "exploiters," morale teams trying to suppress defeatism. But the Government was in a mathematical trap. By the McGifford Formula (even Carl ap Rhys took to calling it that), when x new enemies appeared on the front, the Cabinet had to send x troops to face them *and* increase the "loyalty reserve" in New Nome by $4\frac{2}{3}$—since the chance a government soldier would go over to the rebels was 1 : 3— at the Peurifoy-Runes line. And how could one compute x? How could one trace the comings and goings of a nocturnal enemy living off the land?

And how could the "loyalty reserve" be kept loyal? The currency in which they were paid was all but worthless. The soldiers took to wholesale "commandeering." The black market was glutted with Government matériel. Nighttime in New Nome was laced with screams, with the sounds of smashing and brawling, with tense military challenges and drunken derisive replies. The army authorities dared not deal with the soldiers' outrages on civilians by the time-honored method of condign punishment. When, therefore, the populace inflicted bloody reprisals on soldiers, the authorities dared not investigate either. No one ever discovered who burnt the Carnot Barracks with half of Headquarters company locked inside. Not long before, eight schoolgirls had been dragged onto an army lorry, raped and sodomized, and returned naked to school; and one of the girls had "thought" one of her attackers was a corporal who sold her mother fuel-cell compound from the Carnot Barracks. But also there had been a struggle between HQ company and A company for possession of seventy-five kilos of stolen methamphetamines. In the end, all surviving troops from Carnot Barracks were transferred to the front. That ended the matter—administratively.

The capital of the planet was a city besieged from within, by its own defenders.

Undoubtedly some senior officers made approaches to the Rebels. Soon there were pullulating rumors—of cryptic messages, of anomalous nocturnal visitors, of whores with big vocabularies, of sick leaves that "must" have been something else. Some of these tales the leaderless IDD—nothing is more nihilistic than a police apparatus changing enemies—had fabricated or exaggerated. More of them bore the stamp of that genius for malice characteristic of bored troops. Carl ap Rhys had taken over the Defense portfolio in addition to the Deputy Premiership, and forced the Cabinet to listen to reports of treason, suspected treason, planned treason, condonement of treason; and presently of officers relieved, officers arrested, officers shot trying to evade arrest. The Chamber was in recess *sine die.*

But once Corander's three companies broke the line of the Peurifoy, the situation degenerated quickly into a kind of frantic indistinctness. As the disorganized elements of General Fordyce's division reeled eastward, little Pegrim suddenly reined in the pursuing Rebels and hurled his entire brigade north, taking Yasmy Notch in the rear and driving a strong Government force westward into the valley. And again he held back the pursuit; he lodged a regiment in Yasmy Notch and sent the rest of his troops to clear the mountains of Government patrols and radar pickets, while small Rebel bands picked off the main uprooted government force in the rain-swept valley, dodged around it, and at length streamed through the passes and toward the capital. There was now no front at all.

The Cabinet growled and sneered all night. Carl ap Rhys, nothing if not sincere, proposed to retake the mountains and trap the Rebels on the near side. But the Rebels had had days to organize their ground. Was the Government willing to strip the capital district of most of the loyalty reserve? At 0630 the Cabinet glumly agreed.

The most extraordinary difficulties arose. Computers made massive and inexplicable mistakes in rosters and inventories. Orders transferring whole companies from battalion to battalion, or whole regiments from division to division, mysteriously appeared and turned out to be bogus—after they had been obeyed. One division boarded its surface transport and rolled toward the "front," only to find that its commissary and heavy weapons had been dispatched to a quite different destination—and on the way had been ambushed by Rebel guerrillas—and the orders to return to New Nome to reequip countermanded, reissued, countermanded again, and reissued with a new timetable, *all* the cancellations turning out to be bogus. The computers involved were primitive—the sort of hardware empires send to colonies—but there could be no doubt that some colonial had developed the art of "prefritzing" a computer to a high level of sophistication.

The harsher the measures Carl ap Rhys took to dispel this nightmare of bungling assisted by sabotage, the more loyally the printed press and the news broadcasts supported the Government—in the name of freedom.

The journalists had accepted the moral pretensions of the

Revolution when it was still a revolution. They had caught the habit of reporting the news in terms of Right and Wrong. But a revolutionary war, like any other war, is practical business between two armies, and in the rush of half-secret events, the practical test of Right and Wrong must be simple: Right is whatever is done by the right side, Wrong whatever is done by the wrong side. Freedom was what the Freedom Party did.

However, there was an underground press in New Nome and there were broadcasts from Laing's Land, inefficiently jammed by the Government. Day after day, with fine free-hand scurrility, these reactionary voices told tales of sabotage and consternation that made the Government look as if it were on its last defenses.

The counteroffensive in the Peurifoy never took place, because it was impossible. The civil war had changed into a vast melee of surprise, elusion, and pursuit. Twice, there were Rebel forays into the outskirts of New Nome itself—more noise and symbolism than anything else, but the Cabinet's collective nerve broke and ap Rhys recalled units that had finally succeeded in moving up.

Separate and coincidental mobs murdered three political officers in the same night in towns not fifty kilometers from the capital. (The official press deplored the barbarity. An underground more-or-less weekly called *A Nasty Little Bird* provided remarkable obituaries of the deceased.) An early curfew was imposed. (*A Nasty Little Bird* printed patriotic descriptions of Carl ap Rhys and Olivia Keyes observing the curfew together.) Enforcement of the curfew was left to the military. (*A Nasty Little Bird* published details.)

Long before the Rebels breached the Peurifoy, in fact before they crossed the River Bohr, an old man and a young woman—a somewhat attenuated workingman and a brightly painted young woman—entered an unsanitary little restaurant called Spike's on Spallanzani Street and tried to order lunch. The waitress scratched herself and the young woman looked curiously around while the old man studied the stained bill of fare, on which most of the items were indelibly crossed out.

Old man: "'Slumgullion Des Moines.' What is it?"
Waitress: "Stew."
Old man: "What are moines?"

Waitress: "Anything."

The old man looked politely to his companion; she looked at the waitress and said, "You've been crying."

Waitress, without rancor: "None of your effing business."

Young woman: "How's Spike?"

The waitress started to cry.

Young woman: "Who did it?"

Waitress: "The Specials. Are you going to eat or not?"

Young woman: "They're not likely to come back." She addressed this feeble reassurance to the waitress, but her eyes met the old man's.

That afternoon, the old man installed himself as cook and the young woman as relief waitress. A curious assortment of new customers began to appear—whores, bureaucrats of high and low degree, shabby intellectuals, and spivs.

This was the beginning, and these were the staff, of *A Nasty Little Bird*. The presswork was done across town in a near-bankrupt job-printing shop. In the neighboring loft was a concern manufacturing a shoddy line of woman's suits. Pale, whistling children of the New Poor pushed its little handcarts around to the clothing stores: they were distributing the flimsy gray numbers of *A Nasty Little Bird*.

The print shop was raided. Its pressman and two compositors, along with two handsome women working as cutters and three boys working as runners for Rani Creations, Ltd., disappeared into a van of the Special Police. *A Nasty Little Bird*, with some changes in format, appeared two days later.

The Specials hunted the paper from printer to printer— from the shop that printed the *Record* of the Chamber of Deputies, to a pornography establishment, to an auxiliary pressroom of that redoubtable defender of the Government, *The Independent* itself. The editorial offices proved harder to find.

At length, however, there was a raid on the restaurant. Susan, the relief waitress, was not "on" at the time. One regular contributor escaped detection by being ostentatiously sick, while his woman companion—a swiveling blonde who twice a week appeared to relish the flaccid attentions of the quartermaster general and thus qualified as "Pvt. Thersites," *A Nasty Little Bird*'s devastating analyst of military affairs— quarreled drunkenly with the waiter. The squad of Special Police marched away with six persons in custody, none of whom had anything at all to do with the paper. The old cook had produced convincingly dirty, frayed papers to prove that he was Joe Calabrese. That he was also known to the readers of *A Nasty Little Bird* as Nathan Sparrow, its editor, and that he was in fact a former Minister of Justice, did not emerge. Nevertheless, the old man, still wearing his filthy white apron, clapped a villainous ancient hat on his head, stumped home to "rest" from his ordeal, and never came back. The offices then moved to a brothel.

Before the revolution, the brothel had been a stylish cabaret called The Pink Quail, catering to spaceship officers on surface leave, to the colony's economic elites and their gilded offspring, and to the elites of crime and of Imperial politics. The impudent young ladies who performed on the stage and the blooming young waitresses had an interstellar reputation for being ingenious, tender, and expensive.

The establishment was still called The Pink Quail, but the paint on the walls was peeling, and the paint on the "girls" was thicker. Revolution, Imperial occupation, occupation by the militia, disorder, inflation, and the civil war had changed the pertness of vice to a stale routine of tinny "music" and heavy-flanked "dancing," the peddling of watery drinks, and, upstairs, the endless milking of semen from the groins of depressed or furtive men.

Mustafa Issachar became the palsied, gold-encrusted, patchouli-scented decadent Juan María Inigo Tomás Palomar-Sidonia y Echevarry, self-styled Marqués de Granada, a fugitive from Terra. Nightly he sat in the cabaret, his jeweled claws plucking at the buttocks of the passing waitresses, and after an hour or two tottered up the stairs, assisted by two whores and sometimes cheered on by the other customers.

Hiding Shulamith Wells among the inmates of the establishment was easier at first. She was not as well known by sight as Mustafa. She resumed her career as a waitress named Susan. But her taut, intelligent beauty stood out among the heavy charms of the other women. There were incessant demands from customers for her services upstairs. She refused steadfastly; it became harder and harder to explain why. To remove her from direct solicitation, she was promoted to the stage show and sang two or three short obscene numbers. The curious husky little voice she used turned out, however, to have such an aphrodisiac effect on both the male and the occasional female customers that the pressure on the management rapidly became inexorable.

*　　*　　*

Two days after the battle in the mountains, a farmer from Kraepelin was driving his 2,500-kilo open six-wheeler eastward along the back roads toward the market center of West Hamming, when he saw a soldier sitting on a boulder by the roadside.

He did not expect to see soldiers on that road, he had stayed off the main highway to avoid them, and he did not intend to offer even a solitary soldier a lift. The thought did cross his mind that it was unusual to see one soldier all by himself, that this man might be a deserter, and that somebody could earn a few little favors by turning him in.

Something—perhaps the unnatural stillness of the seated figure—made the farmer glance at it again as he drove past; and at this he stopped the truck in a tumult of shifting load.

The soldier was not sitting on the rock. He was sitting *above* the rock, with some ten centimeters' clearance between the rock and his butt.

The farmer climbed down and walked over to the soldier, who continued to sit motionless, bent forward, his forearms resting on his knees, his hands clenched peculiarly with the thumbs inside the fingers, his head slightly ducked. An explanation occurred at once to the farmer: the man was taking a crap on the rock. But the soldier's uniform was on and intact. The farmer said, "Afternoon," He regretted stopping, but there could be no harm in looking into this, and possibly some profit.

The soldier subsided slowly onto the boulder. A convulsion seemed to seize his knobby frame. After this passed, he rotated and elevated his head in stylized movements. "Morning," he said. He did not sound as if he were contradicting; more as if he were initiating the conversation and thought it morning.

"Afternoon," said the farmer. He liked to keep things straight.

"Afternoon," said the soldier, with identical intonation.

The farmer had a load of produce to deliver in West Hamming in exchange for a plow-robot he knew of, old but in working order.

"Mental," said the soldier.

The farmer, guiltily: "What?"

"That's what you said. 'Mental.' I heard you."

The farmer was positive he had not actually said it. He opened his mouth, could think of nothing appropriate, and shut it again.

Soldier: "I heard that too." He shrugged resignedly. "It's all right."

Farmer: "I got to get going."

Soldier: "You got to get going."

The farmer turned to walk back to his vehicle. The soldier followed him, less than a meter behind, seeming to step exactly in his footsteps and even mimicking his gait. It was notorious that battles made some soldiers mental; it was the shock to their system when they first started killing people, the farmer had heard somewhere. He quickened his pace. So did the soldier. The farmer mounted his vehicle and slid into the cab. So did the soldier. The farmer knew one important thing about loonies: you humored them. He restarted the truck.

The farmer fixed his gaze on the road. It would be better to avoid eye contact with a loony; he did not know why but was sure it was advisable. His peripheral vision caught a movement, however, and he looked. The soldier was bare to the waist.

"You don't like my body," said the soldier. "I can hear quite well, you know." He shrugged.

The political officer assigned to the West Hamming town government was sitting in the mayor's office. The mayor had been hospitalized with the luboes, contracted from a studious young woman serving on one of the agronomy teams. She had also infected the local prefect of police, the town's one practicing attorney, and the district health officer. The political officer undertook to perform all these functions from the mayor's office. Despite this satisfying growth of his job description, he was bored. There were no class enemies in West Hamming.

The sound of a large vehicle stopping outside made him glance out the window. It was an open-bodied truck with six wheels, larger than most farmers in this area could afford. A man dressed like a prosperous farmer emerged from the cab, reached back in, evidently to lock the steering mechanism, reemerged with the keys in a hard fist, said something with a rather oily smile to some unseen person who remained in the cab, and came hurrying into the Town Hall.

A moment later this potential class enemy was in the office, pouring out some sort of farrago about a half-naked loony who read minds and sat on the stones but didn't sit *on* them.

"Bring him in," said the political officer, temporizing crisply.

"I'd rather you came out and—and helped," the farmer said. "He might be violent."

The political officer strapped on his stun-pistol and accompanied the farmer. Seated in the vehicle was a red-haired, pleasant-looking young man in an army officer's protectalls, smoking the stub of a cigar.

"Good afternoon, citizen," said the officer. "I'm Major Thorpe. You're the health officer hereabouts, I take it?"

"Where did you get that cigar?" demanded the farmer suddenly.

The major's eyebrows rose. "Why, you gave it to me yourself not a half an hour ago. I've been taking my time with it, of course. It's a lovely cigar. You must have paid a few million for it."

"You stole it." shrilled the farmer, "while I was inside."

The major held up the cigar. Even the political officer, who had never been able to afford cigars, could see that more than half of it had been smoked away. "That's—ah—what I wanted to talk with you about, doctor," said the major smoothly.

The political officer believed it wrong to lie detectably when the truth would serve. "I'm not a physician, Major. I'm the PO here and *acting* health officer. Dr. Steen is ill at the moment." He added quickly and mendaciously, "I've had some experience in matters such as this, however. Come inside."

The inner room of the District Health Office was fitted up as an examining room. The political officer went over to the cabinet where Dr. Steen, a veterinarian by training and a Type Four alcoholic by calling, kept a rat's nest of medicine, chemicals, sprayskin, old-fashioned dressings, and soiled instruments. He looked for something recognizable as a tranquilizing agent; but the names were strange to him. He said to the farmer with disarming casualness, "Does your doctor give you anything to—ah—to—ah—?"

"Asshole!" roared the farmer. "You got this backward! I'm getting out of here!" He bolted toward the door.

The political officer drew his stun-pistol. The farmer stood still with protruding eyes.

It was at this point that a technicality occurred to the political officer. "Would you mind stepping into the outer room a moment, Major?" He was careful to shut the door on the panting farmer, and then murmured, "Just as a formality, Major, could you show me some identification?"

The major smiled and fumbled inside his protectalls with his left hand. "Don't refer to this aloud, please," he whispered.

The political officer nodded and bent near to look, whereupon something, probably the major's right hand, hit him on the back of the neck.

He woke stark naked on the examining table in the inner room. On the floor was the stark naked form of the farmer, still unconscious, presumably from the effects of stunwaves; and in the man's mouth was the neatly severed half of a luxurious cigar. Of the "major," or of the political officer's stun-gun, or of the political officer's clothing, or of the farmer's clothing, or of the farmer's truck outside, there was no trace.

A lonesome young woman behind the Children's Edu-Toys counter in Wummery's, the 5,000-and-10,000 Unit Store (as it was called, though it was ready to move up another power of ten), saw the young man through her fantasy, which was the one called "Princess of the Imboes," about this beautiful princess on a planet of imboes...For a second, she thought he might be the Terran adventurer who would...but with his clothes not fitting right and his knobby physique, and his never once looking up from the damn Alfa-Print sets, and his big knuckles, she saw he was another damn imbo. Two-centimeter set, a three-centimeter, black inkpad, red, construction-paprite, stickum, notebook. He paid from a stained old wallet, an old married man's, and left.

When they came and asked her afterward, she did not remember seeing him at all.

Pete's Paint in West Hamming was closed. The proprietor, Pete's successor twice removed, had gone off on his bimonthly ethanol fugue. It was not a flourishing business, and no one was inconvenienced.

Several passersby were mildly surprised when an army officer stepped up to the front door of Pete's and affixed a sign reading: RAIDED PREMISES. UNDER SEC. 385 (C) OF THE MILITARY HEALTH CODE, THIS ESTABLISHMENT IS OFF LIMITS TO ALL MILITARY AND CIVILIAN PERSONNEL UNTIL FURTHER NOTICE. BY ORDER, WILLIAM THORPE, MAJOR, SANITARY CORPS. The officer then produced from his protectalls an implement of the type used for changing the treads on heavy ground-contact vehicles, and jemmied open the door with it. One passerby was perplexed to the point of actually stepping closer to gape, at which the officer turned to him, pulled a notebook out of his protectalls, and said, "Anybody here have information regarding the proprietor of this establishment?" The passersby scattered.

Sometime before the Revolution, an Imperial bureaucrat, after misreading a map, had placed the District Garage not in West, but in East, Hamming; and there it remained, out of the way. In it were housed and maintained the vehicles that repaired the public amenities of District Nine: highways, sewers, airstrips, and the like.

With the withdrawal of empire came decay. Empires grow on the competition of bureaucrats for budget; nations decay by putting first things first; and decay had not only opened great gaps in the rows of orange vehicles and machines, but had overtaken the maintenance and field crews themselves. They lived in a routine of bitter excuses.

The chief mechanic lay dozing on the padded seat of a huge half-cannibalized ground-truck when an army officer awakened him.

"Welcome to the Organ Bank," said the crew chief.

The officer: "You're what here?" He whipped out a notebook.

The chief mechanic: "Penis... Chief mechanic."

The officer: "Name?"

The chief mechanic: "Mort... Anderson."

· The officer: "How many on your crew?"

"That depends on whether you count Freddy Havens or not," began the chief mechanic. "He—"

The officer wrote down the name. "Counting Havens, how many?"

The chief mechanic: "Eight."

The officer looked round. The vast, hangar-like structure yielded no other sign of life.

The chief mechanic: "For one thing—"

The officer: "Their names." He wrote down the names and those of the field crew, consulted a watch, jotted down the time, and set about making notations as to the present whereabouts of each crewman. The crew chief expounded his complete system of excuses and fictions.

"Let me get this straight," said the officer ominously. "If I came in here right now, with a truck say, am I right in

(180)

thinking that *for three whole hours* there would be nobody to work on it but you?"

The chief mechanic saw the way to another subject: "Oh! What's the matter with your truck?"

The officer: "What truck?" He slammed the notebook shut and strode to the door. "They should be sending out a bulletin soon. If a deserter comes in with a stolen farm truck, you're to call the provost marshal. If that doesn't strain you too much." He went out.

The chief mechanic composed himself, shut his eyes, momentarily heard the rattle of a stunner from the direction of the door, and went to sleep much faster than he had expected.

It was three hours before he awoke, ill and out of sorts, and decided that he would have to use one of his sick days tomorrow. It was four weeks before he noticed several paint splashes of military color among the civilian colors on the floor.

The Pink Quail was owned by a syndicate of which the only visible member was the pimp, a homosexual who called himself the "manager" of the cabaret and went by the name of Charles Bradford Pirley. He was a fair-haired, aging, neat-bodied man with wide, unaging hazel eyes and a vindictive smile and temperament. He had once been taken into custody by the IDD and released by direct order of its then chief, whom he had admired greatly ever since.

"The whole camarilla was run by a young girl in those days," he would say as he recounted his war experiences in the black market to acquaintances at The Pink Quail, and he would expatiate on her attractiveness. "Only girl that ever tempted me to go bi." He knew himself well and knew she had handled him with great skill: she had released him unconditionally, lightly remarking that she might have to ask him for a favor sometime. "If she'd made me feel grateful, I'd have hated her forever," said Pirley comfortably. "I hate having to be grateful. What a wonderful person! I love her so." He never mentioned that the slim, husky-voiced brunette who had just lent her curious grace to a vulgar ballad up on the stage of The Pink Quail was the same "wonderful person."

One day he was forced to say to her, "I don't know how to cover for you any more, Sue. They're all hot to get you, including the women, and some of them are pretty important. You've brought a better class of customer back here, you know. I hate to see you go, but maybe..."

Sue: "Couldn't you let out that I was your personal property? They'd let me alone then."

Pirley: "Everybody knows what I am, Sue. But I love the easy way you suggested it."

Sue: "I can't leave yet, Charles. There are some people on the way here, and they don't know any other address for me."

Pirley: "I could pass them on to you. You can trust me, Sue, you know that."

Sue: "I can trust you, but *you* can't trust the people who might show up. I don't know even *who's* coming, exactly, and we have no password system. Could I be the Marqués's?"

Pirley: "Oh, come now, Sue! That's just announcing you're on the line. And Sue, I—I don't want you on the..." His voice trailed off, but he looked at her steadily. "It seems to have some sort of importance to me."

Sue: "Of course I won't. Give me a few days, Charles. Please? I know you're taking a big chance for me, and I do try not to exploit my friends, but—"

Pirley: "*You're* taking the chance, Sue. Did you see the bucko that was demanding to have you last night? Do you know who he is?"

Sue, in a low voice: "Specials?"

Pirley: "I think so. And high up. Smart. And lordy, how he wants you! He'd do it on stage. Wait and see, he'll be here again tonight."

The guard detail working the checkpoint east of Perlis had had two exhausting days, and their relief was late again. The sun had almost set.

At last they heard a ground-truck; a moment later a second one.

The first swung into view around the long curve to the west. It was an army vehicle, but not theirs. This one was an open six-wheeler. The lieutenant, the corporal, and the private alluded respectively to two autonomic functions and the Oedipus myth.

The second came in sight: it was their relief. The lieutenant and the corporal said "Ah!" The private recurred to the Oedipus theme.

They then witnessed a strange race between the trucks to arrive *second* at the checkpoint. The truck in front would slow down to let the other pass. The guard truck would then slow down so as not to pass. The truck in front would decelerate further. The guard-truck would patiently hang back.

The lieutenant: "What's Hickey doing that for?" Hickey was their driver.

The corporal: "Because those muzzlers are telling him to. They want to stick *us* with checking that big frigger in front."

The private asked why the *other* Oedipus was slowing down.

The corporal: "Because he don't want to be checked too good, and he figures to arrive while we're changing over."

The relief truck stopped completely. The other vehicle had to arrive first, and the two occupants of its cab faced a suspicious and irritable guard detail. The lieutenant stared at the markings freshly stenciled on the front: "2D BATTN 1ST MIL DCT E S CORPS." He looked up at the figure in major's protectalls who was sitting beside the driver and asked, "What outfit's that, sir? I never heard of any E. S. Corps."

The major hesitated. The driver, who, as was the custom in long-haul driving, had bared the upper part of his anatomy, leaned across the major and answered, "Emergency Supply Corps, sir. Special orders from the Ministry, sir." As the driver said this, his eyes kept shifting to the major's lap in an exaggerated way, as if he were trying to signal.

At the lieutenant's nod, the corporal and private positioned themselves on either side of the vehicle with carbines at the ready. "Got any identification, Major?" the lieutenant asked casually.

The scene froze for an instant. The driver gripped the steering gear with his right hand, the knuckles showing white. The major seemed to be breathing hard, as if in the grip of some violent indecision. The detail waited. The lieutenant sprang up and wrenched open the door of the cab. The major's right hand was resting in his lap holding a stun-pistol on the driver, who sat in strained immobility, his fatigues bunched around his waist but showing a sergeant's stripes, his torso shining with perspiration.

Giving the major no chance to shoot it out, the lieutenant abandoned his grip on the vehicle, seized the stunner in his right hand and wrenched upward, flung his left arm around the major's neck, and threw himself backward, twisting violently, so that he fell atop the gibbering major. The major roared and struggled. One of the men knocked him out with the butt of a blast-carbine.

"Thanks," said the driver. "I'll never pick up a rider again. Thanks, sir. Here's my ID." He held it out.

The lieutenant, shaken and winded by his fall, said, "Mulligan," and the private cast his eye perfunctorily at the plex-icard.

"Looks all right, sir." The lieutenant waved the six-wheeler through the checkpoint, just as the guard truck, full of the jeering and laughing relief, pulled up.

"Good thing you muzzlers weren't in on *that,*" the victorious lieutenant said to them, wiping blood from a cut lip with the back of his hand in a rather dashing way. "You'd have gotten everybody shot up."

An hour later, at headquarters, the major who looked like a quondam athlete running to fat, awoke and inarticulately tried to convince the OG that he had, in some complicated fashion, been made the victim of a case of mistaken identity. "*I'm* the sergeant, *I'm* the sergeant," he yelled. "Don't you see? He had my own blast-pistol on me, hidden in his fatigues in his lap. *My* fatigues, I mean. He put *me* in *his,* and gave *me his* stunner, and made *me* hold it on *him* where you could see it, but *he* had *my* blaster on *me*—"

The OG said coldly, "He had proper identification, Major."

The major screeched, "That was *my* ID. *I'm* the sergeant..."

The OG: "Why didn't you knock him out with the stunner, Major? You'd have got him before he could blast you."

The major: "Think he was that dumb? He pulled the juice-box leads in that stunner."

The OG hefted the major's stun-pistol and pointed it at him thoughtfully.

The major grinned, unflinchingly and nastily. "He told me what he was doing and I *saw* him do it. Go ahead."

The OG pressed the firing stud. There was a rattle, and the major collapsed, unconscious. "Why do they all *argue?*" complained the OG.

CHAPTER 20

FOR a moment, Corander thought he had garbled the address. From the cab of his truck, he stared at The Pink Quail—the crippled dance of the display lights, the pustular scagliola, the torn blinds of the few lit windows.

A stealthy movement in the darkness twenty meters down the street; a man waiting; he seemed to be in uniform of some sort, more a police uniform than a military one. Whatever The Pink Quail really was, it was in trouble.

He could not leave the six-wheeler in this meager little street. He moved it forward, headlights out, until he saw an alley that might be wide enough; backed and filled until he could nose in, and, too late, became aware of several more men, indubitably in police uniforms, in the cul-de-sac. He let the vehicle growl slowly ahead, herding the policemen in front of it, until it was inside the alley; turned on the headlights, and swung out of the cab, waving his blast-pistol at the blinking police and asking amiably, "Mommy, Mommy, why are eleven brave policemen hiding in our alley?"

The leader of the detail, who wore what Corander took to

be a police sergeant's insignia: "What are *you* doing in this alley with that truck, Sergeant?"

Corander: "Leaving it, Sergeant," He thought for a second about the ensemble of The Pink Quail. "While I get laid."

The police sergeant, with a kind of bleak mercy: "The worst venereal disease you can get, Sergeant, is to get arrested by the Special Branch."

Corander: "How long before you go in?"

The police sergeant: "How the hell should I know?" His grievance burst out of him. "The inspector's in there."

She stepped into the cylinder of hard, bluish-pink light, dressed in nothing, apparently, except spike-heeled black shoes and long black gloves; and there was a sigh through the darkened room and then clapping. She held one arm and hand across her breasts, the other forearm diagonally over her hip so that the palm of the spread hand covered her pubic mound. She stood motionless, with the faintest of taunting smiles, then suddenly flung her black-gloved hands aside and up; there was an involuntary gasp and, as the shadows of the gloves seemed to stay behind on her flesh and it could be seen that pieces of black cloth cut in the exact outlines of her gloves were fastened there, loud groans; she looked reproachful, then threw back her head and laughed; and there was a crash of applause and cheering. She had her audience.

> *"There once was a girl,*
> *And her name was Annie.*
> *She had no whatsits,*
> *And a very small fanny.*
> *Her thighs were skinny.*
> *Her calves were small,*
> *And she had no whatsits,*
> *No whatsits at all..."*

At his usual table in the corner, Charles Bradford Pirley settled back in the darkness. The material was stupid, coarse, stale—that dull ballad had been cribbed by the accompanist from some old slut on Terra twenty years before—but this girl projected the most intense sexuality he had ever seen on a stage. With good material, there was no telling...

He had seen nothing so far tonight of the big, hard-mouthed man who had been demanding Sue's services—demanding them in a way that seemed to approach open menace. One of the regular customers, a Pauling Street fence, had said the man was an officer in the Special Police Branch. Whatever the bastard was, he was now missing Sue's last performance of the night, and thus was not likely to show up.

"You'll have to check that weapon, Sergeant," whined the checkroom "girl."

"Of course." Corander turned his belt, holster, and blast-pistol over to her.

He walked toward the sickly mauve door through which, faint as an insect, he could hear singing—one of the whores, no doubt, drumming up trade. Just ahead of him, a big man with a domineering set to his back strode toward the door, flung it open, and stepped into the darkness. That purposeful manner was out of place. Corander followed him. "The inspector's in there." This might well be the inspector. The *maître d'* came over to seat the big man, who pushed him aside and made his way with heavy speed among the tables. The *maître d'* turned to intercept Corander, who pointed to the big man's receding back and followed.

> "...Her whoosis was tiny,
>   Her thingummy small.
> And as for her whatsits,
>   —No whatsits at all."

Halfway to the corner where he could just make out his quarry bending over a lone figure at a table, Corander stopped short and whirled to look at the stage: and there was Citizen Wells, all but naked, the hot light gleaming on her long thighs and on the subtle planes around her omphalos, her eyes shining with her erotic power over the audience, singing a dirty song in a husky voice.

By the time he looked back toward the corner, the big man and the seated figure were both gone.

In the office, the hard-faced man held a plexicard iden-tification five centimeters in front of Pirley's nose. "Inspector Rivers, Special Branch. Any doubt about that?"

Pirley, still bland: "No, Inspector. Just what can I do for you?"

Inspector Rivers: "You know just what."

Pirley pursed his lips and shook his head. "I can't."

Inspector Rivers: "You won't?"

People always thought Pirley a coward because he was a homo. He said, "I can't. *And* I won't. It's up to her, dear boy, and she says no."

Inspector Rivers: "She'll say yes when you tell her twenty armed Specials now surround this place, waiting to move in."

Pirley: "Waiting for what?"

Inspector Rivers: "My signal." He reached over to a humidor on the manager's desk, removed a cigar, and lit it. "In"—the big man looked at his watch—"twenty-five minutes, either I'm going to be in that sweet little muff of hers, or you and she and half the spivs out there are going to be in Special Branch cells."

Pirley could not keep from changing color. "On what charge, Inspector?" At this moment, the office door opened and a knobby, red-haired young man in army uniform started in. "Just a minute, Sergeant," said the manager, a little too shrilly. "Later."

"Sorry," said the intruder, backed out, and shut the door.

"What charge?" Pirley repeated.

Inspector Rivers: "As far as you're concerned, harboring a fugitive."

Pirley could hardly get his next words out: "What fugitive is that, Inspector?"

Inspector Rivers smiled contemptuously. "I see you know. Our little girl 'Susan,' that very special piece of merchandise I'm not good enough to have, happens to be Simon de Ferraris' daughter. Correct?"

Relief and courage made Pirley tremble. The inspector had made a ludicrous mistake. Expose it, and the brute would back down. Now, how could Pirley do that without revealing who "Susan" really was? He set about it cautiously. "Inspector Willis M. Rivers? Identification number three-seven-oh-nine-five?"

The inspector's eyes narrowed at this display of memory, but he nodded, drawing at the cigar.

Pirley: "You don't want to risk drastic action, Inspector, when you're not sure of your facts. One or two of those 'spivs out there' are quite important in your peculiar terms. Now, do you really think Simon de Ferraris' daughter has to earn her living on her back?" He smiled.

The inspector: "I thought you said she wasn't a whore."

Pirley answered, "I didn't say that," and realized a second later that he had fallen into a trap.

Corander realized that the big man and the other had neither come back past him nor crossed in front of the stage. They must have gone out a door somewhere in front of him. He moved along the wall, peering at it and running his hands over it, apologizing to customers whose enjoyment of Citizen Wells he interrupted.

> *"She met a nice boy,*
> *And his name was Dicky.*
> *He had two pimples,*
> *And his hair was sticky.*
> *But his nose was pointy,*
> *And his back was strong,*
> *And his whatchamacallit—"*

He came to a door; it opened to his hand, and he stepped warily through it into a lit corridor.

He passed three shut but silent doors. Behind the fourth there was talking, and it was somewhat rancorous talking. "She'll say yes when you tell her twenty armed Specials now surround this place, waiting to move in."

Another voice said, rather faintly, "Waiting for what?"

The first voice replied, "My signal." After a pause it resumed with a note of ugly confidence, demanding a woman.

Corander opened the door and stepped into the room.

It was as he had inferred: the bully standing in triumph over his pale, rigid victim, who was asking something in a low voice. Seeing Corander, the seated man screamed: "Just a minute, Sergeant—later!"

No need to stay: the big man *was* the inspector, and the blond, effeminate man was trying to protect a woman from the inspector. It was obvious who the woman was. Corander backed out demurely, shut the door, walked in place to make the noise of retreating footsteps, and stood with his ear to the door.

He heard the effeminate man ask about the "charge" and the inspector reply, "As far as you're concerned, harboring a fugitive." Corander held his breath.

The light voice gasped, "What fugitive is that, Inspector?"

Then the bully's victorious sarcasm, ending with "Simon de Ferraris' daughter. Correct?"

It would be easy enough, after all, to go in and kill the inspector. But the policemen were waiting...

The colloquy took another turn. For some reason, the effeminate man had regained confidence and was now trying to bluff the inspector: "...you're not sure of your facts. Do you really think Simon de Ferraris' daughter has to earn her living on her back?" The effeminate man had found the way out.

Corander moved quickly away. He slipped back into the cabaret just as Citizen Wells finished her number by plucking two glove-shaped pieces of cloth off her body and standing nude in the spotlight, laughing uproariously. He ran to the stage, leaped up and over the footlights, knocked the girl's legs into the air with a sweep of his left forearm, and walked to the front of the stage carrying her bare body in his arms.

There was a confused mingling of rage and delight in the audience.

"They're after you. Place is surrounded," Corander whispered between his teeth. "Where are the stairs?"

"To the right." She put her arms around his neck and looked up at him hungrily. The entire audience cheered. Corander made for the open staircase, which led up to a small balcony. He shifted his arms under the girl, flung her over his shoulder with her long legs in front of him and her buttocks uppermost, and went up the stairs two at a time. He heard her chuckling and glanced back; she was blowing farewell kisses to the raucous customers; and he also saw the side door open and, silhouetted, the inspector with a hand on the effeminate man's shoulder, propelling him into the cabaret. Corander threw his head back, laughed, and ran his own left hand over the adorable buttocks.

"Where's your room?" he whispered.

"Left ... stop that ... through here ... oh, you monster! ... up these stairs ... left ... here. Let me down, you rascal!"

He ignored this, carried her into the room, kicked the door shut with his heel, and deposited her very gently on the cot.

He put his lips to her tumbled hair and whispered, "This room miked?"

She pretended to nibble his earlobe and answered, "Yes. Pirley's a blackmailer. I think all these rooms are." She saw what was impending. "Oh gawd!"

Corander: "Viewers?"

Citizen Wells: "Y-yes. I think so. Oh gawd!"

He straightened up. "Just a minute," he muttered. He went to the door and stepped out into the hall, retraced his path, and was about to peer out into the balcony of the cabaret when he heard a murmur of voices.

"I—I'm not sure which room she uses." It was the effeminate manager, temporizing.

"We'll find out, won't we?" came the inspector's drone.

A third voice—the police sergeant's?—laughed.

Corander raced soundlessly back up to the bedroom, bolted the door behind him, and nodded to the girl.

She had taken off the shoes, and sat on the cot with her bare heels digging into the mattress, her arms around her knees, regarding him gravely. Corander felt a pang almost like grief, but totally happy, at the sight—the whole enchanting underside of her that her position brought into view, the black-gloved arms, the wide solemn eyes of a little girl.

"Oh, you liar!" she said, and laughed. But her eyes watched him.

He sat down on the edge of the cot, facing her, put his hands on her shoulders, and made her lie back, laid his head between her breasts, and whispered, "They're Specials. They know you're Simon's daughter. But the fairy's trying to bluff them. He says Simon's daughter wouldn't be a whore, and he's got them nervous. Two of them in the house."

Her susurration was barely audible: "So I've got to be a real whore."

Corander: "You've got to act like a real whore."

Citizen Wells: "Then I'd better take off my gloves." As she removed them, he began to undress, but she said, "I'll do that." Her way of doing it was a pastiche of shamelessness. "You're going to find me a rather surprising whore," she whispered ambiguously, as she invaded his privacies daintily.

He found himself saying helplessly, "Oh, how I love you! how I love you!" He kissed the most astonishing parts of her anatomy.

A few minutes later, he discovered he was taking a virginity. The shock froze him. "Keep going, you bull!" she gritted in a whisper through clenched teeth: "The viewer's in the ceiling." Her eyes were swimming in tears: he kissed them, and kept going.

When he at last fell forward on her, she put her arms around him gently and said nothing; he could feel a tremor in her jaw, however, and knew she was in pain; yet she rolled him over and, putting on a display of loud, desperate lewdness, forced herself and him to all sorts of gross exertions.

"I've read about this," she muttered at one point, half to herself, and at another assured him, "This doesn't call for brains so much as for character." In all the grossness of her performance as a "real whore," there was an indefeasible cleanness about her that was heartbreaking. "Oh, how I love you!" he whispered again, "oh, my darling, I do love you so!"

CHAPTER 21

CARL ap Rhys' face was, for once, expressionless. "We now have," he said matter-of-factly, "a report from the Army Commission investigating the treason at the passes in—"

"Treason?" the Minister of Health broke in sharply. "Does the *report* say it was treason?"

"Who prepared the report?" asked the Minister of Justice in his harsh voice. He was a lawyer named Seiffert, a gray, narrow-skulled, bleak-eyed man with a corded jaw, wide mouth, and conspicuously large teeth; he had devoted much of his career to progressive causes and, having often run afoul of Judge Issachar when that precisian was on the bench, had been gleeful at replacing him. But for several Cabinet meetings now the famous Seiffert style—plunging denunciation of "unproductive interest groups," "elites," "the emptying power structure," "institutionalized privilege," and the like—had given way to a sort of rasping caution. Carl ap Rhys, who as Deputy Premier overtly ran the Cabinet now and ran its meetings, had personally chosen him but was finding him an uncomfortable colleague, particularly after ap Rhys ex-

(193)

panded his new portfolio from Armies and Marine to Defense and naturally assumed control of the police and what was left of the IDD. Seiffert seemed to have conditioned himself over the years to hate policemen.

The Deputy Premier (Minister of Defense): "In answer to the first question—the report does imply that there was treason. In answer to the second—the report is signed by all seven members of the Commission: three officers, two sergeants, and two 'other ranks.' I have copies in case—"

The Minister of Justice: "I didn't ask who signed the report, Citizen Minister. I asked who prepared the report."

The Deputy Premier: "Departmental staff."

The Minister of Justice: "Your Department."

The Deputy Premier: "Yes."

The Minister of Justice: "May I ask—who saw it first, you or the officers who signed it?"

The Deputy Premier: "I really do not know."

The Minister of Agriculture: "You'd know if they'd already signed it when you saw it, Carl."

The Deputy Premier: "I saw it before it was signed. But they could have seen it before that."

The Minister of Justice: "'Could have'... You didn't find out whether they *had?*"

The Deputy Premier: "No."

The Minister of Justice: "But you did make sure you saw it before it was given to them to sign."

The Deputy Premier: "I didn't 'make sure.' I saw it, that's all. Now, as I was—"

The Minister of Justice: "Of course. It was your staff, after all. Did you discuss it with your staff *while* they were preparing it?"

Carl ap Rhys' voice was rising: "Of course. They were my staff, after all, as you say."

The Minister of Justice smiled, displaying his impressive teeth. "You take my meaning. Good! By the way, how many changes were made in that report between the time you first saw it and the time the Commission signed it?"

The Deputy Premier: "Quite a number."

The Minister of Justice: "Were any of those changes suggested by you?"

The Deputy Premier: "A few."

The Minister of Justice: "And how many were suggested by the members of the Commission?"

The Deputy Premier: "How should I know?"

The Minister of Justice: "Half?"

The Deputy Premier: *"How should I know?"*

The Minister of Justice: "Any?"

The Deputy Premier: "I suppose so."

The Minister of Justice: "You don't *know* so?"

The Deputy Premier: *"That's what I said."*

The Minister of Justice: "You saw the draft before and you can see the text now, and you know what *you* suggested, but you can't find anything *they* suggested . . . I believe the expression on your face is what is known as 'glowering.' I haven't met many men who can really gl—"

The Minister of Agriculture said peaceably, "Come on, Charley." But amusement was breaking through his normally prissy countenance.

The Minister of Justice leaned toward the Deputy Premier. "I put it to you, Citizen Minister, that you yourself supervised the writing of the report and that you bullyragged the hapless commissioners into signing it as it stood when it left your hands."

The Deputy Premier mastered himself. "That is a lie," he said in a flat voice. His fury made another effort: "A filthy lie!" He repressed the internal assault, gripping the edge of the table. "There was no pressure on the members of the Commission at all. Much less"—he sneered—"'bullyragging.'"

The Minister of Justice: "Who selected the commissioners?"

The Minister of Health, thoughtfully: "I suppose you did, Carl."

The Deputy Premier: *"Yes I did."*

A pulsing silence. The Minister of Justice watched the Deputy Premier with patient eyes, and just when Rhys opened his mouth to add something, the Minister of Justice said, "Quite so. I thought as much."

The Deputy Premier picked up the stack of copies of the report and almost brandished them at his colleagues. "You're attacking a report you haven't even read."

The Minister of Justice slid a bony hand into his own dispatch case. "*I* have," he said, and held up an identical document.

Control deserted the Deputy Premier altogether. "Spy!" he shrieked, rose in his place, and flung himself out of the room into the garden of the villa.

"Herman," asked the Minister of Health, "will you take the chair, or will we have to wait till Carl comes back?"

The old Premier had, as was his practice now, been watching with a tortoise-like gaze. He said, "We shall recess and read the report," and seemed to withdraw his head into an invisible carapace.

Corander cradled Citizen Wells' dark head under the angle of his jaw.

She wriggled round and bit him viciously on the shoulder.

Corander: "Ow! What was *that* for?"

Citizen Wells: "I was thanking you."

Corander: "You're welcome."

"You and your big, stupid glands," she grumbled. "I rather like them, though." She went to sleep.

"In studying my clients, especially the ones who were guilty," said the Minister of Justice loudly, "I often noticed that such outbursts of rage, though doubtless sincere, fit remarkably well into some prearranged plan of action. I will bet you, your million units against my billion, that now that you've all had time to read his report he—and here he is!"

Carl ap Rhys strode to his place.

The Minister of Justice: "Are there some special financial implications to this report?" Everyone except Rhys turned to look at the Finance Minister, who sat staring ahead of her, white-faced, with compressed mouth and arrhythmically heaving bosom.

The Deputy Premier: "The session will be in order. You have all read the report, which makes it clear that one man's treason was responsible for the disaster in the Peurifoy Mountains. General Fordyce—"

The Minister of Justice: "You supervised the preparation of this report, Citizen Minister, and you yourself said a while ago that it only 'implied' treason. I have now read it—a second time—and I find even the *implication* tenuous. It is more like innuendo. You must have had more trouble with your creatures on the—"

The Deputy Premier: "You are out of order. I am presenting a report, and I have not yet called for discussion...I will pass around a warrant for the arrest of Major General Walter B. Fordyce. I am asking every member of this Cabinet to sign the warrant." The Finance Minister signed. "I can assure you all," continued ap Rhys, "that General Fordyce will receive a military trial before a properly constituted court-martial according to the traditional Code of—"

The Minister of Justice: "Who 'properly' constitutes the court, you or I?"

The Deputy Premier met his stare steadily, "*I* do."

The Minister of Justice: "I think *I* do."

The Deputy Premier: "In peacetime, but in time of war—"

The Minister of Justice: "Is there a state of war legally?"

The Deputy Premier: "The state of war and the emergency powers of the Government that existed during the Revolution have never been legally terminated."

Seiffert's lantern jaw seemed to grow longer. "I don't think the courts would hold that a technical—or malicious—inadvertence in not giving up war powers, even when combined with cowardly unwillingness to declare a second emergency, produces a valid continuity between separate wars."

The Finance Minister: "It's the same enemy!"

The Minister of Justice: "Now, that's the sort of thing I used to say myself."

The Deputy Premier sneered. "Before . . . ?"

The Minister of Justice: "Before I became Minister of *Justice*."

The Deputy Premier: "Where is the warrant?"

"I have it," said Herman Kalino. The others turned to stare at him, and he in turn stared down at the sheet of paper. He had a writing implement in his hand.

The Finance Minister, in a subdued and rather kindly voice: "That's your fading-pencil, Herman."

The Premier smiled. "So it is." He put it down and picked up an ink-pencil. Then he said, without looking up, "Is Fordyce actually in custody?"

The Deputy Premier: "How could he be, without a warrant?"

The Premier: "But is he?"

The Deputy Premier: "No."

The Minister of Justice: "He is at large?"

The Deputy Premier: "Yes."

The Minister of Justice: "You'd better observe the legal niceties, Citizen Minister, because unless I appoint that court-martial I just may undertake the general's defense myself."

The hand holding the ink-pencil did not move. "There was a man named Stalin," said the old Premier softly, "who used to pass death warrants around the table and make his whole Cabinet or Politburo sign them, and he—"

The Deputy Premier, recklessly: "He was wise."

The Premier: "—and soon he had them signing one another's...The report makes much of the fact that the general's son, Wally, is on the other side. How many of us are willing to take full responsibility for our grown children? Olivia, your signature is the first one—besides Carl's—on this death warrant. Are you taking full responsibility for Cathy?"

The Finance Minister sat frozen.

The Premier went on in the same aged voice: "Perhaps in a few weeks, as Carl's murderous hysteria needs new sustenance, your colleagues will be asked to kill you, Olivia, on the grounds that your daughter is Simon de Ferraris' faithful wife—*and* Shulamith Wells' stepmother and childhood friend. I see I have added a new fact to the Cabinet's knowledge. It is new to me, too, but not new to you, Olivia. You were concealing something from us...I shall not sign this. I could tear it up, but Carl probably has duplicates in his attaché case there that you tooled so prettily for him, Olivia...I think I will absent myself while the rest of you surrender one by one. Don't bother to get up." He dragged himself to his feet and trudged toward the door—not the garden door but the one that led through the house into the street. In the doorway, he turned. "I've read the Election Law," he said with a peculiar sad smile. "Come to think, I wrote it." He disappeared.

The Deputy Premier was crisp: "Ch'ien, will you sign, please?"

The Minister of Health: "I think we ought to discuss this some more."

The Deputy Premier: "We can't spare the time. Can't you see, Herman's gone running off to warn Fordyce!"

The Minister of Justice: "I notice you didn't try to stop him. Why? When he told us not to get up, *you* hadn't even stirred in your chair, Citizen Minister."

Through the door came the distinctive howling rattle of ionization. Several ministers leaped to their feet.

The Minister of Justice's unpleasant voice cut through the confused murmur: "There's your reason. I notice, Citizen Minister, that once again you haven't even stirred."

A man in the uniform of the military police burst in, exclaiming loudly, "He was running. A terrible mistake has been made. He came out and started running, and we—"

The Minister of Justice interrupted even more loudly: "*And you obeyed orders.*"

"He came out and started running, and we thought it was somebody who—"

The Minister of Justice: "You needn't deliver the line *perfectly,* my man. You obeyed orders." The other ministers stared at the Deputy Premier.

A knot of men in uniform came in, like the legs of a huge spider, carrying something between them. They lowered their burden to the floor.

The Deputy Premier's voice cracked: "Why *here?*"

It was Herman Kalino's body, bulky, crumpled, hollowed out by a devouring burn.

The Deputy Premier: "*Morons! Why here?*"

The Minister of Justice: "You misunderstood your orders, citizens. We weren't supposed to see that."

A silence fell.

The first guard who had entered coughed and said, "He came running out—"

The Minister of Agriculture: "We know you can do it."

Silence fell again.

The Finance Minister: "Ch'ien, you're a doctor. Why don't you look at him? Maybe he's—"

The Minister of Health: "I like you better this way, Olivia—stupid."

The Minister of Justice: "Citizen Keyes, did you notice when he spoke of signing one another's death warrants, he said 'your colleagues'? He didn't use the pronoun 'we.' He knew he would be . . . the first to go."

The silence resumed.

The Minister of Justice: "He then said a strange thing. He said he had read the Election Law. I think I'll go to some safe place now and read that law."

A Nasty Little Bird appeared with black borders. The headline read: ASSASSINATION. The article began: "Carl ap Rhys has had Herman Kalino murdered." It was a remarkably accurate account of the Cabinet meeting and a straightforward accusation that Carl ap Rhys, using his powers as Defense Minister, had substituted picked killers for the faithful army guard detail, and then had used trumped-up charges against an old and trusted friend of Premier Kalino's to flush the weary old man out to his death.

Then came a paragraph of sentiment: "We need not devote

space to Herman Kalino's life. Our readers know that life. He was the decent and loving father of a world." It looked like the sort of *de mortuis* thing one said in peacetime when a political opponent died, but it was the result of a difficult council of war—the Government was indiscriminately jamming all transmissions—with Simon de Ferraris. It initiated a new Rebel strategy, an attempt to put together a political coalition against Carl ap Rhys.

The last three paragraphs were Orders of the Day:

"Herman Kalino's death is another matter. An ancient principle of justice denies a murderer any legacy from his victim. But Carl ap Rhys intends to inherit Kalino's power.

"The young world now faces a major constitutional crisis. Under the constitutive Election Law, if the Premier does not resign, he can only be replaced by a *newly elected* Chamber. Herman Kalino did not resign. The only power Carl ap Rhys can now legally exercise is the power to set the date of new elections.

"We offer this slogan: *Elections now!*"

One of the more senior of the "girls" at The Pink Quail was a woman of indeterminate age and coloration who worked as a naive blonde named Mandy. Mandy drifted very casually up to Sue, with a tentativeness that showed she had been put up to it by others.

Sue was busy trying to put together in longhand some "Notes on the Constitutional Crisis." She was waiting for John Corander, that great tearing loving oaf, to return with the old judge from preparing a particularly dangerous foray. And her brain insisted on bringing forward images of Herman Kalino's affection for her as a little girl and his pride in her when, not recognizing her, he had known her again as a fellow revolutionist. She did not want to talk to Mandy.

Mandy: "Writing?" That was an unpromising start.

Sue: "Letter." She folded up the sheet of paper and shoved it into a pocket of her coveralls.

Mandy: "Who to?"

Sue made a meaningless gesture.

It satisfied Mandy, who was evidently working toward something else: "We were all waiting to see how long you'd hold out."

Sue, with mock contrition: "It wasn't *too* long, I hope."

This was lost on Mandy, who moved on toward her subject, whatever it was. "He *is* cute."

Sue: "Is that the word? Well, well, perhaps it is."

Mandy: "When you've had yours, I'd like to try him."

Sue: "Sorry, Mandy."

Mandy attempted to be mischievous. "Maybe *he'll* have something different to say."

Sue was astonished at the fury that welled up in herself, but she kept her tone even. "I'll kill you."

Even Mandy sensed something. She laughed nervously. "You couldn't kill anybody." It was obvious she was not sure.

Sue: "I've done it, Mandy. Quite a number of times."

There was a long silence.

Mandy: "What was it like?"

Sue, evasively: "Oh, you know, just—normal." There was more silence, and she found herself adding, with a reminiscent smile: "He's so big and enthusiastic about it, like an enormous goddamn puppy."

Mandy said, "Oh, you meant screwing! I meant killing. What's it feel like?"

Sue looked maliciously into the washed-out face. "Just—normal." Then she relented. "Mandy dear, it's not as good as sc-screwing."

Mandy thought for a few moments. "I know all about screwing," she announced. "So that's what Curly-Pirley meant! That's why you're hiding...I think a lot about death. Not my own, so much...Did you ever kill any women?"

Sue: "Yes. Two. Forget it, Mandy. Killing is overrated. Don't take it up. Stick to what you know."

Mandy: "Screwing is overrated. I know all about it...Being humped by some old coot with hair growing out of his nostrils. You'll see."

Sue: "I will?"

Mandy, rubbing it in: "His ears, too."

Sue laughed. "Did you come to see me because you girls are afraid I'm going on the line."

Mandy was admiring. "How'd you know that's what we were talking about?"

Sue: "I'd think the same way."

With an effort that showed piteously, Mandy achieved an honest statement: "You're young, you see, and—"

Sue: "Not young, Mandy. Just scrawny. Anyway, dear, don't worry. I'm going to stick to my puppy exclusively."

Mandy: "Puppy? Oh, you mean that sergeant. I thought you meant..."

NOTES ON A CONSTITUTIONAL CRISIS

We are an illegal newspaper. How many of us thought, a short time ago when we fought in the Revolution, that there could be such a thing on this planet as an *illegal* newspaper? But illegal we are, and therefore anonymous.

However, we think our readers ought to know that yesterday's first article—which, as we go to press, various official papers are planning to describe this morning as "a paranoiac's guesswork," "wild fabrications," "an insult to the Premier's memory," and "tasteless, conscienceless lying"—was written by Judge Mustafa Issachar, until recently Minister of Justice in the Kalino Cabinet, and still a deputy.

*   *   *

The "guard" who killed the Premier is one Frank M. Turnemi, 46 years old. He joined our army soon after the outbreak of the Revolution, quickly acquired the reputation of being an efficient soldier, and was recruited by the Internal Defense Department for undercover service within the armed forces. He was cashiered by the IDD for using torture, but continued in military service until the end of the fighting; he then obtained a transfer to the Capital District Police. When Carl ap Rhys set up the notorious Special Branch, Turnemi obtained a transfer to that. *Eight days ago,* he abruptly resigned from the Specials, reenlisted in the army, and, on direct orders from the Defense Minister, was assigned to the Premier's guard detail; all this took place in one afternoon.

(202)

In our next issue: the edifying biography of another member of the Premier's "guard."

* * *

The constitutive Election Law provides that unless the Premier resigns to the Speaker of the Chamber, he can only be "replaced" by a Chamber elected within the previous twenty days. This law was drafted by Herman Kalino. Since Kalino was not a lawyer, he worked on the Election Law in the home of, and with the help of, an experienced lawyer, Mustafa Issachar. See above.

* * *

"Spokesmen" for the Cabinet argued yesterday that the Election Law did not "contemplate" the Premier's sudden death. The Law "meant," they said, that a Premier can only be "removed against his will" by a freshly elected Chamber. A Premier's death, they maintained, "has the legal effect" of a resignation. We do not know who these "spokesmen" are—only the official press has seen or heard them. If Herman Kalino had "meant" to say "removed," he would not have said "replaced." Anyway, the Premier *has* been "removed against his will"—and not by a freshly elected Chamber, but by the Deputy Premier. To argue that dying is legally the same as resigning is really to argue that being murdered is legally the same as committing suicide.

Curiously enough, no one has heard from the Minister of Justice on this question. One would have thought that he, of all members of the Cabinet, would have had an opinion to offer. Come forth, Citizen Seiffert!

* * *

Even when Herman Kalino was alive the Cabinet showed itself unable to govern. It was contemptible. It had most of the military matériel on this planet and all the means on this planet for producing more, yet it could not put down an insurrection by amateurs. It had unlimited power over the economic life of this planet, yet it could not—or would not—prevent a disaster that has engulfed the savings of the old, the hopes of the young, the capital of the employer, the wages of the workingman, and all that we had fought the Empire to call our own. It controlled the venal press and all the technology of propaganda, yet no one believed in it. But it had Herman Kalino. He was powerless, held almost a prisoner by his Deputy Premier, but he was there; and because he was there, most of the population declined to rise with the insurgent bands. Now he is gone.

There is now only one way Carl ap Rhys can rule: by fear. He will not mind that—he will rather enjoy it, in fact. He will exploit people's fear of the vast machinery of government. And the insurgents will now proceed to dispel that fear.

Chapter 22

THE other Imperial bureaus had been sacked and burned out when the Revolution broke out, but the Bureau of Currency's stark white building out on Galen Circle was something of a fortress. The Imperial authorities could not conceive that the colonials on Rohan might ever want anything more than they wanted Imperial money—that they might want a currency of their own, for example—and they certainly had never heard of a currency that nobody wanted.

At one point, a single company of Imperial infantry, surrounded and slowly starving, held the Bureau for three weeks against four thousand Revolutionary militia. Then Surabaya took thought; a Pinsker Capsule went out; a flitter from Pradjani's headquarters signaled the order to the survivors in the Bureau, who destroyed the engraved plates for printing the Imperial currency and surrendered. They had proved (a) that good men could serve a bad cause and (b) that the Bureau was impregnable.

This morning its white austerities glared in the warm sun. Galen Circle seemed drowsy; the capital's fuel supplies were dwindling and the vehicular traffic was thin. Even the pedestrians seemed to lack energy, as if waiting for the outcome of some process, somewhere else, in which they had a great stake but played no part. Several had perched on the low wall of dressed stone that surrounded the tiny park in the Circle. One of these idlers, a middle-aged man, opened his battered attaché case and was squandering his neatly wrapped lunch on the tree lizards, tame little six-legged beasts that lived in the park. He turned to his neighbor on the wall, a tall, very thin, bemedaled soldier with a shaven head and a crumpled nose, and asked, "Why do I feel like it was a holiday?"

The soldier replied, "History."

"That's it," the bureaucrat said eagerly, "big events give me this holiday feeling. I say to myself, 'All bets are off now.' I say, 'It doesn't matter.' The little things, you know, don't matter—the deadlines, the things we owe, all those mistakes. Why go in?" He shrugged one shoulder toward the Bureau.

The soldier: "Why indeed?"

The bureaucrat: "I'll sit here for a while, I—"

He had lost his audience. The soldier's humorous face had crinkled into a grin, not at the bureaucrat but at someone across the road, and he had hurried away.

"Ah, Major."

Corander looked up from the wheelchair he was pushing, found the source of the greeting amid the lazy swirl of passersby, and found himself smiling. "T. Walter Hines, I believe."

"An outmoded belief," said the long thin soldier. "The latest scholarship tends to support the theory that I'm M. Roland Worth." He glanced dubiously at the ancient paralytic in the wheelchair. Corander reassured him with a nod. The soldier resumed: "And I take it you're not employed as a major just now."

Corander: "As a male nurse to a distinguished but unhealthy deputy. His name is Rademis. Mine is Murphy."

M. Roland Worth leaned over and inspected the unhealthy deputy, who wagged himself in a vigorous rendition of Levkranz's Syndrome. "A convincing deputy. Except that he reminds me somewhat of somebody who did something..."

"I *am* a deputy," came a precise whisper from the jerking upper quarters of the ancient, "but I *was* a judge, and I sentenced you to a year's hard."

The soldier: "Quite so." He lowered his own voice to a breath: "Judge Issachar."

Mustafa Issachar: "Quite so. I want you to think of me as Deputy Rademis. You were H. Lewis Frame in those days."

The soldier: "Yes, I was, wasn't I?" He sighed. "I was happy as H. Lewis Frame. Is that Parkinson's you're doing? Nobody uses Parkinson's—you have to have something untreatable."

"It's Levkranz's," whispered Mustafa indignantly. "Citizen Murphy, to business!"

Corander: "I'm afraid we must move on, Citizen Worth. It's time for us to walk around the Circle, taking the sun. But you may accompany us, if not otherwise engaged." He let his eyes roam warningly over the men and women strolling past.

The soldier murmured, "Quite so...I shall take the sun *with* you," he said in his normal tone of pompous ebullience, and dropped his voice again: "You seem to have taken up my line of business."

Corander: "In a rather large way."

The soldier looked toward the Bureau. Corander nodded.

Inspector Rivers' return took The Pink Quail by surprise because it occurred in mid-morning. Corander and Mustafa were out at Galen Circle. Sue, on whom the whole responsibility of *A Nasty Little Bird* had fallen for several days, was dozing in her room. Most of the girls were out and others still asleep. Pirley had just come back from a meeting with his syndicate. He faced the big policeman in the manager's office behind the cabaret.

Rivers was bleakly triumphant. "You were wrong—or lying. I've checked. She *is* Simon de Ferraris' daughter."

Pirley could not believe this. On the other hand, he could not have believed that "Susan"—the fugitive, the naked entertainer, the heroine of that haunting bout with the sergeant—had once been the terrible Chief of the IDD, except that he knew it to be so. "Somebody's crazy," he said.

Inspector Rivers: "Or dumb. You. Don't try to put me off this time, Pirley. I get what I want from that quim, everything, or I'm taking you in. And you'll never come out. Things are hotting up now, and nobody's going to ask questions about a little fairy pimp."

Pirley, scarcely above a whisper: "All right, I'll go tell her. Wait here."

As Pirley reached the door, the inspector said, "Oh! and faggot..."

Pirley stopped. "Yes?"

Inspector Rivers: "If you're thinking of trying something, you little faggot, my office knows where I went."

Pirley: "Yes. I see ... I'll—I'll talk to her." He shut the door behind him and raced up to Sue's room.

She lay nude on the crumpled sheets.

"Sue," he said, "Sue!" He took her shoulder and shook her awake. It was the first time he had ever touched her. "Rivers is downstairs. No, no, listen to me. Don't run, listen to me. And trust me ... I want you to let me send him up."

The girl went white. "Pirley, I can't. I can't."

Pirley: "*Nothing will happen.* Let me send him up. Then give me five minutes. Exactly five minutes, and—and he's got to be busy, and he has to have his pants off. But not—but not—"

Sue, with the faintest tremor in her voice: "Five minutes. No penetration. But concentrating on me. And bare-assed. Go to it, Pirley. And Pirley..." She stopped him. "In case things go wrong—" She kissed him softly on the mouth.

At the door, Pirley unscrewed the handle from the bolt, slid the shaft out of its cylinder, and pocketed it. He turned. "Sue, if things *don't* go wrong, promise me you won't hate me either."

Inspector Rivers: "Well?"

Pirley: "You know where the room is?"

The big man walked calmly out of the office. He exuded the aura—the reek—of male power and contempt. Pirley reached into his desk and took out a small blast-pistol, checked it, put it in his left pocket, then moved swiftly to a cupboard and unlocked it. The contents were neat, as Pirley himself was neat; his hands scattered them until he found a gray box labeled "Where is thy sting?" Inside was a large old-fashioned hypodermic syringe, a long needle already in place, and three vials. He retracted the plunger, fitted a vial into the clamp, and, carefully holding the syringe out of sight in his pocket, walked through the stagnant dimness of the cabaret.

Outside Sue's room, he consulted his watch, listened, and heard her whimper. He pushed the door open, in furious haste, but smoothly.

The inspector had arranged the girl to his liking and was

just preparing to cover her, his body hunched over hers like a huge pale turnip. Pirley stepped soundlessly forward; with his left hand parted the man's tight white buttocks, exposing and stretching the rosette; with his right inserted the needle of the hypodermic, turned it, pushing it into the wall of the rectum, and pressed home the plunger; with his left drew his blaster; with his right pulled out the syringe and threw it aside; stepped back and faced the twisting, howling man.

Rivers charged him, but Pirley raised the weapon silently toward the oncoming face. The big man stopped and mastered himself. "What was that?" he said thickly. His pale chest heaved; the flush died from his face.

Pirley: "A sedative, Inspector. A mild depressant. I've changed my mind. Sue, dress. I've decided to give Susan a chance to escape. As you say, Inspector, your office knows where you are. Knowing where you are, they won't expect you back for a few hours. You will soon begin to perspire, and to feel exhausted and sleepy. You will actually sleep for some time. I see you are perspiring already."

The inspector began to curse.

Pirley: "Do be quiet. You can't avoid the effects, and if you annoy me any more, I'll do a few things to you while you're asleep that will ... affect your enjoyment of life, shall we say? You *are* a stupid bastard, Inspector. You've just called me a pervert, but it hasn't dawned on you what that means. I enjoy some things you've never heard of. I enjoy them immensely. You're in the hands of a pervert—totally. Your respiration rate is changing, I see. On schedule. Your speech should, as they say, become dysarthric now."

The inspector subsided, and stood staring at his tormentor with a sort of gathering blankness. Sue finished dressing, in rather mannish coveralls and walking boots; she sat down silently on the edge of the bed.

A hoarse whisper from the inspector: "Can I si' d'—si' duhhh?"

Pirley: "No, you may *not* sit down. When you're weak enough, you'll collapse without asking. Be patient." Silence fell.

A few minutes later, the great white body sagged, heaved itself upright, and toppled. The girl stood up.

Pirley: "Sit down, Sue." He advanced cautiously on the fallen man, rolled him on his back, and examined his eyes. "Ahead of schedule," he murmured. "It was a heavy dose. I think he can still hear me. *Can you?*" he snapped viciously at the inspector.

The inspector's head lolled, and he grunted unintelligibly.

Pirley: "Good. Because I want you to know I lied to you. That wasn't a sedative. It was a modified insulin, a heavy overdose. Your'e in hypoglycemic shock, and you'll die soon, of what they'll put down as 'cardiac insufficiency.' No one will know you were killed, Inspector. This form of insulin works fast—faster than the hormone—and then breaks down in a few hours, completely. And I injected you inside the anus where no one looks for needle marks. It'll all be natural—as *natural* as you were. We'll give you a good send-off. We'll tell your office you died in the saddle. I think he missed the last part. He's out."

Sue said steadily, "I don't think your cover story will work. They can tell if a man had intercourse or not within hours before he died."

Pirley knelt and checked the inert form. "You're right." From his pocket he produced the pieces of the door bolt. "Here. Put these back. I promised him a good reputation, didn't I? What a reputation I'll give him!... Ah, now we get the my-oclonus, and the grabbing movements. That should make it interesting. After a while, the pupils—you see they're very dilated now—will suddenly become tiny, and we'll be too late; we'll be in the midbrain, and the prostate won't respond: but that's not yet. We have time. That is to say, *I* have time. Is the door fixed? Please wait outside, Sue." He bolted the door behind her and knelt to his task, aware of the excited contraction of his own pupils.

The three companions moved around Galen Circle on the walk outside the vehicular channel. A laborer, leaning on a hand power-shovel and contemplating a small hole he had made in the pavement, stooped, picked up a piece of paving, and trudged toward the Bureau, his power-shovel on his shoulder.

A smartly uniformed guard came to attention, boomed, "Good evening, Deputy," and drifted toward the Bureau.

Another guard, less smartly turned out than the first, ignored them and was ignored in turn.

In this fashion the three made a complete circuit, singling their own people out of the throngs: ostensible bureaucrats, dull-faced and unexceptionable; military police; workmen with specialized equipment such as drills, cables, detonators, and cutting torches; the driver of a small, bright red delivery truck (DANGER—ACID), which he had driven halfway up onto the walk; and the policeman who stood hectoring the driver to remove the truck.

A large, six-wheeled lorry was lumbering around the Circle. Its open body, painted a pale, sour green, held a large piece of machinery; its cab was lettered in orange: F. CLOODGE & SONS. As it growled past the three, the driver's mate lifted an arm in unemphatic greeting. The three moved toward the Bureau at a brisker pace.

The next day's *A Nasty Little Bird:*

HOW IT WAS DONE

It took only a small squad of insurgents to capture the Bureau of Currency's fortress on Galen Circle. Some dressed up as workmen, some as minor Government officials, some as police, and one even pretended to be that venerable member of the Chamber of Deputies and former petty larcenist, William Brennan Rademis, who had been much too shaky to get to the Chamber in a long time but whom the official press still likes to call a "stalwart" of the Freedom Party.

One of the insurgents wheeled a large carboy of supposed "engraver's acid" in at the front entrance and past the overweight heroes of Security. At the rear bay, a truck unloaded a supposed printing press. This turned out to be a device which, when it was attached to the ventilation machinery of the building and filled with the contents of the carboy, forced 2,4-delta-hydropilean-drinol vapor into every room and corridor of the Bureau—2,4-delta-etcetera smells like Arcturan violets but it is a powerful anesthetic. Outside, a number of uniformed "guards" quietly compelled the real guards to step inside the building, where they fell asleep, while the pseudo-guards kept everyone else from entering. Inside, an insurgent demolition team, wearing gas masks,

(211)

dragged the unconscious printers to safety, blew up the Bureau's presses, and cut up its plates and designs. Then they drove all the newly overprinted currency to Pauling Park, opposite Special Branch headquarters, and burned seventy billion units.

"Security" at the Bureau comprises 72 persons, every one of whom can feed himself and his dependents out of Government commissaries. The whole invading force comprised 28.

As we go to press, the young intellectual who plagiarized his way through the School of Communications at Borlaug and has sunk to writing the lead editorials for *The Independent* has handed in his copy. He says: "A ruse of this kind proves nothing. Just as it is one thing to rob a bank and another to prove it bankrupt, a raid like this leaves the Government (and the people of Rohan) poorer but not discredited. *Any* government would be vulnerable to," &c., &c., &c.

Well said, Burton Klein! But did you want them to *storm* the Bureau? The whole people of this planet could not storm that building when it was held by one small band of infantrymen from Terra. But the Terrans went back to Terra.

The point is, the Government is one big bluff, and the raiders at Currency have called it.

However, since storming you want, Burton, storming you'll get. Read our next issue.

[Burton Klein had sent over the text of his editorial himself.]

From the same issue of *A Nasty Little Bird:*

THE CASE OF THE POWERFUL CATAMITE

Some of our readers complain that we've gotten too staid. One of them asks, "Why don't you call yourselves *A Clean Canary?*" We'll try to do better. To begin with:

Willis M. Rivers, shield number 37095, Deputy Chief Inspector of the Special Police Branch, is dead at 53. In the line of duty, more or less, Inspector Rivers has killed 23 men, 14 women, and 4 children, with 11 "possibles."

While the insurgents were wrecking the Bureau of Currency, Inspector Rivers was in a bordello, where he died of natural— well—*almost* natural—causes. He died of cardiac insufficiency and vascular collapse. He leaves (as they say) a widow, a secretary, and the young wives of two youthful political prisoners—that on the female side alone. His colleagues in the Specials wonder why, with "suspects" to "interrogate" and prisoners' families to intimidate, Inspector Rivers should have to patronize a brothel. It seems there was another side to the inspector. Ah, but what manner of lover could produce such shattering joys?

* * *

The computer display: "IR786522CASE31935MASTER-SONHC111226257PROGRAM67PROGRAMBEGINS . . . CIT HAS BRT REL RCDS?"

The tax examiner looked severely at the gray little man. "You were told to bring your records with you. *Have* you brought your records with you?"

Citizen Harold C. Masterson meekly indicated the large carton, crammed with bursting envelopes and disheveled paprite forms, that he had just placed on the table in front of him.

The tax examiner looked at the carton for a short while, as if weighing alternative explanations for the carton, then transferred his gaze back to Citizen Masterson. "Well?"

Citizen Masterson: "These are my records, sir—pardon me—citizen."

The tax examiner: "These are the relevant records?"

Citizen Masterson, humbly: "Well, Citizen Examiner, I didn't know what you wanted to ask, so I brought them all."

The tax examiner's patience was rapidly being exhausted. "So, these *are* or are *not* the relevant records?"

Citizen Masterson could not see the display screen; he saw the slight greenish glow it cast from below on the examiner's face, and the effect was alien. "They're all the records I have, Citizen Examiner. Excuse me, Citizen Examiner—"

The tax examiner: "So your records are incomplete." With one finger he poked at his keyboard: "NOT COMPLETE."

The round little man blinked and shrugged helplessly. "They're all I have. Really. Excuse me, Citizen Examiner—"

"Well, we'll soon find out just how incomplete they *are*...Do you have a *respiratory* infection of some sort?"

Citizen Masterson: "I don't see what...No, but I—"

The tax examiner: "Then *stop sniffling*." Then he relented and said humanely: "You have nothing to be upset about, as long as you're *honest with the People of Rohan*." He knew the next line of Program 67 but by force of habit glanced at the display screen, just as it was seized by a horrible alphanumeric paroxysm and went blank. But he was almost sure that, for a few microseconds before the end, he had glimpsed the words: "BUREAUCRATS SCREW YOURSELVES."

Citizen Masterson, like a man who has fallen off a surface ship and continues to swim, all alone in the middle of an ocean, was continuing to try to ingratiate himself. "Citizen Examiner, excuse me, it's none of my business, of course, but do you smell something burning?"

The tax examiner straightened his shoulders and lifted his chin. "Let's stick to the *subject,* shall we?" Fixing Citizen Masterson with his eyes, he pulled open a desk drawer and fumbled for a paprite tablet.

Citizen Masterson: "Of course, of course! I just—"

The tax examiner: "*Just* what do you *do*, Citizen Masterson?"

Citizen Masterson: "Do? Oh! I see. I did own a little—"

The tax examiner: "One thing at a time, *please*." He began to write on his tablet, pronouncing with a kind of scornful distinctness as he did so: "Mas. Ter. Son. Ha. Rold. Seeeee."

Citizen Masterson: "One-one-one two-two six-two-five-seven. Well, I owned a little—"

This time he was interrupted by the flinging open of the cubicle door and the bounding entrance of a large young man in assault armor, complete with still-fuming hopper-pack; he carried a ray-carbine and was accompanied through the door by a swirl of acrid smoke.

The tax examiner, through lips that would hardly obey him, managed to say, "Wrong room."

The trooper looked around at the files. "Better leave, chumlies. In one minute you won't be able to."

The tax examiner rose with dignity and began to assemble some personal possessions, selecting with care, voicelessly forming the word "chattels."

Citizen Masterson: "May I take my records with me, sir?"

The trooper: "They're yours, aren't they?"

Citizen Masterson, timidly: "Would you burn them too, sir? My business has failed anyway. These are *back* taxes." In a rush: "They don't want the money, you know. That's not what taxes are for. They print it, and they don't want it back. It isn't worth anything. Under the Empire, I had a small business. They wouldn't let it grow; the Empire. It was my life; a small business, a small life. Now I have no business. Harold C. Masterson is no longer a reactionary element. Or any element of any—"

The trooper, gently: "Stand farther away, then... No charge for that. Both of you, out. Use the north staircase." He pointed with his huge glove.

"Corander," said Citizen Wells, "do you think you could untwine yourself from my libido long enough to take on a patient?"

Corander: "No."

Citizen Wells: "Wrong answer. Leggo my fundament and listen, you fractious youth. You were a promising psychotherapist once, before you took to high treason and nibbling the behinds of older women; I want you to see a man Mustafa knows. He's old, very dilapidated. But he knows what's under this city."

Pvt. Thersites, the flexible blond military affairs editor of *A Nasty Little Bird*, came to The Pink Quail with some copy. She had, as she put it, milked a good deal of information about the impending trial of General Fordyce from her own general, and she was elated. "Cressida by night, Thersites by day."

In Sue's room, she peeled the clothing from her handsome midsection. "Just a sec," she said; "it's here under my well-informed quarters," delving with two long elegant fingers into a small pocket in the crotch of her panties. "Lechery, lechery; still, wars and lechery; nothing else holds fashion:

a burning devil take them! Here." She retrieved a tiny, closely written wad of paprite and held it out to Sue. "Why, what's the matter?"

Sue said obscurely, "I just remembered something." She shook her head gloomily. "I'm a monogamist."

Pvt. Thersites raised her sleek head as a step sounded in the hall, but did not hurry to restore her clothing. There was a single tap at the door, it opened; and Corander came in, halted at the sight of the blonde with Citizen Wells, and then grinned somewhat apprehensively.

Pvt. Thersites: "Here's Agamemnon, an honest fellow enough, and one that loves quails; but he has not so much brain as earwax. Oh, Johnny, Johnny! How wonderful to see you again!" She threw her arms around him and ground her torso against his torso and her mouth against his mouth.

Corander: "Hullo, Mrs. Penstock—ouch!—Madge—ouch!—never mind, we'll stop at 'Madge.'"

Citizen Wells breathed: "Oh gawd, I *am* a monogamist!"

Citizen Wells began to read Mrs. Penstock's copy:

"'THE WAR, FROM UNDERNEATH By Pvt. Thersites Four days from now, a general court-martial will convene—*not* in the seventh-floor hearing room at the Ministry of Defense, nor at any barracks, armory, or camp, but in Building 6112, a dusty, forgotten army warehouse near the spaceport. Building 6112 is the ideal spot for this particular court-martial. No one will know how to find Building 6112 unless he has been instructed. And with the incessant noise of aircraft no one who gets there will hear much of the "trial."

"'Citizen Rhys, having appointed himself Minister of Defense, has appointed the members of the court, appointed the prosecuting officers, appointed the *defending* officer, and even appointed the spectators. And of course, it was he who appointed the victim: Major General Walter B. Fordyce, Sr., a 57-year-old professional soldier...'"

Citizen Wells: "I like this... Well, well. Good.... This is good."

"'...commanded by the general's youngest son, Wally Jr., a Rebel lieutenant. (The prosecution will make a lot of the fact that the general *nevertheless* signs himself "Walter B. Fordyce, Sr.")

"'The "judges," the three homicidal clowns Carl ap Rhys has picked to destroy General Fordyce for him, are...'"

Citizen Wells: "This is *important*." Her eyes reflected the naked lights in the wan room and seemed to dance. "You're sure of these details? The location of the warehouse? The arrangements?"

Mrs. Penstock, comfortably: "Everything, my child, everything. I just hope my sources haven't dried up for good.

> "*Full merrily the humble-bee doth sing*
> *Till he hath lost his honey and his sting;*
> *And being once subdued in armèd tail,*
> *Sweet honey and sweet notes together fail.*'"

Citizen Wells: "Then we can't run this. No, Madge, don't you see? If they knew we knew all this, they'd change their plan. *And this is the plan for us!* Corander, go find Desmond Feigenbrod."

The QMG's crew finished preparing Building 6112, passed inspection, and drove off. Immediately, a six-wheeled military truck bearing the inscription 2D BATTN 1ST MIL DCT E S CORPS drew up. The driver, a knobby, redheaded sergeant, alighted and, peering at a crumpled trip-slip, approached the nearer of the two sentries.

"Evening, Corporal. This"—he held the trip-slip at various distances from his eyes, as if he were playing the slide trombone—"six-one-one-two?"

The sentry: "I guess so. Six-one-one-two. Whatever *that* is. You can't go in. *I* can't go in either."

The sergeant passed over the trip-slip. It was illegible. "I *think* it says six-one-one-two. That *is* a six, wouldn't you say?"

Sentry: "That's a six all right. All I know is, two things, they put a lot of chairs in today, and you can't go in."

Sergeant: "Tables, too."

Sentry: "*Some* tables."

Sergeant: "But the question is, what didn't they take out?"

Sentry: "They didn't take anything out. It was empty before."

Sergeant: "No sweep, then."

Sentry: "No what?"

Sergeant: "Sweep. Electronic sweep. They didn't do one." He gestured toward the stenciled markings on the truck. "Electronic Surveillance Corps." He lowered his voice. "Listening devices. Looks like a big job. Half the night."

Sentry: "You here to put in listening devices?"

Sergeant: "No, take 'em out. Think they want them listening in?" He hand-signaled the truck. Four other noncoms jumped down and came over, carrying various items of technology.

Sentry: "Who?"

Sergeant: "Same people they don't want *going* in, I guess. Think they ever tell *us* anything? All right, boys, let's get started. Big job. Half the night."

Corander took out the QM-W61 skeleton key Corporal M. Wilson Greene had obtained for him, herded Feigenbrod, Binswanger, and Lieutenant Fordyce, carrying their cutting tools, into Building 6112, and shut the door in the sentry's face.

Someone yelled, "Please rise, the court is coming!" but just then a copter settled noisily somewhere near Building 6112, and only the spectators in front stood up. The cry was repeated and the rest of the audience obeyed hastily. The stone-visaged judges marched in. The law officer and prosecuting officers saluted and reported. The accused was brought in under guard, saluted the court, and placed himself at attention in the dock. The defending officer, sallow and tremulous, saluted and reported. The president of the court read the charge sheet aloud. "Accused Fordyce, do you plead guilty or not guilty to these charges?" The accused pleaded not guilty in a healthy ringing voice. The judges erased momentary frowns of surprise from their faces. A civilian stalked from behind the spectators into the open area before the judges.

"If it please this honorable court, my name is Charles Seiffert, I am the duly appointed Minister of Justice, and I wish to represent the interests of my Department at the trial."

The President of the Court: "*And* just what are the interests of your civilian Department in a military trial, Citizen Minister?"

The Minister of Justice: "If you are familiar with the constitutive laws, General, you will know that my prescribed oath as Minister of Justice binds me to 'faithfully oversee and direct the administration of justice.' It does not distinguish between civilian and military justice. Does the honorable court wish to assure me that no justice will be administered in this trial?"

The President of the Court: "That remark is—is—"

The Minister of Justice: "'Contumacious' is the word you want, General, but the remark was not contumacious. It was not even a remark, but a question. I am listening respectfully. I hear no answer."

The Law Officer: "If it please the court, the court is convened under Section Three-two, Article Eight, of the Military Code. Consequently the trial does not, I believe, fall under the civilian administration of justice."

The President of the Court: "So much for your question, Citizen Minister. I shall consult my brother judges as to whether—"

The racket of another copter interrupted, and as it receded, the Minister of Justice cut in smoothly: "Before you consult your brother judges, General, may I respectfully remind you that you and your brother judges and the Law Officer are all commissioned officers in the army, that you have all taken oaths to 'uphold' the constitutive laws, that the Military Code is *not* a constitutive law while the law establishing my jurisdiction *is* a constitutive law, and that the breaking of your oath is a punishable offense under Section Three-four, Paragraph Eight-two, of the same Military Code you cite?"

The President of the Court: "The court will recess briefly for a conference in—ah—chambers."

The judges and the Law Officer moved toward a small door in the far wall of the warehouse, and the audience began to disintegrate into chattering groups. "Ulrich!" called Seiffert. "*You* can't go in there."

The chief prosecuting officer, in the act of following the judges and the Law Officer through the door, paused without looking round. Two aircraft came in just over Building 6112, rattling the joints of the structure and raising clouds of dust, and the spectators could not hear what the Minister of Justice then said, but the prosecutor went back to his table.

The Minister of Justice was walking toward the defense table when the Law Officer reappeared. The judges followed. Their bearing was noticeably more military than before. To the faintly audible accompaniment of ceremonial bellowing, they took their seats, and instead of waiting for the beating, plosive noise of the copters to subside, the President of the Court Martial began to address the Minister of Justice. Not a word could be made out. Among the other judges and the prosecution, smiles flickered from face to face. Looking stead-

(219)

ily at the Minister of Justice, who stood baffled and red, the President pointed toward the spectators' seats.

The noise rose to an intolerable howl. There was a sharp crack. Building 6112 shuddered. Then, with a screech of tearing metal, the segment of the warehouse where the judges sat began to waver upward, floor and all. Like a huge burst crate, it swung away from the rest of Building 6112 in a lurching arc, dangling on four cables from a heavy freight copter.

For the first second, the three judges and the law officer were rigid; then the giddy swaying of their container broke them, and just as they were pulled upward and out of sight, they were seen to fling themselves on the floor and clutch at each other.

Building 6112 then fell to pieces, and two hundred appalled men and women sat in the open skeleton of the structure and looked around into the wave-guides of a cordon of Pegrim's dusty veterans.

A voice roared, "Hands on top of your heads, and stay absolutely still!" With almost trancelike slowness, the crowd obeyed. A small, incongruous copter with Public Health insignia appeared and hovered just over the lacy trusses that had supported the roof of Building 6112. Dust swirled, stinging and strangling. A ladder unreeled into the hiatus left by the removal of the judges' module.

A somewhat pudgy figure detached itself from the Rebel cordon, clambered over the collapsed shards of the building, walked up to the accused, coughed, and said, "I think I owe you this, Pop."

General Fordyce: "You're a good boy." Following his son's gesture, he swarmed up the ladder into the Public Health copter, which, with a final eructation of dust, darted away.

Lieutenant Fordyce clambered back toward his men. "All *right,* Doggies, let's *move!*" Dog company double-timed to its transport, and the din built up.

Charles Seiffert looked after the vanishing Rebels. "It's pretty," he said to the world at large, "but is it Art?"

"Morally," observed *A Nasty Little Bird,* "it was important to get General Fordyce away from Old Slit Trench and the Giant Midget and Pryke the Proke and Pop Necessity and

Handoid Android (as we affectionately call them at the Ministry of Defense). Politically, this experiment shows that the Government cannot govern. It can hardly even oppress. Elections now!"

CHAPTER 23

EVERY morning the Government went to work with less authority. Pegrim's veterans were now striking almost at will in quick, bloodless raids on ministries and bureaus, sometimes burning records, sometimes jumbling them. In one such raid, the employees of the Agency for Economic Improvement—known to the embittered as "AEIOU" or "the Vowels of Compassion," and notoriously a skinnerbox for the extreme left wing of the Freedom Party—were herded out to some neglected housing nearby and forced to clean the multi-hovels of the actual poor, the New Poor.

Rebels assaulted the Ministry of Justice buildings in regiment strength, one entire battalion swarming through the IDD, which, though it now belonged to Carl ap Rhys' Ministry, had never had time to move its offices. Just as the raid began, the forgotten standing dead-wave generator on the roof came to life and erected its electromagnetic shell, inside which the daylight abruptly dimmed to a yellowish twilight and radiocommunications ceased.

This operation, unlike the rest, was directed by civilians

and was not bloodless. An old man in threadbare black, aquiline and remorseless, and a dark-eyed young woman superintended the destruction—for the most part, highly selective destruction. Only on the IDD floor was there anything like the gutting that had marked some previous raids. Rooms 32 and 40 were destroyed. Thousands of discs were rayed. From time to time soldiers brought certain discs and documents to Citizen Wells, where she stood among the burst-open central files. She bent to the disc-reader; and at length, with a face as pale as ice, went stalking through the smoke of the third floor.

"Reuper," she said to a cringing functionary, "I warned you *never to use torture again*," raised her blast-pistol, and executed him. "It turns out, Hendrix," she said to another, "that you faked the whole case against the Johnstons. You used the Department to murder them," and executed him also.

Swiftly the raiders withdrew, carrying eleven cartons of documentation. The Ministry was set free. The bright sky snapped on.

The rank and file of the Government staffs were by this time responding badly to the stress. Like an army in retreat, they began to lose cohesion. The whisper of "betrayal" which is more terrible than enemy pursuit had its counterpart here in gossip: "X had been too coincidentally absent the day of the raid." "Y had not looked surprised." "Z had smiled." Clean-desk men left letters unanswered and papers in disorder at the day's end. Knots of bureaucrats stood perpetually in corridors and corners, hazarding guesses that turned to rumors that turned to panics. Ninety percent of the daily work of any governmental office consists of making the record and looking busy; it was the ten percent consisting of productive effort that disappeared first.

The razing of Special Branch headquarters, even though that organization immediately set up new offices in commandeered space, gave courage to the citizenry. Moreover, before burning the offices out, the Rebels removed the Specials' files on their "auxiliaries." Rebel squads rounded up hundreds of informers and undercover political policemen, stripped them, sprayed them all over with a nearly indelible purple dye, and released them stark naked—"the shrinking violets"—to make their way to hiding through the terrible streets.

The populace began to show initiative: there were incidents, beatings, a threatened riot. Government troops were confined to barracks after dark. Both the Cabinet and the Rebels knew that New Nome had an incipient mob.

The Cabinet met frequently, under heavy guard. The Minister of Justice sent to ask for a roster of the guard detail, then declined to attend, pleading the press of work. The Minister of Agriculture appeared for one meeting, but not again. The Acting Premier called the Chamber of Deputies into session, naming a date which made it very nearly impossible to comply with the time limit set by the constitutive Election Law on holding elections for a new Chamber. Carl ap Rhys was going to fight.

Citizen Wells: "You rascal! Do you know what you've gone and done?"

Corander: "What a greeting!"

Citizen Wells: "You and that inflamed protuberance of yours have got me all pregnant...Hah! That made you jump a bit, didn't it? Took the smirk right off your beefy countenance, didn't it?"

Corander, tentatively: "You don't *seem* angry..."

Citizen Wells: "'Angry'! I'm happy. Gawd, I'm so happy! Do you know what's in here? There's a little person in here. Right here."

Corander: "Higher, I think."

Citizen Wells: "Here?"

Corander: "About there."

Citizen Wells: "You're so proud of yourself...Well, it's *my* little person now. You didn't take care of it, so it's mine. When it's born, I might let you play with it, if you're very humble. Take your chin out of my belly button, you lust-crazed peasant. Ouch! I'm glad you're happy too, Corander."

Mustafa Issachar: "Be seated, citizens. Brigadier, I take it your staff are all present? Thank you. We have a short time in which to frustrate a very good plot—a matter of three days, now. In these three days, we shall be playing a game of subtle violence, a classical game, composed of many small acts of force within rigid formal constraints. The stakes are high—total, in fact. I shall expound the game for you. It will remind you, perhaps, of chess."

Events were hastening to a parliamentary climax, for Carl ap Rhys' hold on his followers had been weakened by military defeat in the Peurifoy and the plains and by the raids on Government establishments, and he dared not adopt the very means by which he had been made to look ridiculous. He must operate under the temporary appearance of legality.

"He is afraid to break the laws," said Mustafa. "*You* would simply become the legal government. You have behaved most respectably; though you *were* perhaps unkind to bureaucrats and police spies. You have never printed money of your own or enacted laws of your own. You have been wise. You have not set up a rival government. One government is enough for any sensible person."

Carl ap Rhys had already tried unsuccessfully to bend the laws by arguing that Kalino's death was tantamount to resignation, so that he could succeed by a vote of the present Chamber.

"Why did Carl murder Herman?" Mustafa's dry voice faltered. "It may be that Carl was insane. '*Quos deus vult perdere prius dementat.*' But I think Carl murdered Herman because Herman stood in the way of a coalition between an Executive and a Chamber *both* bent on outliving their legal terms."

There was the danger. Carl dared not break and could not bend, so he must *change* the laws. It was easy enough to change an ordinary law—a simple vote of the Chamber would do it, and Carl ap Rhys could still carry that vote. But the law he must change was the Election Law, a constitutive law, and much harder to change. "If more than half of *all* the extant members of the Chamber vote to change a constitutive law, the law is changed. If there is a quorum present and two thirds of those present vote to change, it is changed. Not otherwise. A quorum is anything more than half the deputies. You can now do for yourselves the arithmetic Carl is doing at this moment."

But he proceeded to do it for them. There were one hundred seats. At least three were empty—those of Kalino, Kullervo, and Kullervo's victim. If ap Rhys could muster forty-nine votes, he would be certain of victory; but he could not—so Mustafa assured his hearers. But if only a bare quorum attended the session—again, forty-nine—Carl ap Rhys would need the votes of only thirty-three of them. "And thirty-three votes he assuredly has," said the old judge, and paused.

"He has a very simple strategy available. He will 'purge'

the Chamber. He will throw an armed cordon around it and select the members who can go in and vote."

Mustafa Issachar thought the Acting Premier could count on forty votes and would very likely muster forty-two. "In other words, if fewer than sixty-four deputies attend, we are lost.

"But why not take a leaf from Carl's book and keep *his* supporters out of the Chamber? We cannot. Carl may have some trouble keeping ours out, but the Government surely has enough force to convoy his in. Why not abduct or assassinate his deputies? I think for every vote of his we eliminated, we would throw two doubtful votes his way. I prefer a more conservative strategy.

"The task of smuggling good deputies into place consists of three parts: finding out who they are; finding out *where* they are; and actually getting them over, under, or through that cordon. I have met with Simon de Ferraris. He will marshal as many of his twenty-four deputies as are still alive. I shall marshal my bloc of thirteen and try to win over some more. Brevet Wing Commander Dennis Feigenbrod, Shulamith Wells, and Brevet Major John Corander—stand, please—will coordinate the smuggling—Feigenbrod over, Wells under, and Corander through. Questions?"

Brigadier Pegrim: "Why should ap Rhys wait till our deputies are on their way to the session? Why shouldn't he strike at them now?"

Mustafa Issachar: "He might. But he must be careful. Too soon, and he runs the risk of an outcry that will cost him support. He might chance that, however. Simon has hidden his deputies. I'm trying to persuade mine to hide, but some of them think I'm senile."

Brigadier Pegrim: "What is your guess, sir? How long before he moves?"

Mustafa looked at Citizen Wells.

Citizen Wells said, "Two days."

Corander: "Well, I'll tell you one thing you're not going to do, Citizen Wells. You're not going down into that conduit with our nice new person."

Citizen Wells: "Do you think it would get hurt?"

Corander: "I asked a doctor, and he said no, not unless *you* did. But my instincts—"

Citizen Wells: "I trusted your instincts before, didn't I?

(226)

And what did it get me? Deflowered. Pregnant. And now enslaved to Evolution or something."

Corander, hopefully: "And in love. Don't forget that."

Citizen Wells: "Oh, a woman always loves the man who took her virginity...What will I tell Mustafa?"

Corander: "Tell him you can run it from dry. You can, too. Old Hosig is half sane now; he can do all the wet. I'll talk to Mustafa."

She said in a low voice, "Let me talk to my father first."

Corander brightened. "Now you'll *have* to marry me."

Simon de Ferraris: "Shulamith, you have got to make an honest man of John Corander. What are you laughing about?"

Chapter 24

FOR two days, there was a shadowy war of watchers and counterwatchers. Then Carl ap Rhys moved. Teams of policemen—ordinary Capital Districters, Specials, or sometimes IDD men—suddenly appeared in quiet townships and neighborhoods and took the less wary of Mustafa Issachar's potential supporters into custody.

Morris Dempster was packing his best remaining clothes for the trip to New Nome, patting them tentatively into the battered suitcase and hoping the session would be brief so that he would not have to use his third shirt, the frayed one, when a hog-jawed inspector and three constables arrested him. The charge was sexually molesting an eight-year-old girl. Dempster sat for an unprosperous district on the southern edge of the Plain of Runes. He was sixty-seven, a retired pharmacist, a gentle widower living alone; he was as likely to molest an eight-year-old girl as to be sexually molested by one. Morris Dempster knew every policeman within a radius of fifty kilometers; these were outsiders. He knew that the "arrest" was a political abduction.

"Excuse me," he said timidly. "I was forgetting my kit." He was allowed to go to his old-fashioned "bureau" and came back with a cheap waterproof container for carrying depple, soap, and toothsticks.

His first emotion was more chagrin than fear. He had not believed the message Judge Issachar had sent; he had shooed away the watchers who said they were from Judge Issachar.

His second emotion came as he slumped between his silent captors in the big official groundcar. It sped past the town's police station, and he felt relief. At least he was being taken somewhere where he would not be known. Scandal, whether true or not, was adhesive.

The car tunneled through the loveliest autumn morning under high scattered clouds of pure white, toward what Dempster knew must be his gross, hurtful, probably screaming end in the cellars of the Special Branch, and his third emotion was an unfamiliar, bracing rage.

Peggy Carmichael was arrested for receiving stolen goods. She represented Borlaug, an institutional suburb: the general campus of the University of New Nome was there, a major hospital, a Government research center for plant epidemiology, and what had once been a distinguished preparatory school for boys and girls whose parents hoped to send them for higher education to Terra.

Peggy, whose two marriages had been dissolved by her wish, was forty, had never had children, and now had no lovers. She taught economics at the university, did academic chores at the prep school, and nourished her "independence." When Judge Issachar's message came, she had tartly refused to sell her vote for a few hours of unnecessary watchman service. When two groundcars spilled policemen around her small house, she tried to call her department chairman and the headmaster of the preparatory school, resenting the necessity. But when both men's vidiphone circuits were "busy," she was vouchsafed a vision of herself—the would-be heroine, whose bravery no one would know about, hustled to an ignominious death in the execution rooms of the Specials. She was tempted to make a break for it and get herself killed. Perhaps a neighbor would see *that,* at least.

Instead, when the charge was recited, she asked, like an unprepared student, "What stolen goods?" The answer: "You'll see them at the station." The "station" turned out not to be the local one; nor was it in the capital, for the groundcar turned southwest and took her off through the oblivious day.

Several Freedom Party deputies had refused to go into hiding but at least had been willing to accept surveillance from Mustafa Issachar. One was Lou Gelfinger, the business agent of Local 219 of the Interplanetary Brotherhood of Warehousemen and Freight-Handlers; he sat for a predominantly working-class district near the spaceport. Under Imperial rule, when the Brotherhood really was interplanetary and trade was profitable enough to rob, Gelfinger had become cheerfully familiar with violence. He was used to bodyguards.

The five policemen who converged on the booth in Quong's Diner where Lou Gelfinger was eating lunch saw a spare, stooped, rather helpless-looking man with kinky gray hair and with mournful brown eyes in an old tan face on which the skin seemed to have dripped like candlewax. Opposite him was a somewhat younger man, a typical freight-handler by the look of him, bulbous and unsuspecting. "Brother Kettelbart," said the older man, "let us put on our hats." As if preparing to leave, both men put on roll-brim stocking caps. The arresting officer, a Special, had got as far as "willfully misappropriating" in his prepared speech when one of the other policemen touched him on the arm. Behind the counter, Quong had put on a similar cap. In the corner, Quong's new waitress, who looked like an underage whore, had done likewise. "Brother Gelfinger," said Kettelbart, "let us roll down our brims." The sputter of stun-wave generation began. The five policemen were later found naked in a maternity ward in Borlaug Medical Center, but their groundcar, equipment, and uniforms were not found.

One "arrest" escaped from both plan and counterplan. Granger Kay made his home and practiced law in the provincial town of North Dunning and sat for North Dunning, Dunning's Bridge, and East Armstrong. Though a successful litigator, he was still known at thirty-two to his friends and his wife's friends as "Petey." Cynthia Kay was a handsome, athletic girl. Their daughter Mimsy was one and a half. None of Cynthia's friends had ever taken Petey to bed and he himself exhibited no interest in this method of relieving provincial boredom; and Cynthia, when her friends played cards for one another's husbands, would laughingly decline to join their game. They only invited her out of pity for her situation—they could not understand what she saw in her dull, immature spouse. He was taking on pudge.

He was at work in his neat office above a defunct savings association when the police arrived. He told his secretary to have them wait in the outer room for a moment, locked his office door, called his wife on the vidiphone and told her calmly, "Hide Mimsy with you-know-whom and disappear. Just *disappear*. If the other side finds either of you, it will cost me my life."

She knew his calm tone and took her orders. "You're saying if they get Mimsy or me, you'll give yourself up."

Granger Kay: "Precisely. I love you."

Cynthia Kay: "I love you. I'll kiss Mimsy for you. Be careful."

Granger Kay took a stunner from his desk, courteously admitted the three policemen, stunned them, apologized to his secretary ("This will cover you, Mrs. Flumm"), and, cutting off her desperate expostulations, stunned her; put the stunner in one pocket and a hand-blaster in another, put on a raincoat, filled its pockets with candy from his desk cache, took an SOS gun, his illegal souvenir of the Revolution, from behind the files, limped to the open window with it, destroyed the engine of the police ground-vehicle standing outside; and, taking care not to come down too hard on his beryl-steel left foot, raced up a service stairs and away across the roofs.

The Government agents sent to bring in Cynthia and Mimsy Kay found the cottage deserted. A few doors away, one of Cynthia's friends, abject after a single slap, suggested several places Mrs. Kay might have hidden the child, or be hiding with it; but none of these yielded a clue.

The resident director of Dole House actually shivered as he watched the Agency's program coordinator come down the corridor with Mick Amblaika hobbling after him. Mick, simian on his half-repaired legs, kept looking around him, as always; but this time the apprehensiveness of his skew eyes was replaced by a secret proprietary smirk, and he was humming a nursery tune.

Dole House was the second largest clinic for squeed addicts in New Nome and had by far the largest maintenance program for outpatients. The resident director was a big white-haired man whose once-rubicund presence had, as he knew, slowly collapsed; his face was now merely ruddy and anger-haunted. Once he had pronounced the phrases of his guild with a fine booming dominance ("We cannot attack the problem of addiction until we learn to live with the fact of dependence"), but now, seeing the prim-lipped bureaucrat and his crippled bully-boy approaching, he understood the hideous, inside-out applicability of those phrases.

Squeed addicts were maintained on prylantin, a synthetic euphoriant that blocked the delusional highs of squeed. Although even more strongly habituating than squeed, it was much less destructive. Consequently, in another of the old sonorous phrases, it "allowed the addicts to lead useful lives." Many addicts, however, had taken to squeed in the first place because they could not bear ordinary useful lives, and they still could not. Now, driven out of the casual job market by the diligent New Poor, they were unable to pay for treatment at a private center and were utterly dependent on the Government program. The resident director had complete power over them. He maintained them; he and no one else could transfer them to another Government center; he could disenroll them and leave them to their murderous cravings. "We cannot attack the problem of addiction until we learn to live with the fact of dependence." He had begun to use them—to use the younger women, to use the men spitefully for menial service. They had become *his* narcotic.

He was utterly dependent on the Government for them. Some time ago, the program had been transferred from the Ministry of Health to the Agency for Economic Improvement, and its budget was completely in the hands of a program coordinator there—this Klaensch. And Klaensch used him; the program coordinator used the resident director as the procurer of a group of civil slaves. When Klaensch needed a factional crowd for a Freedom Party rally, or Klaensch wanted informers and spies to work for the Special Branch, or Klaensch asked for petty criminals who would "rob" a political or departmental opponent and leave him half dead, the resident director had learned to live with these new extensions of the term "useful lives."

Then this wall-eyed Mick Amblaika had appeared. He, too, seemed to be in Klaensch's power—the resident director guessed that the long-drawn-out reconstruction of the youth's knees was in some way controlled by Klaensch's "budget"— but whatever pressure had been put on the wall-eyed boy, he seemed to enjoy his tactical management of Klaensch's crowd "work" and showed no fear or rage. In fact, his aura had grown more and more anticipatory and cruel.

Mick Amblaika's grin broadened and his humming broke out into words: "Ladybug, ladybug, fly away home—"

Program Coordinator Klaensch said in his precise way, "Good to see you, Citizen Pimberton."

"Citizen" Pimberton. It was never "Dr." Pimberton.

Mick Amblaika, affably: "Hey there, Pimberton."

The resident director hid his fear.

They all but pushed him into his office. They had come to talk about "tomorrow."

The resident director: "Tomorrow?"

Program Coordinator Klaensch: "The session."

The resident director: "Oh yes, I see. You want spectators—hecklers?"

Program Coordinator Klaensch: "Oh, the spectator gallery will be empty tomorrow." He smiled.

The Rebels' parliamentary War Room was in a disused basement pantry in a home for the aged. Mustafa Issachar, wearing a faded dressing gown that disguised him as a deteriorated inmate, presided over a large map of the continent laid out on a baker's table. He had borrowed a coin collection from a real inmate to use as markers, which he shoved here and there as Shulamith, Corander, and Desmond Feigenbrod brought him reports of the whereabouts of the contested deputies.

"Hakimian's in Safe House Three," called Feigenbrod. Dressed as a male nurse, he was working a small military com-set half hidden among a cupboard full of old pans.

Mustafa plucked a classic British shilling off the map and placed it in one of the twelve rectangles he had ruled on a sheet of paprite.

Shulamith, crisp in the white coveralls of a nurse, came down from the office vidiphone on the ground floor. "Gelfinger reached Safe House Eight, but there were some bad actors hanging around, and Brandy is sending him to Eleven instead."

Mustafa moved a twentieth-century zloty. "Nothing on Granger Kay?"

Citizen Wells: "He *would* go it alone. The only watch we could put on him was his secretary, and he couldn't know *that:* so he stunned her when he made his break. He's disappeared. The Village Bull is working on it upstairs."

Feigenbrod: "I've got one copter over the Perkin-Matsumora-Shockley triangle. You have Dempster, Judge? Dempster's in that triangle, still on Route Twenty-four, same car, headed east, eight kilometers west of Morley Station. But they're bringing Carmichael down into that triangle, southwest on Twenty-two; they're nearly at Matsumora. I can't follow her down; my copter up over Matsumora-Linsker-Borlaug has to watch poor Schmidt. So, if I have to choose between Dempster and Carmichael, which do I follow, which do I drop?"

Mustafa: "Follow Dempster."

Citizen Wells: "Dempster will be nearer New Nome, Judge. Carmichael will take longer to bring to the session when we lift her, so oughtn't we to lift her first?"

Mustafa: "Dempster's old...we don't know what they'll do to him here in New Nome. They might take him to headquarters. They're not set up for that sort of thing out in the hinterlands."

Citizen Wells: "Right. Carmichael afterward."

Some hours later, Corander came in and scowled at the map.

Citizen Wells: "Well, Village Bull?"

Corander: "Have you got something called the Hasping Dam?"

Morris Dempster was taken to a commonplace police station outside the capital. There, the hog-jawed inspector recited the charge to the desk sergeant. The old pervert, he explained, was being transferred to protect him from the little girl's neighbors. The station-house men abused Dempster and deliberately tore his old but sturdy and dignified suit as they shoved him down to the cells. This nearly broke him.

The groundcar that had brought in Dempster was speeding toward New Nome when the hog-jawed inspector, relaxing in the rear seat, noticed something on the floor. "Old fart forgot his kit." He opened it idly. Morris Dempster's old-fashioned suicide bomb exploded, fragmenting the vehicle and its four occupants.

Peggy Carmichael's destination was a very rural police station. Her captors told the locals she had been caught with the swag from a burglary and was to be held incommunicado for a day until she and the stolen property were identified; she had tried to warn her confederates by vidiphone. The locals signed for her. A heavy brown envelope, covered with official stamps and scribbles and called "the evidence," appeared. The locals signed for that, too. "The evidence" was locked in a safe and she was locked in a cell, alone.

Granger Kay had been a good officer in the Revolution until he got a foot burned off leading the forlorn hope in the attack on Langley. Now, sitting on the floor of the gauge room high over the Hasping Dam, munching candy and, with his eyes just above the sill of the paneless window, watching the daylight fail and the white planes of the dam turn into a romantic geometry of pink and gray, he felt...as if this were the end of a long recovery from his wound. His home, his marriage and child, and his legal and political successes seemed for the moment to have been only the pastimes of convalescence.

At either end of the dam, the enemy had posted several men with long-range small arms. They were lower than he, and he could not see over the window ledge for very long without presenting a target for snipers. He unscrewed the infrared sight of his SOS gun and, by mickeying the front prism, made a sort of periscope out of it, so that from time to time he could check to see that they were not rushing the tower along the causeway atop the dam. If they did, he could get most of them with a little plunging fire.

There was no reason to suppose they would rush him. They had only to keep him holed up for (say) ten hours, and he would miss the beginning of the special session. After the session, if they won, they could deal with him at their leisure.

He was sorry to miss the session, of course. He grasped its importance intellectually. But just now he would have been much sorrier to miss this skirmish.

He crawled to the stairhead, descended through the lightless cylinder of the tower several levels, and moved cautiously to a bright strip of light, a tiny window like a loophole—put there, he supposed, to run electrical cables through for limnological equipment or perhaps emergency gear. He slid this window open, drew his hand-blaster, fined down the beam control to needle thinness, and squinted down the waveguide, sighting directly along the dam. After a few minutes, he saw two of the enemy peering from brush cover toward his tower with what seemed to be heavy optics of some sort. He steadied the blaster and pressed the firing stud. There was a screech in the evening stillness, a brief flash of combustion at the target point. A charred body fell from the bushes. "*Nice,* Petey!" said Granger Kay aloud.

Morris Dempster opened his eyes, quickly glanced around his cell, and shut them again. His cellmate, a vast brute with a meaningless chuckle that gurgled periodically in his entrails like borborygmus, was lying on the other shelf bunk and staring blankly at him, silent.

The old deputy had lost track of time. He had long since pawned his watch. The lights here never went out, it seemed. There was no window to the cell, no variation in the bit of corridor he could see through the barred opening in the door, but it seemed to him to be nearly morning—the morning of the session. What had become of his homemade bomb?... And there was a noise, not the sort of noise there was any reason for in a police station, a sort of hiss or endless sigh, like compressed air escaping. Or like anesthetic gas just before an operation. If it was a gas, it smelled harmless enough, like the novelty "Arcturus violets" he sometimes used to sell in his shop. Probably the sound and the smell were really in his head. He did feel ill...

"One pharmacist, slightly shelf-worn," said one gas-masked soldier to the other, checking a written description, "but in generally good condition. The other thing's not ours. Let's go. You take the deputy's nice little feet."

Granger Kay, wide awake, caught the stealthy shuffle outside. He picked up his improvised periscope. The infrared device gave the nocturnal scene an eerie look, a negative look, and the oncoming men showed bright.

They were advancing from both directions along the narrow causeway on the top of the dam, seven from the right bank, four from the left. Their stealth had spoiled their synchrony. The seven from the right were distinctly closer than the other four. That was fortunate for Granger Kay.

He scrambled to the stairs and down to the window slot that faced the right bank, leveled his blaster, and fired into the tiptoeing group. The window was beautifully positioned: his first burst blew away half of the nearest man, the left arm and shoulder of the second, and the face of the fourth. The third man, scorched but not disabled, shrieked, and turned to run; he stepped heavily on the thrashing body of the fourth man and made as if to push the fifth out of his way and off the dam, but the fifth, sixth, and seventh men scampered ahead of him in a jostling panic. Granger Kay killed the nearest man and wounded the next.

No time to do more. He clattered up the stairs; feverishly restored the infrared gunsight to its proper alignment and put it back on the SOS; and, in order to sight and fire, rose above the sill of the window facing the left bank. He was badly exposed, but he had no choice. He could not let the enemy reach the base of his tower.

The group of four was advancing very slowly, perhaps unnerved by the sounds of the horror that had befallen their comrades; at any rate they were caught unprepared by Granger Kay's first combination shot. The radiation killed the foremost man, the explosion of the tracking rocket blew the feet off the man behind him. The other two turned and ran.

Granger Kay crossed to the opposite window. He risked exposure rather than take the time to fidget with the gunsight or go downstairs. The causeway was clear on that side, except for four bodies, motionless and incomplete. The enemy had at least retrieved their wounded.

The two from the left bank who had escaped did not, however, retrieve the man whose feet had been blown off, and his slowly weakening moans haunted Granger Kay's next two hours.

Before dawn, men began to emerge from the Reconstructionist safe houses and make their way—some disguised as policemen, soldiers, sanitation workers, and casual laborers, some sturdily in their own patched clothing—to Benzion's warehouse.

The streets were still silent, except that patrols wove crazily here and there, whisking the alleys and embrasures with searchlights, challenging and admonishing profanely. Most were Rebel squads, openly displaying light blue bands on their helmets and light blue pennons on their vehicles, but a few were Government troops, the least indolent of Carl ap Rhys' remaining "loyalty reserve." From time to time a Rebel and a Government patrol would meet; they swerved apart, shouting obscene banter at each other—a truce of the rank and file.

Rebel patrols picked up several of the deputies and spun them close to the warehouse, which had been silently occupied three hours before by a strong force of Brigadier Pegrim's veterans.

One room in Benzion's was dimly lit; the rest of the warehouse was an intricate hollow blackness. Simon de Ferraris greeted each of his deputies in the lighted room. A few soldiers moved about their tasks, saying nothing. In a corner three indistinct figures sat on a bench: a girl and a beaky old man, and between them a strange creature who shuddered endlessly and cast a gleaming yellow gaze this way and that. Each deputy in turn was sent to a pitch-dark assembly room full of apprehensive rustlings and mutterings.

Chapter 25

GRAY dawn found seventy armored surface vehicles—personnel carriers, weapons carriers, command cars, countermeasure wagons—drawn up in a rectangle around Hooke Place, the muzzles of four hundred assorted weapons pointing outward. On the roofs of the vehicles, swinging their legs and hunching against the chilly air, sat a hundred Government soldiers, watching the streets.

Feigenbrod and Corander reconnoitered the cordon in a small flitter, keeping down among the roofs and darting through the grooves of the streets a few meters off the pavement.

Feigenbrod: "This is illegal. Ooof!" he added, as a laser beam stabbed at them from one of the weapons carriers. He flipped the tiny craft—it was old Simon's, from the kopje—over in a tight Immelmann turn. "Immoral, in fact. Better than getting one's po-po cremated, however."

Corander: "They've got that place sealed off neat and sweet, Desmond. It's going to be hard to get through that."

Feigenbrod: "Harder to get over it. Copters are big, clumsy

things. Even flitters—well, you see how they feel down there about flitters. You'd take a lot of losses, John."

Corander: "Desmond, I think you ought to go back to the Aged and Infirm and take over there till Sue returns. There are still quite a few of our deputies to be heard from. Concentrate on getting them to New Nome. I'll get them through. Forget about the over."

Feigenbrod: "Sound, unromantic thinking."

Corander: "Now, first. Get me where I can get a better look at that MP corporal on the personnel carrier, third from the corner there...

"Good. Good. Very very good." He took off his Rebel brassard. "Here. Have a baby-blue armband. Have a blue-banded helmet. I have decided to join the Military Police. The *Government*'s Military Police. They need men, I hear." From a duffel bag he produced and MP helmet and an MP shoulder patch and put them on. "Do I look sufficiently Governmental? Where's my audio? Ah. When you get back to the Aged and Infirm, Desmond, keep an ear open for me."

Feigenbrod: "Where will you be?"

Corander: "Inside that cordon. If you don't hear from me, tell Sue she'd better have Pegrim break through by main force. Now, set me down. Inconspicuously."

Corporal McBride sat kicking his legs from the roof of his personnel carrier and eyeing the empty streets with total disapproval.

In the first place he had a headache, due entirely to his having hauled his ass out of a warm sack in the middle of the night and brangled this moron carrier through the cold to Hooke Place. There were six morons inside, all warm while he was freezing his nuts off in the autumn air; but on the other hand, they had to smell each other in there, just at the worst time of day for smells, and on the whole, he preferred the bilateral pneumonia he could feel coming on.

In the second place, as everybody knew, there were two—not one, but two—mobs out there in the city. One mob was a natural mob, humpers who hated the Government. They hated it because it governed; also they hated it because it didn't govern; the usual mob. This mob, as Corporal McBride understood the matter, was intent on killing Corporal McBride as he sat on top of his moron carrier. The other mob was a put-up one. It was out there too. He didn't know whom it was intent on killing, probably anybody with brains or character. He himself was safe, because if he had any brains or character he wouldn't be in the army. The leader of the put-up mob was supposed to be a crippled humper named Mick Something, who, as Corporal McBride understood the matter, was On The Payroll...

A solitary figure emerged from one of the small dim streets and came walking across the open space toward the armor—specifically toward his, McBride's, machine. Watching curiously, McBride saw that this hero was a military type; then that there was no Rebel blue on the uniform, which was fortunate for everybody concerned; then that it was an MP officer; then that it was a major; and then that it was the lumpy major who had walked down the hill with him after the shitstorm in the Peurifoy; the major who had told him to go into the MP's. He would like to have a word with that major, and the word was "balls."

This major walked in a perfect straight line to Corporal McBride and looked at him with his "Salute me" look, so McBride saluted without getting off the vehicle, and the major saluted back and snapped, "Corporal, where are the ticket-takers?"

Corporal McBride: "The what?"

The major, coldly: "The checkpoint friggers." He looked at his watch. "The honorable deputies are going to be here soon, and somebody's got to check each deputy to see that it has no thoughts of its own before letting it in." He kept a perfectly straight face as he said this.

McBride could not tell if the major recognized him, so he said softly, "You give putrescent advice, sir. Sir, if you gave any worse advice, you'd be a colonel."

The major raised his eyebrows. "You don't like the MP's? Pity. And you turned down all those lucrative offers in order to join, too!" He surveyed the line of armor right and left. A number of soldiers atop the vehicles were watching him. The major said loudly to no one in particular, "Sitting ducks." He said softly to McBride, "So you don't recommend that I join the MP's?"

McBride looked at the major's MP insignia and answered steadily: "No."

The major: "Who's in that can you're sitting on?"

Corporal McBride: "My men. Six."

The major: "Put one on display and come inside with me." He pointed in a majorly way to the Chamber.

* * *

In the blackness of Benzion's warehouse, a young woman's voice, reedy and astringent, explained the Great Conduit to fourteen quavering Reconstructionist deputies. They were to be fastened together, waist to waist, a meter apart, with a simple rope and belts, so that if one of them lost his grip on the cable, the others could keep him from being swept away.

"Guidon," said the voice, "will be Dr. Jakob von Hosig, who has practiced this route many times. Behind him will come Deputy de Ferraris, then yourselves, and at the end Deputy Issachar, who is also familiar with the Conduit."

Each deputy was issued a waterproof musette bag for the clothing and footwear he intended to wear at the session, and a helmet fitted with a small head lamp.

"You must not—repeat, not—turn the head lamps on until just before you enter the Conduit," said the unseen young woman. "Dr. von Hosig will give you the signal by lighting his. Before you get to the Conduit, there is a long, winding, but not arduous passageway to go through. Parts of it communicate with other underground passages, some of which we know have been discovered by Government agents. Absolute darkness and absolute silence will be the conditions of safety. Are there questions?"

A voice: "Who are you?"

The girl's voice: "I am Shulamith Wells."

A scattered murmur. Another voice: "Forgive me, my dear Miss Wells, but when you were Chief of IDD, you kept your sympathy with Reconstructionism well concealed. And I do not have the honor of Dr. von Hosig's acquaintance. I do not suggest you are planning to drown the entire Opposition, but—"

The unmistakable growl of Simon de Ferraris: "Steenie Smit, come off it. Hosig took me through the Conduit yesterday. Will the honorable deputies stop talking and take their clothes off?"

When Granger Kay had been in the tower of the Hasping Dam for ten hours and knew the special session would begin without him, he felt, if anything, freer. It was as if his personal small war had been severed from the planetary turmoil and had become more definitely his, to do with as he pleased.

He had watched the dawn burst over the storage lake to his left, a conflagration of red vapors and wine-colored ripples, and then steady into cheerful daylight. His mood had likewise steadied. He now wanted to win his war and go home to his wife and daughter—with suitably heroic memories.

Nevertheless, he was sorry to see a black shape advancing and defining itself among the brassy ripples of the lake: a watercraft of some sort—a small harvesting boat for gathering the mutant eelgrass of the lake—an ordinary peaceful boat with some surprising excrescences, projector-barrels, wave-guides. Intruders. Perhaps rescuers.

A voice, preternaturally amplified, howled up from the boat: "Deputy Kay! Granger Kay! Are you all right?"

He shouted back, and was a little put down by the unheroic smallness of his own voice in comparison: "Granger Kay here. Well and happy, thank you. Who are you?"

"Judge Issachar sends his greetings. You may be needed. The session might be deadlocked. Will you join us?"

This, thought Granger Kay, could well be a trap. "What bona fides can you give?"

The boat: "My name is Joseph Holtz and I was just behind you at Langley."

Granger Kay: "Good enough, Joey Holtz. How do we do this?"

The boat: "I keep them busy and you jump suddenly, Captain."

Granger Kay: "Go to it!"

The boat's armament screamed and snapped toward either end of the dam. For a few seconds, there was no reply. Granger Kay thought it would be ironic, humiliating, if the enemy had gone off after their defeat on the causeway and left him there for all these hours, trapped by his own fears. But then hysteria took hold of the hidden men on the right embankment, and they began to fire at the boat. The enemy at the other end joined an instant later. The boat sat in the shining water, rocking gently in its own waves sent back from the shore, and pounded at the sources of enemy fire. The enemy's cover was blotted out by smoke.

Granger Kay put his hands on the sill, hoisted himself up, and dove. The lake was a shock. The glitter had made it look warm; it was icy. He lost his bearings. The weight of his guns seemed to be dragging him under. Then he felt hands on him, and he heard a normal voice say, "This way, Captain."

The Government deputies arrived by sixes in armored personnel carriers and were passed through the cordon at three checkpoints.

Corander strode over and inspected the proceedings, then strode back into the Chamber building, radioed instructions to Feigenbrod at the Aged and Infirm, and rummaged around the dusty janitors' rooms until he found an impressive clipboard. "The perfect disguise," he said to McBride. "You can wear it. I'll wear an expression of bleak dissatisfaction." Each load of Government deputies had evidently been assigned to one of the checkpoints for identification and admittance, and each checkpoint was operating independently, from its own short list. Corander and McBride thereupon opened their own checkpoint, and with much consulting of the janitor's clipboard, admitted five deputies of the Freedom Party right wing and one conservative Independent driven over by Feigenbrod in a "Government" personnel carrier.

The anti-Government mob was now beginning to coagulate in several of the streets leading to Hooke Place. A second cargo of Opposition deputies—three Reconstructionists who were too feeble to attempt the Conduit, and Morris Dempster—were intercepted by a screeching rabble which smoked them and Desmond Feigenbrod out of the armored personnel carrier with bog-pitch, drubbed them unconscious, and carried them away.

At the hour set for the session, the arithmetic in the Chamber was still obscure. Carl ap Rhys and thirty-eight other Freedom Party Left deputies—the Cabinet included—were in their seats. The venerable Deputy Rademis had, as always, sent word at the last minute that he was ill. The Government had also convoyed in two Independents of appropriate tendency. Votes for the Government—forty-one. Or forty, depending on Charley Seiffert.

Mustafa Issachar and five others of the Freedom Party Right had succeeded in entering. The old judge had counted his potential strength at thirteen. But four of his deputies could not be found at all—earlier victims of the Special Branch, perhaps, or casualties in the rebellion. Granger Kay was being pulled from the water at Hasping Dam. Peggy Carmichael had been traced to the village lockup in Perkin. Morris Dempster had been dragged away by the mob. Of the twenty-four Reconstructionist deputies, only old Simon and fourteen others had struggled through the Great Conduit and been welcomed into the dark substructures under the Chamber by the little force of mutinous Capital District police, Rebel sympathizers, whom Citizen Wells had stationed to guard the hatchway all night. Five other Reconstructionists had evidently disappeared into the vortex of rebellion, and four were in the hands of the mob. One pro-Rebel Independent had been brought through the cordon by John Corander; another lay helpless from battle wounds in New Tavistock. Votes for the Opposition—twenty-two.

Carl ap Rhys, concerned for his quorum, had convoyed in nine Freedom Party Doubtfuls, including the Speaker of the Chamber; three others he barred, but one of these, an old woman scarcely one and a half meters tall, had stumped up to the bogus checkpoint and subdued Corporal McBride. Ten doubtfuls, or eleven, depending on Seiffert.

Chapter 26

THE slow, regular tap of the Speaker's gavel emerged from the mumble.

"The special session of the Chamber of Deputies is open. The session will come to order. The deputies will be in order." The mumble ebbed.

Outside, beyond the cordon, the streets were beginning to thrum with a crowd sound, from no particular direction and not factorable into distinct words, except when the thin echo of some harangue crawled over the noise briefly. There were no slogans, no pounding roars, no "Rohan, arise," only a thick bundle of low frequencies.

Inside the Chamber, the Rules of Parliamentary Order, like a great classical choreography, began to lift the dingy theater out of its time and place and to fill it with the imagery of Privilege and Precedence, of a Floor, of Motions. Just as the movements of ballet had begun in the age of duelists with rapiers and carried their grace forward through the age of gunpowder and mass carnage into the age of the meson-vortex filter and the optic torpedo, so debate under the Rules carried on the angry courtesies of great Earth gentlemen dead for centuries. The preeminent word was "Order."

"Order. Order. The honorable deputies will be in order."

Outside, a nervous sergeant raised his weapon toward an advancing civilian. The civilian came on, an intolerable pale beam lanced toward him, he screamed and fell and was dragged away.

Inside: "Unless there is a motion to correct the Record as printed," said the Speaker, and left an interrogative pause, "the Chair will consider the Record for the previous session to have been adopted by unanimous consent. There being no such motion, the Record is adopted and the Chamber will proceed to the Reports of Standing Committees, hearing first the Report of the Principal Standing Committee, the Cabinet. The Chair recognizes for this purpose the honorable the Acting Premier, Deputy ap Rhys." The Speaker sat.

Peggy Carmichael had lain awake all night reasoning out her situation. She could not get to the Chamber in time. That increased the chances of a Left victory, and of her eventual death... But why had they not simply come and killed her? Because of the effect on the doubtful votes in the Chamber. Why had they not taken her to Special Branch headquarters and killed her secretly? Because they suspected their headquarters had been penetrated. *A Nasty Little Bird* said it had. But once they had won...

She accepted breakfast and waited. The hour for the opening of the session passed.

A policeman escorted her to a room containing four chairs and a table that bore the traces of innumerable meals. She was allowed to sit. The policeman stood in important silence. A sergeant, an unbuttoned local, came in with an inspector of the Capital District police and two civilians.

The inspector, a thin man with a shaven head and crumpled nose, gestured wryly toward her and looked toward the smaller of the two civilians. "Citizen Pascal? This is, or is not, the lady you saw running away from the Hobarts' house?"

If they were troubling to frame her, thought Peggy, they could not be planning to kill her—or was this a smooth way of resuming possession of her to take her to the execution rooms? But she could not believe a man so humorous-looking—so attractive, actually—was one of ap Rhys' murderers.

The insignificant Pascal seemed to have become even more insignificant. He whiffled. "I—I couldn't swear, officer."

The inspector, furious: "Couldn't? Couldn't possibly?"

Citizen Pascal: "Really couldn't. Really."

The inspector wheeled on the other civilian: "Is *your* memory intact, Citizen Hobart?"

Citizen Hobart, stoutly: "It is."

The inspector: "Who has the envelope?"

The unbuttoned sergeant produced it.

The inspector: "Be so kind as to open it, Sergeant. Constable, you are a witness to Citizen Hobart's remarks."

The sergeant spilled a fortune in Terran diamonds and pearls and Betelgeuse morblems on the dirty table.

The sight produced a curious sequence of changes in the inspector's countenance: a flash of wild cupidity, a calculating squint, a furtive glance at Peggy, and, on meeting her gaze, a roving look of admiration. Then he was official again: "Well, Citizen Hobart? Are these yours? Constable, take note."

Citizen Hobart: "No."

The inspector, thunderously: "No?"

Citizen Hobart, apologetically: "No. These are not mine. Mine are definitely...different."

Peggy Carmichael, her reasonings overthrown by this scene, could hardly follow the ensuing developments. She heard the inspector say, "This badly spelled document seems to be an affidavit stating that these gems were found in Citizen Peggy Carmichael's domicile and removed therefrom. I take it they revert to her...If you will sign for them, my dear young lady." She was surrounded by rustic apologies and at length found herself walking in the street with the skinny inspector, the scrupulous Citizen Pascal, and the definite Citizen Hobart.

"I am the happy possessor of a groundcar," said the inspector. "May I give you a lift to town? We *may* get the use of a copter and get you to the Chamber before the nonsense there gives out. Forgive me, Deputy Carmichael. My name is C. Richard Baynes. I am not a policeman. *Au contraire.* This is Citizen Hinckley. He is not Citizen Pascal. And this is Lieutenant Fordyce. He is not Citizen Hobart. You make noises. You change color. You are naturally somewhat confused. We shall make our mad dash for the Chamber while you recover your usual poise and grace. I will assist by telling you what happened to the actors originally cast as Hobart, Pascal, and the inspector. Come along."

The Acting Premier stood up, graceful and confident. "Citizen Speaker, I move that the prescribed Order of Business be suspended to take up a bill amending the constitutive Election Law, of which bill due notice was given in the Call to this Session."

A member near him cried out in a triumphant voice, "I second the motion!"

Simon de Ferraris, playing for time, signaled to a young Reconstructionist deputy, who leaped to his feet and intoned, "Citizen Speaker, I rise to a point of order." A ceremonious wrangle arose over whether the Acting Premier, having been recognized for the purpose of giving a report, could use the floor for presenting a motion.

The Opposition deputies had been craning their necks disconsolately, looking for missing colleagues. They stopped and leaned forward, thinking this a hopeful sign. Why hadn't the Acting Premier simply brought his bill to the floor as a Cabinet Report? Why was he using a procedural motion that needed a two-thirds vote to carry? Was Carl ap Rhys unsure of his strength, and had he chosen this way to measure it? Or was there trouble in the Cabinet itself? Heads turned toward Charles Seiffert, the Minister of Justice. He gave no sign.

The Speaker stood up. The pugnacious neutrality of his face withheld all warning of what he was about to say. "The Chair rules that the point of order is not well taken. The honorable the Acting Premier had the floor. Under Rule Sixty of the Rules of this Chamber, a motion to alter the Order of Business prescribed therein is in order at any time when the mover has the floor."

Simon de Ferraris signaled his dismayed followers not to take an appeal from this ruling.

The Speaker: "Such a motion has been made and seconded. It is not debatable, cannot be amended, but requires a two-thirds vote. The question before the Chamber is: 'Shall the prescribed Order of Business be suspended and the bill altering the constitutive Election Law be taken up without delay?' The Chair appoints the following tellers..."

In their respective sections of the theater, Mustafa Issachar and Simon de Ferraris watched the hand vote grimly.

Carl ap Rhys held his block and took seven of the eight

Freedom Party Doubtfuls on the floor. The other Freedom Party Doubtful and McBride's little old woman voted with the Opposition. In favor—forty-eight. Opposed—twenty-four.

The Speaker rose. "The motion is carried; the prescribed Order of Business is suspended. The Chamber will proceed to the bill of which notice has been given."

The Minister of Justice had voted for the motion. He sat unmoved, looking straight ahead.

Across several meters filled with stricken faces, Mustafa Issachar caught Simon de Ferraris' eye, gestured toward Seiffert, and fanned out his hands.

"Citizen Speaker."

"The Chair recognizes the honorable the Acting Premier speaking in support of the bill."

Carl ap Rhys began. He avoided the "effects" that had sometimes made his speeches in earlier sessions faintly theatrical. This bill, he conceded, was timely. It arose out of a tragedy. That, however, did not mean the bill was *nothing* but an expedient to deal with a passing crisis or (he smiled deprecatingly) a political opportunity. It was legislation that would stand on its intrinsic merits.

The Speaker had referred to it as "altering" the constitutive Election Law, but with all respect (his tone here was deferentially plaintive), that was inaccurate. The bill completed that law, remedied an omission. The omission was a very small, technical one. He had served faithfully under Herman Kalino for a long time and at the end of that time had had even more respect for the Premier's care and judgment than at the beginning. One must remember that when Herman Kalino had drafted the constitutive Election Law, *no* one was thinking in terms of a continuation of violence. No one had foreseen that rebellion, guerrilla warfare, and the nocturnal killing of public officials would again be setting men's nerves on edge and turning the freedom of the planet into a terrible game of Guards and Assassins; and so no one had been thinking in terms of sudden death. These things (here he hesitated and seemed to change his mind about something he had intended to say) had happened. Consequently the tragedy had occurred. The tragedy was enormous, the legal omission it had exposed was minute, but the tragedy could not be undone and the law *could* be corrected.

There were many logically defensible ways of completing the law. One, certainly, would be to add a sentence making explicit what one faction already believed was the "intent" of the constitutive Election Law: that when the Premier died without resigning, a new general election must be held before the Chamber could choose his successor. This had a very serious flaw. Where the Premier died suddenly of a natural cause, that scheme would doubtless work well enough; but where violence was involved—or rumored (he added bitterly)—it would invite disaster, because it mandated general elections precisely at moments of the least reasonable, the most internecine, political passion. He asked whether, as a matter of simple prudence, it would not be better at such moments to put off changing the composition of the Chamber until the public mood had sobered...

He went on marshaling arguments in an easy voice, touching time after time on the charges against himself, shrugging them away as if to say, "Farfetched—but what can one expect in times like these?", and contriving to leave the onus for the times on his opponents. Even Mustafa Issachar and Simon de Ferraris found it hard to believe that this reasonable young man could be guilty of what they knew he had done.

When he sat down, the Freedom Party Left applauded delightedly in defiance of the Speaker's steady gaveling. Yet the Minister of Agriculture, with an ambling mildness that hid the finality of the act, left his seat near Carl ap Rhys' and went over to sit next to Mustafa Issachar in the Freedom Party Right. "Judge," he whispered, "he's waiting for news from outside—I watched his eyes. He wants something to come in that door, and it hasn't come. I think he'll break— I could see the strain."

Mustafa Issachar was astonished but rose.

One provision of the constitutive Election Law required that deputies reside within the districts they represented. This made Mick Amblaika's task more difficult.

The first of the Opposition deputies' homes began to burn even before the Speaker's gavel fell. It was Lou Gelfinger's, a clean, unostentatious old house on one of the less tumultuous streets near the spaceport. Gelfinger's married daughter happened to be staying there with her new baby. The arsonists set fires at every point of egress, but one of the blazes sputtered out, and the girl found a way to safety. Against this possibility, Mick had posted men with stunners around the house, but suspicious neighbor-women drove them off. The girl got through unharmed; the infant was unconscious from smoke inhalation.

Mick next sent half his force to the apartment house where a Reconstructionist deputy, a middle-aged engineer named Whipple, lived with his invalid mother. This time, there were two deaths. The old lady died screaming, "I told you so, I told you so, I told you so!" A musician upstairs was sleeping off a club assignment and was asphyxiated in his bed. This fire was an easy job, because the building was ventilated through a single main duct.

The other half of the force, under Amblaika himself, burned the home of a Freedom Party Right deputy named Hakimian. Here the only death was that of one of Dr. Pimberton's patients. Mrs. Hakimian, a burly young woman, caught him in the act of pouring fuel-cell compound around the kitchen and brained him with the edge of a skillet.

Mick Amblaika was unaware of the loss. According to instructions, he had scuttled into a public vidiphone and was placing a call.

Hooke Place waited. All that was holding the anti-Government mob in check now was a convulsive indecision. Frontal assault on that rim of armor would cost hundreds, even thousands, of lives; so much everyone knew; but there was no one in the little streets around the square who knew what to attempt instead. In each street, a new leader appointed himself every few minutes and then was howled down. Some of the crowd wanted to establish snipers in the buildings nearest the open square. Others wanted to approach the cordon under flags of truce and persuade the soldiers to throw in their lot with the People. Rumor drove rumor, and rumor doubled back: The Government had a relief column on the way. The Government was preparing to flee from New Nome. Pegrim was massing an assault force. Pegrim was a prisoner.

The snipers crept up through the buildings and established themselves without consulting the People, but then held their fire because any reply to it would massacre the People hesitating below them in the mouths of the streets, afraid to debouch into the open square.

A chilly wind swept the bright, empty pavement between the mob and the cordon. The soldiers on the vehicles stared into it with watering eyes. To them the paralysis of the mob appeared as simple menace. It made itself felt in Corporal McBride's large intestine.

When Corander came striding out to McBride's personnel carrier and told him that no more customers were to arrive for a bit, the last busload having somehow got themselves lost, the corporal asked for a little time indoors. "Colon," he explained. "Possibly psychogenic. Those buildings over there are crawling with these feebleminded liberty-lovers of yours." He cocked an eye at Corander. "*With* blast-rifles, Major. I've seen five snipers myself—and my retinas are all fritzed by the inadequate diet."

The major was frowning, not across the square but down the line of vehicles to where a colonel and a PO seemed to be breathing by turns into each other's ears. "Something's going to happen, McBride, but I don't think it's coming from the liberty-lovers. Look at the smirk on that PO with the colonel. *They're* expecting something good."

"Oh, that's bad," agreed Corporal McBride. "Much worse in the larger scheme of things than getting a laser beam up your flue. But less personal, if you know what I mean. Sir."

The major: "They keep looking at the Chamber. Waiting for orders or a message. All right, McBride. Take ten. But if you see anything in there that looks peculiar, or secret—it could be a com-set of some sort—get your colon out here fast."

And so it was that a few moments later McBride passed an ordinary vidiphone booth in a corridor and thought to ask himself why an officer—a whole colonel and, by the look of him, a truly dedicated ball-cracker—should be sitting there, just sitting there, with his line-of-duty face on and the phone dead. As McBride went past, the colonel happened to look impatiently at his watch.

McBride considered the matter while relieving himself. This might be what the major was worried about. Whatever that was was due about now, and the colonel had looked at his watch. So there was no time to get out to the cordon and back.

He had the clipboard with him; found a clean sheet of paprite on it, wrote "ECAFTI HSAMMO CPEELS" and folded the sheet in half; checked his stunner; made his ablutions; and trotted back to the vidiphone booth.

The colonel was still waiting.

McBride rushed up to the booth, saluted smartly, slid open the door, saluted again, and snapped aggressively at the indignant officer, "The chief's pretty pissed off, sir." He held out the folded message.

The colonel positively snatched it. A glance at it made his eyes widen.

Corporal McBride leaned over as if to examine the paprite and said helpfully, "Maybe it's in code, sir."

The colonel glared at him but said nothing and bent over to study the enigma in the dim light. McBride gave him a brief dose of stunwaves at point-blank range, wincing at the loud snicker of the weapon; then caught the toppling body, stowed it on the floor of the booth, seated himself in the booth with his feet on the colonel's ass, slid the door shut to hide the colonel from passersby, and waited for something to happen.

He did not have long to wait. The buzzer rasped. McBride punched the dirty white button; the little spotlight flickered on with a sound like piss on a rock and shone in his eyes; the screen lit up and showed a wall-eyed man, actually a kid, grinning at him.

The grin fell from the kid's face and he said: "Where's Colonel Augenblick?"

Corporal McBride: "Taking a shit, if it's any of your business. I'm covering for him. Come on, come on, get it out! You're overdue."

The wall-eyed kid: "Screw you, scumbag. Just tell him Operation Ladybug is doing pretty good. A couple of squeedies took off, but we got plenty left. We did Gelfinger's, Whipple's, and Hakimian's already, and we'll do all the rest. Smit next. Gelfinger's daughter got away, but I hear we cooked Whipple's mother. Old Augie can pass the word to the Rebs now and watch 'em go. Rohan, arise!" He cackled. "'Bye, scumbag." The screen blanked.

McBride stabbed at the red button, darkening the screen and dousing the spot. "Operation Ladybug." Ladybug, ladybug, fly away home. McBride felt genuinely sick. Your house is on fire, your children all burnt...

He held the stunner to the colonel's skull and gave him a long, probably brain-killing, dose; then with a shaking hand lettered OUT OF ORDER on the back of the pseudo-message, folded it over the top of the booth door; stepped out and closed the door, so as to hide the body; and ran.

The major's face paled, but his voice was brisk: "Beautiful work! McBride, you're a scholar and a gentleman and a dirty fighter. Would you mind the store for a bit? I have to go call my friends again."

Corporal McBride: "You're not going to tell Whipple, even?"

A barely perceptible hesitation. Then, harshly: "No. None of them...Listen, McBride, I'm thinking like Whipple. Whipple tomorrow. Tomorrow he won't want this trick to have worked."

"The Chair by agreement recognizes the honorable and learned member for St. Albans, Deputy Issachar, to speak against the bill."

Mustafa Issachar: "Citizen Speaker, if this bill were a technical remedy for a technical flaw in the electoral system of this planet, I would have no fault to find with the Acting Premier's reasoning. But that is not what we are considering. What we are considering here is a new principle of government—or rather, an old principle we had discarded—the principle that the legislature can make or break the executive without consulting the people. Sir, it is a bad and dangerous principle.

"One would suppose that was obvious. The honorable deputies were put here by the people to do certain things they had said they would do; they were put here to make Herman Kalino the executive; they were not put here to make Carl ap Rhys the executive. It pleases Carl ap Rhys to assert that his thoughts are the thoughts of Herman Kalino. Sir, if Herman Kalino and Carl ap Rhys thought the same things, why was not Carl ap Rhys beside Herman Kalino when the murderers fired?

"Gentlemen may howl at the question, but they cannot answer it."

Then, in a voice even drier and more precise than usual, he said he would not claim to speak for Herman Kalino on the strength of his own long friendship with Herman Kalino. He would not argue that, simply because Herman Kalino had drafted the Election Law in the home of Mustafa Issachar, Mustafa Issachar understood the Election Law better than some other man could. But at that time he had had some conversations with the author of the law that might be of some help now to the Chamber. (He peered toward the entrances to the Chamber.)

To the Acting Premier, the constitutive Election Law might be a mere bundle of technicalities, but it was more than that. It embodied a theory, Herman Kalino's theory that political power was a kind of property.

Herman Kalino had always had a vision of government as a great seething hive of bureaucrats, each wretched bureaucrat avariciously building up his power by little obstructions and incomprehensions, frustrating everything he could not meddle in. "Stupidity makes power more *emphatic*," Kalino had said. The more active an agency was in regulating economic matters, the faster it accumulated power; the old socialist had seen this but was unable to yield up the principle of economic regulation, and at last had said, "There's nothing for it, you know, but ruthless periodic expropriation," meaning expropriation of power. The Government itself was ruthlessly expropriating money. Was not inflation a cowardly technique for expropriating accumulated wealth? And yet this very Government, which had made it impossible for citizens to accumulate capital—condensed hope—on the oft-repeated grounds—it was one of the Acting Premier's favorite speeches—that property was power, now proposed to make it possible for themselves to accumulate power, power itself, power growing at compound interest.

And the old judge peered again toward the back of the Chamber.

Steenie Smit lived in a high-rise complex overlooking the desiccated tangles of what had been the Botanical Gardens, and the assault on his apartment needed both halves of Mick Amblaika's gang. They gathered in the dead park.

The wall-eyed youth sat on a stone bench resting his legs. He had a messily drawn sketch. "Garcey, you'll take five men in the passenger lift, that's here; and Finburg, you'll take six in the freight car, here. Pick 'em yourselves. I know how to get the controls onto manual, so I'll be in the basement. There are two stairwells. Two men in each. Murph and Perez north, Tinzer and Gooby south. Smith lives on the twenty-first floor. You four take the passenger car to nineteen. Garcey will wait downstairs with his boys till you're ready. Then walk to twenty and stay on the landings and blow away anyone that tries to come down—except our boys."

The man Garcey, whose drug narcissism had not quite killed his empathy, quavered, "Mick, it's got twenty-six storeys. How about all the—"

Mick Amblaika: "You heard what I said."

A voice nearby: "I heard what you said."

Mick lurched to his feet. His splayed stare whipped from side to side. Ten meters back of him stood the huge tutelary statue of the park, Gregor Mendel in his monkish robes. From behind its base a man stepped into view. He wore what had

(256)

once been a high-ranking army officer's uniform. There was a Rebel blue band across the garrison hat. The officer settled the hat on his gray hair, raised a heavy laser-rifle to his shoulder in the correct manner, sighted, and squeezed off a brief, tight, blinding burst that burned away Mick Amblaika's neck. Then he walked back behind the pedestal of the statue. The voice—it now seemed to come from a trellis fifteen meters to one side—said, "You are surrounded."

Another voice, from behind a low wall on the other side: "Put your hands on your heads and stand quite still."

Perez senselessly began firing at the base of the statue with a hand-blaster and was cut down by a laser beam from behind the wall. Garcey and Tinzer flung themselves to the ground and began to blast the section of the wall from which the shot had come; the wave-guide of the big laser-rifle slid around the base of the statue; the gray head of the officer appeared; and Garcey and Tinzer shrieked and died. Finburg put his hands atop his head, moaning and swaying. Three men tried to rush the base of the statue; two others dashed toward the wall; two ran in one direction after another and stopped. The brown foliage around the trellis and along the wall was afire, the flames ghostly in the sunlight.

Six of Mick Amblaika's "gang" surrendered to the former General Fordyce, now a brevet colonel in the Rebel forces. The rest had thrown away their lives.

For some time longer, Mustafa Issachar opened out the implications of allowing the legislature to change the executive—even once—without express approval from the People. The old judge's fierce, troubled gaze kept turning toward the shadowed entrances through which the missing Opposition deputies should have been arriving, and none came.

Carl ap Rhys also watched the doors as if he were waiting for someone. His followers were all mustered, yet he became more and more visibly angry that no one arrived.

At last Mustafa Issachar seemed to give up on the entrances. He began to tell a story: there had once been a Terran lady, a Frenchwoman she was; a devout Christian priest had tried to edify her with a story of a blessed martyr who, carrying his severed head under his arm, had walked all the way from Rheims to Paris; "Ah, *mon père*," the lady had said, with what passed for wit among the French, "in such cases, the first step is always the hardest." The Chamber now proposed to take a monstrous first step, a step against the nature of free government, with its severed head under its arm; and if it succeeded, it could be confident that the path to oligarchy and despotism would thereafter be easy.

He sat.

Chapter 27

THE anti-Government mob found an effective tactic by mistake. For hours, the populace of New Nome had been converging on Hooke Place, like swamp ants drawn to carrion. Slowly, propelled by sheer congestion behind them, men and women began to move out of the streets into the square. Centimeter by centimeter they came on, leaning back against the milling crowd and here and there turning and burrowing frantically into it.

Corporal McBride watched, fascinated, from on top of his vehicle. The major was inside the building. Abstractly, McBride knew that the approach of the mob was as dangerous as if it had been purposeful, yet there was something comical about the whining, grunting heroes of the front rank.

All around the cordon, the muzzles of weapons began to rise uncertainly.

"Ready! Aim!" cried a breaking voice somewhere.

A huge, authoritative bellow: "Shut up! As you were!" It

was the major, who had reappeared in the shadow of the personnel carrier. "Hold your fire! Colonel Augenblick's orders!" he roared.

"Hold your fire! Hold your fire!" The order was repeated erratically, from twenty points.

"There's your basic echolalia," muttered the major to McBride. "We're all lunatics now."

The reluctant vanguard of the mob—calling out "Quit pushing!" and "Hey, what's the idea?"—worked closer.

The Acting Premier rose and cried, "Citizen Speaker, I call the question."

There was a stir. Ostensibly, this was a motion to cut off debate and face an immediate vote on the change in the Election Law. It had a bright, brisk ring of aggression to it, and the less experienced members leaned forward in anticipation.

But the old men had seen something a moment before that the others had not noticed: they had seen the Government whips break off their busy whispering among the waverers and go back to their seats with somber faces. The Minister of Agriculture's defection had put the Government margin in doubt. If any more Opposition members arrived, Carl ap Rhys would be done for, and it was plain that whatever help or news he had been expecting had failed him. Delay had suddenly become very risky for him. But premature attack was just as dangerous. If he failed to carry his bill the first time, he would go sliding backward down the declivities of power, scrambling and protesting; there would be no second time. This procedural motion was therefore a shrewd test: like the last one, it needed the same margin as the bill itself, and if Rhys won this test, he was ready to vote on the bill; if not, debate would go safely on.

Most of his followers, however, sensed only the fighting style of the move. A deputy behind him bellowed, "Second!" as if Armageddon were at hand. Cries of "The question!" and "Vote!" from the Freedom Party Left.

In the Freedom Party Right, Mustafa Issachar twisted to murmur to the Minister of Agriculture, "We daren't vote *with* him on this to blind his test, and if we vote *against* him we admit we're afraid of a vote on the bill. Awful bad for the waverers." He started to raise a bony fist, thumb downward, for his followers to see.

Among the Reconstructionists Simon de Ferraris wheezed and raised up his vast bulk and rumbled, "Mr. Speaker."

The Speaker said severely, "The honorable member knows that a motion to call the question is not debatable." Snickers from the Freedom Party Left. The Speaker stood up. "That motion has been made and seconded. The vote is on the following: 'Shall debate be closed and the pending question now put?' I appoint the following tellers—"

Simon de Ferraris interrupted: "I rise to a question of privilege, sir."

The Speaker sat down. "The Chair recognizes Deputy de Ferraris for a question of privilege."

Groans from the Freedom Party Left. A furious shout: "He's out of order!" Cries of "Order! Order!"

The Speaker tapped with his gavel and said, "A question of privilege takes precedence."

Simon de Ferraris: "I thank you, Mr. Speaker. The question, sir, is whether the privileges of this assembly, the power to debate and vote, and the privilege of immunity from arrest, should extend to felons."

A genuine gasp. Scattered Government shouts of "Order!" "Expel him!"

The Speaker rapped steadily until silence fell and then said in a level voice, dropping the third-person mode of address, "Do you refer to a member now in this Chamber?"

Simon de Ferraris: "I do, Mr. Speaker."

The Speaker: "Of what felony will you accuse the member?"

Simon de Ferraris: "Of procuring murder, sir."

The Freedom Party Left raged, ignoring the Speaker's gavel, for several minutes. At length the icy, patient voice was heard to be saying, "...or I shall appoint sergeants at arms and have eight disorderly members removed."

Mustafa Issachar to the Minister of Agriculture: "Eight. Enough to shift the vote but leave the quorum."

The tumult gave way before the threat.

The Speaker: "Deputy de Ferraris, questions of privilege may be debated. If your charge stands, the immunity of the Chamber may be withdrawn from the felon. If your charge does *not* stand, you yourself will be guilty of a gross breach of privilege and the Chair will entertain a motion to penalize you. Do you wish to continue?"

Simon de Ferraris: "Yes, Mr. Speaker."

The Speaker: "I will first remind honorable members that

the Chair may adjourn the session under Rule Thirty-seven, if disorder is persistent... Whom do you accuse?"

Simon de Ferraris: "Deputy ap Rhys, Mr. Speaker."

Silence.

The Speaker approved the silence with a nod and in the tones of a judge pronouncing sentence said, "Deputy de Ferraris, you have named the member. You must now substantiate the charge."

Simon de Ferraris: "Since I was last in this Chamber, sir, three of its members are known to have died. One of these was Citizen Kullervo, the talented deputy from Bridgeman West. He perished on a vine in Laing's Land. He was not sufficiently familiar with Laing's Land.

"What brought him to that place? He came there because I was in hiding there, and he intended to murder me. He had been told to do so. Death on a Laing's Land vine is uniquely protracted, sir. The pain goes beyond the ordinary limits of the human nervous system, and even after a man has retreated into unconsciousness, that pain pursues him there and wakens him. No one on a vine doubts that he will die. And Citizen Kullervo did not doubt it. Mr. Speaker, I will not detain this assembly with his long death in the dark waste. Throughout one entire night, hour after hour, he screamed, cursing me, and cursing a man he had already killed, and cursing the man who had sent him to kill me."

The Acting Premier: "Mr. Speaker, I call for the Orders of the Day."

The Speaker: "A question of privilege takes precedence over a motion for the Orders of the Day. Deputy de Ferraris has the floor."

Simon de Ferraris: "Thank you, Mr. Speaker. The man he had already killed, sir, was Henry Meyer, another member of this body. Honorable members will recollect that Meyer's corpse, bearing signs of obscene torture, was found some months ago; and later, after Deputy ap Rhys had coopted the Internal Defense Department for his Ministry of Defense, the Government put out the report of an 'investigation' which 'established' that an IDD agent named Morgan, whose corpse was found in the room with Meyer's, had killed Meyer. It was a false report, sir, falsified by orders of the Minister of Defense, Deputy ap Rhys. Agent Morgan had been fitted with a microtransmitter of the type known in the IDD as a T-Transmitter. This relayed his last seconds of life to Room Thirty-two at the Department. Mr. Speaker, you may remember that there were some disturbances at the Ministry of Justice recently. Files were removed. I have been in touch with some of the—ah—rioters—"

The Acting Premier: "Speaking of felonies—"

The Speaker's gavel fell once. "Deputy de Ferraris has the floor."

Simon de Ferraris: "I have been in touch with some of the rioters, and I am in possession of the official IDD transcript of that last broadcast from Agent Morgan's dying body. You may see it if you wish, sir."

The Speaker: "The Chair will rule on its competence at the proper time. Continue."

The Acting Premier: "Citizen Speaker, I protest! This isn't a question of privilege, it's an impeachment. He's out of order!"

The Speaker: "The honorable member is answering the Chair's request for substantiation. Proceed, Deputy de Ferraris."

Simon de Ferraris: "Thank you, sir. The transcript confirms Citizen Kullervo's dying statement that he had killed Deputy Meyer. Citizen Kullervo neglected to mention, as he lay shrieking in the bog, that he had also killed Agent Morgan. But he did say, over and over, that the man who sent him to kill me, and who suggested he wring my whereabouts from Deputy Meyer, was Carl ap Rhys."

The Acting Premier: "Citizen Speaker, I rise to a point of order."

The Speaker stood up. "Under the Rules of Order, a question of privilege does not yield to a point of order," he said. "Resume your seat."

The Acting Premier did not do so. "The deputy has raised his question of privilege against a member who is dead. He implicates me by incompetent evidence, Citizen Speaker, by alleged hearsay from a dead man—"

The Speaker: "The Chair has not yet opened the question of privilege to debate. Resume your seat, Deputy. Deputy de Ferraris, you have the floor."

Cries of "Hearsay!" and "Lies!"

The Speaker leaned over, rapped his gavel, and intoned, "The Chair will adjourn the session under Rule Thirty-seven if the disorder recurs." He went on even more loudly: "Under Rule Thirty-seven, reconvening the session is at the Speaker's discretion, and he may make it conditional upon excluding members who have persisted in disorder."

The silence was complete. The Speaker sat.

Simon de Ferraris: "Thank you, sir. I am not a lawyer, but I believe the rules of evidence traditionally admit testimony as to statements made by persons who knew they were dying. I heard Citizen Kullervo's statements, or screams, and I will bring witnesses to the bar of this Chamber who also heard them, and we can testify that Citizen Kullervo knew he was dying. But I have not done with Deputy ap Rhys, sir. There is more to my case."

The Speaker: "Continue."

Simon de Ferraris: "Thank you, Mr. Speaker. Sir, there were once three elderly men who had been friends for a very long time, who were loyal companions in the struggles for independence, and who were sometimes called 'the Three Old Men of the Revolution.' After the Revolution, disputes over policy divided the three friends—politically, at least. Yet all three continued in one way or another to stand between Carl ap Rhys and a consuming desire of his. This assembly has had ample evidence of that desire. I shall not waste time reviewing it.

"One of the old men was Simon de Ferraris; and I have told you, sir, how the Acting Premier conspired to have me killed. Another was Mr. Justice Issachar, who became Minister of Justice after the Revolution; and I am prepared, sir, at the proper time to bring forward witnesses to the attempted assassination of Mustafa Issachar and my daughter. My daughter had achieved some fame in the Revolution under a *nom de guerre*, and under that name, Shulamith Wells, was the Chief of the Internal Defense Department when Carl ap Rhys' agents attempted her life." The revelation produced a whisper of repressed excitement. The Speaker raised his gavel and held it poised. The moment passed. The Speaker nodded and lowered the gavel.

"The attempt miscarried, my poor young brother-in-law lost his life in it, and Mustafa Issachar and Shulamith de Ferraris escaped. I confess to you, sir, that there is one witness in this Chamber whom I can *not* bring forward, whose knowledge of Deputy Rhys' complicity in the attempt is direct and complete." He turned to stare at Olivia Keyes. "I have no documents. The attempt was planned—privately.

"Sir, I now come to the third old man, Herman Kalino." Again the sigh of excitement, louder than before, the lifted gavel, and the silence. "You are unfamiliar, Mr. Speaker, with the revelations in that deplorable periodical, *A Nasty Little Bird*." (There was the faintest alteration in the dour face of the Speaker; he looked at Mustafa Issachar.) "The manner is loose-mouthed, the matter is often mingled with smut, but the revelations are true. The editors are men and women who loved Herman Kalino, as did I... as did I. The newspaper charged that Citizen Rhys, Deputy Premier and Minister of Defense, had substituted certain picked men for the soldiers who regularly guarded the Premier's villa, where the Cabinet met; that these picked men were violent men, and picked for their violence from the political police, from prison guards who had been reprimanded or suspended, and in one case from a prison cell; that the Deputy Premier altered the duty roster for the Premier's guard so that these violent men surrounded the villa on a certain night; that on this night the Deputy Premier precipitated a crisis in the Cabinet which drove the aged Premier out of the meeting; and that by prearrangement the Premier was shot down when he emerged from—"

Carl ap Rhys was on his feet. "Citizen Speaker!"

The Speaker's gavel fell. "Deputy de Ferraris has the floor."

The Acting Premier: "I move to table this fabricated 'question of privilege'!"

The Speaker: "As the honorable Acting Premier knows, under our Rule Nineteen, the motion to suspend consideration of a question, or in Old American terminology, to lay it on the table, cannot be made unless the mover has the floor. He is out of order." He stared at Carl ap Rhys. "Resume your seat."

The Acting Premier: "Citizen Speaker, I—"

The Speaker: "Sit down, sir! You know the powers of the Chair." Carl ap Rhys, his face flaming, sat down. The Speaker nodded to Simon de Ferraris.

The old man growled. "I will not tax the attention of the Chamber much longer, Mr. Speaker. The gravamen of these charges is that Deputy ap Rhys arranged for the killing of Premier Kalino. You have seen, sir, and the Chamber has seen, how the Acting Premier responded to those charges: he tried to prevent us from discussing them. I can prove that Deputy ap Rhys planted known practitioners of personal violence among the Premier's guards and that he tampered with the duty roster to put them outside the Premier's home on the night the Premier was killed. I possess every document and I can produce a witness to every spoken order. It will not be hard to prove that the Deputy Premier maneuvered the Premier out of his home and into the gunsights of his killers. But there is an inferential gap. It remains for each member of this honorable body to decide whether the posting of the hunters and the driving of the game constitute a plan of killing. Only one man in this Chamber"—he flung a great rust-smeared hand toward the Acting Premier, who rose and stood waiting—"knows what Carl ap Rhys said to the killers, and he will not tell us in words. I submit, sir, that he has already told us by his conduct." He lowered himself into his seat.

The Acting Premier: "Citizen Speaker—"

The Speaker: "The Chair rules that the question put by Deputy de Ferraris is a question of privilege, which must now be disposed of by the Chamber before the pending motion or any other business can be taken up."

From among the Government deputies, where he had been sitting aloof, the spare form of Charles Seiffert unfolded and said, "Citizen Speaker."

The Speaker: "The Chair recognizes the Minister of Justice, Deputy Seiffert."

The Acting Premier's shout actually trembled: "Citizen Speaker! I asked for recognition first!"

The Speaker rose. "I will read to you from Rule Three of the Rules of Order. 'The Chair will not recognize a member who has risen and remained standing while another member is speaking, provided some other member rises to seek recognition after the floor is yielded.' The Minister of Justice now has the floor. *However*"—he raised his voice to override a rising murmur—"in view of the fact that the question of privilege concerns the Acting Premier so directly, the chair now promises that the Acting Premier will have the floor next *if* he can refrain from further interruption. Does the Minister of Justice have a motion as to the disposition of this question?"

Carl ap Rhys visibly bent his efforts to mastering himself, and sat. The Speaker sat.

The Minister of Justice said with unprecedented hesitancy, "No, Citizen Speaker, I have not prepared a motion. But Deputy de Ferraris has told this assembly that there is an inferential gap, and *I* wish to tell this assembly that I attended the Cabinet meeting during which the Premier was killed and I *am* prepared to come forward as a witness and testify that I observed the behavior of the present Acting Premier just before the killing took place, and it convinced me that...he expected the killing." He sat.

In the dead silence that followed, Carl ap Rhys rose and looked around the Chamber. His face was paler than anyone had ever seen it.

The Speaker: "The Acting Premier has the floor."

The Acting Premier: "Citizen Speaker, I move to table this so-called 'question of privilege.' It has the form of a question of privilege, but I shall show that it is a carefully fabricated sequence of lies which—"

The *crack!* of the gavel cut through his voice.

Simultaneously, a deeper voice roared, "Seconded!" It was Simon de Ferraris'.

The Speaker: "The motion to suspend consideration of a question may *not* be debated, even by its mover." He rose. "The motion has been made and seconded that consideration of the question of privilege be suspended. The motion needs a simple majority for passage. Please sit down, Citizen Acting Premier. You will have the floor again, I promise, when the assembly has acted on your undebatable motion. I appoint the following tellers..."

"Why did old Simon do that?" whispered the Minister of Agriculture.

Mustafa Issachar: "Because if Carl loses this vote, he's lost everything. And if Carl wins this vote, the subject is closed and he can't answer the charges."

The Minister of Agriculture: "Then why did Carl move to table?"

Mustafa Issachar: "He couldn't answer the charges in any case, but this way his disciples think he was gagged."

The Speaker was finishing: "...and the Chair reminds the Acting Premier that under Rule Fifty-four no member may vote on a question affecting himself unless more than one name is included in the resolution or substantive question; and there is only one name in the question of privilege to which this motion to suspend consideration is applied. Shall consideration of the question of privilege be suspended? As many as are in favor will hold up the right hand."

A forest of hands sprang up on the Left side of the Chamber.

The Speaker: "As many as are opposed will manifest it by the same sign."

Hands bristled on the Right, and there were some on the Left. The four tellers conferred in undertones and together walked slowly to the Speaker's dais.

Chapter 28

CORANDER stood atop the personnel carrier and
scanned the approaching mob. A perturbation far back in the
crowd caught his eye—an unusually violent eddying, marked
by flailing arms, around some central figure or figures which
seemed to be wrenching forward little by little. This was
what Corander was looking for. The front of the mob burst
open for an instant and a figure—two figures, actually, one
carrying the other—stumbled out. One was a man in police
uniform, helmetless, battered, unsteady; the other, lying
across his arms, seemed to be a little girl. The policeman
limped toward the cordon, his burden clinging to him and
shivering, and Corander, looking anxiously down the line of
vehicles, saw the snouts of several weapons wavering in and
out of alignment. He jumped down and marched out into the
bright loneliness between the guns of the Government and
the guns of the snipers to meet the arrivals.

The "policeman" whispered, "Major Corander? Granger
Kay. Citizen Wells told me to report to you. How do you like

my camouflage? Her name is Madeline. I have to say she is a very brave girl."

Brandy had been dressed up to suggest unspoiled latency. It was evident the deputy took her to be an authentic child; he gave her a squeeze and an encouraging smile. She had been made up to suggest some wasting illness, but her face was genuinely pale under the make-up, and there was a fresh welt across one cheekbone. She whispered corrosively, "Brave, my ass!" Turning a baleful eye on Corander: "You know what, Johnny? We're on the wrong fugging side. Those dildos out there deserve anything they get." Deputy Kay flushed.

Corander guided them toward the cordon, saying loudly, "That's all right, little darling. Your daddy's in that building there, and he'll kiss you and make you better."

The Speaker: "All tellers concur. The vote is a tie vote, thirty-six to thirty-six, and unless the Chair now votes with the affirmative, the motion to suspend consideration fails of passage. The Chair declines to change the result. The motion fails. The question of privilege remains before the Chamber to be otherwise disposed of. Debate is in order. The Acting Premier has the floor." He sat.

The Acting Premier was nearly inaudible. "I thank the Chair and ask the Chair's indulgence. I should like to reserve my remarks on the 'question of privilege' until a later stage of the debate. I—I do not feel physically able to address the question now. But since both the members who have been granted the floor on this matter have spoken on the accusing side, surely equity demands that... my side be heard now. May the Minister of Finance have the floor?"

The Speaker: "The Chair recognizes the Minister of Finance."

Olivia Keyes was looking at her lover with open dismay, and he met her stare with an infantile compound of pleading and blind will. She rose uncertainly, and he turned and walked toward the rear of the Chamber with the gait of a fainting man.

"Mr. Speaker," she began, "I hadn't expected to make a speech on this subject, and I hope the honorable members will excuse my—my disconnected way of talking."

Mustafa Issachar, grimly, to the Minister of Agriculture: "She may do us in yet."

The Minister of Finance took a deep breath and continued: "I don't know anything about Deputy Kullervo's attack on old Simon...on Deputy de Ferraris. Perhaps it took place. He may even have said what Deputy de Ferraris says he did. I can't tell. I wasn't there. I understand my daughter was there, but I have been told she was in labor at the time, giving birth to Deputy de Ferraris' child, so she can't have been aware of what precise words Deputy Kullervo used when he was dying out in the bog. It strikes me as strange, when I think about it, that Deputy de Ferraris should say he was out listening carefully to Deputy Kullervo when his wife was in labor far from any doctor. But it doesn't matter.

"Because if a man is dying in his bed, he might think about things and make a—a serious statement. I can see why that kind of deathbed statement is respected by the law, as we've heard it is. But this man, I mean Kullervo, was not dying in bed. He was in frightful agōny, or we were told he was. And if he was hysterical and cursing, and in this—this unbearable pain, why are we so sure he was telling the exact truth? And he is the only man who said that Carl—that the Acting Premier had anything to do with his, Kullervo's, killing of poor Meyer and trying to kill Deputy de Ferraris."

Mustafa Issachar whispered, "Mark my words, she's going to dish us."

The Minister of Finance: "Now when it comes to the attack, so-called, on Mustafa Issachar and Sue de Ferraris, *that* I know about. I was there myself. Carl—that is, the Acting Premier—wasn't, but I was. It wasn't an attempt to murder them, it was..."

The Chamber listened raptly.

Of the five anti-Government men whom the anti-Government mob had beaten unconscious, Desmond Feigenbrod was the first to regain his senses; but for some reason he could not regain all of them, or any of them entirely. His sight hardly worked at all. He could shut his eyes and see darkness; he could open his eyes and see whiteness, featureless whiteness, a paler kind of nothing. He listened; he heard nothing. His mouth and nostrils were pervaded by a cold, attenuated aroma; the smell at least was real; it was nothing he could identify, but it was a threatening smell. He felt cold, not cutaneously; the cold went through him, stiffening him. Rigor mortis. The thought took hold.

What saved his wits was his proprioception. His proprioception centered on a vast yearning to urinate. It reported little else—but the good news was enough. He began to feel contusions and bruises through the cold; and something else: he was tightly bound. He was lying naked on something hard and smooth, like a slab. There was a sheet over him. He knew where he was.

"Honorable deputies," he called tentatively. It was more like a croak.

Morris Dempster croaked, "That is not the Recording Angel. An assistant perhaps?"

As Carl ap Rhys stepped from the Chamber into the inner lobby of the old theater, he dropped the pretense of feebleness and hastened toward the row of seven doors that led to the outer lobby and the street. At one edge of his mind he was fleetingly aware of the thought that he should head for a door at one end or the other of the row, where he would be a little less likely to come face to face with someone entering; but his body was impatient, and he found himself approaching the middle door so quickly that it was opening toward him and two men were coming through it before he could stop.

With a flickering series of shocks he saw that one of the men was a policeman and was carrying a child in his arms, a little girl with a burned face. The diversionary maneuver at the Rebels' homes had failed in some way. Klaensch had bungled, perhaps had talked. The Opposition would exploit this mistake too. Carl ap Rhys stood trying to calculate. The second man, a knobby russet-topped soldier, stared at him sharply.

The Acting Premier turned around and walked back across the lobby, veered toward a staircase that led down to the lower levels, and broke into a run.

Carl ap Rhys was upflow of his pursuers in the bellowing darkness of the Conduit. He had not quite knocked out the drowsy guard at the trapdoor, and the man had recovered his senses quickly enough to clamber after him and catch a glimpse of the direction he had taken.

John Corander clutched at the cable, squinted into the cold, percussive spray, which smelled like rotting honey, counting head lamps that bobbed and flickered ahead and behind him; six ahead, four behind; all was well. Far behind the eleven was a twelfth glimmer, doubtful, intermittent, the head lamp of the policeman posted under the Chamber hatch. The pursuers struggled forward—moving faster, Corander supposed, than their lightless quarry could. They would over-take him soon, or at least drive him up into the streets, where Pegrim's brigade were hastily posting patrols over every known exit from the Conduit. And yet there was no saying what a psychotic's terrors could drive him to; prodigies of cunning or endurance were clinically possible.

Handhold by handhold the line sidled into the queasy surge. Corander watched the foremost head lamp. Its light reached him discontinuously; he was looking for a regular off-on pattern which was the arranged signal that Rhys had been sighted; but for an interminable straining interval, the light was interrupted randomly.

Then he perceived a steady rhythm behind the stochastic one, and then that light went out altogether; soon the next head lamp in line took up the rhythm; and then that one winked out altogether; the next began to switch off and on, off—on—off—on; then the next. There remained two lights in front of him.

The plan was to darken the head of the line and make it impossible for their quarry to be sure how close the nearest hunter was; the policeman in front had been chosen for his singularly powerful hands and arms; he was to seize Rhys' hand when his own found it on the cable and then to wait in the darkness, gripping his prisoner with one hand, the cable with the other, until the second man came up and switched on his lamp.

Even hand-switching the lamps on and off was dangerous while working along the cable in the wrenching currents. For the man at point, the seizure of Carl ap Rhys would be fearsomely dangerous: with one maniacal contortion the hunted man might tear his captor and himself from the wet metal clue. Twice, as Corander pulled himself along with weak, heavy arms, he thought he heard the ghost of a shout up ahead, but each time, the same tone recurred just after-ward among the mingled frequencies of the Great Conduit. His own need was projecting the shout onto the noise. The noises began to fill and overfill his skull; he could no longer sequence his thoughts among them; he must stop listening.

Then, some way ahead, a head lamp came on, and next to it another. The point man had caught Rhys, and the second policeman had reached them and switched on his light and the first man's. At once the other two lights came on.

Suddenly the foremost lights whipped from side to side, and the movement ran down the row toward Corander: Carl ap Rhys had broken loose, lost his hold on the cable and was being swept down the Conduit, each policeman lunging to grasp him one-handed as he passed. The lamp ahead of Corander bobbed wildly sideways. Then the policeman's hand must have slipped from the cable. The lamp tossed palely in the churning foam; its rays picked out the policeman's thrashing hands as he tried—futilely—to swim against the overwhelming flow; he was flung nearer to Corander; and ahead of him came, not so much a seen human—though Corander's lamp shone for a fraction of a second on a blurred face with an enormous open mouth—as the point source of a shriek, unbelievably heard through the numbing roar. Corander launched himself toward the policeman, stretching his arms from the cable to the floating man like a rope about to snap; a chance wave tumbled the policeman's body into reach; Corander caught his upper arm; the policeman seized Corander's sleeve with one hand, then the other; the two men strained toward each other; the current twisted Corander backward; the policeman reached the cable behind Corander, clutched at it, and held safely on; while Carl ap Rhys was carried, his high screech lost in chaos, toward unbirth.

The Minister of Finance was saying, "...easy to look back afterward and see all sorts of sinister meanings in Carl—in the Deputy Premier's behavior. I don't blame anyone for analyzing it to death. I've thought about it and thought about it myself.

"But what I can't see is how Carl ap Rhys is supposed to have *forced* Herman Kalino to rush out into the street. Isn't that the key to it all? The argument was about Wally Fordyce, General Fordyce; and it doesn't matter, does it? whether the Deputy Premier was right or wrong about General Fordyce— who would have thought the Premier would go rushing out into the street in the middle of the *night* to get help for a friend, when that friend hadn't even been arrested yet?..."

Meanwhile, someone had come into the Chamber and was in converse with a deputy in the shadows under the balcony; and presently the deputy came down the aisle and handed the Speaker a slip of paper.

The Minister of Finance: "So what it really comes down to is that Herman, poor impulsive, wonderful Herman—"

The Speaker's gavel tapped softly. He stood up. Olivia Keyes broke off, her eyes fixed on him. "Forgive me, Citizen Minister," he said. "For the first time in my life I am deliberately violating the Rules of Order. I think you ought to know, Olivia, and the Chamber ought to know, that this discussion is now...pointless. The Acting Premier is believed to be dead."

A hum of bewilderment started and grew unchecked. The figure of the Finance Minister grew rigid; her face whitened and lost its definition; she toppled. The Minister of Health scurried and bent over her. The Speaker stood silent, and whether his face was ironic or tender no one could say.

The Minister of Health looked up at the Speaker and shrugged.

. The Speaker stared down at the recumbent form of Olivia Keyes. "The Chamber will be in order. This seems as good a time as any to tell this assembly the truth. It was unfortunate that the Acting Premier did not stay to hear the arguments for his innocence advanced by the Finance Minister. They might have convinced him, as they convinced me. Instead, he tried to run away. He was leaving this building when he met some citizens coming in. They were, it seems, ordinary unsuspecting citizens who knew nothing of what had been said here." He paused. "The guilty flee when no man pursueth. Citizen Rhys apparently thought they had come to seize him. He escaped into some species of sewer or conduit through which, as he and I were given to understand, some of you earlier had seen fit to come to this session. I am not familiar with it. The note I have been handed says that he has been swept away by the current in that conduit. Am I to take it he has perished miserably in subterranean darkness? If so, it is...a regrettable simplification of our affairs." His eyes sought out Mustafa Issachar and Simon de Ferraris. "I should imagine that some of the honorable members would like to caucus. Does the Chair hear a motion for a brief recess?"

"No," said the Finance Minister. "Thank you. No. What a farce that would be!" She sat, chalky and still shaking, and the others stood around her.

Simon de Ferraris: "You could serve without portfolio. It might keep the Left from going outside the system now."

Mustafa Issachar: "We need some hypocrisy for a few years, Olivia. Yes, we do. To recover."

The Finance Minister: "No, Simon. No, Mustafa. There's nothing political about this. It's personal." She laughed; a cruel laugh, apparently directed at herself. "Don't make the same mistake Carl did. I made it too. He thought of me as...you know the Terran phrase, 'a clinging vine'? But Simon, *you* know what a clinging vine really is. Wu, help me to find some safe transport." She stood up, holding onto the Minister of Health. "Goodbye."

The two old men watched her go out, an attractive woman, the delegates making way for her with excessive, eye-lowered courtesy.

Simon de Ferraris: "Charley Seiffert's compromised himself, but let's talk to Charley."

Mustafa Issachar: "Charley was right when they were wrong. They'll never forgive him for that. But let's talk to him."

The two old men, stared at curiously but left alone, made their way through the babble.

Official word came out to the cordon that a flitter would arrive in a few minutes to take away a Cabinet minister who had fallen ill; it was *not* to be shot at. Corander, uncomfortably fragrant in a uniform whose owner, one of McBride's squad, sat naked and cursing in the personnel carrier, looked doubtfully over at the mob, which had now edged to a stop a few meters from the armor. The wave-guides of the ordnance swept silently back and forth along the front of the crowd, and the terrified eyes of the men and women swept the cordon, back and forth.

"Might set *them* off again," said Corander to McBride, shrugged, and then, coming to a decision, hurried into the Chamber building, forcing his exhausted legs to a sprint.

Shulamith was taking care of things alone at the Aged and Infirm.

Corander: "Did you say this Carmichael was coming in in a flitter?"

Citizen Wells: "It ought to be here in a moment, Village Bull."

Corander: "Divert it. Have it come directly here." He rattled instructions.

A few minutes later, a small black flitter whirred in a graceful arc around the cordoned area and began to settle toward a landing. There was a vague, hostile *"Oooo"* from the crowd; a lone sniper in a distant building opened fire, and a lance of violet light struck at the little ship, but the sniper could not track it.

Corander to McBride: "Whose opfrag is that down the line?"

Corporal McBride: "Twenty-eighth, sir."

Corander shouted: "*Twenty-eighth!* One burst! take that sniper out!" The heavy weapon coughed, and the facade of the building exploded. "Good!" yelled Corander. *"Hold your fire!"*

A second flitter, bright green, appeared over the sniper-infested buildings and joined the first, skimming low over the mob and leaving a frightened mass shriek as its wake. Corander nodded in approval.

The two craft hesitated in midair, wheeling like two animals eyeing each other, then landed.

Corander: "Corporal, there's a woman in the green flitter. Go see her safely in."

The Finance Minister came out of the Chamber building, assisted with histrionic solicitude by a sergeant-technician. She shook him off and walked unsteadily toward the two flitters, obviously puzzled as to which she should take. The crowd spotted her, and a deep-throated roar arose. She paid it no attention. The hatch of the green flitter opened and Peggy Carmichael stepped down just as the bellow of the mob swelled; it seemed to strike her like a physical blow, and she braced herself defiantly, then saw Olivia Keyes and understood. The two women passed each other; their eyes locked momentarily; Olivia Keyes said something and Peggy Carmichael replied; they went their opposite ways.

Corporal McBride came trotting back and reported, "The young-looking old muff said, 'Could *you* have done better?' and our muff, the middle-aged muff, said, 'Yes.' I've noticed that about women."

The two flitters took off, each as if the other did not exist. The crowd was in motion again.

Chapter 29

TAP . . . tap . . . tap . . .

The knots of apprehensive men loosened. The low, vexed mutter and the thready little descants of accusation and excuse trailed off. The Speaker stood.

Tap...tap...tap. The squeaking of chairs. "The session will come to order. The honorable deputies will be in order." Silence. "The honorable member who raised the question of privilege which, though moot, is still before this Chamber now asks leave to withdraw it. Is there objection to the Chair's granting that permission? There being no objection, the question is withdrawn. Now an undebatable motion comes before the Chamber for vote. The question is: 'Shall debate on the main motion, to alter the constitutive Election Law, be closed and the question on that main motion be put?'"

Stunned and planless, the Freedom Party Left held together this time, but it had been reduced by two and was joined by only one of the Freedom Party Doubtfuls and two of the Independents. The Opposition was augmented by Granger Kay and the newly arrived Peggy Carmichael. Thirty-nine for, thirty-three against; not the necessary two thirds.

The Speaker announced the defeat of the motion. The main motion, the Election Law reform, once again came before the Chamber.

The Minister of Justice: "Citizen Speaker."

The Speaker: "The Chair recognizes the honorable and learned Minister of Justice, Deputy Seiffert."

The Minister of Justice: "Thank you, sir. Sir, the measure before us cannot pass. That is a mathematical certainly. The honorable deputies know the numbers. If they do not, why are they all sitting there scribbling sums on little bits of paprite?

"When this session began, Citizen Speaker, the supporters of this wretched measure might conceivably have carried it. I for one was planning to vote against it."

Cries from the Right: "How can you say that?" and "Not so!" Granger Kay: "Oh, Charley! That ain't the way I heard it!" McBride's little old woman: "Shame on you!" The Speaker's gavel.

The Minister of Justice smiled. It was as if the visor of an ancient helmet smiled. "I did vote to take it up before the other business of the Chamber, yes. I had agreed, before coming to this Chamber, to do so. In return for that promise, the Acting Premier agreed not to bring the measure forward as a Cabinet measure. My honorable friend the Minister of Health has authorized me to say he struck the same bargain with the late Deputy Rhys.

"Citizen Speaker, I see looks of perplexity around me. I am used to that, but this time there is reason for them. Why should the Minister of Health and the Minister of Justice have cared whether the measure was called a Cabinet measure? We did *not* care. Then why did we let ourselves be counted as 'doubtful' rather than 'opposed' in the calculations of the Acting Premier? Because, after some of the pressures we had recently undergone, the Minister of Health thought it only just that Citizen Rhys should misread us, and I as Minister of Justice thought it healthier.

"Of the forty-eight of us who voted to suspend the Order of Business, then, at least two intended to change sides when the substantive measure came up; another, my honorable friend the Minister of Agriculture, has already done so; and two others—the chief proponents of the measure—have left his chamber. Meanwhile, two known opponents of the measure have arrived. The measure cannot do better than forty-three to twenty-nine. It will fail.

"But why should anybody at all vote for it? Sir, I am not one to go about lightly attributing lofty motives to others. My first thought was, this change would attract a good many deputies who had made themselves unpopular and could not win reelection at this moment, and who would drag out their membership in this body until the quadrennial elections swept them away—hoping, I suppose, that some great revulsion of popular sentiment would take place in the meantime and rescue them. Perhaps they would even do away with quadrennial elections and turn themselves into a House of Lords. But then I realized this solid, normal, self-referring motive did not apply here. It could not possibly actuate anyone but an imbecile now. For what if we did prolong the life of this alienated legislature by some technical tricks? What would be the likelihood of a turn of sentiment in our favor? None. In fact, we would make sure of the opposite. The present civil warfare has been cleverly managed. I have to compliment my honorable friend opposite"—his square white teeth showed at Simon de Ferraris—"on his contrivance. But not even he could restrain the masses, whom we have defrauded economically and now propose to defraud politically, from throwing us out—out, and our Chamber out with us... Deputy Carmichael has handed me a note to the effect that the masses, or at least some healthy specimens of masses, are now pressing against the perimeter guard outside.

"Sir, anyone who seeks to put off a general election must be doing so from the highest motives. He must want to immolate himself, and all the rest of us, and this planet's young institutions, and this planet's lively hopes, in some sort of left-wing *Götterdämmerung*. I am a man of the Left, but to such an idealist I could only say, 'Bah! You are altogether too good for us. Go away.'"

His voice dropped abruptly back to a conversational tone. "Everybody here, Citizen Speaker, saw me plotting with Deputy de Ferraris and Deputy Issachar during the recess. My colleagues of the Left probably muttered to one another, 'What's Old Shovel-Tooth up to now?' *This* is what:—" and he ran rapidly through the bargain he had struck. He would support half the present Reconstructionist deputies for reelection; Simon de Ferraris would support two thirds of the present Freedom Party deputies—Left, Right, and Doubtful.

After the general election, Seiffert would back de Ferraris for the Premiership and serve in his Cabinet, along with Mustafa Issachar. This bargain would last one year.

"Some of the honorable deputies, sir, have run out of paprite, and others have used up their erasers. Let me spare them further work. If all the present Freedom Party deputies run for reelection, forty to forty-two will have safe seats. If all the present Reconstructionists run, ten to twelve will have seats as safe as I can make them.

"That sounds like a very good bargain for the Freedom Party. It is. But, Citizen Speaker, Deputy de Ferraris, though a Reconstructionist, is no fool. He counts on winning most of the contested seats. He might. He might very well. But even if he does, and even if he favors those Freedom Party deputies who have supported Judge Issachar today, he will have given safe seats to some twenty members of the committed Left. And his own party cannot really win more than a bare majority in this Chamber; so that when the bargain runs out in a year, the poor fellow may have to go in for coalition politics. I asked him a few minutes ago how the prospect of coalition politics appealed to him. He answered, 'I will prove I can rise above principle.'

"Sir, I am as fond of perorations as the next man, but I will forgo one. This is no time for high resolves. This is a time for simple arithmetic." He sat down.

The Speaker surveyed a silent Chamber. "If there is no request for the floor—" he began.

At the rear, a figure in police uniform rose. "Mr. Speaker."

The Speaker: "The Chair thinks it recognizes the honorable member for North Dunning, Deputy Kay."

Granger Kay: "Sir, I had some trouble getting here, and I would like to feel that being here was worth the trouble. The bill can die in two ways—it can dwindle away by failing to get the two-thirds vote it needs, or it can be repudiated by a solid majority of this Chamber. I prefer the latter. I therefore move to table the pending question."

A figure stood up at the rear of the Freedom Party Left. "I second the motion."

The Speaker: "I will translate the motion from the Old American. It has been moved and seconded that consideration of the proposed alteration in the constitutive Election Law be suspended. Unless I hear objection, we will proceed by voice vote. I hear no objection. As many as are in favor of the motion say *aye*."

A roar of *ayes*.

The Speaker: "Opposed, *no*."

A few calflike *nos*.

The Speaker: "The ayes have it; the motion is passed; the proposal to alter the constitutive Election Law will not be considered further. The Chair is now in a quandary."

The green flitter that had delivered Deputy Carmichael to the Chamber was pursuing a pseudo-random course at high speed five hundred meters above the sunny expanse of the capital. The two men aboard were still under orders to confuse the Government's traffic analyzers, if any. Citizen Hinckley, at the controls, had lost his runt-of-the-litter look and was singing a waltz song in a loud, hoarse baritone,

> *"Free in the sky, soaring so high,*
> *Something, something as happy as I."*

The man who called himself C. Richard Baynes, still in his inspector's uniform, conducted an imaginary orchestra.

As he turned to shush the brasses, he saw something through the cabin window that interested him. "Hinck, my lad," he said quietly, "that's Maxwell Square over to the right. I want to go look at it." He leaned over his friend's shoulder and pointed.

Hinckley: "Looking up an old flame?" He guffawed and took the flitter in a wide, swooping curve toward the great sallow bulk of the Central Crematorium.

Baynes: "Around the other side, Hinck. Right. Look at that."

Five figures, naked males, were moving in a wavering single file, keeping close to the side of the building and pressing their hands against it almost as if they were blind men feeling their way.

Hinckley muttered, "Ugh! Somebody must of thrown the whole plant into reverse." He set the flitter down on the deserted square, near the corner of the building. "Hey, wait, you're not a real inspector!" But Baynes was out of the hatch and advancing on the mysterious nudes.

Seeing a police officer striding toward them, three of the naked men turned feebly to flee, another leaned against the building wall and slowly collapsed down it, gasping, and the man in front stood facing Baynes with doubt, astonishment, and laughter in his bleeding face.

Baynes: "A representative of the police was on hand to congratulate Citizen Feigenbrod on his recent resurrection. Hullo, Des."

Feigenbrod: "It *is* you. Do you realize that Ma has been waiting dinner for you *six years?*" He blinked convulsively and started over. "Denny, what are you doing in that uniform?"

Baynes: "Impersonating an officer."

Feigenbrod turned and shouted to the three men who were tottering back to the doorway from which they had emerged. "Come on back! It's all right, he's my—he's my buh—my bruh—"

Baynes: "This is better than a parable."

"My quandary," said the Speaker, "is this: The Chair must now return the Chamber to the prescribed Order of Business, which calls for the Report of the Cabinet. But who is to report for the Cabinet?"

Simon de Ferraris: "Mr. Speaker."

The Speaker: "Surely the honorable member does not claim that *he* speaks for the Cabinet."

Simon de Ferraris: "I wish to suggest a way of proceeding."

The Speaker: "The Chair recognizes Deputy de Ferraris for the purpose of making a helpful suggestion."

Simon de Ferraris: "Mr. Speaker, our problem is that we have no Premier or Acting Premier. Let us elect an Acting Premier. The Acting Premier must, under the unchanged constitutive Election Law, announce a date for the general election. Let that be his report to this session."

The Speaker: "The Chair will entertain a motion to that effect."

The Minister of Agriculture so moved. The Minister of Health seconded. The Speaker ruled it to be a motion for making a General Order, debatable and requiring a simple majority; he called for debate. Silence. There being no objection, the Speaker put the question, "Shall the Chamber now elect an Acting Premier to speak and report for the Cabinet, and shall the Acting Premier then announce a date for the holding of the general election?" The ayes roared out. A lone voice: "No."

The Speaker: "The ayes have it; the General Order is made. Nominations are in order for the office of Acting Premier."

The Minister of Justice nominated Mustafa Issachar. The

(283)

Minister of Agriculture seconded. Simon de Ferraris moved that nominations be closed. The Minister of Health seconded.

The Speaker: "The motion has been made and seconded that nominations be closed. Under Rule Forty-one, this is not debatable and it may be carried by a simple majority *provided* that no more than one name has been placed in nomination." The ayes roared out. There was a thin scattering of *nos*.

The Speaker: "The ayes have it. Nominations are closed. There being but one nominee, unless there is objection, the Chair declares the honorable and learned member for St. Albans, Deputy Issachar, to be the duly elected Acting Premier. There being no objection, the Chair congratulates the honorable and learned deputy and suggests that he communicate as quickly as he can with the troops outside and with 'the mutable, rank-scented many' who are about to disembowel us." He made no effort to gavel down the ensuing cheers of victory and simple relief, during which the old judge could be seen, but not heard, announcing the date of the general election.

Mustafa Issachar, Simon de Ferraris, and Charles Seiffert then hurried from the Chamber.

Chapter 30

CORANDER looked sharply at his naked new wife, who had begun to bubble with laughter, apparently at nothing.

She said, "I was thinking of the day I sent for you to go catch my poor old father, so I could lock him up out of harm's way in my own little jail. Remember what you said, and I promised I wouldn't?"

"Yes."

"I'm glad I didn't castrate you, Corander."

"*How* glad, citizen?"

"*This* glad."

"I'm glad too. Oh, you beautiful bare citizen, I'm glad too!"

About the Author

DONALD BARR had a nearly normal boyhood in New York City, though he went to a progressive school. But after starting Columbia as a math major and finishing as an anthropology major, he went into the Army, which made him successively a math teacher, an Italian interpreter, and an OSS man in Germany. Continuing in this erratic ("versatile") style, he has been the literary editor of a magazine, a teacher of English at Columbia (hired by the professor who had given him "No Credit—for non-fulfillment of work"), assistant dean of engineering and applied science at Columbia, founder there of the famous Science Honors Program for gifted high-school students and the Talent Preservation Project for high-school under-achievers, a National Science Foundation bureaucrat, headmaster ("innovative," "reactionary") of the Dalton School in New York, and currently headmaster ("easygoing," "moralistic") of the Hackley School in Westchester. He is the author of three bushels of literary criticism, four fluid ounces of poetry, a well-known ("controversial") book on education, children's books on mathematics, anthropology, engineering, and nuclear science, and a previous science-fiction novel, *Space Relations*. He is married and has four grown sons.

FAWCETT COLUMBINE
SCIENCE FICTION & SCIENCE FACT

Large-format books by the masters of the genre.

CURRENT BESTSELLERS
from POPULAR LIBRARY